"Fans of Neill's Chicagoland Vampires series will rejoice to see the next generation in their spin-off. Featuring her trademark snarky characters and colorful backgrounds, this is a fun and action-packed urban fantasy launch."   —*Library Journal*

"*Wild Hunger* is a great start to this spin-off series, with plenty of action, political intrigue, [and] chemistry between the main characters, and I already can't wait for more."
—Booklovers for Life

"Neill's storytelling takes you along for a wonderful ride full of great characters, effortless description, and imaginative magic."
—Galaxy's Edge

"It's a great spin-off for Neill, and promises a long story arc . . . and some serious romance for the future."
—Kings River Life Magazine

"Chloe Neill introduces a wonderful new series with some fantastic characters . . . a great start to a terrific urban fantasy/paranormal series."   —The Reading Cafe

"Neill does a wonderful job of giving readers a glimpse of the past while setting the stage for this new series. Elisa is all sorts of badass."   —Readaholics Anonymous

"Fresh and exciting with all the elements I love in a good urban fantasy series."   —Caffeinated Reviewer

"Neill balanced the humor, fantasy, crossovers, and new and exciting into a world we couldn't get enough of . . . reinvented with new amazing characters and circumstances."   —Tome Tender

WICKED HOUR

An Heirs of Chicagoland Novel

CHLOE NEILL

BERKLEY
New York

BERKLEY
An imprint of Penguin Random House LLC
penguinrandomhouse.com

Copyright © 2019 by Chloe Neill
Excerpt from *Some Girls Bite* copyright © 2009 by Chloe Neill
Penguin Random House supports copyright. Copyright fuels creativity,
encourages diverse voices, promotes free speech, and creates a vibrant culture.
Thank you for buying an authorized edition of this book and for complying
with copyright laws by not reproducing, scanning, or distributing any part of
it in any form without permission. You are supporting writers and allowing
Penguin Random House to continue to publish books for every reader.

BERKLEY and the BERKLEY & B colophon are registered trademarks of
Penguin Random House LLC.

Library of Congress Cataloging-in-Publication Data

Names: Neill, Chloe, author.
Title: Wicked hour / Chloe Neill.
Description: First edition. | New York : Berkley, 2019. | Series: An heirs of
Chicagoland novel ; 2
Identifiers: LCCN 2019020176| ISBN 9780399587115 (paperback) |
ISBN 9780399587122 (ebook)
Subjects: | BISAC: FICTION / Fantasy / Paranormal. | FICTION /
Fantasy / Urban Life. | GSAFD: Occult fiction.
Classification: LCC PS3614.E4432 W53 2019 | DDC 813/.6--dc23
LC record available at https://lccn.loc.gov/2019020176

First Edition: December 2019

Printed in the United States of America
1 3 5 7 9 10 8 6 4 2

Cover art by Tony Mauro

"Uneasy lies the head that wears a crown."
—WILLIAM SHAKESPEARE

WICKED HOUR

ONE

While humans slept, monsters raved.

Maybe it wasn't technically a rave. There weren't any glow sticks or electronic music, or club kids with crazy hair and fluorescent clothes. There were a few dozen shapeshifters and a sprinkling of vampires—and one not-quite witch showing off the mural she'd painted in a literal wolves' den.

I was one of the vampires, an unaffiliated Rogue in a city of Houses—including the House led by my parents. The artist was my best friend, a woman with sorcerer parents who'd said no to magic and yes to brushes and paints. And tonight, a lot of champagne.

Lulu Bell stood near her artwork—dozens of female bodies of all shapes, sizes, and shades—champagne flute in one hand as she gestured with the other toward the painting and spoke to a rapt audience. She was petite, with a shining bob of dark hair that framed her pale heart-shaped face and green eyes. She'd paired a multicolor tunic with gray leggings, red heels, and enormous dangling earrings, and looked very much the part of the artsy girl.

Music shook the air around her, heavy on guitars and drums. Her audience was in clothes that were heavy on leather. The shifters, members of the North American Central Pack, were mostly wolves, and they were similarly handsome. Strong men and women whose energy seemed palpable, as if their vitality were sturdy enough to actually thicken the air.

"She looks happy." The man who'd spoken stood behind me, his dark skin and short dark hair contrasting sharply against his brilliantly colored short-sleeved button-down shirt.

He was Theo Martin, one of Chicago's supernatural Ombuds—liaisons between humans and Sups. In his particular case, a former cop with a good brain and a minor obsession with superheroes and, as I'd learned, the comics they lived in.

I was an OMB staffer, at least temporarily. Roger Yuen, the city's new Ombudsman, had given me a gig when my plan to continue working for Paris's Maison Dumas had fallen apart. I'd been helping Theo and Petra, another Ombud, address supernatural problems that cropped up in Chicago; I'd keep helping them until the grant money ran out—or the mountains of OMB paperwork finally disappeared.

"She does look happy," I agreed. "At least some of that is sheer relief. She's been worried about finishing it in time. The Pack wouldn't reschedule the party."

Pack-brewed beer was being introduced in the Pack's bar today. They'd wanted the mural completed by the time the party started, and they'd refused to negotiate with Lulu for a different deadline. Shifters weren't usually picky . . . except when it came to business.

Theo sipped a glass of brown beer that looked more like chocolate than booze. Then coughed. "It's . . . intense."

"Good intense or bad intense?"

He swirled the liquid in the glass, dark beer against pale foam. "I feel like I need a knife and fork. You should try it, Elisa. Your tastes are, you know, different from mine."

"What with the blood and all," I said dryly.

Theo grinned a crooked smile. "What with."

Now or never, I told myself, and took the glass he offered, then a hearty sip . . . and was overwhelmed by flavors. It was sour and tangy and complex and smoky.

Theo was right. I wouldn't say it tasted good, exactly, but its complexity was impressive. Someone had worked very hard to make so many flavors bloom and blossom.

"I don't know that I ever need to drink it again," I said, looking at Theo. "But it's . . . an achievement."

"I don't want to drink an achievement," he said. I couldn't really argue with that.

He gestured toward Lulu. "Should we go say hello?"

Lulu was still holding court across the room, nodding at a thin man with bowl-cut white hair. I watched her, waited until she finally raised her gaze and looked around, then lifted my glass. She gave me a wink, returned to her conversation.

"Done," I said. "Actual discussion can wait until she's made it through her court of admirers." Which gave us time to look around the room. You couldn't beat the people-watching at a Sup party. In addition to the shifters, there were a handful of the scantily clad nymphs who ruled the Chicago River—several of them being wooed by Pack members—and a few vamps from Chicago's other Houses.

"Hey!" Turning the word into a melody, Lulu squeezed between me and Theo, linked her arms with ours. "Is everyone having fun?"

As if on cue, one shifter threw another across the room, the move echoed by tinkling glass. Onlookers cheered and applauded.

"Ain't no party like a shifter party," Lulu said. "'Cause a shifter party don't stop after drinking a reasonable amount of booze."

"I'm not sure anything else could top this," Theo said. "This may be the last party I ever need to attend."

"It's a great party," I said to Lulu, kissing her cheek. "And the mural looks amazing. Congratulations."

"To Lulu!" Theo said, and we lifted our glasses.

"Thank you, thank you. I'm still shocked I got it done." She lifted her gaze to the crease where the wall met the ceiling. "I'd avoid touching that corner," she said with a pixie smile, "unless you want to wear paint."

"I do not," I said. "And I doubt even shifters would get drunk enough to climb the actual walls."

"One never knows," she said, and was beckoned by someone across the room. "I'll catch you later."

"Have fun," I said, and she moved through the crowd again.

A hush fell over the room. I looked around, thinking she was about to make a speech, or I'd been wrong about the effect of booze on shifters and someone actually was inching up the mural. But that's not why they'd gone silent.

"Well, well," Theo said, gaze on the corridor at the other end of the space. "Look who's back in town."

I scanned the crowd, and my gaze came to a halt just as Theo's had done.

Connor Keene, the prince of wolves, had come home.

If "swagger" was a mood, he'd perfected it.

Connor was tall and broad shouldered, hard muscle under taut, sun-kissed skin. His hair was dark and wavy, his eyes pale blue under thick brows. His jawline was chiseled and marked by a sexy dimple in the chin.

He was the son of the North American Central Pack's Apex, and he moved into the room like a prince among royals. I'd have called it arrogance if he wasn't able to back up his words with action. Even if I didn't know that beneath that wicked facade there was competence, care for those within his circle, and an unquestionable loyalty to the Pack, I'd have put money on his being Apex one day. His power was strong enough to send eddies of magic swirling in the room.

It had been weeks since I'd seen him, since we'd fought back a group of fairies intent on destroying Chicago by replacing our world with theirs . . . and he and I had shared a shockingly good kiss.

It was strange to have kissed someone—to have *wanted* to kiss someone—who'd driven me crazy as a kid. But he'd grown up, become a different kind of man.

He'd stayed in Chicago to help us fight despite Pack obligations that would have otherwise sent him across the country. But when our battle was done, duty called again. Not in Alaska, but in the Pack's Midwestern territory, where he'd been sent to solve problems that arose as the Pack traveled cross-country.

We'd texted while he was gone. He told me about the drama he was dealing with, the internal and external politics of the Pack. I told him about my daily interactions with paperwork and Supernaturals. Having been raised a vampire—the most political of Supernaturals—I was smart enough to understand the subtext: The prince of wolves was making time for me.

It took only a moment for his predatory gaze to track through the partygoers and land on me. When surprise and pleasure flashed in his eyes, I was very, very glad that I'd skipped denim and leather for a body-skimming midcalf dress of deep vampire black. I'd left my sword and scabbard at the loft, but I'd tucked a dagger into a thigh garter, and my red heels were thin and high enough to serve as literal stilettos in an emergency. My hair, long and blond and wavy, was loosely tied at my shoulder with a thin ribbon of deep crimson velvet.

Connor began to cross the room, making his way toward me like a missile locked on its target. Anticipation was like an electric charge across my skin.

When Connor and I had been kids—and hadn't liked each other very much—I'd seen him with plenty of girlfriends. All shades, all shapes, all sizes. Always gorgeous. I hadn't been jealous of them, but I'd definitely been curious, wondering what it was like to be the object of his attention, to be the one he was walking toward.

It was a thrill. A song, low and sexy and seductive.

"Brat," he said to me when he reached us. The nickname was a holdover from our icy childhood, but his tone was plenty warm. "Theo."

"You never call," Theo said. "You never write."

Connor kept his gaze on me, and I could all but feel my blood heating from the power of it. "I wrote the ones that needed writing."

The words were a thrill, the emotion still a shock. As was the fact that we'd grown from irritating enemies to . . . something very different.

"How was Colorado?" I asked.

"You do some skiing?" Theo wondered.

Connor shook his head. "Shifters in Colorado who don't acknowledge the Pack's existence had some objections to our riding through what they call their territory."

Theo nodded. "I'm assuming the Pack disagrees?"

"The Pack does, but it's handled. For now."

I took a guess. "Because the Pack made it through Colorado, but you still have some thoughts?"

"Feelings linger," he agreed, gaze on me. "I'm leaving again tomorrow."

Disappointment covered desire like a heavy cloud. But before I could ask for details, another shifter slipped to Connor's side.

He was male, with pale skin, dark blond hair, a trimmed beard, and angular brows. His eyes were hazel, his mouth a firm line. There was something familiar about his face, his magic. But I couldn't place him.

The shifter whispered something to Connor, face turned away so we couldn't read his lips.

After a moment, Connor nodded. "Ten minutes," he said, and the man walked away without so much as a word to us.

"He's friendly," Theo said.

"Who was that?" I asked. "He looks familiar."

"Alexei Breckenridge," Connor said.

My grandparents were friends with the patriarch of the Breckenridge family, Michael Sr. But the family was less friendly with my parents. Alexei was our age, but I hadn't seen him in years, and probably only a handful of times before that.

"I didn't know Brecks mingled with the rest of the Pack these days," I said.

"He's one of the few," Connor said dryly. "The Brecks prefer to live within the human world. But Alexei's good Pack. If not entirely sociable."

"Everything okay?" I asked.

"It will be. Business as usual. And I'd like to talk to you about that." He looked at Theo. "Mind giving us a minute?"

"No problem," he said. "I'm going to see a shifter about some meats." He cut through the crowd, disappeared, leaving Connor and me alone.

Connor looked down at me, a corner of his mouth lifted in a smile that was partly cocky, partly unsure. He knew exactly who he was. But we were both still figuring out who *we* were. Our beginning had been sandwiched between years of teenage sniping and weeks of separation. Uncomfortable, given I generally preferred clear steps. Rule books. Plans and procedures.

"Hey," he said.

"Hey back. It's good to see you," I ventured, and his face lit, his smile widened.

"It's good to see you, too, Lis."

"The Pack's good?" I asked quietly, not wanting to force him to spread internal struggles through the room, and betting he'd tell me more than he'd said in front of Theo.

"Drama," he said. "Almost as bad as dealing with vampires."

"Oh, that's funny."

"I thought so."

We stood there for a moment, just looking at each other. Want and trepidation dancing in the air around us.

"I'm going to Minnesota," he said. "I'd like you to go with me."

I stared at him. "You want me to go to Minnesota with you."

"Yes. Grand Bay, on the north shore of Lake Superior. Beautiful place. My cousin—a second cousin, actually—is being initiated into the Pack, and I'm going. Night to drive, night to attend the initiation, night to drive back."

"Why would you want a vampire at a Pack initiation?" They were notoriously secretive events, just for family and close friends.

"Maybe I'm interested in your company. Does there always have to be an ulterior motive?"

"I'm a vampire. So yes."

A corner of his mouth lifted. "Colorado wasn't the last of the Pack's troubles. The initiation is happening within a clan—a small community—that's got issues."

"What kind of issues?"

"That's the question. The clan is being mum on the details, and I want a firsthand look at it. I *need* a firsthand look, but I know I'm biased; you won't be. And in case there's trouble, I know you can handle yourself."

"You're using me for my sword?" I asked.

"Isn't that the vampire specialty?" His eyes gleamed.

"One of several," I said.

"So that's a yes?"

I wanted to say yes. To drive away with him into darkness and woods, to give ourselves a chance to be together without the pressures of Chicago or our families or their expectations. But this wouldn't be a vacation, and it wouldn't be without its own pressures.

I looked around at the crowd. The Pack had noticed Connor and I were talking, and several shifters were watching circumspectly. Others were being perfectly obvious about it, and their gazes were cold. To their minds, vampires were arrogant, calculating, high-maintenance, manipulative. They weren't going to bother hiding their disgust that a contender for the throne was giving attention to a vampire.

I didn't see Miranda—one of the Pack's shifters who tended to hang out here at the HQ. She had feelings for Connor—and negative ones for me, and not just because I was a vampire. Considering her attitude when Connor had announced he was staying in Chicago—and the fact she thought he'd breached his duty to the Pack—I also suspected she had designs on the throne, the desire to be Apex and take the crown from the Keene family. She probably wasn't the only one.

Their derision was more dangerous than they imagined. Not just because I was fully capable of taking care of myself—vampires were arrogant for a reason—but because their interest in turn made *it* interested.

I was vampire. But I wasn't just vampire.

There was more to me than fangs and immortality: There was the monster that lived inside, created—as far as I'd guessed—of the same fragmented magic that had allowed me to be born, as the first vampire ever created by birth, not by bite. I had no name for it—hadn't wanted to give it one—so I referred to it only as the monster, and I worked to keep it hidden. A difficult mission, given it tended to overwhelm me when I was vulnerable—when blood had been spilled, when danger was high, when other monsters threatened. And pushing it down again was a test of my control.

Connor knew the monster existed; he was the only one I'd trusted with that information, and even he didn't know the full origin story. Lulu and Theo suspected there was something unusual; they'd both seen me in berserker mode. But I hadn't told them anything. My parents were completely in the dark—about the monster, the effect, my theories about why.

Connor suggested I use the monster and the power it provided instead of pushing it down, which might keep it from overwhelming me. In the last two weeks, I'd been trying to let it stretch, to give it space. Not a partnership, but an acknowledgment.

This, I decided, was one of those times. I let it rise and stretch, shift and undulate beneath my skin, see the world from my eyes— but not quite enough to color my green eyes the monster's particular shade of crimson. I met the shifters' gazes, let them see I wasn't intimidated and was more than willing to fight. That I looked forward to it.

Most of the shifters turned away—whether bored or satisfied or intimidated, I didn't know. But I suspected this wouldn't be the only time they looked at me like that, or doubted Connor's judgment. I wanted to learn more about him, about us. But given those looks, I wasn't sure an initiation—a private shifter event— was the right vehicle.

"I don't know," I said, looking back at him.

There was a flash of surprise in his eyes; Connor wasn't used to being turned down. And the teenager in me was a little too excited that I'd been the one to deliver it. "What does that mean?"

"It means I appreciate the invitation, and I'd like to see the initiation. But we both know there would be . . . consequences."

"Consequences." His voice was flat.

"The Pack doesn't much care for me and you being in the same room together. And if that room's being used for a secret Pack ceremony? It's going to be controversial. You're going to take heat for it. And your father might, too."

His flat expression became a cocky smile. He took a step toward me, close enough that I could feel the heat of his body. "There's something you should know about me, Elisa."

His voice was barely a whisper. His words a challenge.

"What's that?"

"I can handle my own heat. And I don't care much about controversy. Let me know," he said, mouth hovering near mine. Then he stepped away and smiled, his expression satisfied and cocky, before disappearing into the crowd.

TWO

My heartbeat had finally started to slow, my vampire reserve sliding back into place, when Lulu found me a few minutes later.

"Where's he off to?" she asked, picking a pastel-colored petit four from her small plate.

"I don't know. Alexei Breckenridge delivered a message, and he had to handle it."

"Ah, the mysterious grandson."

I looked at her. "You know him?"

"Sure. Everyone makes it to HQ eventually. But he doesn't deign to talk to the likes of me."

"Because you aren't Pack?"

"Probably because I'm not old money. Brecks," she said with a little distaste. She selected another cake, bit in, screwed up her face. "Ugh. Raspberry. You want?"

I held out my palm, and she dropped the half-eaten cube into it.

"It's good," I said when I'd eaten the leftover. "I like it."

"You're insane. Raspberries are the devil's balls."

"I . . . have no response to that."

"Good. I don't want to eat or talk about them. Tell me about your business with the prince."

"Is it worth saying that my business isn't yours?"

She snorted. "No. All your business belongs to me. It's part of the rental package." She inspected the remaining petit fours, settled on a glossy chocolate cube.

I gave in. "He's leaving for Minnesota tomorrow for a relative's initiation. Grand Bay, Minnesota. It's on Lake Superior."

She frowned. "Damn it. If he doesn't prioritize being in Chicago over his, you know, family and friends and biology and future position as Apex, your relationship is never going to get off the ground."

I kept my face blank, drawing out the enjoyment of irritating her as long as I could. Because friendship. "Yeah," I said dryly. "When you put it that way, he's being a real jerk."

"I just want you out of the loft of an evening now and again."

I looked at her, brow arched. "Am I interrupting plans? Do we need a 'sock on the door' situation?"

"Lord no," she said, sliding her empty plate onto a nearby cocktail table that was already stacked with them, then dusting off her hands. "If I was any less interested in surfing Chicago's dating scene, I'd be . . . Well, it's literally impossible for me to be any less interested."

That meant both of us spent time in the loft we'd been sharing since I'd come back to Chicago. Because she was as generous as she was talented, it was probably time to fess up.

"He wants me to go with him to Minnesota."

"Wait. What?" Her eyes popped wide. "That's huge!"

"Yeah," I agreed. "It is."

"You'll have to talk to your dad about the political ramifications. And Yuen about getting time off."

I lifted my brows. "I haven't decided if I'm going."

She just snorted. "Of course you're going. Your dad will be thrilled, because alliance. Yuen will be cool with it because you'll be escorting a shifter to a shifter cultural event. That's right up the OMB's alley."

"That sounds filthy."

"So it does." She looked me over, nodded decisively. "You're going to Minnesota."

But I was much less sure.

It was nearly dawn when we climbed out of the self-driven Auto taxi in front of Lulu's loft in the Near North Side neighborhood. And we carried a bag of leftover appetizers and a growler of beer we hadn't been able to turn down.

"How pissed is she going to be?" Lulu asked after we swiped our way into the building and she pulled out keys to unlock the door.

"She" was our third roommate. Eleanor of Aquitaine, a cat of sleek form, black fur, and a refusal to answer to anything shorter than her full name.

She wasn't technically a demon, as far as we were aware, but she had the same general disposition and attitude.

Door unlocked, Lulu pushed it open slowly. We looked down and found the hallway that led into the loft empty of cat.

"Shit," Lulu muttered. "That's not a good sign."

"No, it's not."

"Well, into the fray."

We went cautiously inside, closed and relocked the door, then peeked around the corner—a vampire and the daughter of two sorcerers checking the battlefield for their frenemy.

We found her on the ledge beside the horizontal stripe of windows, stretched and languid in the light of the lamp we'd left on for her.

Eleanor of Aquitaine opened one green eye, found nothing remarkable in our arrival, and closed it again.

"We've gotten the cut direct," Lulu said, crossing the loft to put the appetizers in the fridge.

"Growler?" I asked.

She looked back at it, grimaced. "I don't want to drink it. I appreciated the drink I had—like that time I drank that shooter of parsnip soup—but I never need another one."

"Same," I said. "At least for the beer. I've never had parsnip soup."

"You didn't miss much."

I put the bottle on the counter. "Can you mix it in with your paint? Make something creative for the Pack?"

"Something that smells like coffee and booze and old house-plants had a baby?"

"I mean, if the shoe fits?"

Lulu pulled a stool from the island, slumped onto it. "I am beat." She ran her hands through her hair, and I could see the smudge of shadows beneath her eyes. "I'm glad the mural is done. Glad the Pack is happy. Glad the party is over."

"It's gorgeous, and of course they are, and you're always glad when a party is over."

"I'd rather work than make small talk with strangers." She yawned, glanced back at the windows. "You don't have much time before dawn. You'd better get packed. Or to bed."

The horizon was just beginning to blush.

"It would be stupid to go, right? To ride on the back of a motor-cycle six hundred miles with the likely future Apex of the North American Central Pack and invade a sacred Pack ceremony?"

"You didn't mention having your first weekend getaway with a guy you said you were 'falling for.'"

"There's that," I admitted. "I'm not worried about spending time with him. I probably should be, since going out of town is a big step, and we can't possibly be there yet. We've barely been in the same state at the same time."

"You've known each other for twenty years. Your parents are friends."

"Yeah, but is it a date? Or since he wanted my opinion, is it some kind of detective job?"

"Does it matter? I mean, you'd check both of those boxes."

"True."

"Do you want to go?"

I thought about it. "Yeah. But that doesn't mean it's a good idea."

"Who cares if it's a good idea? That you want to is reason enough. He can ride the hell out of that bike, and you're immortal. You'd be the guest of the likely future Apex. You've got a degree in Sup sociology, and you get to witness a sacred Pack ceremony. And yeah, because of his traveling, you're not exactly dating."

Lulu frowned, chewed the edge of her lip as she considered. "That's not to say you don't have to be careful. Having a relationship with a shifter is going to be a challenge. You'll have to be wary of the Pack. Be smart. Yeah, you're a vampire, he's a shifter, and you're going into his territory. Miranda already hates you."

"She wasn't at the party."

"So I noticed. I haven't seen her around the building for a few days. Maybe she's in Alaska, so she's Jeff and Fallon's problem." Fallon was Connor's aunt, Jeff her husband. They'd led the Pack to Aurora, Alaska, when Connor had decided to stay and fight with us.

Lulu frowned. "And she may be gone, but there were still a few shifters giving you and Connor dirty looks."

"Noticed that, did you?"

"Hard not to. But you're a damn vampire, and you aren't going to be scared away from a man who's into you because strangers have their panties in a twist."

I grimaced. "I'm imagining hairy, naked bikers in lacy thongs."

"Wolves in panties. Panty-wolves." She waved a hand. "The point is, you're immortal, and I figure you probably ought to take advantage of that. What's the worst thing that could happen?"

"I could be staked."

"That's pretty unlikely. But we still haven't gotten to the real reason you should go."

"Are we nearing the end of this countdown?"

"I'm building dramatic tension. You should go"—she paused, presumably for more drama—"because this is your fucking thing. Getting out there and mixing it up. Not sitting in a damn office or being a Supernatural bureaucrat."

"*Hey,*" I said, a little hurt by the comment. "My life got turned upside down, and I got a job in my field in a matter of days. And the Ombuds are good people." Good, rule-abiding people.

"I know," Lulu said. "You did the best you could when Dumas left you high and dry, and I'm still angry about that. You didn't mope. You got a job, and you're contributing to your community, and you're helping pay the rent, which I like. But a desk at the OMB is not your destiny, Lis."

"My destiny?" I asked, a little surprised that she'd come up with something so . . . supernatural. Lulu worked with shifters, had a vampire for a roommate. And usually preferred to leave the woo-woo to us.

"Your destiny. I shouldn't be an accountant. You shouldn't be a bureaucrat."

"What should I be?"

"I have no idea," she said. "You're still evolving. You were teenage Elisa, Paris Elisa, transition Elisa, and now . . ." She shrugged. "We'll see. But you're going to be a hell of a lot closer to finding it out there—in the woods with the wolf—than in an office writing reports about River nymph dynamics."

"It was a very good report. There were eighty-seven footnotes."

"And a graph," Lulu said, then walked to the couch and lay down on her back, eyes closed. "Woods, wolves, whiskey, and an invitation from the prince himself. This is the kind of thing you don't say no to."

"Maybe," I said, unconvinced. I stood up. "I'm going to bed before the sun does the stake's work."

"If you go tomorrow, I'm eating the rest of your yogurt. You buy the expensive stuff."

"I think that's entirely fair. But I'm probably not going."

THREE

Of course I was going.

I hadn't been certain when I woke up. I hadn't been certain when I'd brushed my teeth in the dark, or drunk a mug of coffee and half a pint of blood, or when Lulu and I practiced sun salutations in front windows that showed the dark city beyond.

I'd once used yoga to help me control the monster. Now I practiced to give it some exercise, to give us both some breathing room. It seemed to help, but it had been very quiet at the OMB, so the theory hadn't yet been field-tested.

The monster stretched and moved as I did, filling my limbs with a warmth to which I was growing accustomed. Its awareness increased, too, so I had two views of the world, two opinions. Maybe because I'd given some ground, it didn't try to overtake me, was content to exist beside me.

At least for now.

"Downward-facing shifter," Lulu had said as we bent over, hands and feet on the floor, butts in the air.

"I don't encourage you to say that in front of any Pack members."

She blew hair out of her face. "Because they don't enjoy the healing effects of yoga?"

"Because they don't like being called 'dogs.'"

She humphed as we moved our body weight forward into a modified plank, then lowered our legs, arms still stretched and chins lifted. "You're on their side now."

"I'm not on anyone's side. I'm supernaturally neutral."

"Then you're a perfect candidate to attend and witness a Pack event. It's a very sociological thing to do."

We moved backward, settling on our knees, foreheads on the floor and arms stretched in front of us.

"You're going to call me," she said. "I want updates about the shifters, including Connor, and proof of life." She adjusted her elastic headband. "A stack of empty coffee cups would suffice."

"I'm more than the sum of my caffeine addiction."

"Yes. You're also a lot of blond hair and sarcasm, and a big chunk of 'crush on the guy you'll be traveling with.'"

"That's quite a profile, Lulu."

"I probably need to paint you."

I decided to let that one go.

Lulu had been right—about the trip, not the painting. There was still no need for that.

I showered and dressed, threw a few things into a backpack, grabbed my scabbarded katana, and requested an Auto to my ancestral home.

Cadogan House sat on lush and green grounds in Chicago's Hyde Park neighborhood, a gracious building of white stone in which nearly a hundred vampires had lived since the late eighteen hundreds. I'd lived there until I'd moved to Paris at nineteen, had explored the dozens of rooms and hallways, every inch of the rolling lawns and gardens, and even a few of the tunnels that ran beneath the House to access points across Chicago.

The Auto dropped me off in front of the imposing black fence, and I walked to the gate, smiled at the guards.

"Elisa Sullivan, here to see my parents."

"Parents?" asked the guard on the right, a pale young man who looked dubious at my claim. He was young and human, as the House guards often were, and maybe hadn't gotten the memo.

"Seriously, Curt?" asked the other guard dryly, a curvy woman with dark skin and shorn hair. "She's the bosses' kid."

"Vampires can't have kids," Curt said.

The woman looked at me apologetically, flipped the switch to open the gate. "Please excuse him. He'll be more familiar with the family history when you come out again."

"What are you—" he began, but the woman cut him off.

"Thank you," I called out, and slipped through the opening gate. A sidewalk and stairs led to the arched portico that guarded the front door, and I walked inside to the reception desk, added by my parents after one too many security breaches.

"I'm—"

"Of course you are," said the man at the desk before I could respond. "Your parents have been advised of your arrival, Ms. Sullivan. They're in his office." He gestured grandly down the hallway.

Very efficient, but it made Cadogan House feel less like a home than like a hotel. It also reinforced my decision to live outside the House. I loved my parents, but Cadogan just felt stifling.

I walked into my father's office, ready to pitch the idea of my attending the initiation as a kind of diplomatic attaché, and found him and Roger Yuen talking, drink bottles in hand, and both wearing running shorts, singlets, and sneakers.

"Hey," I said, meeting their eyes, because that was less traumatizing.

"Lis," my father said. He was tall and lean, with blond hair that nearly reached his shoulders, currently tied back. His eyes were the same green as mine. "I'd give you a hug, but we've just finished a run."

Yuen lifted his hand. "Hey, Lis."

"Hi," I said, then again when my mother walked into the room with a bottle of blood and considerably more clothing—a singlet, cropped leggings, and running shoes. She was lean like my father,

her long dark hair pulled into a ponytail, which was part of her uniform. Her skin was pale, her eyes light blue.

"No hugs," she said, pointing at herself. "I am disgusting."

"So I hear. Training run?"

"We're going to do the Chicago Marathon," my father said. "There's a new Supernatural division."

A good idea, since many Sups—vampires included—could easily outrun humans. "That's cool. How did today's run go?"

"Not as fast as I'd have liked," he said, and slid my mother a glance.

"I beat him by fourteen seconds," she said with a grin. "Fourteen delicious seconds."

More than twenty years together and my parents were still very much in love, with humor and competition the background music of their relationship.

"They both smoked me," Yuen said. He had medium brown skin, dark hair, and dark eyes and, like my parents, the build of a long-distance runner. "But I'll be in the human division," he said philosophically.

"And you're going to do great," my mother said, taking a sip of her blood. Then she looked at me. "How was the party?"

"Good," I said. "Lulu finished the mural, and everybody seemed to have a good time. That's actually why I'm here."

"Did you have too much of a good time?" my father asked, eyebrow arched.

"No. Connor invited me to Grand Bay, Minnesota, to attend a Pack initiation."

The room went quiet, and the reactions were priceless: My mother looked pleased. My father looked displeased. And Yuen looked giddy.

"An actual initiation?" he asked.

I nodded. "For his relative. This particular clan has a base in the North Woods, so he's invited me to go up with him."

"I'm torn between pointing out that you're an adult," my father said, "and driving to his home to threaten him within an inch of his wolfish life."

My mother snickered. "That wouldn't do much for Pack-House relations."

"Those aren't the relations I'm worried about."

"Oh, my god," I murmured, and felt my cheeks heat. "I'm only here to talk about the politics. I'm not going to discuss the rest of it."

My mother grinned at me. "I want to discuss the rest of it. You and Connor! On a trip! I need to call Mallory."

Mallory was Lulu's mother. "You absolutely do not," I said. "Look, it's a big deal that a vampire would be going to a Pack event, so I wanted to check with you first, get your okays." I smiled at Yuen. "Super handy that you're already here. Saves me a trip."

"I also appreciate efficiency," he said with a smile.

"At the risk of putting you on the spot, are you okay with it? I'll have to miss a few nights of work. I'm not sure how many yet, but I'd guess at least three—two to travel, one for the event."

"We'll miss you at the office," Yuen said, "but it's a fantastic opportunity to strengthen the relationship and learn more about the Pack and the ritual. I've heard it's beautiful."

"There will be Yeats," my mother said with a smile. "There always is."

Yuen looked at my father. "Are there any vampires in the area?"

My father frowned. "Near Grand Bay?" he repeated, then considered. "I recall there may be a small coven near there. Ronan is the Master, last I heard."

Covens were communities of Rogue vampires that lived together but weren't organized into formal Houses recognized by the Assembly of American Masters.

"Will he have a problem with my being in the area?" I asked.

"I wouldn't think so. He has a reputation for honesty and careful decision-making. But also for being particularly concerned about the reputation of his community, the concerns of the humans around him. So as long as you don't wreak havoc, you should be fine."

"Wreaking isn't really my style," I said. "But Connor did say there's some conflict in the clan, and he wanted a second opinion from an outsider."

My father seemed to visibly relax. "So it's a working trip."

"Sure," I said, well aware that was what he needed to hear. My mother just patted his arm.

"This will be a really good opportunity for you," she said. "You and Connor can get to know each other better"—my father cleared his throat, loudly—"and you'll have a pretty amazing learning opportunity. I say go for it."

"I reluctantly agree," my father said, but there was humor in his eyes.

"Concur," Yuen said. "As your employer," he added with a smile.

I checked the clock on the wall. "In that case, I'd better get going. Only so many hours to travel before the sun comes up."

"Be safe," Yuen said. "And check in occasionally."

"I will, to both." Besides, I'd have a shifter on my side.

The Auto dropped me off in front of the Keene house, and I climbed out as moonlight and shadow raced across the peaks and valleys of the family's porch-wrapped home. In addition to the immediate family, two or three of Connor's aunts and uncles—I always forgot the number—lived there, too. If the business was the Pack's public hub, the house was its private refuge.

The neighborhood was quiet, many of the house's windows still dark. But the first floor was lit, pale curtains drawn. I'd been afraid I'd find a gleaming Auto against the curb to whisk us north while the landscape passed us by.

But there was no Auto; there was a bike, low and dark and impressively built. Her name was Thelma, and Connor had transformed her from rusted frame to dark siren after god only knew how many hours of work.

I walked closer, ran fingers across the buttery black leather that covered the seat, carefully quilted in a diamond-shaped pattern. There was a second seat behind the first, just a little higher, but still close.

The house's screen door screeched open, and Connor walked onto the porch, lips curving as he saw me. He wore jeans and a black motorcycle-style jacket that looked like it had already seen a lot of miles.

With his dark, wavy hair and blue eyes, he looked every bit the rakish prince. Gorgeous, devilish, and just a little dangerous.

"I wasn't sure if you were going to show up," he said, coming down the steps.

"I wasn't, either. But I'm here."

He stopped when he reached me. "Controversy?"

"Beaten out by curiosity."

"Brave girl," he said with approval. Frowning, he scanned my face. "And your . . . enhancement?"

We'd taken to calling the monster my "enhancement" over text message in an effort to keep it secret. And that he felt he had to raise the issue at all put a hard stone of guilt in my belly.

"I'll be fine."

He looked at me carefully, judging, considering, and my guilt melted away. There was a softness in his eyes that spoke of concern, not fear; he wasn't afraid I'd hurt his family, but that I'd be hurt.

"The yoga is helping," I said. "Letting it stretch, giving it some space. And if there's an issue, I'll just run into the woods."

His smile was canny. "A tried-and-true method for shifters, as well. There will be plenty of woods where we're going."

"Which is where, exactly?"

Connor grinned. "Very unvampiric of you to show up without the full details."

"I can be spontaneous when necessary." And I knew when to pick my battles.

"We're going to a former resort in Grand Bay," Connor said. "North shore of Lake Superior. Two dozen cabins plus the main lodge. Couple of saunas, several firepits. Humans couldn't keep it afloat, so the clan bought it and adapted it. Some of the cabins are empty; we'll stay in one of those."

"You've been there before?"

"Spent several summers there when I was younger, hanging with the family." He tapped the seat. "You good riding on Thelma?"

I thought, *Yes, please*, but said, "I can manage. As long as you keep her upright."

His grunt made it clear how unnecessary he thought the warning was. "SUV would be easier. Auto easier still. But they're . . ."

"Safe?" I offered, and he smiled thinly.

"Sterile," he said. Then he stepped back, looked me over. "Boots and jeans and jacket are good. You might want to pull back your hair. I've got a helmet," he said, and pointed to the smaller of two that hung from the bike's handlebars. He looked at my scabbard. "I presume that's nonnegotiable."

"You would be correct. I presume we won't be traveling in daylight?"

Connor smiled. "That would defeat the point of bringing you along, wouldn't it?"

"Unless you wanted vampire charcoal, yes. But this seems an awfully roundabout way to get it."

"I don't want charcoal," he said, leaning in, gaze locked on mine as he moved in for a kiss. "Vampire? That's a different matter."

The screen door slammed. "Con."

Connor sighed, lips curling into a smile. "The Apex's timing is impeccable, as always," he whispered, lips nearly against mine, then stepped away. "Pop."

Gabriel Keene, head of the North American Central Pack, came down the steps. He was an imposing figure. He had Connor's strong build, but different coloring. His tawny, sun-streaked hair reached his shoulders, and his eyes were the color of whiskey. He wore jeans, boots, and a Henley-style shirt of slate blue.

He glanced at me. "Elisa. I guess you've decided to visit Minnesota."

I smiled at him. "I haven't seen nearly enough Paul Bunyan statues lately."

"You'll get your fill this weekend. And of cheese curds and hot dish."

"As long as there's coffee, I'll be fine."

"You should be good there," he said, then glanced at Connor. "Anything happens to her, and there will be hell to pay."

I almost objected to the assumption I needed protecting until Gabriel looked at me, grinned.

"And same goes for him," he said, his smile knowing. "Try to keep him out of trouble."

"Sure. I mean, that hasn't worked during my first twenty-three years, but maybe I'll have a sudden run of luck."

He grinned. "You decide you need backup, call us."

"We'll be fine," Connor said. "And Alexei's going to join us en route." He glanced at me. "We're going to meet him outside Schaumburg."

I wasn't sure if I was glad I'd be able to learn more about Alexei—or disappointed it wouldn't be just me and Connor.

"Good," Gabriel said. "That's good. Let's chat for a moment." He beckoned Connor a few feet away. My hearing was good enough that I could have listened in, but I turned back to the bike, pulled back my hair, and plaited it into a loose braid.

A minute later, I heard the sounds of backslapping as they embraced.

"Bon voyage," Gabriel said, then headed back into the house.

I glanced back at Connor. "Everything okay?" I asked. But I could read the concern in his eyes clear enough. Not fear—Connor wasn't the type to be afraid—but unease.

"Just another warning about your safety and the future of Supernatural relations in Chicago."

"So no pressure."

"None," he said with a grin. "Let's get moving."

Connor stowed my backpack with his duffel in the small cargo box. I resheathed my sword so it hung at my back, then pulled on the helmet and fastened it, adjusted my braid.

Once helmeted, Connor threw a leg over the bike, pushed up the kickstand with a heel, took his seat. "Your turn."

I moved behind him, put a hand on his shoulder, and tossed my leg over, grateful for yoga flexibility. The thickly padded seat was perfectly comfortable, as was the nearness to Connor.

"You good?"

"Yeah." But I wasn't entirely sure what to do with my hands.

He turned back and looked at me, his smile cocky and classic Connor. "I like seeing you back there."

"So far, I like being here," I said, giving him back the same smile. "We'll see how it goes."

He chuckled. "There's a bar behind you if you want to hold on to that. Or"—he reached behind him, took my hands, and pulled them around his waist—"this is an option."

When I gripped him, body warm beneath my hands, he shifted his body and mashed the starter with a booted foot. Thelma roared to life—a deep, low rumble that pulsed through bone and muscle like a second heartbeat.

And so we rode into the night.

*   *   *

It being Chicago, traffic was thick as molasses even in the dark. We battled cars and trucks and a few other bikes on 90 as we drove toward the meeting place, and the stop-and-go didn't exactly give me a good sense of what it was like to ride the open road. Connor could have bobbed and weaved on the bike—I'd seen him do that as a teenager—but he rode relatively sedately, staying with the flow of traffic as long as we were making forward progress.

Alexei—or the man I assumed was Alexei, given the shielded helmet—pulled behind us on a cherry red bike just past Schaumburg. He followed us, staying a few yards behind, until traffic cleared. Then Connor opened up the motor, and we absolutely flew. Thelma cornered like she was part of the road, a slot car tied to asphalt.

My heart raced every time he accelerated or took a curve at speed . . . which was often, and I had to stop myself from giggling maniacally. Connor might have grown from the cocky teenager he'd been, but there was still a shimmer of the wild about him. I gripped his hips tighter every time he did it, which probably just encouraged him.

We passed fields and farms and fast food and very occasional wildlife. A pair of deer frozen and staring in the middle of a corn-field. A raccoon, eyes flashing in our headlight as it scampered along the side of the road. And the approximately one million bugs that struck our helmets.

We'd ridden for a couple of hours when Connor pulled into a gas station with a diner along a dark stretch of road. The building gleamed in the darkness, and semis idled in the parking lot's dark corners. We parked, removed our helmets. Alexei pulled up beside us, took off his helmet, pushed a hand through his hair.

"Coffee," he said.

"Seconded," I said, then climbed off the bike, still feeling phantom vibrations from the bike's motor, and rolled my neck.

"You okay?" Connor asked.

"I'm great," I said, not bothering to check my crazed smile. "That was amazing."

"I'm glad you liked it, 'cause we've got several hours to go." He smiled, ran a hand through his hair. "It's the scenic tour of Wisconsin tonight. Albeit in the dark."

"My favorite time of day," I said, and tucked in locks of hair that had escaped from my braid. "It's nice to get outside the city. We weren't really a road-trip family. Much less a motoring one."

"I'm shocked to hear that," Connor said as we walked toward the door, his voice dry as toast. "When I think vampire, I think camping and muddy hikes."

"My father was a soldier—four hundred years ago. He's gotten used to high thread counts and temp control."

"And what about you?" Connor asked, with what sounded like challenge in his voice. He held open the door as a man reached it, then walked through, sleeping child limp in his arms. *"Thank you,"* the guy mouthed silently, carried the kid to a minivan.

I glanced back at him. "Are you asking me if I can hold my own?"

"Yeah, I am."

We walked into the small alcove between exterior and interior doors. There was tile on the floor, paneling on the walls, and an old-fashioned gumball machine in a corner, topped with a pile of real estate brochures.

I arched an eyebrow. "Not that I need to prove anything, given we fought the fairies together—and won—but I've walked forty miles of Hadrian's Wall, hiked Lac Blanc in the dark, spent three nights in a tent in the snow in the Pyrenees. That acceptable?"

His mouth twitched. "Yeah. That should do it."

"Yeah," I said, pushing through the interior door. "I thought it might."

*   *   *

We sat down at a booth along the diner's front glass wall and ordered black coffee, which the pinafored waitress delivered in plain stoneware mugs.

I took a sip, grimaced at the harsh bite of what tasted like liquid creosote.

"Coffee's shit," Alexei said, staring down into it.

"It's pretty bad." I looked at Connor. "I don't suppose there's a Leo's in Grand Bay?" Leo's was my favorite coffee shop in Chicago.

"Leo's is good coffee," Alexei said. The most words he'd said directly to me so far, and since we agreed, I considered it a good step forward.

"No Leo's," Connor said. "But there will almost certainly be coffee, and it will probably have 'north' or 'moose' or 'lake' in the name."

Alexei grabbed a half dozen sugar packets from the condiment holder, ripped off the tops, and emptied them into his mug. He piled the leftover paper into a neat little mountain, then took a sip of the coffee-flavored sugar, swirled it around his mouth.

"Did that help?" I asked.

"No," he said, putting down the mug and wrapping his hands around the ceramic to warm them. "Just makes it sweet."

"Alexei has a bit of a sugar problem," Connor said.

"Sugar isn't a problem," Alexei said. "It's a solution."

"You riding dirty?" Connor asked.

Alexei humphed.

"How much you carrying?"

Connor's voice, dropped to a whisper, had gone so serious, I thought we'd shifted to talk about transporting contraband across state lines. Especially when Alexei reached into a small leather backpack, pulled out a wrinkled and folded paper bag.

He unfolded the top, poured the contents on the table. But where I'd been expecting to see drugs or contraband, I found a hoard of candy. There were gummi bears, sour sharks, licorice, and lemon drops. A rainbow of taffy, a sleeve of candy wafers I didn't think they even sold anymore.

"You're hilarious," I said to Connor.

He smiled at Alexei. "Told you that would make her nervous."

"I won't apologize for being law-abiding."

"Long as you aren't a square," Alexei said, tracing the shape in the air with his fingertips.

I rolled my eyes. You could take the shifters out of Chicago, but that apparently meant bringing along their inner fourteen-year-olds.

"Shifters," I muttered, and took a square of banana taffy. "Sarcasm tax."

Alexei almost—but not quite—smiled.

I unwrapped the taffy, read the joke on the inside of the wrapper. "'Knock, knock.'"

"Who's there?" Alexei asked. At least he was game enough for a bad joke.

"'Orange.'"

"Orange who?"

"'Orange you glad you ate this delicious taffy?'" I read.

Alexei's expression was grim. "That's moronic."

I smiled, handed him the wrapper. "You'll have to take that up with the taffy people. Tell me about Alaska," I said to Connor. "Has everyone made it to Aurora?" I popped in the candy.

Alexei snorted, stirred his coffee, metal on ceramic making a tinkling sound as he mixed.

"Almost no one has made it yet," Connor said. "They take their time. It's a tree," he said, and unwrapped a bundle of silverware. He put the spoon on the table. "Main branch," he said, then added the fork and knife so the blunt ends of all three touched, but the functional ends were fanned out. "Secondary branches," he said, pointing to the fork and knife. "Most of the travelers take the main branch, but there could be as much as two days of riding between the first and last riders. That's a long column with potential stragglers, and it's hard to defend. So we use the branches. Two separate groups of shifters edge out from Chicago on routes that run alongside the main branches, but between fifty and a hundred miles apart. They ride ahead, scout territorial problems."

"And provide a shield," I guessed.

"Exactly," Connor said approvingly. "They can close in from the sides if necessary, but they give the main Pack plenty of room to move. And spreading them out—keeping the main group smaller—tends to keep the locals calmer."

"Tends to," Alexei muttered. "But does not always."

"Thus your last two weeks," I said to Connor.

"Thus. Shifters in Colorado. Vampires in Arizona. Among other problems."

"How's Riley? I forgot to ask last night." Riley was Lulu's ex-boyfriend, a hunk of a shifter who'd been wrongly accused of murder when the fairies had worked to take over Chicago. We'd helped secure his release, and the moment he'd walked out of his cell, he'd joined the caravan.

"Better," Connor said.

"He's the knife."

I looked at Alexei. "Leading the line?"

Alexei nodded, sipped his coffee.

I looked at Connor. "You want to tell me why Gabriel thought we might need backup?"

"'Cause the clan is run by assholes?" Alexei suggested.

I shifted my gaze from him to Connor, brows lifted.

"The leader's arrogant," Connor said. "I called my great-aunt Georgia to get the details about the initiation, found out there's been some dissent in the ranks over the last few months. Clan elders versus young guns, as far as I can tell, but I don't think I'm getting the whole picture."

"You think they'd hide something from Gabriel?"

"Yeah," Connor said. "A Pack's not like a vampire House. There are more of us, but we're spread over a larger territory, so the local outfits tend to act like fiefdoms. That's fine by the Apex. As long as everyone is treated well, things are run fairly. But sometimes they aren't. I don't know if that's the situation here, but we're hearing grievances, and the responses from the clan leaders don't engender much confidence."

"And that's where we come in," I guessed, and Connor nodded.

"Ought not pull the sword unless you have to," Alexei said.

I smiled thinly. "Vampires don't pull swords unless they mean to use them."

He made a sound I thought was approval, but how would I have known?

"I'm going to gas up the bike," Connor said, rising and pulling bills from his pocket, tossing them onto the table. "Pay that, will you, Alexei?"

He gave me a meaningful look, then walked out, leaving the two of us alone. And, I thought, trying to get us to talk to each other.

I looked at Alexei, found him looking back at me.

"How's your family?" I asked him.

"They're Breckenridges."

"Rich, fancy, and condescending?"

A corner of his mouth lifted. "Pretty much. Yours?"

I considered my answer. "They're Sullivans. Political, particular, and very focused on Cadogan House."

"I think we're supposed to be enemies."

I looked up at him. "Are we? I mean, I know there's no love lost, but I didn't know there were active grudges."

"I'd call it more lingering resentment."

I nodded. I didn't doubt he was telling the truth about his family—they were Brecks—but I think he was being sarcastic about the rest. His voice was so flat, it was hard to tell. On the other hand, there were shifters who didn't like me, and they hadn't bothered to mask the emotion, so I decided to play along.

"Okay. We should put on a good front for Connor, though. Especially since he went to all the trouble of assuring we'd talk to each other."

He nodded, cast a dour glance out the window. "I don't care for conversation."

"So I gathered." I finished my coffee, slid to the edge of the booth. "I'm going to do you a solid and let you out of it early."

He looked at me, skepticism in every inch of his face.

"I have no argument with introverts," I said.

"I'm not an introvert," he said, sliding out of the booth to stand beside me. "I'm just a misanthrope."

I grinned. "Then I guess it's a good thing I'm a vampire."

He was smirking when I turned back toward the door. I considered that a victory.

When the bill was paid and the gas was pumped, we gathered outside again. Alexei took off first without a word to me or Connor, taking the lead for this portion of the trip.

"He has a unique sense of humor. Dry as a bone."

Connor smiled. "It took me a while to catch on to that. Figured he was just an asshole Breckenridge. He's quiet around those he doesn't know. But he'll talk the ears off those he trusts. He's smart, savvy, and loyal. And loyalty matters."

I couldn't argue with that.

FOUR

We saddled up again and headed northwest. Two more hours slipped by beneath a rising crescent moon that shone among a million diamond stars. We pulled off the freeway near our third (or fourth?) cheese curd castle, then drove through flat pasture to a small town with little more than a grocery store and a gas station. We turned into a neighborhood of tidy ranch houses with flowers on small porches, then into the gravel driveway of a low brick house. Flowerpots flanked the door, and a wrought iron bench held court beneath a picture window.

Connor turned off the bike, pulled off his helmet.

"Our second and final rest stop," Connor said as the porch light came on, illuminating the front door.

"No Alexei?" I asked, pulling off my helmet and rolling my neck.

"He's going to drive ahead, check the lay of the land."

"That's very vampiric of you," I said with a grin, throwing back his comment.

"We occasionally have strategic thoughts," Connor said with a smile. "But we try to avoid them as much as possible."

A woman stepped outside. She looked to be in her late thirties or early forties, with light brown skin, dark wavy hair that just reached her shoulders, and the wiry form of a distance runner. And she wore a tank top over yoga pants and running shoes so brightly pink, they nearly glowed in the dark.

That she was shifter was obvious from her energy. She was also stunning, with wide hazel eyes, a generous mouth, and apple cheekbones.

"Connor," she said, and held out her arms. She was just a little shorter than me, and nearly dwarfed by Connor when they embraced. He pressed a kiss to her cheek.

"It's good to see you."

"And you. It's been too long." She put her hands on her trim hips, looked him over. "I think you've gotten taller." She glanced at me, smiled knowingly. "And definitely more interesting."

Connor smiled, and it was warm and happy. "This is Elisa Sullivan."

"Of course it is," she said with a smile, then reached out a hand. I walked up to meet them, and we shook, shifter power tingling in her touch.

"Marian Decker. It's lovely to meet you."

"And you," I said. "Your shoes are amazing."

"Right?" She looked down at them. "Running is my best friend and my worst enemy. But just seeing these makes me smile." She opened the door, waved us in. "Come on in. Let's get acquainted."

The house's interior was lovely. It had been gutted and remodeled, small rooms replaced with an open living and dining room, carpet replaced by hardwood floors, heavy cabinetry painted white. It was cheery and happy, and that was helped by the two giggling little girls who'd been captured in the arms of the man I guessed was their father.

"I'm Arne," he said, a tall man with square shoulders, light skin, and short blond hair so pale, it was nearly white. The children squealed beneath his arms. "And these are Maddie and Roxie."

They laughed as he swung them back and forth.

"Elisa," I said. "It's lovely to meet you."

"You know me," Connor said, tilting his head to look at the girls. "Hello, ladies."

They stopped wiggling to look at him. "You're the prince," said the older girl, who I guessed was six or seven. She had light brown skin and curly hair pulled back into a bouncy tail.

"Something like that."

"I'm a wolf!" said the littler one, closer to three or four, and bared her teeth menacingly. She had her sister's coloring, but her hair was darker and made a halo around her face.

"A terrifying wolf," Arne said, and put them carefully down. "Now, go play."

The younger girl put her thumb in her mouth, held out her hand automatically for her sister's. The older girl took it, and they ran down the hallway and turned in to another room.

"We've just finished up some soup," Marian said. "Creamy chicken and wild rice, because we're in Minnesota, of course. Would you like some?"

"I'd love some," Connor said, then glanced at me.

I was starving, so I nodded eagerly. "As long as it's not any trouble."

"Zero trouble. Sit down," she said, gesturing to the table as she moved to the stove, where a blue enamel pot was waiting. She pulled down bowls from an overhead cabinet, plucked a ladle from a crock near the stove, and began to fill the bowls.

"That smells amazing," I said as the scent of chicken began to slip into the room like smoke.

She brought the bowls to us—stoneware of a deep ocean blue— along with folded linen napkins and silver spoons.

"What would you like to drink?" Marian asked. "Coffee, water, tea? We've also got a fridge full of pop for company."

"Water's fine," Connor said. "Riding always makes me thirsty." He glanced at me.

"Water's fine for me, too. Thanks."

"Easy enough. I'm going to make some tea, and you're going to eat. Arne?"

"I'm fine. You want help?"

"No," she said, making a shooing motion with her hands toward the table. "Sit and chat. I'll get this."

"She uses this fancy tea," Arne whispered as we tucked into our soup. "Has it shipped in from the UK, and she won't let me touch it."

"Shifter," Marian called out as she filled a red kettle. "I can hear you whispering."

"Also shifter," Arne said back to her. "I know you can."

Marian rolled her eyes, but a smile tugged at the corner of her mouth.

"The soup is wonderful," I said, blowing on another spoonful. The chicken was tender and moist, the broth almost obscenely buttery, the wild rice the perfect texture between chewy and soft.

"Thank you," she said, adjusting the gas flame beneath the kettle, stray water droplets hissing in the heat. "It's Arne's grandmother's recipe."

"Your grandmother is a genius," Connor said to him.

Arne accepted that with a nod. "How was the drive?"

"Good," Connor said. "Weather was fine, cops were few, and the vampire only screamed once."

"There was no screaming," I said dryly. "He managed not to drop the bike, although there were a few close moments."

"There were no close moments," Connor said, giving me a sly smile that put a bloom of heat in my chest.

"How do you know each other?" I asked, looking between Arne and Connor.

"Marian's one of Georgia's kids," Arne said. "Marian's sister, Cassie, is the one whose kid is being initiated tomorrow. So they're cousins of some variety."

"And William is Cassie's son," Marian added.

"Big family," I said, and Arne smiled.

"You're telling me. It was like marrying into a small college. Probably not unlike Cadogan House."

"Only different by degrees," I agreed.

"Will we see you at the initiation?" Connor asked.

"Unfortunately not," Marian said. "The girls have dance recitals tomorrow, and we promised them we'd both be there before the initiation was scheduled."

"It looks like the girls are doing well," Connor said.

"They're adjusting," Arne said. He glanced at me. "We used to live at the resort, but we left when the girls were younger. Decided they needed a different upbringing. Less violence, and more honesty."

"Honesty?" I asked.

Arne looked at me. "The shifters in Grand Bay still pass as human."

I lifted my brows. Supernaturals had been out of the closet for more than twenty years. "Why?"

"Partly habit, I think," Marian said as the kettle began to whistle. She turned off the burner, poured water into a mug. "The clan's been at the resort for decades, and they never had a reckoning, I suppose you'd say, with the community. They've been part of it for decades, and it's a relatively close-knit relationship. They both root for the high school hockey team. Shifter kids go to school with humans—"

"Which screws up everyone's sleep schedule," Arne said.

"Totally," Marian agreed. "They're integrated, is what I'm saying, even if the humans don't know it."

"I don't get why they'd go to all that trouble," I said. "Is the community anti-Sup?"

"Not overtly," Marian said. "There's a vampire coven in the area, although they keep to themselves."

"Ronan's group," I said.

Marian nodded. "You know him?"

I felt Connor's curious stare. "Only that he keeps to himself. My father knows him, but not well. I didn't think the coven was closeted." Or nothing my father had said had given me that impression.

"They aren't. But it's a small group, and they live several miles outside town. In my experience," Marian said, "humans simply don't think much about them. More odd neighbors than Sups. Which, frankly, is pretty much how humans saw the resort—an odd community."

Nodding, I savored the last bite of soup, licked the spoon clean.

"More?" Marian asked, walking over and claiming a spot at the table with her mug.

"No, thank you. That was perfect." And I didn't want to slosh on the next part of the ride.

"The shifters don't admit that's the reason, of course," Arne said. "That they want to keep their standing among the humans. They say the issue is privacy. If humans don't know they're shifters, humans won't watch them, obsess over their magic, try to use them for it."

"It's probably a little of both," Connor said, and glanced at me. "About a third of the Pack still passes for humans."

"So many," I said quietly. So many unable to be honest. Tied by circumstances, or decisions, to pretending. It bothered me more than I would have thought, probably in part because I'd been able to be an "obvious" vampire. There'd been no need to hide—and it wouldn't have even been possible, given my parents' fame.

"They spend a lot of time trying to hide who they are," Marian said quietly. "We didn't want our girls growing up like that, having to worry about every little thing they did or said, whether that would spill the secret. So we left, found a new community, and have been completely up-front."

Arne nodded. "It seemed to us that if any parents were going to worry about their kids being friends with shifters, it would be easier to be be honest. For the parents to make a conscious decision."

"Worked for us growing up," Connor said. I think he'd meant to include me. And while he was partially right—my childhood had been as "normal" as my parents could make it—humans had a very different relationship with vampires than with shifters. Shifters were intriguing; vampires were dangerous.

"It's worked pretty well here. A few parents opted out, but the girls have a really nice group of friends." Marian fished the tea bag out of her mug, set it aside. "We're happy here. And if we need to be with the clan, the Pack, we can go to Grand Bay."

"And Grand Bay?" Connor asked. "What are you hearing from there?"

Marian's brows lifted. "You should know, since you're headed that way, no?"

"We are," Connor said. "But it always seems wise to check."

"You heard about Paisley?" Marian asked.

He frowned. "Who's Paisley?"

"Young female shifter who died." Marian turned her gaze toward Arne. "What's it been, a couple of weeks now?"

"Thereabouts," Arne said.

Marian nodded. "Hit-and-run," she said, then sipped her tea. "She was walking or running—we aren't sure—along the old main road, by the resort, when she was struck by a car. The car didn't stop."

"How did they find her?" I asked.

Marian sipped, nodded. "One of the clan elders, a man named Loren, had walked to a coffeehouse up the road and found her in the middle of it. It was a Saturday night, and Loren believed one of the locals imbibed too much, kept driving because they'd been drinking and knew there'd be a heavy price to pay."

"What did the sheriff say?"

"Same conclusion," Arne said, "as far as we're aware. No one saw or heard the vehicle, and if any of the locals know anything about it, they aren't talking."

Marian nodded. "She was one of the younger shifters—the up-and-comers, you could say. The younger generation has tried to distance themselves from the clan's elders."

"In what ways?" Connor asked.

"For one, they're lobbying to be public about who they are. They want to be honest about their identities, and the elders aren't interested in it. They're also angry about the resort; they want to revitalize the grounds, and the elders aren't interested in that, either."

"We don't know that there's any actual fighting per se," Arne said, looking at Marian for confirmation. "But there's definitely tension."

"The more things change," Connor said philosophically. "How does Georgia feel about all this? She's an elder, after all."

"Mom likes what's familiar," Marian said. "She'd deal with changes if she had to, but she's mostly content."

There was gentle rapprochement in her voice, as if Marian hadn't agreed with her mother's position.

We sat quietly for a moment, sipping our drinks and listening to the girls' bubbly chatter from the other room.

If I was being honest, this was not at all what I'd expected to find on this trip. A happy family of shifters acting like any other happy family might and letting me—an obvious outsider—sit companionably in their home.

"There are more interesting rumors coming out of Grand Bay, you know," Arne said.

"What rumors?" Connor asked.

"Some sort of bigfoot," Arne said. "Supposedly."

"The Beast of Owatonna," Marian said. "Or that's what they're calling it."

Connor arched a brow. "What's the Beast of Owatonna?"

"Minnesota's answer to Bigfoot," Marian said with a grin. "A big and hairy creature that supposedly stalks prey in the North Woods."

"Are we sure humans haven't just seen shifters in their native forms?" I asked.

"That would be the simplest answer," Arne said with a smile. "And logical. But the sightings came from clan members, not humans."

"They find any evidence?" Connor asked. "Footprints, scat?"

"Not that I'm aware of," Arne said, glancing at Marian for confirmation.

"Nope," she said.

"God only knows what happens in the North Woods. Probably young guns screwing around, maybe hoping they get caught by the humans. Either way, it's the kind of thing that might attract attention, and the clan doesn't want that."

A squeal echoed from the room at the end of the hall, and little feet quick-stepped toward us. The older girl ran to her father. "I didn't hit her," she said quietly, and rested her head on her father's arm.

"Mommy!" The younger girl stomped into the room, eyes streaming. "She hit me with her doll."

"No, I didn't! I didn't!" The older girl paused. "She hit me first!"

"I did not!"

I had a flashback to similar scenes twenty years ago, when Connor and I were kids of about the same age and fighting over toys, running to our fathers to solve our disputes. I glanced at him, found him smiling knowingly back at me. I guess he'd been thinking the same thing.

"*Girls,*" Arne said, firmly enough to stop the rising hysteria. There were sniffles, but the yelling stopped. "We don't hit each other, do we?"

In answer, the little girl burst into tears.

"And I think it's nap time," Marian said, pushing back her chair. "Girls, quiet time, now."

That created another round of screaming as they stomped dramatically toward the back of the house.

"Excuse me," Marian said, and followed them.

"Poor kids," Arne said. "Adulting is hard, but you couldn't pay me to be a kid again. All those hormones, still figuring out the world." He shook his head. "Crazy thing is, give them fifteen minutes of quiet time, and they'll be best friends again. Biology is a fickle mistress."

"We'll get out of your hair," Connor said, rising from his chair. "We need to hit the road, anyway. Thank you for the refreshment and the conversation."

"Please don't feel like you have to go," Arne said. "This is a minor skirmish in the War of Daughters."

"No, we're on a deadline. Sunrise," he said, nodding toward me.

"Right, right." Arne looked at me curiously. "I think you're the first vampire I've ever met." He grinned. "You seem pretty normal."

"Please excuse my husband," Marian said, coming back into the room. "The running has finally scrambled his brain."

"For a vampire, she is pretty normal." Connor looked at me, his smile so tender and warm, my heart fluttered like wings in my chest.

"Adorable," Marian murmured, sliding her arm into Arne's. "Do you need anything for the road?"

"We're good," Connor said. "But thank you for the offer."

They walked us to the door, and we exchanged hugs.

"I like you," Marian whispered as she embraced me. "And I like you for him," she said when she pulled back, meeting my gaze. "Take care of each other."

We hit the road again, interstates and farmland eventually turning into coastal cities marked with ironworks and rocky shores, which turned into divided highways through tall and pointed trees.

It was two hours before dawn when Connor pulled off the main highway, taking a silent and dark road that seemed to run parallel to it—probably the old main road Marian had mentioned— to a spur that led to the former Superior Shore Resort & Lodge, according to the peeling sign at the edge of the drive.

The drive was narrower than the road had been, and rutted with potholes. It wove through the property around cabins of assorted sizes, past overgrown lawns and wild-looking shrubs. Connor brought the bike to a stop in front of a stand-alone cabin near what looked like the edge of the property. He turned off the bike, and we pulled off our helmets and sat for a moment in the quiet that embraced us.

Wordlessly, we climbed off the bike. Connor walked into the grass and turned a quiet circle as he took in the grounds, or what he could see of them in the darkness.

The cabin was a neat rectangle of honed logs with a steeply pitched roof. A couple of steps led to a small wooden porch held up by wooden posts, a white rocking chair moving subtly back and forth in the breeze.

When I looked back at Connor, his brow was furrowed.

"What's wrong?"

He shook his head, still frowning, and ran a hand through his hair. "It's been a few years since I've been back, but it's not as well-kept as it was. The potholes, the grass. Maybe the young guns had a point there."

"I like it," I said, and he looked back at me. "It looks real. Lived in and homey."

"Is 'homey' what vampires say when they mean 'shabby'?"

I grinned at him. "Good to know you think I'm tactful, at least. How does the clan support itself? I mean, they had to buy this land, right? Buy food, at least what they don't hunt or scavenge?"

"They work," Connor said. "They pooled money to buy the resort, and everyone puts in for the mortgage. They spend some money on their needs, put some money into the communal pot. Elders are retired, so some of that pot supports them directly. And they don't live extravagantly, as you've seen. Shifters aren't much into material possessions."

"Because they have the moon and the woods and the cheese curds?"

"Not necessarily in that order, but yeah. For their security, vampires prefer to live high. To have the protections of wealth. Shifters prefer the opposite. To blend. To go unnoticed."

We took our bags and walked to the door, and he pointed to the large dark green shutters installed over the windows. They looked like slatted ornamental shutters but for wide hinges that would allow them to close and hooks that would keep them that way. "Sunlight protection."

"That's a relief. Does the clan get a lot of vampire visitors?"

He looked back at me, eyes full of meaning. "No."

He'd put thought into this, I realized. Thought and time to make sure I'd be shielded if I decided to come. Warmth spread through my belly.

Connor flipped up the welcome mat with a booted toe and flicked out the key someone had stowed there. He unlocked the door, held it open for me. "You're invited in, if you need the invitation."

"Only by etiquette," I said. "Not magic."

Inside, the decor was simple, a mix of vintage outdoor prints and gear and North Woods kitsch. The wooden walls gleamed golden beneath brassy light fixtures. There was a couch in front of a fireplace and a dining table in front of a small kitchen. The table was small and forest green with matching ladder-back chairs, all of it well-worn, the corners rubbed down to pale wood from hands and feet and legs, the corners softened by others' lives.

It smelled of woodsmoke and cinnamon and, beneath that, wolf. Magic and pine resin and loamy soil. The scents of wilderness and wild.

"Why did the resort fail?" I wondered, putting my backpack on the small kitchen island.

"They built the divided highway we came down," Connor said, dropping his duffel onto the floor. "That pushed traffic off the scenic route, and hotels that weren't close enough to the highway failed. The clan took advantage." He looked up, gestured toward the hallway. "The bedroom's down there. You can take that, and I'll take the couch."

I hadn't been sure how we'd handle the sleeping arrangements, and appreciated that he was willing to make the sacrifice. But I didn't need to be coddled. "We can flip for it."

He pointed to the sliding-glass patio door. "That doesn't have shutters, but the bedroom does. So this isn't chivalry. Or not just."

"In that case, thanks."

"You're welcome."

He smiled at me, and I was suddenly aware of the fact that we were alone together in a cabin in the woods of Minnesota.

"You want something to drink?" Connor asked.

I grinned at him. "Is it last night's beer, or . . . ?"

Connor grinned. "Local. Much paler than the Pack's version."

"Then I'll take one."

While he checked the refrigerator, I walked outside the small porch. Firepits along the curving lakeshore winked like jewels among tall and stately evergreens. And beyond them, the sound of soft waves filled the air.

I walked toward the lake, footsteps crunching over a mulch

path that ribboned along the shore. Water lapped, slowly and steadily, against the rocks, and crickets chirped in the grass nearby.

"It's peaceful out here," I said quietly when Connor moved behind me. "And shifters really like fires," I said, gesturing toward the closest firepit, where Adirondack chairs circled licking flames.

"It's part of lake life," he said. He handed me a bottle, then clinked his against mine. "Fire keeps away the chill, smoke keeps away the bugs, and it's a chance to connect with friends, especially when you're preparing for a long winter indoors."

I sipped the beer, liked it immensely. It was lighter and crisper and went down a lot easier than the Pack's brew.

"I don't know what we're going to do with an entire growler," I muttered, and caught his soft laugh.

"It wasn't that bad."

"I'm sure it wasn't," I said. "But we aren't craft beer aficionados. We drink cheap pink wine out of plastic cups." I looked at him. "Did you know they make chocolate wine?"

His lip curled in distaste. "That's disgusting."

I laughed knowingly. "Oh, but it's not. It's delicious. At least until the second bottle."

Connor offered a long-suffering sigh. "I'm going to have to learn you about good alcohol." He shook his head. "Back to the point—if she didn't like the beer, why did she take a growler?"

"Because she loves you guys. Generally," I added. "Not you specifically. You drive her crazy."

"Mutual."

I smiled. "The Pack hired her for the mural, let her show it off at their party. She's never had an easy time fitting with humans or Sups. The Pack gave her space to be herself, probably more than she even knows. I think that's been good for her."

"I think it's been good for the Pack," he said. "She's a pain in the ass, but manageable."

I chuckled, sipped.

He took another drink of his beer, then set the bottle aside. He turned toward me, gaze heavy as if he was preparing to unburden himself about something very serious.

And then a sharp howl split the air.

Connor tilted his head toward the sound, one of the most wolfish things I'd seen him do, frowning as he listened, interpreted.

Until the howl became a scream.

The beers were left behind, and we took off running.

FIVE

We ran across the resort toward the sound of voices, the wild blossoming of magic. The wind had picked up, that magic swirling farther, faster, in response.

Along the way, we passed what looked like the resort's former main lodge, a dozen cabins, and a few piles of rubble that I guessed had once been buildings, but time or neglect had stripped them of the title.

Connor was right. The resort hadn't been kept up. Paint left to peel. Lawns gone to dirt and scrubby weeds. Overturned and rusting picnic tables. You could see the bones of the resort behind the mess, but it would take time and care to carve the decay away again.

We saw no shifters until we reached what I guessed was the far edge of the property, given the thick treeline. A half dozen men and women stood near a woodpile that was surprisingly straight and tidy given the rest of the resort's condition.

There was chatter—agitated, excited, confused—not unlike the magic in the air. And the voices went quiet when they realized someone had joined them—and realized who that someone was.

I wondered if that reaction bothered Connor. Not the pause, but the implicit acknowledgment that he was different. Pack, but different.

The monster shifted, wanting to touch the magic, wanting access to that power. I ignored it.

"Everything okay?" Connor asked.

A man stepped up to him, beefy and strong and nearly a foot taller than Connor. His skin was ruddy and freckled, his hair short, red, and spiky. His eyes were small, blue, and suspicious, his nose Roman in profile and knobby from being broken. "Who the fuck are you?"

Connor looked completely implacable. "I've gotten taller since I last saw you, Clive, but you should still recognize me."

Clive's eyes went wide, and he moved back a step as if to get a better view. "Keene? Holy shit, man." He reached out, gripped Connor's arm in one of his enormous hands. Connor returned the gesture. "My bad. It's been too long."

"A few years," Connor agreed. "This is Elisa."

The shifter nodded. If he recognized my face or my name—or realized that I was a vampire—it didn't show on his face.

"What happened out here?" Connor asked. "We heard screaming."

"One of our shifters, Beth, was attacked."

He moved aside, gestured to a female shifter who sat on a small bench along the mulch path. She wore a T-shirt and shorts, and her skin was pale, her hair nearly as light. A set of crimson scratches stood out starkly across her cheeks. Bruises blossomed around puncture marks on her arms, and her lip was cut and bleeding.

Shifter blood was a powerful thing—full of magic—and the monster became more insistent. It stirred, curious. I was afraid to force it down too harshly, for fear that might make it fight back. And this wasn't the time or place to let it go, especially when I wasn't sure I'd be able to push it down again. Instead, I focused on staying calm, on breathing through the magic.

Two more shifters, both female, sat on either side of Beth. One was pulling gauze from a plastic first aid kit. She folded a mound, pressed it to Beth's arm.

All three women wore strips of black fabric, like emblems of mourning, around their arms. For Paisley? I wondered.

There were footsteps behind us. We looked back, found Alexei had reached us. He gave me and Connor a silent nod.

"This is Alexei," Connor said, and gave him the basics. "Who attacked her?"

Clive cleared his throat. "She said she was attacked by an animal out near the big woodpile."

"An animal?" Connor asked.

"Something with fur," Clive said. "Fangs, claws. That's all we know so far. We just got here—me and my girl, Jae." He pointed to the shifter with the gauze, who had pale skin, a fall of straight dark hair, and dark eyes.

"The other girl is Maeve. She got here first. We haven't questioned Beth yet, just made sure the immediate area was clear, then got her treated. We asked her to wait to shift until we talked to her, looked around."

"Have you told Cash?"

Clive rubbed a hand over spiky hair. "That was the plan. He's apparently at the cataracts preparing the site for the initiation."

"I'd like to talk to her," Connor said.

Clive looked at Connor, back at the girl, debating whether Connor was an acceptable substitute. "That works for me. Let me just give them a heads-up." He walked toward the women, talked to them as he gestured back at us.

"Cash?" I whispered.

"One of the clan elders," Connor said quietly.

Clive gestured us over. Connor moved to the women, while Alexei and I stayed a few steps behind. "Beth, I'm Connor. We're in town for Will's initiation—me and Elisa and Alexei."

She nodded.

"Tell me what happened."

"I was getting some firewood," she said, and gestured to the woodpile.

"Do you do that often?"

"Often?" she asked.

"Is it part of your routine?"

"Oh," she said. "No. We wanted a firepit, and the box near the pit hadn't been refilled, so I volunteered. I grabbed two pieces, heard something in the woods. Got a little excited, because I thought it might be a rabbit or a deer, and I could use a good run."

She looked up at Connor for confirmation, and he nodded. "Go on."

"I put down the wood again, very quiet in case I needed to bolt, then walked really quiet toward the edge of the woods. I saw something—a flash of fur, I think—and then something hit me from the other side." She touched fingers gingerly to the left side of her head, where the skin had started to purple.

"Hit you with something?" Connor asked.

"No, I think it was an arm or paw. It wasn't rough or hard on the outside, like a log or pipe or something. But it had force behind it. Anyway, that hit me, and then it moved again. It was fast, and it was big. Huge claws," she said, and pointed to her cheek.

"An animal?" Connor asked.

"Some kind of animal. I don't know what specifically. It was really close—and really big. The only thing I saw was fur. I hit it back, made contact. There was strength beneath the fur, but not much muscle, if you know what I mean? Kind of . . . stringy strength."

"I understand," Connor said.

"There was a howl," Alexei asked. "My cabin's on this side of the resort. Was that you?"

She shook her head.

"It was me," said Maeve, the third shifter. Early twenties, with tan skin and brown hair that fell straight to her shoulders, bangs long enough to partially hide her dark brown eyes.

"I was heading out for a trail run," she said, gesturing to her shorts and tank. "I smelled blood and called out. I found her on the ground. I yelled for help."

That explained the scream.

"Something was crashing in the trees," she continued. "Moving away from us. I thought it might have been a bear or something. They're active right now, trying to eat up before hibernation season. And there was a bear attack a few weeks ago near Boyd."

Connor shifted his gaze to Beth. "Did it look like a bear?"

"Not really," she said, and looked guilty at the admission, as if she was letting Maeve down.

Connor nodded. "That's fine. It's better not to jump to any conclusions. Did you smell anything?"

She frowned, shifted her gaze down as she considered. "Nothing but Pack," she said, and looked up again. "No animals. But we were upwind, and the wind was really strong."

"What about unfamiliar magic?" I asked.

"Like sorcerers?" Beth's gaze darted to mine, then away again. "Vamps?"

"Or shifters," Connor said. "Any kind of magic that didn't seem common or usual. Or maybe no magic at all?"

Beth lifted a shoulder. "I don't know. Nothing unusual, I guess."

"There are rumors about a beast," Maeve said.

"What kind of beast?" Connor asked, voice quiet and careful, as the chatter dipped to silence around us.

"Something big," Maeve said quietly, and goose bumps lifted on my arms at the warning in her voice. "Something stronger than us. Something that's out there hunting."

Despite the warning in her tone, her eyes glittered, and I wasn't sure if it was fear or excitement about the possibility of a hunt—or a battle.

"Details?" Connor asked.

"Only what we've told you so far," she said. "No one's gotten a good look at it. No one has really seen."

"Because it's nonsense," Jae said, closing the first aid kit with a click. "Maybe there's an asshole in the woods. Maybe there's an asshole in the clan. But there's no mythical beast."

Maeve didn't seem to like that pronouncement, made an expression that said she'd eaten something sour—or held back salty words.

"Did anyone see or hear anything else?" Connor asked.

"Not that I can think of," Beth said. Maeve just shook her head, and then shifted her gaze to the lawn, where a man approached.

He was tall and lean, with a short crop of white hair that was perfectly styled. I guessed he was in his late fifties, and he eschewed the shifter denim-and-leather uniform for pressed khakis and a polo shirt of blue-and-green stripes. He looked less "shifter" and more "insurance agent."

Gaze scanning the scene, he saw us, nodded, headed in our direction. "Loren," he offered with a smile. "And you're Connor Keene. It's been a few years."

This was the elder Marian had mentioned, the one who'd discovered Paisley. He nodded at Clive, got a nod in response. He was handsome in the way of sharp and precise men, and wore his power comfortably.

"It has," Connor agreed, shaking his hand. "This is Elisa Sullivan and Alexei Breckenridge."

"Of the Chicago Sullivans and Breckenridges," Loren said, blue eyes shining. "Welcome to our home." Loren glanced back at the women. "Everything all right here? I was just in the lodge and felt the magic. Thought I'd check it out."

"Beth was attacked," Connor told Loren, and gave him the details.

I looked back at the women, and noticed Beth and Jae didn't seem especially thrilled to see Loren. Because he was an elder, I wondered, or because they just didn't like him?

Maeve wasn't watching Loren; she was watching me, and didn't bother to hide her animosity. Because I was vampire, because I was here with Connor, or possibly both, I guessed.

"Animal attack" was Loren's conclusion.

"Maybe," Connor said noncommittally.

"We should let her shift," Loren said, nodding to Beth as if offering her permission.

That was part of the magic of shifters: Transforming into animal form healed any wounds incurred in human form. A neat trick, but unfortunately one that didn't work the other way around.

Beth nodded. "I would. I'd like to get back to my cabin."

"Take care of yourself," Loren said supportively, then turned back to us.

"You might consider putting a guard on her tonight in case this was personal," Connor said.

Loren smiled, but there was a tightness to it he didn't quite manage to hide. "This isn't Chicago, and we take care of each other here. Issues are resolved quickly; we don't let them fester."

"What about the Beast of Owatonna?" I asked.

Loren's laughter was booming and broad. "Thank you for that," he said when he'd calmed again. "A fairy tale created by humans who don't realize they have no need for cryptozoology. The Supernatural realm is more than sufficient to fill their nightmares."

"You think the Beast is a shifter?" Alexei asked.

"Of course," Loren asked. "Humans don't know that we live here, so when they see a shifter in wolf form—larger than the average wolf—they draw their own conclusions. It's the nature of humans to exaggerate."

Loren struck me as the type happy to exaggerate if it enhanced his own position.

"There are, of course, always believers, regardless of the silliness of the idea. You must be tired," Loren said. "I'll handle this, let you get some rest."

"Appreciate it," Connor said, but his smile wasn't reflected in his gaze, which kept its suspicious edge.

"A tidy dismissal," I whispered when Loren walked over to the girls and we turned back toward the cabin. "Did we find the monster Marian mentioned?"

"We found something," Connor said. "But I don't smell anything other than Pack, and apparently neither did they. They also didn't detect any unusual magic, and Beth's injuries are consistent with a wolf attack."

"From a shifter," Alexei said, "but not one they recognized?"

"That's an issue," Connor admitted. "We don't know Beth, don't know how skilled she is in fighting. Maybe someone just got the best of her, was too fast for her to make a positive ID. Maybe someone didn't like Beth, saw their opportunity."

"And ran off without doing her much harm?" I wondered. "Or telling her how she'd pissed them off?"

"Also good questions," Connor said. "She didn't go to this woodpile regularly, so the attack couldn't have been planned to match her schedule. And, again, they ran off when they were confronted. That's not very dedicated if they were trying to make a hit."

"Put like that," Alexei said, "it seems random."

"We could look around," I said. "There could be fur, footprints. Maybe even a trace of magic or scent in case there was something they missed."

Connor smiled. "You just earned your room and board."

"I haven't had any room or board," I pointed out. "But I'm glad to hear they're on the agenda."

"I'll take a look," Alexei said.

"I'd appreciate it," Connor said.

"Did you see Beth and Jae didn't seem thrilled to see Loren?"

"I did," Alexei said. "They looked wary. Suspicious." His gaze fell onto a pile of lumber and debris that might once have been a cabin. "I think there's some rot in the resort."

"Yeah," Connor said. "I think you're right."

"Are the black armbands because they're mourning Paisley?" I asked.

"That would be my guess," he said.

"Armbands?" Alexei asked, frowning back toward the wood-pile. "I didn't catch that."

"Only the young ones wore them." Connor sighed. "We'll have to dig into this more, but tomorrow, since the sun will be rising soon." He looked at me. "How long do we have?"

I looked toward the eastern horizon. Dawn was creeping closer, her rosy fingers grasping at the edges of the horizon. "About thirty minutes," I said.

"Do you feel it in your bones?" Alexei asked.

I looked back at him, smiled. "No, but I can see it with my eyeballs."

"Hilarious." He looked at least faintly amused.

"Let us know what you find," Connor told Alexei. "And be careful."

"Always," Alexei said, then pulled a peppermint from his pocket, unwrapped it, popped it into his mouth. And disappeared into the woods.

Back at the cabin, I organized my gear in the bedroom. When I came back into the living room, I found Connor had arranged a blanket and pillow on the couch, but I was alone in the cabin. He came in through the front door a moment later.

"I was just closing the shutters," he said, and locked the door behind him.

"You sure you'll be okay on the couch?"

"I'll be fine. I've also slept in a tent in the mountains. Rockies, not Pyrenees, but I imagine sleeping on rock in a freezing wind is pretty much the same all over the world."

"Our tragedies bring us together," I said.

He snorted, took off his watch, placed it on the kitchen counter, along with the contents of his pockets, then toed off his boots.

"You were good with Beth."

He looked up, brows lifted.

"You handled her well, I mean. You were thoughtful and polite, and you worked to put her at ease. But you did it with authority."

"Not bad for a former punk."

I bit back a smile. "You still have some punk in you."

"Will I get in trouble if I call you a brat again?"

"Yes. There were two of them—the things that attacked her. She didn't realize it, but there would've had to be at least two. One to hit her, one still moving. Because the one that hit her was behind her."

"That's my thinking, yeah."

Silence fell.

"Does it bother you?" I asked, breaking it.

"Does what bother me?"

"The fact that conversation stops when shifters see you."

He went still, watched me for a quiet moment. "Yes. It's part of who I am. Part of who I want to be. But it makes me . . ."

"Separate," I said, and he nodded.

"I think we've switched positions," I said. "You've always been the prince, but when you were a kid, it didn't really matter. Gabriel was in control, and that was that. But you're older now. You've, I guess, come into your power. People are curious about you. Maybe wary of you. And wondering if you're the next Apex. The next leader of the Pack."

"Yeah," he said. "They see me for what I might be. Some for who I actually am—they're the good ones. But most for what I might be able to do in the future. The possibility I can make things better or worse for them."

I nodded, shifted my gaze to the window and the dark trees outlined beyond it. "For me, it's the opposite. When I was a kid, I was a novelty. The new thing. The first thing. There was a little of that when I came back from Paris, but now the novelty's somewhat worn off because I'm a vampire with a real job. That's not nearly as interesting, at least for humans. But I'm still . . . separate. I know how that feels."

"Yeah, I imagine you do."

I studied him. "You know, you've changed a lot. Grown up a lot. It's strange to witness. But good."

"Because you wouldn't be here if I was still pulling your pigtails?"

"I would not." I smiled with teeth. "But you can try it if you'd like."

"Oh, there are things I'd like to try."

"And that's a little strange, too."

"Being flirted with?"

"Being flirted with by you. You usually had an entourage of ladies hoping to bag the next Apex."

"And you dated vampires."

I pointed at myself. "Vampire, so."

"And yet," he said, gesturing to the room, "here we are."

Silence fell, and because we were still getting used to each other, it was about halfway between comfortable and awkward, and on the verge of both.

"This is going to be complicated," I said.

"No," Connor said, stepping forward. "I don't think it's going to be complicated at all." He put a hand at my waist, pressed our bodies together.

Here we were. On the cusp of something, even without considering whatever the hell was happening at this compound. But when he kissed me, the rest hardly seemed to matter.

Ten minutes later, I fell asleep to the howling of wolves. This time, it seemed they howled not in fear or alarm but in solidarity. Because dawn was coming, the night was nearly done, and it was time for rest again.

SIX

I blinked awake in darkness at dusk, howls issuing across the resort again.

Shifters, I realized, were the roosters of the supernatural world. And I thought it best not to mention that observation to Connor.

I sent Theo a message, gave him a brief update with a promise to call if we learned anything else. And when my stomach growled, I looked at the closed bedroom door and thought longingly of the kitchen that lay beyond it.

I'd managed not to steer Connor into a relationship talk, into defining what we were doing. And I wasn't so comfortable with him that I'd shuffle out of the bedroom in a T-shirt, hair a bird's nest. I got up, moved around quietly to shower and condition a few hundred miles of wind out of my hair, dress in jeans and a fluid green V-neck T-shirt.

I found him still asleep on the couch. He was shirtless, one arm thrown behind his head, the other across his abdomen, and a striped camp blanket ruched at his hips. He was much too tall for the battered leather couch, so his bare feet were propped on the opposite armrest.

There was something disarming about seeing him—tall and muscular—squeezed onto the sofa, the sensation amplified by his bare chest and the dark lock that curled almost innocently over his forehead. He was a powerful shifter, a powerful alpha. But he was also a man who'd slept in discomfort, so I'd have a bedroom to myself.

He was honorable. Or at least had *become* honorable after his puckish teenage years. Either way, that was where he'd ended up. And we'd ended up here together, in a North Woods cabin surrounded by shifters and the beast that seemed to be haunting them.

I tiptoed into the kitchen, found a coffeemaker ready to brew, and turned it on. I sampled green grapes from a pile in a bowl of fruit, then opened the refrigerator and stared. He'd fetched the beers last night, so this was my first view of the fridge's contents—and the dozens of bottles of blood inside.

"You think that's enough?"

I glanced back, found Connor sitting up, running a hand through his hair and looking a little concerned that it might not actually be enough.

I arched an eyebrow. "How much blood do you think a vampire drinks?"

"I'm not entirely sure."

"A couple of bottles a night," I said, "depending on whether I'm injured or training heavily." I did a quick guesstimate. "There have to be at least a hundred in here."

"I figured it was better to err on the side of caution."

I raised my brows. "To avoid my snacking on shifters?"

He grinned. "Maybe I erred a little far. I don't want you to starve. And I actually asked Miranda to stock the fridge. She, let's say, poured herself into the task."

"That's truly awful."

"I just woke up" was his defense.

That Miranda had bought the bottles probably explained why she hadn't been at the party. She was here instead.

"I'm sure Miranda was thrilled to help," I said dryly.

"She wasn't, of course." He smiled, but moved closer, rested his arm on the door, and peered inside. "Did she get anything good? I didn't pay much attention last night."

"She bought the most ridiculous—and probably the most expensive—options. Nothing basic. Nothing simple. Everything with flavors and seltzers and swirls."

Brows raised, he took out a bottle. "Free-range, shade-grown vegan blood product." He looked at me. "Why would a vampire want vegan blood?"

"Why would a shifter buy it for a vampire?" I countered.

"Touché. Probably to insult her." He slid the bottle back into its slot. "Is there something in here you can actually drink?"

"I'll be fine." I preferred my blood unadulterated or flavored, but I'd live. Because I was immortal. "I appreciate the gesture. It was thoughtful."

"It wasn't meant to be. As you pointed out, I'm trying to keep you from snacking on us. It's good, practical Apex behavior."

"Said the man who chases prey on four legs. Why is Miranda even here? Is she close to your family?"

"Coincidence, or so she says. She's got friends in the clan, and had already arranged the visit."

"Hmm," I said vaguely, fairly certain there was nothing coincidental about it, and grabbed the simplest flavor I could find—"Hint o' Lemon." I closed the refrigerator, twisted off the cap. "Would you like a drink?"

He looked at the bottle for a very long time, a man facing a tricky dilemma. "If I say no, will you think less of me?"

"Don't you eat prey on the run?"

"Isn't that a book title?"

I just lifted my eyebrows.

"I'm a wolf," he said, eyes flashing like he'd already made the shift into that form.

The coffeemaker finished its cycle, and he poured a mug, passed it to me, then poured one for himself.

I took a drink of the blood, bit back a grimace at the tang. And swallowed a mouthful of coffee to erase the aftertaste.

"Well, Mr. Wolf, what's on our agenda tonight?"

"Initiation," he said. "But first we'll go pay our respects to the other elders."

I grinned. "That's very . . . politic."

"If you call me a vampire again, I'll make you drink the vegan blood."

"I'd like to see you try."

Connor snorted. "After the initiation, we'll have dinner with my family. It's tradition for the initiate's family to host a meal."

"What do wolves eat to celebrate a new member of the Pack?"

"An old member of the Pack," he said, and laughed when my eyes widened. "That was a joke."

"I know," I said. Or I mostly had.

He smiled. "It depends on the locale. Since we're in Minnesota"— he paused to consider—"herring and moose?"

"Yum," I said with false cheer, uncertain about both choices.

He turned, and I caught a flash of something dark on his flank, just above his right hip. It was ink and what looked like letters. "Since when do you have a tattoo? I saw you with your shirt off, like, two weeks ago."

"It was dark that night, and we were fighting."

It hadn't been that dark, and it would take a particularly uninterested person not to notice his torso in great detail.

"Arms up," I said. "I want to see it."

"I don't need to be inspected."

"As the inspector, I disagree. Come on," I said with a grin, and twirled a finger in the air.

"I object to being objectified," he said, but his cocky smile said exactly the opposite. He raised his hands and turned.

Across the side of his hip, in a thick font that looked medieval, were Latin words drawn with a very skillful hand in a deep crimson.

"'*Non ducor, duco,*'" I read. "What does it mean?"

"Roughly: 'I'm not led; I lead.'"

"Once again, surprisingly politic for a shifter. You sure you aren't part vampire?"

"Watch it."

I grinned. "Based on the timing, and because you don't exactly look happy about it, I'd say you got drunk with a bunch of shifters while you were traveling."

"I wasn't drunk, Holmes. But I was outplayed in a game of darts," he admitted. "Barely. And this was the cost of my loss."

"It's a very pretty cost," I said. The letters were sharp and crisp, the ink dark and immaculately applied. I liked the look and the phrase. "It doesn't disappear—heal itself—when you shift?"

"The wound heals, closes. But it doesn't affect the ink." He sipped coffee, cocked his head. "Can vampires get tattoos?"

"Same issue. Healing closes the wound, but doesn't affect the ink."

"It occurs to me that I haven't seen you naked. Do you have any?"

"No."

He smiled. "You wanna play darts?"

"I do not," I said with a laugh. "But I could eat. Human food," I added. "Do you cook?"

"I make a very good grilled cheese sandwich. You?"

"Only coffee," I said. "But it's very good coffee." And that was something.

"I can probably manage to scramble eggs."

"Then I can probably manage to eat them."

He lifted his brows. "Are you asking me to make you breakfast, brat?"

"Room and board," I reminded him, and sipped the blood. "That was your offer."

He looked mildly irritated to realize I had a point, but turned back to the refrigerator, shoved aside bottles to reach a carton of eggs, a stick of butter, and a bottle of cream. While I sipped coffee, he cracked eggs into a bowl, added a splash of cream, waited for a small skillet to heat and for the plug of butter he'd put in it to melt.

"You look like you can handle cooking well enough," I said when he poured the beaten eggs into the pan.

"Better than you can bake. I remember the Cadogan House fire."

I pursed my lips. "The Cadogan House fire was not my fault. Who lets a kid bake without supervision?"

He grinned. "I think you mean, what eight-year-old vampire wanders into the kitchen alone during a House barbecue because she wants a cupcake and, when she can't find one, decides to make it herself?"

Me, obviously, but at eight, I hadn't realized that ingredients had to be carefully measured and that frosting was more than sugar and food coloring.

"It was only a small fire."

He moved the eggs around with a spatula. "Get two plates, will you? Cabinet above the sink and to the left."

I drank the rest of the bottle to get it over with, then came around the counter, found plates and forks. And when Connor began to spoon up soft yellow curds of scrambled eggs, I held out a plate for a scoop.

I took my portion to the counter, sat down on a stool.

He served himself, turned off the burner, and moved the pan, then put his plate near mine. But instead of digging in, he put his hands on the counter, arms braced, brows knit. "Before we go to the initiation, I wanted to . . . explain some things."

"Okay," I said with a nod, expecting a primer on how to deal with the clan. The rules, the etiquette we hadn't had time to discuss before the trip.

Instead, he ran a hand through his hair. "I've had no shortage of women," he began, then paused.

I lifted an eyebrow. Not the conversation starter I'd expected. And I realized he seemed more than a little unnerved. For the first time that I could remember, he didn't seem entirely sure of his steps.

Connor looked at the floor, brow creased. "I'm struggling a little bit. I don't usually struggle when talking to women."

He really did seem unsure of himself. "Are you about to tell me you've dated everyone in the resort?"

"What? No. I'm talking about us. About the cabin and the bed."

"Okay," I said again, still confused, but a lot more intrigued.

"I'm used to being slick," he said. "Suave. The prince surrounded by potentials. It's kind of my thing. Or was. After the fight with the fairies—fighting with you—and after two weeks of traveling and thinking, I acknowledged that being that kind of prince wasn't enough for me. Not anymore."

My heart pounded, as if it understood something the rest of me hadn't yet. "What kind of prince do you want to be?"

He looked up at me, blue eyes shining as if they were lit from within. "The kind that's good enough for you."

I grasped at words, but they scurried away, totally uninterested in being wrangled to express my dizzying emotions. "I don't know what to say."

He smiled. "Of course you don't. You're confident, Elisa, maybe a little arrogant. But not smug. Not cruel. You're a skilled fighter and intelligent and funny, and you have a very charming obsession with rules."

"So the things that made me bratty as a child make me a very good adult."

The smile became a wicked grin. "Your words, not mine. You want to be good, to be skilled. But you can still empathize. You care about justice and doing the right thing. And you keep doing the right thing even when you're afraid of what's inside you."

I didn't flinch at the reference to the monster because the sentiment was so complimentary. It was odd to hear myself described that way by him—a guy I'd spent nearly twenty years mostly wanting to slug.

"I've been very privileged," I said. "And I was taught—just like you—the very clear differences between right and wrong. You're confident," I said with a smile. "Maybe a little arrogant. Occasionally smug, but never cruel. You're a skilled fighter and intelligent and funny, and you have an occasionally charming obsession with breaking rules. You also care a lot about doing the right thing. You care about your people. You travel to help them, risk yourself to help them. You're good enough for anyone."

"Even after harassing you for most of your teenage years?"

I couldn't help but grin. "You were a holy terror, but let's acknowledge my role in that, too. While I will deny everything if you bring this up again in the future, I could be . . . bratty."

"Big admission," he said, his smile as wide as mine. "I don't believe in fate. But maybe we just needed to be ready for each other."

We just looked at each other, smiling.

"I love my parents, my family," Connor said. "But I'm aware I was spoiled because they considered me the prince. The Apex in training. I had attention and love. I was encouraged to take chances, and I was forgiven if I screwed up. I was praised for being cocky because it was a sign of being alpha. Showed I was on the right path.

"That's the thing about Apex," he said. "Being Apex is about listening to the Pack, doing what's best for the Pack. Acting on behalf of the Pack. If you aren't confident enough to be who you

are, to care about those who you care about, you're not alpha
enough to be Apex." He paused. "It's Alexei's fault I grew up."

"Is it?"

Connor nodded. "He's always been more serious than me. Not
as serious as you," he added with a grin, "because he's still a
shifter. But he has . . . an old soul.

"We were out on a run," he continued, "scrambling around in
the woods. Chasing rabbits, turkeys, deer, whatever. We heard
this really odd sound—some kind of bird, but nothing like what
we'd heard before. So we followed it, found a pond in the middle
of a field. There was a full moon, and it was shining down on this
water, and the water was perfectly still. Except, in the middle, was
a bird."

He frowned. "A crane, I think. A sandhill crane. White, with
black-tipped wings and a spot of crimson right at the top of its
head. It was alone in the middle of this water, the light reflecting
off its feathers. And it was . . . majestic."

He stared into middle distance, as if watching the memory play
back. "It was alone, as far as we would see. No other birds—no
other wildlife. Just this one single crane in the middle of this sil-
very water." He ran a hand through his hair. "I was—I don't
know—eighteen or so. We shifted back, and I made some stupid
joke about food, and let's hurry up and go. I'm sure it was witty,
but it was callous. And he said something like, 'It can fly. We
stumble around in the dirt, and it can fly. We should see what it
has to tell us.' And then the bird spread its wings and lifted up,
droplets of water flying behind it like a trail of stars. It was one of
the most beautiful things I've ever seen."

"I bet it was lovely," I said, imagining the scene clearly.

He settled his gaze on me again. "You'd have appreciated it.
And after that, I began to appreciate things more. Alexei has
depth. And for the first time in my life, I wanted to have some of
that depth. Some of his gravitas. Does that sound ridiculous?"

"Not even a little. It sounds important."

He smiled, seemed relieved that I thought so. "It was."

"While we're being honest, can I make a confession?"

"Sure."

I cleared my throat, had to work myself up to it a bit. "As a kid . . . I enjoyed it when you got in trouble."

He threw back his head and roared with laughter. When he'd calmed down, he wiped at his eyes. "Sorry," he said. "Sorry. It's just—that's not a confession I'd have ever thought you'd make. I know you enjoyed it. You weren't exactly subtle, Lis. That's one reason why I called you brat."

He smiled at me, and there was something so open and unguarded about his smile that it tugged my heartstrings. Vulnerability wasn't something I saw very often in Sups, much less in the man who wanted to lead them. I let myself enjoy that smile, that moment, and thought how much time had changed us.

Something beeped, and we both looked toward the sound. Connor's screen was on the counter, flashing with light and buzzing with sound.

"Hold that thought," he said, and maneuvered around to check it. "My alarm." There was resignation in his voice as he turned it off. "I set a reminder. We need to get moving."

I looked down at the plates of eggs that had gone cold, and probably a little rubbery. "You still hungry?"

"Yeah. You?"

"Yeah," I said, smiling as I picked up a fork, and began to shovel in eggs.

He grinned, did the same thing. And for a moment, we were kids again, supernaturally hungry and unselfconscious about the need.

"Oh," he said, swallowing a mouthful. "And since I cooked, you have to do the dishes."

Dammit.

* * *

The resort was quiet when we walked back toward the lodge. There were lights along the path, but the firepits hadn't yet been lit. These shifters didn't appear to be early risers.

"Let me take the lead with the elders," Connor said. "They know you're coming; they've been informed. But that doesn't mean they won't play insular and offended."

"Well," I said resignedly, "this will be a fun wake-up call."

We took the stairs to the lodge's porch, magic growing stronger as we entered the building. We followed the sounds of talking and conversation to the lobby, where a dozen shifters lounged on worn leather furniture. There was a fireplace on one side of the room and a bookshelf on another, and they flanked a third wall of windows that overlooked a large lawn.

Magic was plentiful. Sunk into the cracks and crevices of wood and furniture, and stirring in the air as shifters communicated, moved, watched us pass.

We took the stairs to the second floor. The vintage North Woods look continued here, with golden log walls, patterned carpet, and old fishing and hunting gear on the walls. We steered down a hallway with named rooms—Superior, Michigan, Erie, Ontario—branching off, and into the final room on the right.

It looked like a former ballroom: vaulted log ceiling, river stone fireplace, plenty of windows. Threadbare stacking chairs edged the room, and there were more well-beaten leather couches and folding card tables in the middle of it. Shifters were scattered throughout, but I didn't see Loren, Georgia, or the other members of her family. The space smelled of smoke and cigars, and magic peppered the air.

A man, leather-skinned and tendon-lean, came toward us as the other shifters watched. He wore jeans, boots, and a T-shirt, all of them equally scarred. His face was deeply lined, his hair a gleaming mix of black and silver that shagged to his neck.

We met in the middle of the room. "Keene," he said. Unlike Loren, he didn't offer a hand.

"Cash."

He turned his gaze to me, briefly evaluated the threat, then shifted back to Connor. "Welcome to the resort, to clan territory. And who's this?" Cash asked, although he obviously knew.

"Elisa Sullivan," Connor said. "Daughter of Ethan Sullivan and Caroline Merit."

"Vampire," Cash said.

"Maison Dumas graduate," Connor said. "OMB staff. Daughter of two Pack allies. Katana expert."

I wondered if he was justifying my being at the compound—or his interest in me. Maybe both. Whatever the reasons, Cash's expression didn't change. I guess he didn't care much for vampires.

"How's Beth?" Connor continued rather than waiting for commentary on my qualifications.

"She's fine. Shifted, healed."

"Good," Connor said. "What about her attacker? Did you find any evidence in the woods?"

"Evidence in the woods?" Cash's tone was dry, and other shifters around the room chuckled. "Of what? There are hungry animals, shifters we know, shifters we don't. Nothing more, nothing less. This was probably someone Beth pissed off who hasn't come forward yet. Her generation has a lot of . . . conflict."

"Does it?" Connor asked mildly.

"Look," Cash began. "The clan's getting younger. There are a lot of whelps around here, and they spend a lot of time talking and thinking. They have a lot of opinions."

"They've shared those opinions with you?"

"Some." His eyes went dark. "Nothing that needs to concern Chicago."

Connor managed a surprisingly imperious expression. "I think Chicago can be the judge of that."

Cash rolled his eyes. "They complain about not being known to humans, but they don't know what life is truly like. What humans are truly like."

"And the black armbands?" Connor asked.

Like the women last night, several of the younger shifters wore the black armbands. And none of the older shifters had them. Because they hadn't been as close to Paisley or because they mourned differently?

"In honor of a shifter who recently passed." Cash's tone wasn't complimentary.

"Paisley," Connor said, and Cash didn't quite manage to hide his surprise.

He nodded. "You know her?"

"I didn't. You don't like the armbands?"

"I don't like the display of mourning. Life begins; it ends. That's the cycle, and it's perfectly natural, perfectly in tune with nature. I don't approve of the sentiment or of the fact that they're wearing something intended to distinguish them from others. Paisley's death was a tragedy. But that's all it was. You can't go around assigning fault to every act of god. We're shifters, for god's sake."

"So you think one of the younger shifters might have attacked Beth," Connor said.

"It's the most logical solution. I suppose it could have been someone outside the clan. A rogue shifter."

"Are there many out in these parts?" Connor asked but, given his tone, just for form. "Rogue shifters?"

"Few here and there. They aren't part of the community. They don't reach out much."

Connor made a noncommittal sound. He walked to the window, looked out over the dark resort. "You heard about the issues en route?"

Cash went to a couch, took a seat, and spread his arms along the back. He was showing arrogance, that he had nothing to hide. But there was a tightness around his eyes.

"To Alaska?" he asked as if he had no interest in the answer.

Connor glanced back at him. "The Pack's return home. No one from the resort joined the caravan."

"Look out the window," Cash said, turning his gaze to it. "We don't need to go anywhere to recharge. We have everything we need right here."

"Recharging isn't about woods. It's about Aurora, as I'm sure you know."

"Whatever. No one told me leaving was obligatory, so we didn't leave. If you had issues, not our doing."

"And I take it you don't think there's anything to these beast rumors?" Connor asked.

Cash rolled his eyes. "Trouble-mongering and wild imaginations."

Connor watched him for a minute. "Okay," he said. "I appreciate the time and the talk. We'll see you at the initiation."

"We?" Cash asked.

"Me and Elisa," Connor said, voice dry because the answer was obvious, and Cash certainly knew that plan ahead of time.

All eyes in the room shifted to me. "No vampire is attending an initiation," Cash said, leaning forward.

"I was invited," Connor said mildly. "She's my plus-one."

"No fucking way." The shifter who said it was older, probably Cash's age, with a barrel chest and silver hair and beard. His skin was suntanned, his eyes blue and hard. He wore jeans, a button-down shirt with sleeves rolled up at the wrists, and dark motorcycle boots with chains across the instep.

"Everett," Cash said in warning.

Everett's lips compressed into a thin, unhappy line, but he held his peace.

"As you were informed before we made this trip," Connor said, "we'll be attending together, and with Georgia's and the Apex's blessings. If you've got a problem with that, you're welcome to take it up with the Apex. Or, if you're not interested in a trip to Chicago, with me. Now."

Tension and magic rose in the room, swirled in invisible eddies.

Cash sat back again. "I don't know you or your old man like some of the others do. Not like your aunt does. You're Pack, and that gives you a right to be here and an invitation. We aren't looking for trouble. We're looking to be left alone, to live our lives. We have nothing to hide here."

"Including from humans?" I wondered.

Cash looked at me, jaw tight. "What we do in our territory is no business of humans." *Or of vampires* was his silent addition.

Connor let those words hang, apparently didn't feel it necessary to respond to them. "We appreciate your hospitality. If you want to talk to me about anything else, we'll be here for at least a few days."

That was a longer trip than we'd discussed, so I guessed from Connor's expression he was testing the clan, watching their reactions to the possibility we'd be around for a while.

"You're staying past the initiation," Cash said.

"I don't see that we need to be in a hurry," Connor began, shifting his gaze back to the windows. "Like you said, you have everything a shifter needs right here."

SEVEN

"We'll take the bike," Connor said, then glanced at me. "Unless you prefer a vehicle to protect your . . ." He circled a finger over his head.

"My head?"

"Your hair."

I just lifted my brows.

"Just checking," he said with a teasing smile. "We are going to an event, after all."

"An event for shifters, which means most of them will probably be in T-shirts and boots. And I revise my prior conclusion: You're still a punk."

"I prefer 'thorough.' Your impressions of the shifters so far?"

"Cash is worried."

Connor looked down at me. "Worried?"

"He sat down on the couch—moved away from you. He wasn't going to show you any deference. Casual disdain," I decided.

"Okay," Connor said.

"But that's not what was in his eyes. That wasn't casual, and I don't think it was about you. It was worry or concern. He didn't like you asking questions, because I don't think he's comfortable with whatever the answers might be."

He studied me before turning the bike, picking up his helmet.

"What?" I asked, a little unnerved by the intensity of his stare.

"You're good at this."

I lifted my brows. "Did you think I wouldn't be?"

He grinned. "I've never known you to half-ass anything. But this isn't just practice. It's . . . innate. A kind of instinct for reading people. You've got it."

"I'm a vampire," I said.

"A lot of people are."

"No, seriously," I said. "I mean, I appreciate the compliment, and I'll take it. And you told me you wanted to know what I thought, so I assumed you were serious and I paid attention."

"Good."

It was my turn to smile. "But vampires—" I paused to gather my thoughts. "Wolves are predators, but they're predators—mostly—of animals. You understand land, animals, their behavior. We hunt humans. We know how to watch them. It's our nature."

"Have you ever bitten a human?"

"No. Have you?"

His smile was lazy. "Only when asked."

I just rolled my eyes, picked up my helmet, but paused before getting on the bike. "I want to ask you something. Not about biting," I added at the flare of heat in his eyes.

"Okay," he said, his response quick and sincere.

"Did you bring me here, into this compound and this lodge, to piss them off?"

Heat flashed in his eyes. "I don't use people. You're here because I want you to be here."

"But?" I prompted when he paused.

"But, yes, I'm paying attention to how they react to you. Because they're a microcosm of the Pack."

My belly quivered at the admission and the implication. He anticipated—planned—that I'd meet the Pack. Not just as a Sullivan or a vampire or an Ombud. Because somehow, despite years of pushing it away, we'd found something important between us.

Connor tucked a lock of hair behind my ear, and I could all but feel my heart melting. Then he dipped his head toward mine.

"*Elisa,*" he said, so softly that the word was nearly a breath, hardly a prayer. My eyes drifted shut, awaiting the kiss I knew would follow. Eager for it.

"Just remember," he said, moving his lips to hover near my ear, "that shifters can manipulate people, too."

Then he pulled back, turned away, and threw a leg over the bike.

I gave him a narrow-eyed stare. "That was really mean." But I liked the way my heart thudded in response.

"And effective," he said with a cocky smile. "Let's go for a ride."

I climbed on behind him and planned my revenge.

We rode northeast, dipping away from Lake Superior and into the hinterlands of Minnesota. The road became curvier and steeper, forest giving way to rocky hills and striking drops. We disappeared into a tunnel carved into hard rock, the orange lights along the wall flashing as we sped past them.

After ten or fifteen miles, we left the divided highway, and Connor slowed the bike to pick over a gravel road bordered by evergreen trees and steel gray boulders.

He came to a stop at the end of a line of vehicles—bikes, trucks, and SUVs—parked along both sides of the road. We dismounted, removed helmets, ran fingers through tangled hair. And, without the bike's rumble, could hear the sounds of happy children and chatting adults through the whisper of leaves.

A few muscular men and women stood around in black shirts and pants, casting suspicious gazes at us before looking away.

"Security?" I asked.

"It's a private event," Connor said. "Especially since humans don't know what they are."

"Where are we going?" I asked. I'd expected to see a park shelter with coolers and balloons, or an overlook where shifters had swagged streamers and drank beers. Instead, trees made a canyon on both sides of the road.

"You'll see," he said with a smile, and offered his hand.

I took his hand, enjoyed the satisfaction that flashed in his eyes when I linked our fingers together.

Connor ducked into the trees, and we followed a well-worn trail I probably wouldn't have seen if I hadn't been with him. We walked maybe a quarter mile, and I was glad I'd opted for boots without stiletto heels, which wouldn't have worked well over uneven ground and loamy leaves. As the sounds of celebration grew louder, we passed birch trees with curled silver bark, hard-edged boulders that looked like they'd been spewed from a volcano, and delicate white flowers sprouting in blank spaces in the undergrowth. And behind it all, a soft static that it took me much too long to realize was water.

A long, dark shape slithered across the trail, and I stopped short, only just managed not to squeak.

"What?" Connor asked, fingers tensing around mine. "What's wrong?"

"Snake."

"It was harmless. Just a garter snake."

"Don't care. I don't like snakes."

He looked at me. "How do you not like snakes?"

"Biological mandate," I said. "They slither. I don't like things that slither."

"But you both have fangs."

I slid my gaze to him. "Shifters and skunks both have fur."

"Fair point."

"You have no issues with animals?"

"I'm not afraid of any animals, reptilian or otherwise." His smile was cocky. "I'm wolf and human. That's two Apex predators for the price of one."

"Or twice as much trouble in one package, depending on your

perspective. And I'm pretty sure if you were being hunted by a great white shark you'd have some fear."

"There's a solution to that: Don't swim in the ocean."

I couldn't argue with that logic, and skirted the edge of the trail, where the snake had disappeared.

The sound grew clearer as we edged toward a creek, water trickling like tiny bells over rocks as it raced ahead of us.

And suddenly, the ground disappeared.

We reached the literal end of the trail—and the world opened up. Forest gave way to stone—a rust-colored plateau half as big as a city block. Connor stepped down from the trail, offered me a hand as I jumped down beside him and moved forward, stared openmouthed as I turned around.

Not just a plateau, but waterfalls. The creek had rounded behind us, spilling over a stone cliff before tumbling over cataracts below it, then moving through a narrow groove in the rock across the plateau. Tiki torches had been lit along the edges, casting flickering light and shadows across water and the stone bluffs along the far side of the plateau, black and red and orange stone marked with trees and what looked like a high trail. Even with the dark dome of the sky above us, it was like being in a canyon of color.

For the second time tonight, I was speechless. "I don't have the words," I managed, walking toward the rockbound stream. There were pools of water here and there, collected in smooth divots in the rock that had been worn by time or rain or the stream itself. The water disappeared over the edge of the plateau on the other side.

I walked forward and watched it tumble down another set of cataracts, lights from more torches glittering like diamonds.

"What do you think?"

"It's . . . amazing," I said, looking back at him. "Absolutely amazing."

"It should probably be a state park," he said. "But it's privately held, and the owner's a friend of the clan."

I turned around, found Alexei standing right behind me.

"Jesus," I said, feeling bones jolt against skin as I startled. "What is wrong with you?"

He grinned. "Did I scare you?"

"You disturbed me."

"I scared you."

"No, that's not really the emotion."

"You should probably look down," Connor advised Alexei.

He did, saw the small dagger I'd drawn in the blink of an eye, held near his groin.

Connor leaned forward. "Did she scare you?" he asked Alexei, whose expression was dour.

He lifted his hands. "Initiation's a bad time to pull a knife on a shifter."

"And you shouldn't startle a vampire when she's surrounded by shifters in a foreign territory." But I slipped the dagger away again.

"Truce," Alexei said, and took a step backward, putting a little more space between us. The boy could learn.

"I thought you weren't armed," Connor whispered.

"It's a very small dagger. You never know when you're going to need one."

"For the sake of peace," Connor said, "try to keep it hidden."

"I'll do my best."

"You did the introductions?" Alexei asked Connor.

"We did. Cash was an asshole."

"So, as expected." He looked at me. "You appear to have survived."

"I mostly stood there and tried to look stern."

"Wise choice," he said with a faint smile.

"What did you find last night?" Connor asked.

"Nothing useful. Ground in the woods didn't hold footprints. No fur, no scent of non-shifter blood."

"In other words," Connor said, "no sign of the animal."

"Zip."

Clapping and whistling split the air around us, and we followed the others' gazes to the movement at the top tier of waterfalls.

Shadow and light began to shimmer across the rock and water as shifters carrying candles and torches moved across the plateau, walking toward the middle falls. In the arms of a smiling brunette with sun-kissed skin was a smiling baby boy. His cheeks were flushed pink, his hair pale blond. He looked to be about nine months old, and he gnawed on his fist like it was a favorite snack. Behind them a man followed with tan skin and the same shade of blond hair as the child, although his was longer and shaggier, reaching his shoulders in what I considered classic shifter style: halfway between "hair metal" and "cologne model."

"That's Cassie with the baby," Connor said, gesturing. "Her husband is Wes, and her mother is Georgia. All of them are McAllisters."

Georgia was tall and pale, with long legs and a generous build topped by a bouffant of black hair with a streak of silver just above her eyes. She had a face that would have been called "handsome." Strong features, with sharp blue eyes and a wide mouth with a beauty mark at the left corner.

"So Georgia is one of your parents' cousins?" I asked.

"My mother's cousin," Connor said. "Their mothers were sisters."

"Big family."

"My mother has to keep a list."

"I bet." I glanced at him, saw pleasure and pride as he watched his Packmates assemble, prepare to welcome another into their fold. "You were initiated, weren't you?"

"I was. My parents, aunts, and uncles were there. It's where Jeff stood up to my father for the first time. I think that was before you were born."

"Old-timer," I said.

"Maybe. But I got to wear a crown."

I narrowed my eyes at him. "Seriously?"

"Well, technically it was a coronet," he admitted with a shrug. "But that's close enough."

"I'm jealous."

"Of course you are, brat. You did always love a good crown." He slid his fingers into mine, squeezed, and trained his gaze and satisfied smile on those who gathered on the plateau beside the trickling waterfall.

I could hear the murmurs around us, surprise and whispers moving through the crowd like a wave as they observed their prince, their would-be king, and the vampire he'd brought to the ceremony and publicly joined himself with. If their magic was any indication, their emotions were mixed. Some were confused, others surprised. A few were angry, but since I didn't know anyone here other than the few we'd met last night, that could have been prejudice or preconception talking.

I wondered if I should be concerned, glanced at him, and found him looking at me, brow lifted in amusement.

"You're a very loud thinker," he said.

He couldn't have known what I was thinking, but when I realized I'd tensed up, I figured it was easy to guess.

"If you're going to focus on shifters," he said with an easy smile, "focus on me."

A whistle cut through the air, high and sharp as a blade. We looked up at the waterfall, where a man with suntanned skin, gray hair, and a thick but neatly trimmed beard in the same shade looked down at us, hands clasped together. He was short and compact; his arms were strong beneath the short sleeves of a button-down shirt he'd paired with khakis. That was practically shifter formal wear.

"Bowling team uniform," Connor whispered, and I bit back a chuckle.

"Another elder?" I asked.

"His name is Patch," Connor said. "He's their, let's say, spiritual leader."

"That means he picks the best whiskey." It was Alexei's voice that whispered beside me, and damned if I hadn't totally missed his sidling up to me again.

"How do you do that?" I asked.

He lifted a shoulder. "We're wolves. We stalk prey. This should not be a surprise."

I rolled my eyes and demanded better of my predatory senses.

"We are gathered here," Patch said when the crowd quieted, "to welcome William Avery into the arms of this territory, into the arms of this clan, and into the arms of this Pack."

There were hoots and shouts of approval, a few hearty claps.

"I've known Cassie and Wes, and of course Georgia, for a very long time. We all have. They're part of the family we've grown here. We've watched Cassie learn to cook—and occasionally battled fires because of it."

Sister from another mister, I thought.

"We've seen Wes's skills with a bow and arrow grow. And those times he isn't so skilled. And now they've made this beautiful baby boy."

He reached out his arms. Cassie pressed a kiss to the baby's forehead, then handed him over to Patch. The child went big-eyed, clutched at Patch's beard.

"May your life be long," Patch said. "May your love be deep. May your laughter be loud. May you be strong and proud and happy. May you remain a member of the clan, a member of the

Pack, a wolf until your days are no more. May you find peace in the world around you, solace in the woods, and your family waiting when you return."

He leaned in, whispering something into the child's ear, then stood straight again. "You have the object?"

"We do." Wes held out something long and silver. Patch took it, draped it around the child's neck.

William immediately popped it into his mouth.

"Military dog tags," Connor whispered. "Wes's father was in the Army, killed in duty."

"Shifter?"

"Yeah. Bribed a doctor to let him skip the physical after he ran the quarter mile in record time. Wes wanted to enlist, follow in his footsteps, but shifters were banned by that time, and there were no bribes to be had."

A damn shame that was, given shifters were stronger and faster than humans, could heal themselves, at least under certain circumstances, and had a pretty good disguise. The ban was less practical reality, I figured, than human prejudice and jealousy.

"I hereby deem you, William Avery, a member of the Grand Bay Clan. And with the acknowledgment and approval of the Apex, a member of the North American Central Pack. Blessings on you and your family, and congratulations."

He handed the child back to his parents as applause and shouts rang through the darkness, echoing off rock and water. The baby clapped and tugged at the dog tags as his parents, smiling and misty-eyed, looked on.

After a moment, Patch held up his hands again. "We also have responsibilities," he said, shifting his gaze back to the clan. "We are to hold this child. To protect it and keep it safe. It is our responsibility to keep the clan strong for little William, and give him a home to always return to."

A few more shouts and agreement in the crowd.

Then Patch closed his eyes, held up his hands, and began to recite. "'I will not be clapped in a hood / Nor a cage, nor alight upon wrist.'"

Goose bumps lifted on my arms as the shifters around me, Connor included, began to join in the recitation. "'Now I have learnt to be proud / Hovering over the wood / In the broken mist / Or tumbling cloud.'"

"Yeats?" I asked quietly, and felt Connor's eyes on me.

"Yeah. You know it?"

"Educated guess," I said, and thought of my mother, the vampire with the master's degree in English literature. "My mother told me he was important to shifters."

"Probably was a shifter," Alexei said philosophically.

"We don't have any certainty about that," Connor said. "And we aren't going to out a man who didn't want to be outed."

"The woods are our home," Patch continued. "The mist our secrets. The clouds our ceiling. We are Pack, and we are proud."

This time, the sound of approval was nearly deafening, as shifters clapped and yelled and stamped hands or feet or stone against stone. Magic rose and built until the water itself seemed to vibrate with it, the cascades tumbling in time to the rhythm of their applause, until it reached a crescendo of happiness and union—and then fell into stunned silence.

I moved to a defensive position almost automatically, until I realized there was no fear, no imminent attack. Just awe.

I followed the line of their gazes, looked up at the sky, and stared at the ribbons of green that swam and pulsed in the clearing above us.

"Aurora borealis," Connor said. "Not usually seen this far south. But occasionally, when conditions are just right . . ."

The colors shifted, expanded, contracted, until they faded from view. And like the end of every fireworks show I'd attended as a child, people began to mill about awkwardly, not entirely sure if they'd seen the end or should wait around for more.

"I'm going to interrogate Georgia," Alexei said, breaking the silence.

Connor lifted his brows. "About the attack on Beth?"

"No," Alexei said, pulling a cord of red licorice from his pocket. "About the dinner. I want to discuss hot dish." With that, he walked away.

"It's an interesting journey, waiting to see what comes out of his mouth," I said. And wished he'd left me some licorice.

"It always is. What did you think of the ceremony?"

I looked up at Connor, found his face somehow even more beautiful in the shifting glow of torches on water. "It was beautiful. Powerful. And I can tell it means a lot to the Pack."

"I wanted you to see it."

His tone was so serious. So grave. "What do you mean?"

"This. I knew you'd be interested in the event, because you're curious. And I wanted to get your thoughts on the clan, because you're smart. But I particularly wanted you to see it. It's important to me, Lis. The union, the coming together of the Pack. The celebration of what is Pack. I wanted you to see it," he said again. "And I wanted you to be here with me."

My heart seemed to swell, emotion tightening my throat. "I'm glad I'm here," I managed. "And not just because I'm curious."

He smiled. "But you are."

"Of course I am," I said, and looked around. "I know this is a rare occasion, and rarer that a vampire gets to experience it. So thank you for that. For giving me the opportunity."

"You're welcome. And not to ruin the mood, but given this is the biggest group of clan members we're likely to see at one time, and while we're waiting for the crowd to thin"—he tipped his head toward the shifters who had clustered around the newest Pack member and his family—"any impressions?"

I'd been trying to be polite, to keep from studying or staring at anyone too closely at an event where my behavior—if not my presence—was being hotly debated. But if he was inviting me . . .

I pretended to survey the waterfalls and the high bluffs that surrounded them, but let my gaze drift across the shifters who stood or sat on the rocks, chatting or minding children whose hands and feet were in the small pockets of water in the rock, splashing joyfully. It looked entirely normal. Entirely typical. Just people socializing the way people did, supernaturally or otherwise. They looked happy. But there was something beneath it. A tension, not just in the magic, but on their faces.

If you looked at the group as a whole, the twenty-thousand-foot view, they looked relaxed. But if you looked carefully, more closely, they were on alert. Eyes scanning the edges of the waterfall. Never more than a step away from their children.

These shifters, predators in their own right, were acting more like prey. As if they feared something higher up the food chain.

"There's more fear," I said.

"Fear?"

"Apprehension," I said after a moment, testing the word. "They know something's off. I don't think they know anything in particular, but they've got concerns." I looked at him. "Do you feel anything like that?"

"I can sense the change in the magic, the tension of it. Like a string pulled too tightly. The energy is different. But you see more than I do. I honestly think you have a gift."

I looked back at him. "Come on."

"No, I'm serious." He narrowed his gaze. "You aren't psychic, are you?"

"No. I'm nosy, and I like to watch people, and I tend to notice the . . . discrepancies, I guess."

Connor grinned. "Is that why you like rules? Because they prevent discrepancies?"

"It's one of the reasons. I also like level playing fields and people who abide by the rules. Present company excluded."

He snorted. "I interrupted your review. Keep going."

I blew out a breath, took another look. Noticed the groups, the clusters, of shifters. That they were grouped together wasn't necessarily unusual; that happened whenever people socialized.

Here, the young and old shifters seemed to stand apart. Again, not necessarily unusual. Maybe they wanted to talk to the people in the same generation, those who were facing the same issues. But there seemed to be tension. Not fear or apprehension this time, but suspicion in their glances at one another. Sneaky looks, side-eyes, and armbands.

"Young versus old," I said quietly, and Connor nodded.

"I'm wondering how much is caused by his attitude."

"Leadership matters," I agreed. "Hard not to learn that lesson growing up in a House with a Master. No one is perfect, but the Cadogan vampires respected my father. Same for the Pack and your dad."

"Yeah," he said. "Until you find the groups like this where the Pack is no longer number one."

"And what is?"

"That's what we have to figure out."

Cassie, Georgia, and the others began to descend from the top tier of the waterfall and head toward us.

"All right," Connor said. "Let's go meet the family. And keep the rest of this to ourselves."

EIGHT

H ey, Connor," Cassie said, pressing a kiss to his cheek when they'd descended to our level of the cascades. "It was wonderful of you to drive up."

"Glad to be here," he said, shaking Wes's hand. "My parents send their regards."

"Appreciated," Wes said.

Cassie looked at me, eyes appraising above a bright smile. "And you must be Elisa."

"I am. It's nice to meet you. And thank you for the invitation."

"I wasn't aware I had a choice," she said, sliding a grin toward Connor.

"Don't be dramatic," Georgia said, stepping up to us with Alexei.

"Aunt Georgia," Connor said. "This is Elisa."

"Welcome," Georgia said, frowning at a smudge of something she tried to wipe from her grandson's face. "Lovely ceremony, wasn't it?"

"It was beautiful," Connor said.

Cassie smiled, danced in place to keep the baby smiling. "And Will was surprisingly well-behaved."

Right on cue, the baby burped, gurgled spit-up across his front and his mother's new dress.

"He has good timing," Connor said with a grin.

"We'll see how good his timing is," Cassie said, putting the baby into Connor's arms before he could object. But he situated the baby like a champ, tucking him into his hip and tapping at his little round belly with a fingertip so Will flashed his toothless grin.

I hadn't grown up with many babies—seeing as how I'd been the only baby vampire—but I did find them fascinating. Since that probably wasn't a thing a human mother wanted to hear from a vampire, I kept the thought to myself.

Will reached out, grabbed a lock of my hair, began babbling at it.

"Sorry," Cassie said. "He's in the grabby stage."

"Not a problem," I said with a smile, and offered up my index finger. The baby dropped my hair, wrapped his chubby fingers around mine and smiled like a madman.

It twisted my heart a little to see Connor holding Will, the depth of his enjoyment—and match that against my biological weirdness. And the likelihood I couldn't have children.

What would I be forcing him to give up? I wondered, and hated the way the question tightened my gut.

I forced myself to ignore it, to shake off the worry. We'd *just* started dating. Planning was fine, but it was unfair to both of us to put that much weight on the relationship. We'd cross that bridge—that very large and unstable bridge—when we came to it.

A kid came running back toward us, a teenager of thirteen or fourteen with hair in tiny blond tufts at the top of her head, like fuzzy little ears. She was thin, with the slightly awkward build of a girl still growing. She reached Cash, who stood a few yards away, and stopped, nearly out of breath. "You have to come."

He frowned down at her. "What's wrong, Ellie?"

"There's . . . Someone hurt Loren. He's dead."

Connor turned back to Cassie, carefully shifted the baby back into her arms.

"Show me," Cash said, and the girl nodded, turned around again, and took off.

Connor, Alexei, and I followed them at a jog. Georgia walked behind us, along with the other shifters who'd heard Ellie or seen the commotion.

We moved toward the edge of the plateau, then jumped down the five-foot drop to the next level. The creek narrowed here, the rest of the space overtaken by trees and undergrowth. There was another trail, and we followed it to a small wooden bridge that arched over the creek.

Ellie led us onto it, then pointed to the water below.

Loren lay in the shallows at the edge of the creek, arms and legs spread like an "X" marking the site of his own death. And by the look of him, that death had been hard.

His body had been horribly mauled. His skin had been cut, ripped away, streaked with bruises. Bones were broken, exposed. His clothes had been shredded and lay like streamers from a ruined party among the leaves and stones.

Something settled heavy in my gut. Sorrow and sympathy mixing with anger. Death was a bastard. Death was a waste.

Was this the thing the Pack had anticipated? Feared? The reason they'd seemed uncomfortable? Maybe they'd scented death, the dark smear of it beneath magic and joy and tumbling water, but hadn't known its source. Or maybe they'd been the ones who'd done this, who'd left this body to be found by a child, the possibility of which only made me angrier.

The scent of blood was faint—streaks across grass here and there, not the pools that should have gathered given the sheer number of his injuries, the depth of his wounds. But even in small amounts, it was still the blood of shifters. Potent and full of magic. Enough to make a vampire literally drunk on power.

The monster stirred, curious. I let it look, let it see, let it evaluate. But not too close—still well hidden behind my eyes. Fortunately, its interest was only mild. The power was interesting, but the death repelled it.

I blew out a breath and rolled my shoulders, trying to push out some of the tension. I happened to look over and found Georgia's gaze on me, face drawn and brows furrowed.

My heart thumped once, hard, and I swallowed down fear, kept my face blank. Maybe she'd think I was just dealing with a little run-of-the-mill bloodlust.

Georgia finally shifted her gaze back to Loren, then to the child. "Ellie, go back to the cataracts."

Ellie prepared to argue, but a hard look from Georgia sent her on her way.

"I don't coddle children," Georgia said as Ellie disappeared down the trail. "But she's too young to see something like this." She sighed heavily, and there was grief and weariness in the sound. "What the hell is happening in our clan?"

Connor put a hand on her shoulder, squeezed.

Cash pulled out his screen, tapped it. "It's Cash," he said to whoever answered. "We're at the waterfall. And we've got a dead resident."

"The security guards didn't come back this far?" I asked when Alexei had joined us and we'd moved several yards from the crowd.

"I doubt it," Connor said. "They'd have checked around the waterfall since that's where the event was held, but not far beyond that."

"Whoever left him here believed someone would find him."

They both looked at me.

"What do you mean?" Connor asked.

"He wasn't killed here," I said. "He was left here for someone to find."

"Psychic?" Alexei asked, just as Connor had.

"Observant," Connor corrected, narrowing his gaze as he looked at me, considered. "What do you see?"

"He looks like he was attacked by a wild animal—something

with teeth and claws—not a knife or a gun or fists. He'd have bled a lot, but there was no blood where he was placed. No smears of it on the ground, on the plants. He's tall and in good shape, and presumably would have put up a fight, but the grass around him wasn't trampled down. He wasn't killed here."

Connor nodded. "Wild animals certainly cache food, but we'd have seen evidence if they'd dragged something this large through the brush. And you're right—there isn't any evidence here."

"Which means this wasn't an attack by a wild animal," Alexei said grimly. "Humans or Sups did this."

"Which ones?" Connor asked. "And why leave him here for the rest of us to find?"

"Someone who wanted to ruin the initiation?" Alexei asked. "Or make a statement?"

"Could be either or both," Connor said. "That's what we'll have to find out."

The sheriff was younger than I'd expected, a sturdy man with suntanned skin, short brown hair, and brown eyes set beneath dark and angular brows. His jaw was square, his chin equally so, but with a dimple in the middle, his bottom lip a little fuller than the top. Handsome in a rugged way, and probably in his late thirties. And he definitely wasn't a shifter.

He wore a wide-brimmed taupe hat in the same shade as the perfectly creased uniform.

"I'm surprised his first thought was calling a human sheriff," I whispered.

"Clan's doing what humans would do in this situation," Connor whispered back. "Call the authorities and let them come in and handle it. It's the cost of pretending to be human."

Along with the cost of turning over control to humans, I thought. Was that worth it? Given the looks of displeasure on some of the younger shifters, they didn't seem to think so.

The sheriff examined the scene, hands resting on his loaded belt as he scanned what remained of Loren. After a minute of review, he looked over the crowd, pausing when he reached me and Connor, then turning back to Cash.

"What was happening here?" he asked.

"Baptism at the cataracts," Cash said solemnly.

As cover stories went, a baptism wasn't terribly far from the truth.

"Not a very auspicious one," the sheriff said.

"No, it isn't."

"You hear anything? See anything?"

"Nothing," Cash said. "One of the kids was playing, found him, came back and told us."

"Looks like he's been mauled," the sheriff said. "A man was killed by a bear in Boyd a couple of weeks ago. Blew a tire while driving down a fire road, was attacked while putting on the spare. His dashboard screen caught the whole thing."

He scratched his jaw, the stubble making a *scritch* sound. "Looked a lot like this. Maybe he was taking a walk on the property, was attacked, taken down. I don't see a weapon wound."

"I don't, either," Cash said. "Just these scratches, the bites."

As silence fell, I looked at Connor, wondering about all the things that hadn't been said. Cash hadn't mentioned the attack on Beth last night, and either the sheriff hadn't noticed the fact that Loren had been placed there, or he'd decided not to mention it in front of us.

Connor shook his head just enough to give me the signal. We weren't going to talk, either. Not now.

The sheriff turned away from Cash, settled his gaze on us again. It wasn't difficult to guess that he'd done so because we were strangers. We were the odd men out.

He walked closer, pulled off his hat, ran a hand through his short hair.

"Ken Paulson," he said, and didn't extend a hand. "I don't know you."

"Connor Keene. Georgia's my great-aunt. We're here from Chicago for the baptism."

"We?" the sheriff asked.

"Me and my girlfriend." He reached out a hand for mine, and I took it, squeezed, offered a smile that I hoped skirted just between shy and sad.

The sheriff looked me over, but if he recognized our faces or biology, he didn't mention it. "You see anything unusual?"

"Not until this," Connor said, gesturing to the scene. "We were talking with the family when a child ran up, said she'd found a body. You've seen the rest."

"I have." He shifted his gaze to me.

I met it, worked to look sheepish. And being a vampire, and skilled at fooling humans, I apparently pulled it off, as he settled the hat back on his head, looked at Cash.

"He have family that needs to be notified?" Paulson asked.

"If you mean biologically, no. We're his family as far as it matters. Which means I guess we'd better call the funeral home. Or do you have to call the medical examiner?"

"County doesn't have an ME right now," Paulson said. "We contract with Lake County, but it could take two, three days before they can get someone down here. And autopsies aren't mandatory."

"Oh, that's right," Cash said. "You mentioned that when Paisley was hit. I'd forgotten." But the calculation in his eyes said that was a lie. He knew very well what the rules were.

"Your people are having a hard month," Paulson said. "I don't see any need to add to that by forcing a discretionary autopsy. Especially since this looks like a wild animal attack."

And just like that, I thought, any chance of figuring out exactly what had happened to Loren disappeared. A very tidy result for Cash, which made me even more suspicious.

"We'll search the woods," Cash said. "Look for signs of wild animal activity, for the bear, if that's what this was. We don't want to feel useless here," he added. "We need to feel like we're contributing."

The sheriff adjusted his hat. "Unfortunately, I don't have people to offer up for that, either. Not since they made us a satellite office. I can call in, ask for help from Duluth, but I'd rather not if you can handle it. We don't want word of attacks to spread, not with fall-color season approaching. Would be more helpful to locate the animal, get it down, get it tested."

Cash nodded. "We'll contact Flanagan's regarding the body, the service. And we'll take pictures of anything we find on the search, keep you updated."

"That's agreeable," Paulson said. "I'll check in with you later."

"What the hell was that?" Alexei whispered when Cash led the sheriff back toward the trail. "Doesn't Cash want to know what's happening?"

"Or the sheriff?" I wondered. "No autopsy, no search, for a body that's been brutalized?"

"I don't know what's going on," Connor said as he watched, gaze tracking the men's retreat. "But I don't like it."

It took only a few minutes for Cash to return, boots cracking dry leaves and hard grass across the trail, with Everett in his wake.

"The sheriff is content to let you investigate a homicide?" Connor asked, not bothering to hide his incredulity—or his suspicions.

"Did you not hear the part about the bear attack?" Everett's tone was aggressive.

Connor didn't spare him a glance. "I'm hearing a lot of things. Why did the sheriff walk away?"

"We have an arrangement," Cash said. "As long as we mind our own, he doesn't interfere. Helps that the county's short-staffed. Makes it easier for him to pass the ball."

Connor cocked his head to the side. "You aren't trying to stonewall the investigation, are you?"

"You'd better remember where you are," Everett said. "This isn't Chicago."

"Everett," Cash said, but Everett shook his head.

"No, Cash. They think they can come up here and tell us what to do? They arrive, and trouble starts. I say that's not a coincidence. I say we send them back home."

"A good thing, then," Connor said, "that you don't run this particular show." Then he turned his gaze back to Cash, as if Everett wasn't worth even a moment's time. "You got issues with the Apex's leadership, you take them up with him. You have issues with me, I'm here, and I'm ready. But maybe, instead of arguing like children, we could concentrate on the member of your Pack who's been murdered?"

Magic had risen with each word, each punctuated sentence. And by the time he was done, the other members of the clan were watching, listening.

Waiting.

"We don't want humans in our business," Cash said. "If we have problems, we prefer to solve them on our own. We take care of our own," he said, each word a punch of power and magic. "And we make a nice donation to the sheriff's campaign to ensure it stays that way."

Apparently done with the explanation, Cash looked over his people. "Something attacked Loren. Maybe his luck ran out, and there was a wild animal. But I've yet to meet a shifter taken by a bear, so we are going to figure out what happened here."

There were rumbles of agreement in the sizable crowd that had gathered.

"Everett, you coordinate getting Loren to Flanagan's."

The barrel-chested man nodded.

"John, you check Loren's cabin," Cash said to a dark-skinned man with dark hair and a thick beard. "See if there's anything amiss there. Everyone else, either get back to the resort, keep an eye on the kids, or stay here to help us search. We'll split into teams," he said. "Look for scat, footprints. Anything that tells us what attacked Loren and where it went."

"Elisa and I will take the woods to the east," Connor said when shifters began to volunteer for assignments.

"No fucking way!" Everett, arms folded across his chest, shook his head.

"Excuse me?" Connor's voice was low and threatening.

"Everett," Cash said, a low warning, but the man shook his head.

"She's a stranger, and a vampire, and this isn't our property. For all we know, she was involved."

I started forward, but made myself stay in place because of the hand Connor put out to stop me. He kept his gaze—cold and flat—on Everett's. "You want to be very careful before you accuse friends of the Pack, of my family, of murder."

"I didn't say she actually killed him. Point is, we don't know, do we? This is enough of a clusterfuck without involving strangers."

"She's no stranger to me or mine," Connor said. "And her being a vampire isn't a weakness—it's a strength."

Cash and Everett gave me head-to-toe appraisals. Cash's gaze was at least considering; Everett just leered.

"How is she a help?" Cash asked.

"For starters," Connor said dryly, "she's a predator with night vision, and she's been trained by Chicago's Ombudsman. She's exactly who you want looking for evidence. Refusing to let her assist doesn't make you safer; it makes you look guilty. Elisa," he said, shifting his gaze to me, "would you like to enlighten them with what you've noticed already?"

"For starters," I repeated, looking at Cash, "he wasn't killed here." And I told them what was missing from the place where Loren's body had been, for lack of a better word, dumped.

Cash watched me carefully. "You have had some training."

I ignored the statement and asked a question. "Did everyone in the clan know about the initiation?"

"Yes. Everyone knew," Cash said. "Why?"

"Because if they all knew it was happening here tonight," Connor said, "leaving the body here wasn't an accident."

Cash worked his jaw, as if chewing over words. "Fine. Take the vampire if you want. She's your responsibility. We've wasted enough time," he said, irritated magic nipping at the air with needle-sharp teeth. "We find out who or what killed Loren, and then we deal with it. Get moving."

The shifters were content to ignore me, light and magic flashing as they transformed, dropping clothing and exchanging bare skin for paws and fur. Moments later, a dozen wolves, a couple of coyotes, and the sleek, dark form of a panther dispersed to look for a murderer.

Connor glanced at Alexei. "You mind going back to the resort, staying with Georgia and the others? I'd feel better if you were there. And they'll be working on dinner."

"Incentive," Alexei said, then gave a salute and headed wordlessly back to the trail.

"You mind?" Connor asked, pulling off his jacket.

"It's your party," I said, then winced. "Sorry."

"It's all right. I know what you meant."

"You want me to put the clothes on the bike?"

For the first time in hours, he smiled. "They'll be fine where they fall. Take a step back, would you?"

I did, pulling my dagger in case anyone got brave while Connor was midshift.

"Good call," he said, and clothing dropped to the ground.

I watched him, let my gaze linger on that dip at the bottom of his spine, just before the ripe curve of his gorgeously toned butt.

"I can feel you staring at me," he said without turning around.

"Then you're very perceptive. Can you understand me when you're in wolf form? I mean, is your understanding the same as when you're a human?"

"We pretty much just divide everyone into 'food' and 'not food' and go from there."

I was sure he was joking. Well, mostly sure.

"I hear you, and I understand you," he said. "But the understanding of human words is . . . different. Less like hearing the individual words than understanding the concept. The same applies when I'm human. I understand animal concepts—smells, sounds, instincts—differently than when I'm wolf."

"What about scritches?"

He grinned. "Scritches are appreciated in any form. And here we go."

Magic sparked, ignited, circled his body in shimmering waves. Light filled the air, bright as a camera flash, and put the trees and boulders in sharp relief. I shielded my eyes.

When the magic dissipated, I glanced back. A wolf stood where Connor had been. Large and strong, with silver fur and the blue eyes that were undeniably his, even in this form.

He padded toward me, moved by my side, just close enough for his haunch to graze my leg. I looked down, decided this wasn't the time or place for scritches. A grimmer business was at hand. "You want to lead?"

He bolted.

"I guess that's a yes," I said with a grin, and ducking my head, pushed off to race after him.

That we were moving quickly made me feel better about being in hostile territory—and not just because we were going too fast to notice any slithery things on the ground. The trees and under-growth were so tangled that I couldn't see more than a few feet in front of me, or more than a dark sliver of sky above the canopy. All that flora smelled rich and green and a little funky—the com-mingled scents of decay and rebirth and traces of the animals that lived here.

The slope increased gradually until we reached the crest of a granite-pocked hill that overlooked the lake, the road ribboning a hundred feet beneath us, the lake a dark blanket at its edge.

We stopped to look over the pale break of waves, the single golden dot of a boat on the horizon moving south. Nose lifted, Connor scented the air, seeking the clue that would tell us who—or what—had hurt Loren. I glanced around, but saw nothing on the trail nearby, or strewn across the hard rock, that would mark a murderer.

Below us a lone wolf howled, its cry rising through the air to circle around the cliff. A second wolf answered it, then another, until the air was an orchestra of sound, a chorus of harmonized voices.

I doubted many vampires had borne witness to this, had been able to stand in the midst of the Pack and listen to its sonata. I closed my eyes, let the monster have its chance to hear as the howls rose and fell, wound around one another. Some carried the melody—the main portion of the song—while others sang or yipped around the edges, adding their own stories to the larger book. It was astoundingly beautiful and yet hauntingly sad, even though I knew it had a practical purpose.

"They're checking everyone's location, right? Making sure they're all safe?" I looked down at Connor, and he lifted his gaze to me, but his eyes were unreadable.

"At the risk of insulting you, and I'll apologize in advance for that, could we have some kind of signaling system when you're in wolf form?"

He continued to stare at me. But it seemed chillier.

"One paw scratch for yes, two for no? And not like one of those counting horses," I said, reading his expression perfectly. "I don't want you to perform for me. I just want to be able to communicate with you."

I made myself continue to meet his steely gaze, unreadable though it was, because it seemed important that I not look away.

"One for yes, two for no, and three for 'you're being a brat'?"

He scratched once.

Then he scratched three times.

I probably had that coming.

NINE

We walked for nearly an hour, following this wing of the trail over and around hills marked by god-strewn boulders. The trail appeared to dead-end at another creek that channeled through the high granite walls.

"End of the trail?" I asked him.

I sensed the lightning spark of power before I saw it, and this time managed to close my eyes. The light of his transformation still flashed red behind my lids. When darkness fell again, I opened them to find him naked beside me, hands on his hips.

"Yeah, unless you want to go rock climbing." He lifted his gaze to the thirty-foot ledge on the other side of the cold, dark water.

"Not at the top of my list. But if we might find anything over there, we should probably follow it through."

"We won't," he said, moving closer to the water, crouching in front of it. "I don't smell Pack—or anything else—past here. The water's deep, and if anyone tried to cross it, they'd have had to take a good swim."

"Eliminating their scent trail," I guessed, and Connor nodded.

"At least for a bit." He rose again. "Long enough to mask their direction. I'd rather search with a scent, a footprint, something. Not randomly stumbling around."

"We need more information," I said.

"Yeah." Frowning, he rubbed his neck.

"Are you okay?" I asked. "You seem . . . uncomfortable. Is it the paw scratching?"

There was laughter in his eyes. "No. It was a good idea, but your delivery sucks. Something is . . . strange out here. Something . . . off."

"Magic?"

He looked back at me. "I don't know."

"Hold on," I said. His was the only magic I could feel, but I'd let myself be ensconced by it. So I closed my eyes and tried to filter it out, along with all the other scents and sounds that wove through the woods.

Connor and I had left trails of magic along the path, shimmering ribbons of power that wove through the trees. But there was another trail, and this one was . . . different. Still shimmering, but not a ribbon. Not fluid or continuous, but sharp and broken. Angular, like a fork of lightning.

I opened my eyes, looked at him. "There's magic, but I'm not entirely sure how to describe it. I think it's broken."

"Broken," he said, staring deeper into the woods as he considered. "Yeah. I see that. But why?"

"I have no idea. I don't know what would make someone—or their magic—leave a trail like that. Illness? Or the effect of some foreign magic?"

He looked back at me. "Like magical sabotage?"

"Or magic by choice. Because someone in the Pack tried magic, and it did something very, very bad. I didn't detect anything like this with Beth."

He rubbed his temple. "I was just thinking that. But it was windy last night, could have dissipated faster. The air is still tonight. Let's check this area," he said. "If the magic is strong enough to detect it here, maybe that's not all they left behind."

We nodded and split up. He moved back to the bank of the

creek, and I moved to the edges of what passed for the trail, looking for broken branches or other signs someone had passed through.

It took only a moment.

I was moving away from the water when something flagged my attention. I wasn't sure what I'd seen—something different enough to have my brain clicking to alert—so I stepped back, looked around. Then crouched in front of a boulder on the edge of the path.

There was grass around the base, and it was trampled flat as if someone had moved near the rock—stood or sat on it—and flattened the grass in the process. They also left a set of footprints that definitely weren't human.

The marks had the general look of paw prints—toe impressions atop a central pad. But the impressions were elongated, as if the pads were longer and more narrow than a standard wolf's. And they were massive.

"Connor," I called out, and heard footsteps behind me a moment later. "Tracks," I said, pointing toward them. "And I don't think they're yours."

He studied them.

"They look canine, right? But they aren't shifter."

"No," he agreed. "They aren't. Too wide, too long."

I held back the obvious joke and was inordinately proud of myself.

"Whatever made them was very large and very heavy," he said. "That's what she said."

I couldn't help but grin. "I'm glad you said it. I was trying to be serious. So what could make them? A really big dog? A wolverine?"

Connor stood. "There's been no canine in North America big enough to do this in tens of thousands of years. I don't know any living creature that makes prints like that—Supernatural or otherwise."

"What about a cryptid?"

He gave me a dry look.

"What? The Beast of Owatonna is the best lead we've got."

"That's not a lead. It's ignorance disguised as science."

"Okay, then let's add some science into it. Maybe we don't need to figure out if this is the Beast. Maybe we just need to figure out what the Beast actually is."

He blinked. "That's not bad."

"I'm feeling very intellectually spry today."

"Then riddle me this," he said, turning back to me. "What looks like a cryptid, but smells like Pack?"

"Like Pack," I said, leaning around him to look at the track. "That's all you smell?"

"That's it."

"Then I have no idea, unless you've got a Pack member with a really unusual podiatric condition."

"I'm not aware of any. Take photos, will you? I don't have my screen."

"Because you're naked," I said and, reminded of that, had to work very hard to focus on his face.

His smile was wide, cocky. "I am, yes."

I pulled out my screen, took pictures of the footprints. "How about I send these to Petra?"

"The conspiracy theorist?"

I smiled. "She's not just a conspiracy theorist." She was an aeromancer and led the OMB's technology squad. "She's also into cryptids."

Connor's gaze went flat.

"She's very good with research," I added. "And Theo and Yuen are there, too. Maybe someone has an idea."

Connor sighed. "Send away."

I did, sending the photos to Petra and Theo and giving them both an update about Loren, Cash's reaction, and the search, and I asked Petra to check out the pictures and let us know if she found anything interesting. Then I put the screen away again, looked up.

At his face, obviously.

He glanced at the sky. "Let's get back to the cascades, see what everyone else found." He grinned at me. "Assuming we can make it back by dawn."

"If that's a dig at my speed, you have four legs, and I only have two."

"At least you acknowledge that's a weakness, vamp."

"You wanna test me?"

"At the moment, I can think of many more things I'd rather do to you, Elisa."

My heart quickened at the knowing look in his eyes. The wolfishness. "I think at the moment we'd better concentrate on the search." But I put a hand against his bare chest, felt his heart pulse beneath my fingers. Want and need rose up so quickly, they nearly swamped me.

Connor smiled, and there was nothing pleasant in it. Just the harsh acknowledgment of the need. "Maybe I better shift again."

"I think I can control myself," I said, but it took another five seconds before I put my hand down again.

"There you go," he said with a smile, then took that hand and stepped back onto the path. "You know, when we get back to the cascades, you'll need to help me out—I'm not entirely sure where my clothes are, and mine won't be the only ones out there."

"I can point you in their general direction."

"Good enough," he said.

We walked side by side, vampire and naked shifter, back to the waterfall.

* * *

We returned to find the waterfalls nearly empty, only a few piles of clothing scattered here and there. The shifters who'd finished their searches had apparently dressed again and left.

"I guess Cash wasn't in a hurry to discuss the evidence," I said when Connor had dressed again. "Maybe he went with Everett to the funeral home?"

Connor surveyed the area, his expression going grim. "He should at least be out here managing the investigation. Waiting for everyone to report in. If a member of my clan was murdered, I'd be out there searching right along with them."

"Cash isn't you," I said. "Maybe he didn't like Loren. That would explain the indifference."

"Yeah," Connor said. "It would. But we've got a dinner date at Georgia's. If we don't tell him what we found until tomorrow, that's his loss."

"Because we're going to keep looking," I guessed. "And we're more reliable."

His smile was warm. "I like that I never have to explain things to you twice."

Rain, soft and misty, had begun to fall when Connor pulled the bike in front of the cabin. I was glad I'd taken a photo of the tracks; there'd probably be nothing left of them by tomorrow.

I walked around the building, scanning for any trace of that same broken magic. And found nothing.

"No broken magic," I said when Connor joined me.

"Could be on the other side of the resort," he said. "Or maybe it didn't come back here, whatever it is." We walked to the front door, and Connor pulled off his boots. "I want a shower."

"Okay. Do I need to do anything for dinner? Prepare anything?"

He smiled in amusement as he unlocked and opened the door. "Like whip up some steaks?"

"Or whatever."

He opened his mouth, closed it again. "I've actually taken care of that," he said. Then he walked to the duffel bag he'd left near the kitchen, pulled out a growler of thick, dark liquid. "I brought this."

I stared at the bottle and the dark brew that sloshed inside it. "Do you hate your family?"

"It wasn't *that* bad."

"It wasn't bad," I agreed. "It was just . . . a lot. But maybe they'll have more of a taste for it."

Connor put the growler on the table, headed down the hallway, pulling his shirt over his head. "We're beginning Scotch trials when we get back. And you might need a drink after hanging with the family."

While he showered, I checked my screen for messages from Petra. There weren't any, so I toed off my shoes and sat down on the floor. My monster had handled the initiation just fine, but past results didn't guarantee future success, as my father enjoyed saying in his not infrequent pep talks about mental toughness.

But Georgia had looked at me and seen . . . something. My eyes hadn't changed color, and I hadn't gone berserker. Maybe she'd only detected the magic, had felt the *otherness* about me. Either way, that was the most awareness I was willing to grant her.

So I crossed my legs, put my hands on my knees, and closed my eyes. I focused on my breath—in, hold, out. In, hold, out, until I could feel the remaining tension slip away, and the monster no longer peeked over my shoulder, looking for a way out.

I opened my eyes when I heard the water turn off, and half-expected to see Alexei staring at me again, but the room was still empty. Just me and the monster.

Feeling chill, if not exactly more energized, I stood up and stretched out, pulled a colored lip balm from my backpack, reapplied, then flipped over my hair, finger-fluffed it, and flipped it back again. I checked myself in the mirror that hung over the couch—the frame made of birch logs—and decided I was presentable.

"Best I can do," I said, and prepared to sup with the family.

Georgia's home was four cabins away from ours, so it was only a short walk. But I still made him carry the growler.

"Door's open," Georgia called out before Connor had even put a hand on the knob.

"I suppose I shouldn't mention the importance of security," I said.

He snorted. "No, vampire. You should not."

"Welcome," Georgia called out when he opened the door and amazing smells spilled through the doorway. She stood in front of a kitchen island, mixing something in a blue ceramic bowl with an enormous red spoon. She'd added a red apron to her ensemble, and switched out the formal shoes for furry house slippers.

There was food everywhere. Stacks of meat on plates, bowls of vegetables in various stages of preparation, two cakes—one pink, one covered in coconut—on a nearby table.

Like vampires, wolves could eat. That was a vote in their favor.

The scent of food was matched in strength only by the variety of magic in the room. Layers of it, probably because Georgia's home had been a meeting place for shifters, a place where her family gathered and their magic had lingered.

"Georgia," Connor said, pressing a kiss to her cheek, "thank you for having us."

"You're family," she said. "And you're welcome. What's in the bottle?"

"NAC Industries' first stout," he said. "We call it the Alpha Stout."

Of course they did.

Georgia arched a narrow painted eyebrow. "Is it good?"

"It's . . . distinguished," he decided. I couldn't disagree with that, so I didn't challenge him. But then she looked at me, and I had to work hard not to look away.

"Is it good?" she asked again, gaze narrowed.

"It's complex."

Her mouth twitched. "Put in the fridge, or in the deep freezer down the hall if it needs to get cold fast. Cassie is upstairs with the baby. You should go find Wes. He needs help with the Triumph. Something about the starter, I think."

"Okay," he said, but glanced at me.

I recognized that gleam in his eyes. He was seeing oil and bolts and steel, and hearing the purr of a well-running antique. I also knew the division of labor in shifter houses tended to fall along traditional gender lines: Ladies did the cooking; men did the mechanics.

"I'll be fine," I said.

Connor pressed a kiss to my lips. "Be good. I'll be outside if you need me. Take care of her," he told Georgia with a grin, then walked toward the door.

He hadn't been fazed by kissing me in front of his family, or leaving me alone with them. For the first time, I realized we hadn't just "met" his family on this trip. He'd presented me to them—to his best friend, his relatives, his (theoretical) allies. He'd introduced me to shifter families whose lives didn't seem all that different from humans, to a clan of shifters who'd never feel comfortable inside the Pack. He'd told them who I was, stood for me, and allowed me to stand for myself.

This trip hadn't been entirely—maybe not even mostly—about an initiation or a monster.

He'd been introducing me to the Pack.

This was . . . a beginning.

Surprise and pleasure made my heart beat a little faster.

"So," Georgia said, "you can entertain me with stories of big-city life while I slave over this damn dough."

I had to blink my way back to the kitchen and the conversation. "I could help you," I said.

She looked at me, brows winged up in surprise. "Vampires can be helpful?"

"Yes, at least as often as shifters are open-minded."

Georgia chortled. "Touché."

I smiled at her, liking her already. She was up-front, unbowed, and straightforward. I walked toward her, glanced in the bowl. There was a mass of shaggy dough, combined but in need of some work.

"I can knead that if you want to move on to something else."

She looked down at the dough, then up at me with suspicion. "You know how?"

"I went to college in France. I can't bake, but learning the mechanics was, let's say, not optional."

"*Oh là là,*" she intoned, then put down the spoon, walked away from the bowl. "Get to work."

I glanced back, found Connor still standing in the doorway, arms crossed and head tilted as he watched us, amusement on his face. "Go," I told him, and he gave me a wink, disappeared.

I made room on the counter and looked around, found a scoop buried in a crock of flour, and sprinkled some on the countertop. Then I tipped the bowl so the dough slid onto flour and began to work, just as I'd been taught. Fold the dough in half, push to stretch, fold it again. Turn, repeat until the dough was smooth and the gluten stretchy.

"I take it you aren't ready to run away from us quite yet," Georgia said as she moved to the stove, pulled out a silver baking dish that sizzled and sent out the ambrosia smell of roasting meat.

"I grew up with vampires," I said. "My standards are low."

"Clever," Georgia said, and moved the chicken—two birds

with cracklingly crisp skin that was nearly translucent over herbs tucked beneath it—onto a large white platter. I had to work not to reach out and grab a bite.

And realized I hadn't been the only one interested in the surroundings. Maybe because of the food, maybe because of the magic that permeated the cabin, the monster had awoken.

It wanted to move through the rooms, feeling out the magic, caressing the inchoate power. *Not now,* I said silently, willing it to stay down. The first rule of the monster was not letting the monster be seen by strangers, especially since Georgia had already seen *something.*

But the monster believed it had been pushed down enough this trip, and it didn't want to retreat again. Not when the magic was so enticing. It fought me for access, trying to shove my consciousness down so it could stand in my place.

"Tell me about yourself," Georgia said while I fought in silence and couldn't spare the strength to form words.

I stared down at the dough, pushing the bread, folding, folding, folding, like every pleat and turn would diminish the monster.

I'd let it breathe, I thought, anger rising. I'd given it space. And this was the thanks I got.

Silence was stretching between me and Georgia, and I was growing desperate. How long ago had she asked me about myself? How long had I been staring at this dough, trying not to let the claws push through?

I promise, I told the monster. *I'll give you room. I'll let you breathe. I'll let you run and fight. But not now, please.*

Push. Fold. Fold.

Finally, it relented and loosened its grip. I'd been tense—my legs and torso braced in the battle—and its release nearly had me pitching forward.

Push. Fold. Fold.

The second rule of the monster was not discussing the monster with strangers. So I forced myself to smile, made a production of stretching a ball of dough to stretch the gluten. Not ready yet.

"Sorry," I said, the only word I could manage, and hoping my voice was casual, but still not meeting her eyes. "Did you say something? I think I got a little carried away with the kneading. It's not ready yet."

"Apparently," she said, her tone careful and very unconvinced. "I was just saying you should tell me about yourself."

Push. Fold. Fold.

"Well," I said, "you probably know all the interesting bits."

There was a moment of silence while, I guessed, she debated whether to call me out or let it go, at least for now.

"I know how to do my homework," she said, her tone a little lighter now, and I relaxed incrementally.

"I spoke with my sister yesterday," she continued, "and she gave me the details. It's not often the would-be brings around a date."

I nearly smiled at "the would-be." "How often?" I wondered.

"Never, actually."

"Hmm," I said mildly, though I was thrilled to be the only. I liked those odds.

"I'm twenty-three," I said, answering her previous question. "Bachelor's degree. Both parents live in Chicago and are associated with Cadogan House. I'm not. I love coffee, am very good with a sword, and enjoy long walks on very dark beaches."

Georgia looked up at me, grinned. "You have a handout to pass around with all that on it?"

"Laminated card."

She chuckled. "Cute. Connor's a good one, or he's become a good one. To tell you the truth, I wasn't sure how good he'd turn out when he was younger. Not because he was wild—kids should be a little wild. But he was cocky. You need self-confidence to be Apex, not cockiness. Cockiness gets you in trouble. Gets the Pack in trouble. But he seemed to settle down."

"He's changed a lot," I said. "We didn't like each other growing up very much."

"He was a little brat."

I chuckled. "He always called me 'brat.' I wasn't spoiled. I was lucky and privileged, and I liked playing by the rules. He liked doing whatever he wanted to do, and because he was the prince, they usually let him. Sorry," I added, wincing. "That sounded insulting to his parents."

"Not insulting," she said. "Honest. Not because he's a Keene, but because he's a shifter. We aren't what you might call helicopter parents. We want our kids to follow creeks, get scraped knees, learn about beestings the old-fashioned way. Part of that's our connection with the world. Part of that's how we believe kids learn—by experiencing, not by being told.

"He did a lot of his learning by himself or with the help of his friends. Some who were good, some who were bad. For some, it takes tragedy to make that change, to move to that next stage. Hurting themselves or someone else to realize they can be something different. I'm glad he didn't have to learn that way."

The door opened, and Miranda walked in, a wine bottle in each hand.

My dislike aside, she was a beautiful woman, with an athletic body, light brown skin, and dark hair that swirled in loose curls around a face dominated by her dark eyes, thick brows, and a scattering of freckles.

"I found the pinot," she said, and stopped short when she caught sight of me. The air in the room seemed to chill. "Oh, good," she said, lip curling. "The vampire's here."

"I take it you've met," Georgia said.

"In Chicago," Miranda said. "She's very important down

there." Ignoring me, she put the bottles on the counter, began to dig through a kitchen drawer.

"Well, she's not in Chicago right now," Georgia said matter-of-factly.

"I'm not," I said. "And don't really care if I'm important."

"Then you're a fool," Miranda said, closing the drawer with her hip and putting a bottle opener on the countertop. "Power and authority are the only things worth having."

Given my parents had both, and I lived under the umbrella of their privilege, I turned back to my job. I smoothed the surface of the dough, tucking the ends beneath it to make a smooth, tight ball. "I think this is ready," I told Georgia.

"In there," she said, pointing toward a linen-covered basket. I dropped the dough in, seam down, and covered it with the plastic wrap that sat nearby.

"That's for tomorrow," she said. "Tonight's is baking. Can you check that?"

"I'll do it," Miranda said, moving around me to the oven. She opened the door, sending the scents of yeast and butter and herbs wafting through the kitchen.

"Five more minutes," she pronounced, then closed the door again.

"Is there anything else I can help with?" I asked, ignoring Miranda's haughty stare, but still not meeting Georgia's eyes.

I still felt too vulnerable for that.

Before Georgia could answer, there was a knock at the door. Georgia wiped her hands on a towel, opened it.

A girl with pale skin and straight brown hair stood beneath the porch light, a paper-wrapped bundle of flowers in hand. "Happy initiation day!"

"Hey, kiddo," Georgia said, then held open the door. "Come on in."

The girl was petite and slender and very human, despite knowing about the initiation. How much more did she know? I wondered.

She was probably eighteen or nineteen, with brown eyes, a slender nose, and wide smile. She gave Georgia a hug, then extended the bouquet. "For you," she said. "To celebrate."

"You are a doll," Georgia said, then looked around at us. "You know Miranda, and this is Elisa."

"Connor's Elisa?" she asked brightly, then came toward me, eyes aglow. "It is so good to meet you!"

"Thanks," I said, shocked when she gave me an embrace as warm as the one she'd given Georgia. And she smelled rather deliciously like—

"Who has doughnuts?" Alexei walked into the kitchen, looked around, then settled his gaze on the girl. "You have doughnuts?"

"No," she said. "Do you have doughnuts?" She certainly smelled like them.

He looked perplexed by the question. "Why would I have doughnuts?"

"Exactly," she said, pointing at him. She looked at me, smiled. "I'm Carlie Stone."

"Elisa," I said lamely, given she already knew my name, then pointed. "This is Alexei."

"I know who you are," she said with a smile, then shifted her gaze to Alexei. "I don't know who you are."

He humphed, apparently irritated he hadn't been recognized. In fairness, I'd lived in Chicago my entire life, and I'd seen him only a couple of times.

"Carlie is human," Georgia said, putting an arm around her shoulders. "But we don't fault her for that. We've been friends with her family for many years. And she's done us a favor a time or two."

I guessed Carlie did know it all.

Connor stepped into the room with Wes, and when his gaze landed on Carlie, his eyes went wide. "Well, well, well, look what the cat dragged in."

"Connor!" Carlie said, and ran into his arms. He smiled with brotherly affection.

"How are you, squirt? It's been a while."

"I'm good." She stepped back, squeezed his arm. "You got muscles."

Connor grinned. "I grew into them. How are you? How's the bakery?"

"Donut Town will always be Donut Town," she said with a rather infectious grin. She looked at me. "My family runs it. It's up the road."

"Best doughnuts on the north shore," Georgia said, and Carlie grinned.

"You just like it because we keep shifter hours."

"That's part of the allure," Georgia agreed. Then she looked around, clapped her hands together. "All right," she said. "Now that everyone's here, let's eat before this gets cold. Grab a dish, and we'll put it all on the table, eat family style."

I grabbed a cloth-covered basket of buttery rolls, while Connor picked up the platter of chicken. And we headed into the dining room to have our fill.

TEN

Cassie brought Will, now in a onesie dotted with spot-eyed puppies, downstairs. He sucked drowsily on a blue pacifier.

"Dinnertime was a success," she said, placing him in a white reclining contraption that looked like it might have been engineered by NASA. He stirred when she moved her hands away, opened his eyes wide and verged on a fuss, until Wes tapped the top of the device, and it began to swing gently back and forth.

The baby's eyes drifted shut, his little body relaxing.

"Do they make those for adults?" Alexei asked.

Miranda walked in with a glass bowl of green salad, stopped when she saw Connor. Their eyes met, magic rising as they watched each other.

"Miranda," he said.

"Connor." She put the bowl on the table with an extra snap of sound, slid her gaze to me. "I see you followed through on your promise to bring a vampire onto clan property."

"I always follow through. Thank you for stocking the refrigerator. Very thoughtful."

Her smile went thin, mean. "I hope I bought something she can drink."

"You did great," I said. "She's very appreciative."

The cheer in my voice just made her scowl more, which, of course, had been the point.

"Are we going to have a problem?" Connor asked, tone mild.

"No," Miranda said. "As long as you remember your place." She moved a step closer, anger burning in her eyes. "You aren't Apex, and you aren't in charge here. And they don't take kindly to input from strangers."

This time, Connor moved closer, so the tips of their shoes nearly kissed, but looked over her shoulder, as if he couldn't be bothered to meet her stare. "You remember that our memories are long. And I won't forget your sowing discord in the Pack."

"Our memories are long," she agreed. "And I won't forget your disloyalty to the Pack."

"Children," Georgia said, moving into the room with the bottle of wine Miranda had found. The word was part question and part warning, and the magic between Miranda and Connor shattered like glass.

"Sit down," Georgia said, this time the words softer, and we all moved around the table.

I followed Connor's lead, taking a chair beside him. Georgia took the seat at the head, Wes and Cassie on the other side near the baby. When Miranda, Alexei, and Carlie took seats, Georgia looked at Connor.

"Is there anything you'd like to say?"

"About the food?"

She worked to hold back a smile. "About the occasion?"

"Oh, well." He put his hands on the table, looked around at everyone, settled his gaze on Wes and Cassie. "I've already said congratulations, so I'll just say that we're glad to be here with you celebrating this moment. It's a big deal when the Pack gets a new member. And especially when the new member is family."

"'Cause it changes the odds in his favor," Alexei murmured, and the others chuckled.

"That helps," Connor acknowledged with a warm smile. "But

it's not the only reason. Family is family; family matters. It's good to be here with you, and we appreciate the warm welcome."

Miranda coughed an objection.

"Very subtle, Miranda," Connor said quietly, voice flat.

She just rolled her eyes, looked away.

"We appreciate it," he said again, looking at Georgia. "And this food. So let's eat."

"Hear, hear," Georgia said, and we all raised our glasses.

I didn't think it was an accident that none of them held the Alpha Stout.

The meal was one amazing dish after another. The chicken was juicy and perfectly flavored with butter and herbs. There were warm yeast rolls, carrots and asparagus, and a casserole dish of cheese potatoes covered in crispy tater tots.

If this was hot dish, I was in. And I felt very much like my mother's child.

The conversation flowed naturally, from Grand Bay news, to Pack updates from Chicago, to very polite questions about my parents and Cadogan House.

"The idea of living in a giant dorm always seemed suspect to me," Georgia said, stabbing an asparagus spear.

"Masters and Novitiates have a special relationship," I said. "A kind of connection that makes them more like family than roommates."

"Does that make it better?" Wes asked. "That's like living at home with your parents." He gave Georgia a wide smile.

"Very funny, child. Maybe you should go visit the vampires. See how they live."

He looked at me. "That a possibility?"

"Probably so. As long as you aren't afraid of fangs."

When the eating slowed and Carlie excused herself to go back to the bakery, Connor pushed back his plate and took a contemplative sip of Alpha Stout he'd finally managed to convince some of them to try. Only the Chicago shifters—Miranda and Alexei—took him up on it, and Alexei made it only halfway through his glass.

"I don't want to ruin a lovely evening," Connor said, "but I'd like to talk about Loren."

"We'll talk," Georgia agreed, picking a tater tot from her plate and popping it into her mouth. "Someone should."

Connor looked at Cassie and Wes. "I'm sorry to bring this up, but he was left at the initiation. Were you having trouble with anyone?"

"We've discussed that," Wes said, draping his arm protectively across the back of Cassie's chair. "And the answer is no. We don't have issues with anyone, and no one has issues with us, at least that we've seen. We're family people. We tend to keep to ourselves."

"We think it's more likely they wanted to make a statement," Cassie said, gaze on Wes. "The clan was together. The event was special. You leave the body there, you make a statement."

Connor nodded. "Did anyone have any particular problems with Loren?"

"I don't know of any real issues," Georgia said, and she sounded convinced. But Cassie and Wes exchanged a look that said there was more to dig through here, more to consider.

"What about Cash?" Connor asked. "He seemed pretty eager to keep the investigation as low-key as possible."

"That's Cash," Georgia said. "He doesn't like humans, doesn't trust them. Barely trusts anyone who isn't clan. Certainly doesn't trust anyone who isn't Pack," she said, with some chagrin, as she looked at me.

"Cassie?" I asked quietly. "Wes? Do you know of any problems with Loren?"

Cassie winced, looked apologetically at Georgia. "I don't want to speak ill of the dead."

"It's not ill if it's the truth," Georgia said. "So spit it out."

"It's just, there were some general complaints," she said. "About how he didn't really listen to concerns when they were brought to him. Same for Everett and Cash. The younger shifters want change. They want to revitalize the clan, the resort. They don't feel like they're being heard."

"And me?" Georgia asked, spine snapping straight. "Are people having words about me they aren't willing to say to my face?"

"No," Cassie said kindly, and put a hand over her mother's. "You care about the clan, and everyone knows that. Everett and Cash and Loren are . . . old-school. They care about staying in control. And sometimes, that's at the expense of the clan."

Georgia sat back, breathed in deeply, and took that in, waited for it to settle.

Cassie, concern in her eyes, looked at me. "I don't know about anything specific, but—"

She looked at Wes, who nodded and said, "Tell them."

"Loren was with Paisley before she died."

The room went silent.

"How do you know?" Connor asked.

"I saw them. They were walking together along the main road. There's a coffee shop about half a mile up. It's a nice walk, so I assumed that's where they were going. I was driving on my way into town. I waved, but I don't think either of them saw me. Or at least they didn't acknowledge me. I ran some errands in town, came back again. And that's when I found out what happened."

"I thought Loren found her after she was dead," Connor said, which was what Marian had told us.

"That's what I heard, too," Georgia said, frowning and shifting in her seat, as if literally discomforted by the information.

"That may still be true," Cassie said. "But it's not the entire story. And it didn't look like they were having a very good time."

"What do you mean?" I asked.

"It looked like they were arguing about something. I mean, I couldn't hear them. I could just see that they were talking kind of . . . energetically, I guess. Neither one of them looked particularly happy. I just figured they were disagreeing about something."

"Did you tell anyone?" Connor asked.

"No," she said. "There didn't seem any point. Cash, the sheriff, and Loren decided it was an accident."

"It could have been an accident," Georgia said. "Paisley had no enemies. She was young, sweet. Naive but kind. Full of life. There's no reason anyone would have wanted her dead—Loren or anyone else."

Maybe not. But there were a lot of reasons for murder. Revenge was only one of them. She could have seen something she wasn't supposed to. Or had something that someone else wanted.

"It was a horrible accident," Georgia said, "and there's no evidence of anything else. We have enough tragedy to focus on without creating more trouble for ourselves."

Connor looked at her for a long time. "We found a print in the woods," he said. "Big animal. Vaguely wolf but much bigger than anything else we've seen."

I nearly pulled out my screen to show her the photograph, when Connor gently squeezed my knee. A sign to keep that to myself, I figured, so I just adjusted my napkin.

"Bigger?" Georgia said, leaning forward. "What's bigger?"

"We were hoping you'd have some idea—since you live here," he added.

"No," she said, and glanced at the others, who seemed just as baffled—and concerned—as she did.

"Whatever made the prints smelled like Pack," Connor said, delivering the final blow.

"No one in the clan would have killed Loren," Georgia said. "We live with the clan, day in and day out. We'd know if someone

was capable of—of what was done to him. We'd know," she said
again, stabbing a finger into the table to make her point.

"Okay," Connor said. "You'd know more than me. But you'll
tell Cash what we found? Just so he'll know, too?"

Georgia nodded. "I will." But she pushed back her chair and
rose, and walked back into the kitchen without another word.

The mood when we prepared to leave was much darker than it had
been when we'd arrived.

Connor picked up the mostly full growler as we stepped out of
Georgia's cabin onto the porch; I had a container of leftover
chicken I was already planning to eat for breakfast.

Georgia stepped into the doorway behind us. "Elisa."

Her tone was concerned, serious, and I had to steel myself, prepare myself to turn around and meet her gaze.

"Yes?" I asked as innocently as I could manage.

Her brows met at a point between her eyes. "The power," she
said. "It's fighting you."

Cold ran down my spine like ice water, and I had a vision of
my mother's face—tear streaked and sobbing—if she discovered
what I really was.

"It's fine," I said, and could hear the tightness in my voice. "It's
handled."

"Is it?"

Connor glanced back from the edge of the porch, brows lifted
at the fact I'd stopped following him.

"It's fine," I said again, this time my voice harder. I immediately regretted my tone, but could hardly apologize when I
couldn't admit what I was apologizing for.

"I don't think you believe that," she said, her gaze intense on
my eyes. "But if you change your mind and you want to talk, I'm
here."

That couldn't matter. It just couldn't.

* * *

"You want a drink?" Connor asked when we returned to the cabin and he'd squeezed the growler in with the blood in the refrigerator. "Maybe that Scotch we discussed?"

"Rain check," I said, shaking my head. "I'm still digesting dinner." I was also worn out—physically, emotionally. It had been a long night. And given tonight's events, I suspected tomorrow wouldn't be any easier.

I pulled off my boots, sat down on the couch, and let my head fall back. And opted not to tell Connor what his aunt and I had discussed. He didn't need any more drama piled on.

"Same," he said, taking a seat beside me, weariness in his movements.

"We aren't leaving tomorrow," I predicted.

"I think I need to stay." He turned his head to meet my gaze. "I can get you home if you need to go, but I'd like you to stay, too."

I reached out and took his hand, big and warm, in mine. "We rode up together. Might as well go home the same way."

He squeezed my hand. "I'd say I'm sorry for dragging you into this, but that's why I wanted you to come. At least in part."

"Yeah. I'm sorry for it, for you and your family and the Pack."

"Me, too." He sighed. "There's a small part of me that dreads the possibility of being Apex because I'd have to deal with idiocy and self-aggrandizing shifters and poor decision-making."

"And the rest of you?"

His eyes went hard, and there was purpose in them. "Is thrilled about the possibility of getting to deal with idiocy and self-aggrandizing shifters and poor decision-making."

"You know, you can be a little scary sometimes."

He snorted. "Says the immortal with berserker powers."

I meant to hide my flinch, but didn't quite manage it.

"That was intended as a compliment," he said, and I nodded. "But I'm sorry if it didn't feel that way."

"It's fine," I said, but still felt that hollowness in my gut that came with having my weakness pointed out. Ironic, given my strength was part of the problem.

"I like Carlie," I said, trying very much to change the subject. "She's really friendly."

"Doesn't have an evil bone in her body," Connor said. "She's a good kid, loves her family, respects the Pack. Saw me change when we were kids—that's how she knows about Sups. I tried to tell her she'd imagined it, that I'd been working on a magic trick and every other excuse I could think of. She didn't buy any of it, said she didn't care if I was a werewolf, because I'd taught her how to ride a bike. It was as simple as that."

"And you and Georgia seem to be close, but you didn't tell her about the photographs of the tracks we found."

"I think it's best to keep the evidence in our hands," Connor said. "I trust her, but I don't trust the clan. So we'll do our own search, let them do theirs. Maybe we'll both end up in the same place."

That would be its own magic trick, I thought. "If it helps, I don't think she's involved in the murder. Or the cover-up."

"I don't think so, either. Or at least not directly. But she's an elder. That means she bears responsibility." Connor sighed. "I should update the Pack," he said, and pulled out his screen, and placed it upright on the coffee table.

He tapped and the ringing began, and his father's face appeared a moment later.

Gabriel Keene's hair was pulled back in a headband, and his face had been coated in pale pink slime. "Children," he said nonchalantly, nodding at us in turn.

"I have many questions," I quietly said.

"As do I."

"I'm being made up," his father said, eyes flat. "Your nieces and

nephew are visiting, and they decided I needed a makeover."
There were giggles off camera, and his eyes grew wide. "No mascara. My lashes are plenty full." He looked back at his son. "Is there some reason I might need to immediately drive to Minnesota? As soon as I wash my face, at any rate."

"Sorry to burst your bubble, but no. But that's not to say something isn't happening out here."

"Tell me," his father said. "*Slowly.*"

Connor managed not to smile. "There's definitely clan infighting. One of the elders was killed, his body left at the initiation. And we found tracks near the spot where his body was dumped. Animal but not like anything we've seen. They smell like Pack—like clan. And there was magic, but splintered."

His father's brows lifted. "Well. That's a lot. How was he killed?"

While Connor gave him the details, I sent him the photographs we'd taken on the trail.

"Not Pack," Gabriel concluded. He must have been viewing the photos on the same screen he was using to communicate with us, because he was squinting at something to our left. "Not human. Nothing I've seen before. But they smelled like Pack?"

"They did," Connor said.

"And broken magic," he said. "That's a new one. Maybe a disorder? A spell?"

"We don't know," Connor said. "But we haven't sensed it at the resort."

"Hmm," he said. "What's the infighting?"

"Young versus old, it seems. The younger shifters are, I think, sick of passing, of hiding their identities."

"Exactly what I told Cash a decade ago. There's no point in hiding. Not anymore." He shifted his gaze to me. "We can thank vampires for taking most of the heat there."

"Sorry not sorry," I said, and Gabriel smiled.

"What's the next move?" he asked.

"They'll plan the memorial," Connor said. "If there's a schism in the clan, we'll probably see evidence of it when they make those plans. Memorials are a big deal in the Pack," he said, shifting his gaze to me. "The celebration of life, the reunification of the body with the earth."

"That will be telling," I said. "If the clan had any involvement in his death, if someone was angry at him, it might come out in those discussions."

"Might," Gabriel said. "Unless they're savvy enough to hide it."

"Nothing hidden regarding the murder," Connor said. "But we'll see."

"When were you supposed to come back?" his father asked.

"Tomorrow," Connor said, glancing at me. "But we're negotiating."

"If both of you can swing it, I'd like you to stay a couple more days. I don't want whatever has infected the clan to spread to the rest of the Pack. It needs to be isolated and rooted out. If they get suspicious, say—I don't know—that you're staying to pay your respects to Loren."

A tiny hand holding a tiny pink brush sneaked into view. It smashed bright pink powder onto Gabriel's cheek, leaving a splotch.

"Thank you," Gabriel said, voice and eyes flat. "That's very pretty."

A child giggled.

"I'm also open to your driving home immediately," Gabriel said. "Please."

"I wouldn't want to interrupt your grandchild bonding time," Connor said with a grin. "And I don't mind staying."

"I can clear it with the Ombudsman, if that would help," Gabriel said. Then added, "Not on the walls, Milo."

"I think Yuen will understand the delay," I said. "But it probably wouldn't hurt for him to hear from the Apex."

"Done," Gabriel said as tiny glitter stickers were pressed to his face. "Feast your eyes on the Apex of the North American Central Pack in all his glory."

"Heavy is the head that wears the crown," Connor said, "and is covered in glitter stickers."

When the call was done, Connor settled back onto the couch again, ran a hand through his hair.

As if by instinct—and where had that come from?—I curled into him. Connor made a sound of satisfaction, wrapped his arms around me.

"You sure you're fine with staying?"

"I'm too intrigued to leave," I admitted. "As long as Yuen's good with it."

"I'm pretty sure he will be when he's advised you're helping solve a supernatural murder."

"Which is, ironically, what the sheriff's office would be doing if Cash hadn't paid him off."

"Yeah," Connor said ruefully. "This place is more of a mess than I'd imagined. So I'm glad I have backup."

"It's a shame you can't rely on Miranda for that."

"I could rely on her if things got hairy because she's Pack, and she's Chicago Pack. But no, she won't take a silver bullet for me."

"I'll make you a deal," I said. "You take an aspen stake for me, and I'll take a silver bullet for you."

"Deal," Connor said, and lowered his mouth to mine. The kiss was soft, almost teasing, and enough to have my blood speeding.

But dawn was coming, and my eyes were growing heavy. I yawned, apologized. "Sorry. Biological mandate."

"No worries," he said. "I'm not in any hurry. I mean—don't get me wrong. I want you. And want for you, Elisa, is a powerful thing." He brushed his lips over mine. "A powerful thing," he said again, and kissed me softly. "But we don't need to rush. Especially not when the wanting is so much fun."

I smiled against his mouth. "There is something . . . intoxicating . . . about the anticipation."

"There absolutely is," he said slowly. "And the other reason I can wait?" He slipped his mouth across my jaw to my ear and whispered, "Because I know it will be very, very worth it."

ELEVEN

The next evening—since we were now on a mission—we walked across the resort toward the lodge instead of beginning the drive home. Tonight, the shifters would decide on Loren's memorial. That discussion would be very telling.

My screen chirped, and I pulled it out, found a call from Petra. I accepted it, watched her face appear on screen. She had light brown skin and wide, dark eyes, her hair and brows both dark but for the golden highlights in her hair.

"Talk to me," I said as we moved off the main path and into the shadow of some trees. "But be quiet about it."

"Two things," Petra said. "First, Theo and I passed your update along to Yuen, and Gabriel Keene also made a call. Yuen says be careful, provide a further update when you can, and keep an eye on your six. Do you know what your six is?"

"I do," I said, lips twitching. "Why didn't Theo respond?"

"Because all hell has broken loose."

My heart gave a thud, and I imagined flying monsters and magic battles. "In Chicago? What's wrong?"

"Oh, nothing with Supernaturals. Theo just discovered a copy of *Mindmasters* number four is up for auction today. He's bidding. Yuen's actually along for moral support."

I'd have sworn my mental brakes squealed as my thoughts ground to a halt. "A copy of what?"

"What's the condition?" Connor asked before Petra could answer.
I just stared at him.

"What?" he said with a grin. "That's an important comic. First
appearance of the Silver Champion."

I frowned. "He's the one who went from killing werewolves to
working with them, right?"

"That's him," Connor said. "And they fought together against
Captain Goliath."

Seeing his face light, I realized we'd talked about this before—
years before, when Connor had been fourteen or fifteen. He'd
had an enormous collection of comic books, but he'd reached the
age where he didn't think it was cool to be into anything, at least
as far as his shifter friends were concerned.

My parents had taken me to his house for dinner, where we'd
also been joined by Lulu and her parents. While our parents had
talked, we'd hung out in the basement, a shabby den that had been
newly stuffed with boxes of comics.

"Are you finally moving far, far away?" Lulu had asked.

"Comics," Connor had said, flipping through one. I'd sidled
behind him, looking over the panels. They'd been beautifully
drawn, with watercolor tones and expressive lines.

"Who's the Silver Champion?" I'd asked.

"Werewolf killer," he had said, then closed it and tossed it into
the nearest box. "And before you get snarky, brat, he comes
around eventually. Every man has a journey," he'd added with
attempted gravity. He sat on a weight bench in jeans and a T-shirt,
lifting a dumbbell and trying very hard to look like he wasn't
trying very hard. "I'm getting rid of them."

"Why?" I'd asked him. "You love comics."

He'd shrugged, began to do curls. "I'm growing out of it.
You're still children," he'd said with a cocky grin. "You wouldn't
understand."

He'd been a punk but correct. I'd been thirteen, had my own

collections that straddled childhood and adolescence. Holographic nail polish—which was becoming a Very Big Deal for girls older than me—and the vampire Barbies I hadn't played with in years but couldn't bear to part with.

"I understand plenty," Lulu said, snorting as she kicked her feet onto the coffee table. "For example, I understand you're going to have to spend a lot more time lifting those weights."

He'd been whip lean then, didn't have nearly the muscle he'd eventually grown into. "Why don't you come over here and lift it, witch?"

Her eyes had fired; she hadn't liked that word. "Why don't you shove it, puppy?"

They'd argued like that for fifteen more minutes, until Connor or Lulu—or maybe both of them—had stormed into some other part of the house. I'd peeked into the closest box, found a battered book of manga, and settled in to read.

"The comic is in mint condition," Petra was saying. "Theo saved up."

"Good luck to him," Connor said. "Nice addition to anyone's collection."

"So Theo and Yuen are currently indisposed," I said mildly. "You said you had two things—what's the second?"

"Second, I have information regarding your cryptid," she said.

"Give it to me, baby."

"The Beast of Owatonna," she said, drawing out the words like a storyteller around a crackling fire.

"Ha!" I said, and poked Connor in the arm.

Petra's expression fell. She looked disappointed we hadn't responded with confusion and surprise. "You already know about it? Then why did you call me?"

Connor rolled his eyes. "We know it's nonsense. Local hokum."

"A shifter suggested the Beast of Owatonna was involved," I explained. "But we're nowhere near Owatonna."

"And the footprints were made by a real creature," Connor muttered.

Petra rolled her eyes. "The story only begins in Owatonna. It does not end there."

"Few good stories do," he said.

I put a hand on his arm. "For the sake of argument, why do you think this is the Beast of Owatonna?"

"Because the shoe fits," she said. "Or the footprint, anyway. Like you guessed—the track wasn't made by any known domestic or wild animal, and certainly not by anything that's native to the area. Too long, too wide."

"But it matches tracks made by the Beast?" I asked.

"Technically," she said, "we don't know that, because there aren't any confirmed tracks of the Beast. But," she said, raising a finger, "the Beast is wolfish but bigger. Stalks prey throughout north and central Minnesota, usually at night. Prey is usually livestock. Sheep, cows, roosters. And, drum roll, there are multiple reports of attacks on humans."

"What kind of attacks?" I asked.

"The humans generally report they were assaulted by big, hairy, canine-type creatures. Some reports have them on four legs. Some reports have them on two. Chasing, lacerations, torn clothing, bites. And one alleged incidence of interspecies flirting."

"Someone was propositioned by the Beast of Owatonna?" Connor asked.

"That's the story. Mildred Farmington of Albert Lea, Minnesota, says she was walking back to her home from her neighbor's house when the Beast approached and began to flirt with her." Petra looked down, frowned at something offscreen. "Quote, 'She was wooed weekly for approximately seven weeks, at which time she told the Beast she was unwilling to make a commitment, and the Beast moved on,' unquote."

Connor whistled. "And humans think Sups are bizarre."

"Humans are the strangest of all," I said. "At least we have a magical excuse. Tell us more."

Maybe—okay, almost certainly—this wasn't really the Beast of Owatonna. But maybe, like many other tall tales, the tales had some origin in fact. Maybe there was some clue we could glean out of the stories.

"It's a carnivore. Has a taste for chickens—they tend to go missing when the Beast is roaming. It's more active in the summertime. Not active at all in the winter."

Much like a hibernating bear, I thought.

"Prefers to hunt after one o'clock in the morning, during what they call the 'wicked hour.'"

"Is that like the witching hour?"

"Wicked," Petra said, "as in the Beast is selective about who it eats."

"What do you mean, 'selective'?" Connor asked. "It only eats the plumpest, most tender humans?"

"A tried-and-true plan of attack, but no. It's *morally* particular. The Beast's victims have always done evil deeds. There was a deer poacher, an insurance fraudster, a lady who ran a Ponzi scheme and bilked a dozen Minnesotans out of their pensions."

Connor just rolled his eyes. "So the Beast was punishing white-collar crime."

"You sound skeptical," she said, her tone entirely reasonable. "And I understand that. But if you're going to believe in human-eating North Woods beasts, better they do a good deed along the way by ridding the world of the wicked."

While I was still 90 percent convinced the Beast of Owatonna was nonsense, she had a point.

Maybe Loren's attack had been random, the result of some animal we hadn't yet identified. But if it wasn't random, wasn't just an attack, then someone had selected him. Someone had attacked him on purpose. Why? Because of something he'd done? Something he knew? Something the attacker was afraid he might do?

I thought about the violence that had been done to his body. It looked like punishment. So who would want to punish Loren? And for what? And did Paisley have something to do with it?

"Thanks for taking a look," I said after a moment. "We appreciate it."

"You find any more evidence, send it along. And, Elisa?"

"Yes, Petra."

"Beware of government types in ill-fitting black suits. You never know who else may be looking for the Beast."

She ended the call then, a nice bit of dramatic flair for the *X-files*-worthy send-off. I slid the screen back into my pocket, cleared my throat before looking up at Connor. And seeing the expected know-it-all expression on his face.

"We had to ask," I said. "And notwithstanding the Beast, she's ruled out any native animals. So it's progress. And we'll keep an eye out for the feds, just in case."

He just rolled his eyes.

There was more magic in the lodge today, spilling beneath the closed doors like smoke from a very energized fire. It wasn't broken, but it did have an edge of heat that said discussions about Loren's memorial were not going smoothly.

The shifters hadn't even made it upstairs, but were clustered in the lobby—Cash, Georgia, and Everett standing in front of the fireplace as shifters around them yelled out their concerns.

We worked our way through the edge of the crowd, Georgia giving us a small nod in acknowledgment, and watched as a young shifter did the same on the other side of the horde. Maybe nineteen, tall and on the lean side. He was pale but had sun-kissed skin and dirty-blond hair that was combed forward to flop over his face. Brown eyes topped by thick brows, a square, narrow jaw, a wide but thin mouth.

"Loren doesn't deserve a memorial," he said, eyes hard. "He brought nothing but trouble to the clan."

"Kid's name is Traeger," Connor whispered.

"Loren was an elder," Cash said.

"Not because the clan wanted it," Traeger insisted. "He's not even a wolf. That means he's not Pack. Not really."

Even I knew that wasn't the rule; the Brecks were panthers, and Jeff Christopher was very much a tiger. All of them were Pack. But there were murmurs of agreement in the crowd.

"I'm coyote," Everett said. "That doesn't matter, either, and you know it. We're family as far as family's concerned."

"He's Pack," Georgia agreed. "By choice and by blood. The Pack isn't just wolves." She looked at Connor for confirmation.

Connor glanced at Cash, doing him the courtesy of getting his approval before entering the fray, and when he got the nod, he looked at Traeger. "She's right," he said. "Pack is geography, self-identification. He's a shifter in our territory, says he's a Pack member, then he's a Pack member."

"Fine," Traeger said. "So he's Pack. Then he's not *clan*. He's not part of our family. Not by blood. He married in. That doesn't mean shit."

"These are all technicalities," Cash said, frustration clear in his voice. "We get that you had issues with him, Traeger. But he was part of our community, one of our elders. He did his part to work for the clan, and his death was violent. The least we can do is give him honors in death."

Traeger made a sound of frustration, shook his head.

I thought the least they could do was find his killer, but maybe that was just me. For all their nerves the night before, the clan didn't seem to be much interested in diving into the cause of Loren's untimely death. Was that avoidance? Guilt?

I looked at Traeger, wondering how deep his dislike went—and what "troubles" Loren might have caused. And if Traeger's anger over them might have moved him to murder. Considering the number of injuries and the amount of damage done, someone had been very, very angry at Loren.

Traeger seemed angry enough to kill. But we'd all been angry at someone sometime, and very few of us actually committed murder. And there was no evidence linking Traeger to the death, at least not yet. But maybe we could have a few words. . . .

"The memorial will go forward," Cash said, which sent a new wave of sound through the crowd. Some approval, some anger. "We'll address the details—whether he'll be honored with song, with magic, with sacrifice—in private council." His gaze landed on me, suspicion keen. "This isn't the time or place to have those discussions."

Cash looked away, spread his gaze across the shifters at large. "The clan accepts violence is inevitable. Nature is not soft, and neither are we. Nature is hard, and strength is rewarded, and sometimes we must fight for what we want."

I glanced at Connor, wondered what he thought of the clan's liberal attitude toward violence, and found cold disapproval in his eyes.

"Because of that," Cash continued, "we hold the sheriff—the human justice system—at bay so the clan can make its own decisions. But the injuries done to Loren were not sanctioned by the clan, and no one has presented evidence they were warranted. If I find out any of you were involved, there will be hell to pay."

This time, Traeger was the recipient of Cash's cold gaze. Maybe Cash, too, believed Traeger was capable.

But the chill in his eyes disappeared—blanked out—when a

hush moved through the room, filling it with utter silence. And a cold spill of magic followed in its wake.

The hair on the back of my neck lifted. I knew that magic.

Vampire.

I turned around, watched the crowd slide apart, smooth as the slice of a dagger.

He walked through them, the shifters giving him hard looks and ample space as he made his way toward Cash.

He was a handsome man, with dark brown skin and cropped black hair, brown eyes topped by a heavy brow, and generous lips just a little heavier at the bottom, and edged by a short beard. He wore a black tunic of stiff linen with a short collar and a V-neck, pants in the same stiff fabric, black shoes, and a silver cuff on his right wrist. He wore no sword, carried no other obvious weapon. But he was the one in charge, if his square shoulders and stern expression were any clue.

Two vampires appeared behind him. A man, tall and broad shouldered, with tan skin and dark hair—short on the sides, waved back on top—and a woman with pale skin and blond hair in a complicated braid around the crown of her head. They wore tunics of the same style, same color as the first vampire's.

If the shifters objected to vampires walking through their lodge, they didn't say it aloud. But Connor moved a step closer to me.

"Ronan," Cash said, nodding at the vampire in front. This was the vampire my father had mentioned.

"We heard of Loren's death," Ronan said. "We come to offer our sympathies."

"Appreciated," Cash said. "Loren was an elder, a statesman, and he'll be missed."

There were obviously some who disagreed with that assessment, including Traeger. But they kept their mouths shut. They might debate whether Loren was clan, but he was plainly a shifter.

So they presented a unified front to the outside. To the vampires. Shifters versus the world.

"I always appreciated his thoughtfulness," Ronan said. "He was a cautious and careful man. And above all, he loved the family that he found here and desired to protect it. The authorities were contacted?"

"Sheriff Paulson came out," Cash said. "Took a look at the scene, agreed with us that an animal attack was probably to blame. We searched Loren's house, didn't find anything. Found nothing compelling in the woods indicating his death had anything to do with the Pack."

That wasn't even close to accurate. And while my first instinct was to wonder if Georgia had told Cash what we'd found, the fact that Cash's gaze shifted to Connor—and contained a pretty obvious warning—answered that question. He knew the truth, but was holding it close. Maybe there were some in the room who believed him regardless. But I wondered.

"I'm not surprised to learn your people were not involved," Ronan said. "Are there any leads outside the community?"

"Those avenues are being explored," Cash said, and I'd have called bullshit if the moment had been right.

"If you learn anything, I'd appreciate an update," Ronan said. "In case they pose a threat to my people, as well."

"Of course."

"I'll also admit to some . . . curiosity . . . about your guests."

Ronan turned to me, evaluated. His eyes were intense, curious. Not unfriendly, but the inspection had the calculating edge I'd come to recognize in vampires, who often gauged the value of the fellow fanged by their political usefulness. I'd seen plenty of similar looks when I'd met single vampires curious about the only born vampire—and the prize I'd make.

"Elisa of Cadogan House," Ronan said, taking a step closer.

"Elisa," I corrected. "I'm not a member of Cadogan House."

He lifted his brows. "I wasn't aware, and assumed wrongly. I apologize."

"No apologies necessary. I respect Cadogan House greatly. But I'm not a Novitiate."

"I see," he said, but puzzlement remained in his eyes. He looked at Connor. "The son of Gabriel Keene."

"In the flesh," Connor said stiffly and with more heat than I'd have expected. Surely he didn't think of Ronan as a threat to the Pack. That wasn't Connor's style, and it wasn't consistent with his usual swagger.

"A pleasure to meet you," he said. "I've heard much about your father, your Pack. Both are very well respected."

"Appreciate it," Connor said shortly.

"I hate to be rude," Cash said, "and we appreciate your thoughts, but we're in the middle of planning Loren's memorial, and there's work to be done yet."

Ronan looked dismayed, put a hand over his chest, bowed slightly. "I apologize for the interruption. Perhaps I might have a word with Elisa while you continue your discussions?"

"Fine by me," Cash said with a thin smile he directed at Connor. Another challenge, I thought, this time to test if Connor was brave enough to send me off with a vampire.

Connor looked at me, and while there was undeniably concern in his eyes, they held trust, at least for me. Because I didn't think there were many others he trusted at the moment.

"Elisa is her own person," he said, "and doesn't need my permission."

I caught snickers from more than a few shifters in the room who apparently thought the notion of my autonomy was hilarious. While I wasn't entirely sure I wanted to go with Ronan, I was certainly not going to hesitate in front of them. And since the night had barely begun and I was already sick to death of troglodytes, I decided something quite the opposite was in order.

I turned to Connor, let my eyes silver, and heard the gasp in the crowd. But his eyes, wide and wild, stayed on mine. I put one hand against his chest, the other into his hair, pulling him down to me. And I kissed him, let magic spill and rise around us.

It wasn't politic of me. But it was very vampiric.

His lips curving against mine, Connor put a hand at the small of my back, pressed me forward, and kissed me without regret, without trepidation. He let the others feel the power of it, the *strength* of it.

By the time I pulled back, there were whistles in the crowd, and Connor's eyes were glittering with desire and amusement. A pretty good combination of emotions, I figured.

"Be careful," I said, then turned to Ronan, extended a hand toward the door.

There was a smile on his face before I turned away, walked through the gauntlet of shifters, and felt pretty good about my place in the world.

I walked through the lodge to the back patio, steam from the hot tub fogging the air with humidity and the scent of chlorine. I was half-surprised to find it worked, given the resort's repair needs, but someone had apparently determined it was a priority. Maybe not so surprising, given we were in Minnesota, where heat was an important commodity.

"That was quite a show," Ronan said when he met me on the porch. The other two vampires stayed near the doors, just in case.

"It felt necessary," I said.

"The Pack—and the clan—is patriarchal in many respects. And that you are a vampire discomfits them."

"So I've heard. I understand you're local."

"We have a small coven northeast of here. Unaffiliated, like you."

"And you're friendly with the clan."

"Friendly enough," he said, strolling to the hot tub and gazing into the water. "The clan generally keeps to itself, has the traditional distaste of vampires. We also keep to ourselves, although we are honest about who we are."

It was hard to miss the subtle disapproval in his voice or to disagree with it. "You think they should tell the community they're shifters?"

"I think they should have the benefit of making that decision for themselves," he said. "But I also believe the costs of honesty are not what they were when Cash and the others were in their prime."

"How many are in your coven?"

"There are twelve at present. Ten of us are employed by or with humans. I'm a physician. Attended Cambridge when Queen Victoria ruled much of the modern world. And learned most of what I know after that," he added with a grin.

"That must have been fascinating."

"It had its moments. Most of them immediately before and after the Ripper."

"I bet."

He looked me over, brow furrowed as if he was working through a puzzle. "And how was it to grow from child to adult as a vampire? That must have been fascinating."

He seemed genuinely curious, probably at least in part because of his medical background, so I didn't give a snippy response.

"It just was," I said honestly. "Impossible to compare it to anyone else. I aged normally, stayed away from sunlight, ate plenty of chocolate chip cookies."

His smile was broad. "I'm very glad to hear that. How long will you be in town?"

"To be determined," I said.

Ronan nodded. "We would be happy to host you and Connor at our home while you're in town. It would be . . . fascinating to learn more about Chicago's vampires and shifters."

"I'm not sure how long we'll be here, but I appreciate the gesture."

Connor came outside, joined us.

"Everything okay?" I asked.

"We're getting there. Details to work out, and we're making our way through them." He slid his gaze to Ronan. "Everything okay here?"

"Fine," I said. "Ronan has invited us to the coven if we have time. I told him we'd see."

Ronan smiled at him. "If there's anything I can do to assist the clan or the investigation, I would be happy to offer my services." But he kept his gaze on me, kept the words aimed at me.

"We've got it," Connor said, the words short and clipped.

"Then I'll leave you to it." Ronan held out a hand to me, and we shook, magic tingling beneath my fingertips. Then he walked into the dark, the other vampires falling in line behind him.

I turned back to Connor, noticed the tightness around his eyes. "Are you all right?"

"Vampires," he said, the word nearly a growl.

Since he seemed pretty displeased by the categorization, I pointed at myself again. "Vampire," I reminded him.

This time, he actually did growl. "I don't like being manipulated."

"Manipulated? What did he do?"

"Glamour. You didn't feel it?"

I looked to the spot where they'd disappeared into darkness. "I could feel his magic—but just of the general vampire variety. He didn't try to glamour me."

"It felt like he was trying to keep us calm, relaxed."

That was classic glamour, used once upon a time to keep humans eager for the bite of a hungry vampire.

I put my hand on his arm. "I'm sorry. There was no need for him to use magic at all; he already knows the clan, and apparently has a decent enough relationship with them. I wonder if he was aware of it, or if it's just habit."

"Just habit," Connor repeated, heat in his voice now, "to manipulate us?"

"Habit, and totally wrong." Connor's eyes had gone to ice. He drew a very hard line here, which I could appreciate. "He made a specific decision to use his magic on you now. And there's no excuse for that."

That I'd defended the Pack—against a vampire—seemed to loosen some of the tension from his shoulders.

"Vampires don't get a free pass just because we share some biology," I said. "Same for you and the Pack."

"Same," he agreed. "It's a violation. He also noticed you."

"Noticed me?"

"Seemed interested."

I snorted. "If he was interested, it's because I'm a vampire from Chicago. This close to the city, it would be weirder if he didn't." I looked at him, gave him a friendly elbow. "If I have to get jealous every time a shifter 'notices' you, I'd never have time to do anything else. You attract a lot of attention."

"I guess that makes us a very interesting pair," he said.

"I guess it does." I gestured to the lodge. "How's it really going in there?"

"Testily. It's elders and a few others, and they've deigned to let me join them."

"So thoughtful."

Connor grunted. "It's going to take a while to get through the rest of it—the clan has a very particular list of protocols, and every step has to be negotiated. I need to do that on my own. Can you entertain yourself for a few hours?"

"I can keep myself busy. I could start by talking to some of the shifters."

"About?"

"About Paisley. She's the best link we have to Loren's death, so that seems like the logical place to begin."

Connor frowned, crossed his arms. A lock of dark hair fell over his temple; he ignored it. "You think he was killed because of what happened to her."

"I think it's the best lead we've got." I gestured to the lodge doors. "And Traeger is pretty pissed at him, pretty insistent he not get any posthumous honors. Maybe I'm wrong, but he seemed very capable of taking Loren out."

"Yeah," Connor said. "I had the same thought. You'll be careful out there?"

"I will. And you be careful in there." I looked back around the compound, the nearly identical cabins. "But first, can you point me in the direction of Paisley's cabin?"

TWELVE

Paisley's former home, a little larger than our cabin but with similar architecture, was on the opposite side of the resort, tucked into a sliver of coast between tree line and shoreline. The remains of logs smoldered in a firepit nearby, sending a ribbon of smoke into the air.

The blinds were drawn, but light shone through the slats, and I could hear the low *thrum* of bass from a screen. I knocked on the door, listened for footsteps, and, when I heard nothing, knocked again.

There was muttering before the door was yanked open. "Jesus, George, the music is turned down. Go to sleep and—"

The man who'd answered the door—a shifter about my height, with dark skin and short dark braids—looked at me, eyes widening.

"Oh, shit. You aren't George."

"Nope."

"Sorry, sorry." He leaned out of the doorway, looked left and right. "He's got tinnitus or something. Complains about the music even when it's not on." He looked back at me. "Did you hear it?"

"Only a little when I got close."

"That's fine, then." He paused, looked me over. "You're the vampire. Ellen?"

"Elisa."

"Right. I'm Dante Jones. You need something?"

"Actually, I wanted to ask you about Paisley, if I could."

Pain crossed his face, a clench in the eyes, in the muscle, that I'd have bet he felt as keenly in his heart.

"Connor has been asked to help find out what happened to Loren." That was the truth, even if not all of it. "I understand Loren may have been the last person Paisley spoke with. And they're both gone now. . . ."

I let the implication hang in the air, watched understanding dawn in Dante's face.

"You'd better come in," he said, and held open the door, looking around outside again before closing the door behind us.

The interior, like ours, hadn't changed much since its resort days. The same knickknacks and decor, although there were a few more rugs here and there, framed photographs, colorful blankets that made the space feel less like a vacation cabin, more like a home.

The front rooms were roughly the same size as ours, but the hallway branched down to the left, led to a few different doors. The air was tinged with spices—cinnamon and cumin—and the citrusy tang of sour fruits. And once again, healthy magic. I still wasn't entirely sure if the absence of broken magic meant anything—or what had caused it in the first place—but it felt important that I hadn't found it yet in the resort.

"You can sit," he said, and gestured to the couch. "You want anything to drink?"

"No, thank you. I'm good."

"I'm going to have a root beer. We have some Goose Island from Chicago."

"Then I'll change my answer," I said with a smile. "I'd love one."

He nodded, pulled two frosted bottles from the refrigerator, popped the tops, and walked them over.

"You live here alone?" I asked, sipping the drink, which was ice-cold and delicious.

"With my girlfriend," he said. "She works overnights in Grand Bay. I work for the clan here at the resort. I'm an electrician."

I smiled at him. "That's handy, having a contractor in-house."

"It does come in handy," he said, and sipped his own drink. "She was my younger sister," he added after a moment, gesturing to a photograph above the fireplace.

I rose and walked to it. Dante and Paisley stood in front of the lake, Paisley holding up an enormous fish. She had her brother's coloring—dark brown skin and eyes—and nearly identical short braids. She smiled broadly, obviously proud of the catch, while her big brother looked on, hand on her shoulder.

"She liked to fish?" I asked, glancing back at Dante.

"I don't know that she liked it. She was good at it." He frowned. "Paisley had a way with pretty much everything. Had instincts, could learn quickly. I took that the first time she went out fishing with me. Probably five, six years ago. She nailed that big boy in fifteen minutes." He shook his head in wonder, still smiling, but grief pulled at the corners of his eyes.

"I'm very sorry, Dante."

He nodded, lips tight.

I straightened the picture, then walked back and sat down on the couch. "You know Loren was murdered, and it was . . . bad."

He nodded. "I heard."

"Do you know what she and Loren spoke about before she died?"

"I don't. Loren was an elder. Paisley was young, but interested in clan politics, I guess you'd say. I don't know if that's what they were talking about, but it might have been."

"I understand she was killed while walking near the old main road. Did she walk that way often?"

"Sure," Dante said. "She was a runner. Was doing what she called her 'long run' that day."

"She was training for a race?"

"Some kind of marathon," he said. "Or 50K. Is that a thing?"

"It is. A long-distance race, then."

"Yeah, I think that's it. It was her long-run day, and she liked to run on the main road. Open, good visibility, good surface, but not much traffic. She was upset about something that day. I mentioned that to Cash, but there's no evidence her death had anything to do with that."

"And you don't know what she was upset about?"

He shook his head.

"Would she have told Loren?"

Dante opened his mouth, closed it again. "I don't know. Maybe." He considered, nodded, seemed relieved by the possibility. "Yeah. Maybe that's what they were talking about. She was going to him about some trouble. Something that concerned her." He narrowed his eyes, staring at the floor. "Maybe something to do with the clan, with politics. She was interested in that kind of thing—how the clan was run."

Or, I thought, she was talking to him about something he'd done that concerned her. Confronting him about that. But I didn't need to mention that to him now.

"Was she seeing anyone?"

"Oh, sure. She was dating Traeger. One of the younger shifters. They'd been dating for about two or three months."

It was the first time I'd heard them linked. Why had that taken so long? And given that Traeger didn't seem to be one of Loren's biggest fans, what did that mean?

"I miss her," Dante said, and I looked up at him, recognized the fresh grief in his eyes. And felt bad that I'd stirred that up.

"She sounds like a wonderful person. And it sounds like you had a great relationship."

"We did," he said. "We did. I'm sorry she's gone. I think the clan's less because of it."

* * *

I asked Dante for directions to Traeger's cabin, then walked outside, breathed the fresh air, and tried to clear my mind.

On the walk, I considered the possibility Traeger was behind Loren's murder. Maybe the fact that he and Paisley were dating hadn't been common knowledge, but that seemed odd in a community this small. On the other hand, the clan did seem to have an obliviousness problem.

I crossed a lawn with a sandpit for horseshoes, a handful of rusting chaise lounges, and a swing set for children. And then they stepped in front of me.

"Well, well, well," Miranda said. "Looks like we found her."

Maeve and Jae—the women who'd helped Beth after she'd been attacked—stood behind her. All three wore their anger like battle armor. All three looked ready for a fight.

And what kind of fight? I wondered, and gently tested the magic in the air. Not as strong as Connor's, I gauged, but healthy and whole. No broken magic among them.

"Hello, Miranda."

"What are you doing out here, vamp?" Miranda asked. "Sneaking around our compound? Poking into things that aren't your business?"

My blood fired, began to heat. Miranda had picked the wrong night to bait me. And I wasn't the only one irritated. The monster shifted, stirred, offered almost lazily to join in, take care of the problem. Reminded me of the promise I'd made. The release I'd promised.

Not yet your turn, I told it.

"It's not your compound," I said. "And as you're well aware, I'm here with permission, so I don't need to sneak around."

"What were you doing at Dante's house?" Jae asked, and I shifted my gaze to her.

I wanted to throw out a sarcastic answer, but realized that wasn't the wisest course of action. And at least one of us needed to think through our decisions. "He agreed to talk to me about Paisley's death."

"What about it?" Miranda asked.

I considered what Connor had said about evidence, keeping information close to the vest. "Figure it out," I said darkly.

Her gaze narrowed, and she tacked, shifted. "That was quite a show you put on in the lodge. Quite a little performance."

"I don't consider kissing Connor a performance," I said mildly, but of course it had been. And it had apparently touched a nerve, confirming my theory that Miranda didn't just want the Pack—she wanted him, too.

"Okay, so it's a ploy, right?"

I watched her for a moment, taking in the haughty tilt of her chin, the prickle of irritated magic, the fight in her eyes.

"A ploy?" I asked.

Her eyes gleamed. "For more celebrity. For the thrill of it. To piss off daddy. Dating a shifter. So risqué. So dangerous."

I couldn't help it; I burst out laughing, which just put more sourness in her expression and had Maeve and Jae moving closer.

"You think my father—who orchestrated an alliance between Cadogan House and the Pack, and was chosen by the Pack as a bodyguard for convocation—would be mad I'm dating a shifter?"

Her eyes didn't change, stayed hard and cold as glass. "Hanging all over him, more like. His little princess, wasting all that magic. Wasting all those political opportunities."

That one hit deeper, and I didn't like it.

Miranda moved forward. "You're not going to end up with him, you know; you can't. And you know he can't be with a vampire. Not if he wants the Pack, which he does. Which means you're just wasting his time."

She didn't know anything about my family, about vampires.

Probably didn't know that much about Connor, frankly. But she'd managed to land another blow in a spot I hadn't even realized was weak.

I didn't think I'd flinched, but her smile said otherwise. "You know he's just having a little fun, right? A little rebellion, because he can't afford you. That means you're temporary. A distraction. So why don't you take yourself back to Chicago and your fancy little house and quit putting your nose where it doesn't belong?"

If she was so certain that my being a vampire mattered, I might as well give back a little of my own. I let my eyes silver—and had to hold back the red that wanted to shine through, that wanted the fight on its own, thought it deserved the fight—and watched her throat work as she swallowed. Her own magic filled the air, the paranormal equivalent of fur lifting at the back of her spine. A reaction to a threat.

Good. Better a threat than a joke.

"I'm no princess," I said, voice low and dangerous. "Maybe you're used to prey that slinks around in the dark or humans who avoid you because, deep down, they know what you are." I leaned forward, stared into her eyes. "I'm not human, and I'm not prey, and I know exactly who you are and what I am."

"You want to fight me?" Miranda said, each word bitten off like something foul. Something rotten.

"If you need to see me in action to believe I've got skills, I'm open to that. If you think I'm going to back off just because you can grow claws, you'd be dangerously wrong. Frankly, I don't really think it's a good use of your time, given the clan is apparently being stalked by a killer."

"No one is stalking the clan."

"Loren would disagree with you," I said. Harsh words, but true. "If you really want to test me, you can pick the time and place. If you have thoughts about Connor's choices, you should take them up with him. I'm not his keeper, and I'm not trying to run his life. You might try that strategy, too. Because the one you're currently trying is pretty dumb."

Her eyes went hot. "What did you say to me?"

"You've told Connor you wanted the Pack," I said, and let my gaze slip to Maeve and Jae, watched uncertainty creep into their eyes. "If that's really true, and you think Connor can't win Apex while he's dating me, shouldn't you want him to date me?"

"I don't—"

"Because that would give you a clear path to Apex, right?"

"It's not that simple."

"Because you want the Pack," I said, "but you want him more. This isn't about me, Miranda, and it's not about the Pack. You're just pissed off because he's not interested in you." I kept my gaze on her, but could see Jae and Maeve shifting uncomfortably. She'd probably lured them on this little errand by explaining how I was using Connor, using the Pack. They hadn't known her well enough to guess it was all sour grapes.

"I deserve him," she said, voice high and a little panicked. "Me. I'm Pack. I'm wolf. And I've been by his side for years. Where the fuck were you? In freaking Paris, living it up."

I'd been in Paris, trying to hide the monster while I bled from katana and Krav Maga training, not that she cared about the truth. But I was nearly out of patience.

"Here's the thing, Miranda. Nobody owes you anything. Not Connor, not the Pack, not the world. You want to fight him for the Pack? Then fight. Quit sniping at me, at him, and fight. Maybe you'll get lucky, and maybe you'll win. Maybe the Pack will select you. But even if you win, it doesn't end with the two of you on the throne together. You don't get to pick his partners for him."

Miranda seethed for a minute before Jae touched her arm. "Come on, Miranda. Let's go."

But Miranda wasn't quite done. "Mark my words," she said

through bared teeth. "The Pack belongs to shifters. And I'll do whatever I have to do to ensure you'll have no part in it."

With that, she turned on her heel and walked away.

"Game on," I muttered into darkness. "Game on."

I wanted to hit something—technically, both of us did—from the frustration of dealing with Miranda. I wasn't afraid of her; she talked too much, and did too little, for fear to take hold. But she knew just where to strike to do maximum damage. If she put that cleverness to good use—helping the Pack—instead of fixating on Connor, she could probably do a lot of good.

"Maybe the Beast of Owatonna could find her," I muttered, and strode toward Traeger's cabin. "She's plenty wicked."

Still fuming, I knocked on his door.

It took a few seconds, and the door opened, Traeger sneering at me through the crack. "You at the wrong cabin, vamp?"

"Thank you for acknowledging my biology," I said, and enjoyed the irritation that flashed in his eyes. "And no. I'm here to talk to you."

"I don't have anything to say to you or anyone else."

"Charming attitude."

"I'm not here to charm anyone, much less a vampire."

"Yeah, you mentioned that. You were dating Paisley when she was killed."

"So what?"

"So, I bet you knew her better than anyone else."

"Yeah, I did. Why do you care? She's gone now."

"She is. And I'm wondering about that."

Pain crossed his eyes, as sharp and brutal as the pain I'd seen in Dante's. But it changed, mutated into anger, hot and bitter.

He turned and walked into the cabin, leaving me in the doorway, then sprawled onto the sofa, stared into the dark window beyond. "Ask your questions and get out. Like it matters, anyway. The clan is what the clan is. Cash and Everett and the others are going to do whatever the hell they're going to do, and what we think doesn't matter."

Taking the invitation, I moved inside and closed the door. In the air was only typical shifter magic. Nothing broken, nothing splintered.

I looked around. This was one of the smaller cabins, and it was even shabbier than ours. Cabinets worn at the edges, surfaces not entirely clean, pop cans here and there.

It was interesting how each family started with the same basic structure, the same cabin, which almost evolved to fit their personalities, their lifestyles. I didn't see much forward progress here.

"It matters to me," I said, moving toward the couch. I glanced down at a club chair, the brown leather faded and crisscrossed with scars, considered sitting, but opted to stand. Given his attitude, I'd rather stay on my feet. Prepared in case he pounced. Literally and figuratively.

Traeger's eyes went cold, mean. "Maybe you're a big fucking deal in Chicago, but you're nothing here. So why don't you take your questions and get out and leave the rest of us to our business?"

There was a lot of anger here. And because of that, I opted for honesty. "Because I think something's going on in this clan. I'm not entirely sure what, but there are a lot of angry people. And two people are dead. I'd rather there not be more."

He just looked at me, his face hard.

"Did she have any enemies?"

"Paisley? No. Of course not. She was a good person. Nice. She was friendly to everyone."

"Do you think her death was an accident?"

His lips pressed into a thin line. "I wasn't there, was I? No one was. Clan says it was an accident."

"And what do you think about that?"

"The clan is what it is. It runs the way it's always run. What I think about it doesn't matter."

"Who do you think killed Loren?" I asked.

He looked out the window. I'd have put his age at nineteen or twenty, and that made him seem even younger. A child angry at the world's unfairness. "The fuck do I know?"

"You'd know better than me," I said. "You didn't like him."

His expression didn't change, but he also didn't disagree.

"In the lodge, you said he brought trouble to the clan," I said. "What did you mean by that?"

"He was a dick, and he's dead. So why does it matter?"

"Because someone cared enough to murder him," I pointed out. "Did you know he was the last person to talk to Paisley before she died? And she was angry about something when that happened?"

Angry magic crackled in the air. He hadn't liked the suggestion that Loren and Paisley had been together—or he hadn't known about it. "Said who?"

"Said the people I've asked. You know anything about that?"

He stood up so quickly I nearly flinched with surprise; then he moved toward me. "You're a fucking liar. I want you out of my house."

I was getting real tired of being told what to do by shifters. And the monster was interested in the sharp whip strike of his anger. "Are you afraid of someone asking questions?" I asked quietly, keeping my voice low and refusing to move, to step back.

That challenge put a spark in his eyes. "I'm not afraid of anything."

"Loren?"

"*Anything*," he said, voice low and threatening. "Even nosy vampires."

The door opened. Georgia walked in, grocery bag in hand; behind her, Connor carried two more. They put the bags on the counter, went very still as they read the scene. And I looked back at them, trying to figure out why they'd just walked into Traeger's cabin.

"Hey," Connor said carefully, taking in our positions, the fire in Traeger's eyes, as he evaluated the situation. Assessed. "What's up?"

"Traeger and I were just having a conversation," I said, and looked up at him, refusing to step backward.

I could feel Georgia's cautious but heavy stare, like that alone might be enough to hold Traeger back, to keep him from doing something stupid in front of the prince. Or to him.

"Trae, can you help me put these groceries away?"

"In a minute," he said. "I need air. There's a smell in here." Without waiting for Georgia's response, he stalked outside, slammed the door behind him.

Georgia looked back at me, dark brows lifted. "What pissed him off?"

"Generally, the clan. Specifically, me." I shifted my gaze to Connor. "He and Paisley were dating. Says he didn't know Loren was the last person to see her alive or that they were arguing. I tend to believe him."

"Loren was an elder," Georgia said, pulling boxes and jars from the bags, setting them on the counter. "He talked to all the clan members."

"Not all the elders are dead," Connor pointed out.

She put a box into one of the cabinets, closed the door again. I guessed she wasn't optimistic about Traeger coming back to finish the job. "Trae has nothing to do with any of that."

"You're sure?" Connor asked.

"Do you mean, would I know if he'd killed an elder of this clan?" Her voice was dry as toast. "Yeah, I feel pretty confident I would. Look, he's hot-tempered," she said, putting both hands on the island countertop and leaning forward, eager to make us believe her. "He's young. It's typical behavior. He's learning what

being alpha means, and it takes some longer than others. Especially given his history."

Given the meaningful look she aimed at Connor, I assumed
she'd given him some of that history—and he'd tell me what I
needed to know.

"Georgia, you're family," Connor began, "but something is
going on here, and everyone seems to be ignoring the obvious.
One of your elders is dead, and Paisley before him. Maybe Traeger is involved, and maybe he isn't. But the denial isn't helping
anyone."

Her eyes flashed, hot with fury. "I'm not in denial, and you'd
best remember where you're standing and who you're talking to,
whelp. I've been a member of this Pack—and this clan—a little
longer than you."

"I know," Connor said, not unkindly. "Maybe you can talk to
Traeger, find out if he knows anything else. And maybe you can
talk to Cash and Everett, tell them about Loren, Paisley, their
fight. Maybe they'll pay attention. Because—and I'm going to be
honest here—I'm getting really fucking sick of this clan."

He strode to the door, slammed through it.

I walked to the door, but paused. "Not even Connor can save
the clan alone," I said. "Think about that."

THIRTEEN

"Come here," he said when we walked outside. "I need a minute."

He took my hand, and we walked together along the path that led to the water. Waves lapped gently at the smooth stones that made up the shoreline.

Someone had built a cairn in a flat spot, a tower of round rocks stacked one on top of another, successively smaller as they neared the top. The builder had left a white flower perched on the smallest stone, which made the pale petals seem even more fragile.

Cairns were often used for burials in places where rock was easier to come by than soil. They left behind a visible and tangible mark of the person who'd come before. This one was small—less than a foot high, only a few inches wide. And I wondered if it had been placed here intentionally. For Loren or for Paisley. Or maybe for the clan, because of the hits it had taken.

We didn't stop walking until we'd reached the very edge of the land, an outcropping of stone that jutted stubbornly into the water. Connor wrapped his arms around me, stars spinning overhead, the only sound the soft *thush thush* of the waves and the beating of our hearts.

Silence fell, and I closed my eyes, matched my breathing to the waves until my mind was calm again.

"It talks to me," he said, chin atop my head.

"What does?"

"The lake. The woods. The stones. Not in words—it's not a Disney movie out there—but it has a kind of heartbeat, too."

A shifter's relationship with the earth was unique among Supernaturals, but it wasn't often they talked about it. Maybe they wanted to keep that relationship to themselves; maybe they didn't want to weaken their leather-and-chrome and ass-kicking reputations.

"What do they say?" I asked. "The lake, the woods, the stones?"

"That they're glad you're here."

"I'm glad the stones are here, too. Because otherwise we'd be standing in Lake Superior, and the water looks very, very cold."

Connor leaned down, dipped fingers into the water. "Definitely chilly."

He stood up again, and before I could move out of the way, pressed his wet and freezing fingers to my face.

I couldn't help the squeal forced out by the icy bit of lake now dripping into my shirt. "Oh, you will pay for that."

"Come at me, vamp."

"Not now," I said, shaking out the water. "That's too obvious. I'll take my revenge when you don't expect it. And it will be devastating."

He just snorted.

"Is the memorial arranged?" I asked quietly, loath to bring up the clan again, but knowing we had plenty to talk about.

"Tomorrow night," Connor said. "No one is happy, which I guess is a sign of a good compromise. I won't be able to take you," he added, uncomfortable or unhappy about the admission.

"I assumed. It's fine. It's for the clan. Did you learn anything else?"

"This isn't the first time the sheriff has deferred to the clan to handle criminal matters. However much they're paying him, it's effective."

"Effective if they want to be left alone, and get no real criticism of what goes on internally."

He smiled. "Once again, I don't have to bother explaining things to you."

"Well, not supernatural manipulation. I was born to that. What's the deal with Traeger?" I asked after a moment. "Does he have the cabin to himself?"

"His parents are dead—both killed in a drunk-driving incident four years ago. Both of them way over the legal limit. Father and mother both on the bike, and father turned into the path of a semi. Killed them both instantly. Georgia took him in until he was old enough to live on his own. Still checks in on him. He eats dinner with them most nights."

"He's got plenty of anger," I said. "I think he knows something more about what happened to Loren."

"He said that?"

"Not in so many words. But he was hiding something—his tone, his body language. He doesn't bluff very well."

"And he didn't know they'd argued?"

"I don't think so, which raises a different question: If he wasn't angry with Loren for that, what was he angry about?"

"A good question. I'm a little surprised he talked to you at all."

"Well, Paisley's brother, Dante, talked to me. Traeger mostly talked *at* me. He's a punk. And not the good kind."

"The good kind being yours truly?"

"Of course. Hot and redeemable. Not necessarily in that order."

He chuckled, put a hand at my back. "And what else is wrong?"

I didn't want to tell him. Wanted to handle my own battles. But she was a member of his Pack, and if we were going to have a chance at this, at overcoming everyone else's attitudes, we were going to have to be honest. Something that was in short supply in Grand Bay.

"I can tell you're disturbed," Connor said soothingly.

"Miranda, Maeve, and Jae stopped me on the way to Traeger's. Miranda had some thoughts she wanted to pass along. About me and you."

"Did she?" His tone went flat.

"Yeah. In particular, she's got a lot of thoughts about who you should be spending time with."

He muttered a curse.

"I can handle myself," I said. "And I can handle her. But you should watch your back. In case you needed any more proof, she does not want to hand the Pack over to you."

"She has nothing to hand over," he said calmly. "The Pack does not belong to her. And if I have my way, it never will." He sighed heavily, pulled me closer again. "Damn, Lis. It's been a really long night."

"It's barely midnight."

"Don't ruin the moment, brat."

I smiled against his chest. "Just keeping it real."

We decided food was the way to go. We'd take a break, recharge, and figure out a plan of attack. Someone in the clan knew who'd killed Loren; the body, the trail, the prints all smelled like clan, not like something foreign. We just needed to figure out which clan members were involved.

I'd forgotten about the leftover chicken for breakfast, but it went down well with beer and, in my case, a bottle of blood. Even if it made us both a little uncomfortable to partake of Georgia's generosity after we'd parted on bad terms.

"Let's go to the firepit," Connor said. "Sit outside. Enjoy the evening. It's beautiful out there, and the fire will be relaxing. And maybe we could even talk to some shifters."

I smiled thinly. "You're inviting me to interrogate your Pack-mates?"

"No," he said firmly. "I'm inviting both of us into someone else's conversation—which isn't quite the same thing." But he didn't look entirely convinced of his own argument.

"Okay," I said, and finished the bottle of blood. "Let's go to the firepit. But I reserve the right to ask inappropriately probing questions."

He just rolled his eyes.

The weather was cool and just crisp. I grabbed a jacket, and we walked across soft grass to the firepit nearest our cabin, found a crackling fire and four shifters sitting in Adirondack chairs around it. Two chairs were empty.

"Can we join you?" he asked.

"Sit," said a shifter on the opposite side, his face silhouetted between bright fire and dark lake. "Take a load off."

Connor took one empty chair, and I took the chair to his right, sipped the bottle of beer as I considered the company. Some of the shifters watched us, considered. Others watched the fire or the lake.

"I'm Rose," said the woman beside me. Her skin was tan; her hair was short, dark, and slicked back. She wore a tank top over leggings; a wide, tasseled scarf was bundled around her neck. She pointed to the older woman beside her. "This is Patsy," she said, then moved counterclockwise around the circle. "That's Gibson, and my sister Ruth."

They all acknowledged the introductions. Gibson was a young man with dark skin and cropped hair. Ruth looked a lot like her sister, if maybe a few years younger.

"Connor," he said, and they laughed. "And this is Elisa. She doesn't bite. Unless you ask nicely."

The shifters chuckled good-naturedly, seemed to relax.

"You've stirred up Cash," Rose said, drinking from a plastic tumbler. "He's usually pretty low-key, but he doesn't like being questioned."

Connor stretched out his legs, folded his arms. "I'm not questioning him. I'm questioning what the hell is happening in this clan that two people died in a matter of weeks. Coincidence bugs me."

"Loren had his place," Gibson said. "He was—as all the elders are—concerned about keeping the clan together, keeping it stable. I can't fault them for that."

"I can," Connor said, "if saving the clan hurts the individual shifters."

Gibson lifted a shoulder. "Who's to say it does? Things are different out here than they are in Chicago."

Beside Rose, Patsy shook her head. "That's an excuse, and you know it, Gibbs." She looked back at Connor. "Describe this resort, physically."

Connor frowned at the fire as he considered. "Comfortable. Kitschy. Dated."

"Bingo," Ruth said, pointing at him. "Frigging bingo."

"Bingo," Rose agreed. "It's dated. The grounds are the same. The cabins are the same. We don't want to spend communal money on fancy decor, fine. But the place is falling apart. The floors are stained. The edges are worn. The dock disintegrated five years ago, and it still hasn't been replaced."

"I thought there was a dock," Connor said, lifting his gaze to the waterline. "I figured I just misremembered it."

Rose nodded. "There was a dock. It wasn't original, so it wasn't replaced." There was disdain in her voice.

"Hell, shifters weren't original," Ruth said, "and that didn't stop us from moving in."

"Right?" Rose agreed. "I'm fine with not changing things, with retro. But when things start to fall apart, and we pretend it isn't happening? No. Unacceptable."

"You're stagnating," I suggested.

"Something like that," Ruth said, nodding. "We're so busy

protecting the clan that existed twenty years ago that we aren't paying attention to the clan that exists now."

"Why the obsession with the past?" I asked. "What's the appeal?"

"They were at the top of the pile back then," Rose said as the fire popped, sent up a spark that blossomed in the air like a Roman candle. "The resort was basically new, the elders young and strong. Cash and Everett were married. There was money in the bank, and being a shifter was still secret. And because of that, sexy."

"You've got a secret power," I offered, "so you're basically a superhero."

"Exactly. Times were good—or seemed to be in hindsight. There was always the usual drama. Humans curious about the 'cult' that lived together in the abandoned resort, humans who came around to freeload or preach, someone's wife runs off with someone else's husband."

"Or wife," Ruth said with a grin.

"Or that," Rose agreed. "Those were golden times."

"So what happened?" Connor asked.

"An investment in some kind of restaurant lost us some money. Cash's wife died, and Everett's ran off, and they both got grouchier. Normal wear and tear on the resort evolves into shabbiness and dilapidation. That entire generation got older, had kids. And never stopped talking about when things were better. Kind of lived in the snow globe of those better days, if that makes sense."

"It does," Connor said. Brow furrowed, he looked like he was considering saying something else, but wasn't quite sure whether to voice it. And lifted his gaze and looked around the shifters, considered. "And the newest generation. They want different things?"

"Different and better," Gibson said. "They don't much like the elders, don't agree with how they're running things. Unhappy with the resort's condition, unhappy with how Paisley's death was handled."

"They have the strength to make a change?" Connor asked.

Gibson whistled low, and the discomfort the question had triggered was keen in the irritating prickle of magic. "Let me put it this way," he said, "and I'm sure these ladies will disagree with me if I'm wrong."

That elicited a chuckle of agreement.

"I don't think Cash, Everett would survive a takeover," he said quietly, voice barely audible above the crackle of the fire. He didn't want his voice to carry beyond the circle. "They aren't strong like they used to be, and they don't train like they once did. Complacent, I guess. But I don't know of anyone who'd challenge them. Who'd want the clan bad enough to take on that fight."

"No other alphas?"

"Not at the right age," Ruth said. "Teenagers who aren't ready, young parents who aren't interested." She shrugged. "They thought they'd have better lives in town, so they went to Duluth, Minneapolis, Chicago."

She sounded certain. But I wasn't so sure. Not given what we'd seen . . .

"What about Georgia?" I asked.

"Female," Rose said. "For better or worse, clan's patriarchal, like most of the Pack."

I could accept that that was the pattern, even if I disagreed with the necessity of it.

"So why do you stay?" I asked.

"Just look," Ruth said, gesturing toward the lake. "And listen." Quiet fell, revealing the songs of humming frogs, the sounds of water on the rocks, the crackle of the fire, the wind through the trees to our left. And somewhere beyond it, the sound of laughter.

I looked in the direction of the trees, half expecting to see lights or movement.

"It's the Stone farm," Connor said, gaze lifting to the thin tower of smoke that rose over the canopy. "Probably having a party over there."

"Carlie's family?" I asked.

He nodded. "She and her grandmother. The clan's territory extends right up to their property line at the edge of the woods."

"Technically," Gibson said, "clan territory runs just past the woods, but the Stones are good people, and we don't worry too much about that."

"Now that you've grilled us," Rose said after another quiet minute, and another sip of beer, "I feel like we should interview you."

"All right," Connor said. "That's fair."

"You're taken, right?" Ruth asked. "I mean, I play for a different team," she added with a grin, "but we have a younger sister."

Connor slid me a glance, smile slow and sly. "I'm not currently accepting applications."

Since we hadn't discussed exclusivity, I figured that answer was more than fair.

"Damn it," Ruth said with good humor. "Ah, well." Then she cleared her throat, the sound a little nervous. "But that wasn't the real question. We want to know about your intentions with the Pack."

Connor watched her for a moment. He didn't ask what she meant or that she clarify. Just considered the question like it was one of the most important he'd ever been asked.

And maybe it was.

"Apex," he said.

"You want to be Apex?" Ruth asked carefully.

A tricky question, I thought. Did an alpha predator and presumptive Apex "want" to be Apex? Or was it just an unquestionable state of being?

"I am alpha," he said, looking at each of them. "And my father is Apex. It's up to him and the Pack when his tenure is done. Up to the Pack to determine whether I'm next. But I don't intend to step away."

There were considering nods. Ruth had opened her mouth to ask another question when screams cut through the darkness, echoing around us in a cloud of sound with no apparent starting place.

Silence fell again. We stood one by one, quietly and slowly, and we waited, bodies tense and still, for another sound to penetrate the quiet.

There was another scream. And this time, the direction was clear.

It was coming from the Stone farm.

"Carlie," Connor said.

Clothes were discarded and light flashed as humans became wolves, shifters running full out toward the possibility their human friend was in danger. Or worse.

Connor looked back at me. "Go," I said.

"You're sure?" He searched my face.

"I'm sure." I flipped the dagger from my boot. "And I'm armed."

He slipped a hand through my hair and pulled me against him, kissed me hard. "Follow the trail. It's a good half mile to the farm. There's a V just before you get there. Go left."

"I'm right behind you," I assured him. "Be careful."

He nodded, ditched his clothes, and ran.

Dagger tucked away again, I took off after him.

FOURTEEN

I was fast, but they were faster—proving that four supernaturally enhanced legs were in fact better than two.

As I pushed through the darkness, it worried me that I couldn't even hear their footsteps ahead—until I realized it was smarter to track them by magic rather than by sound. I reached out for that, caught the sizzling trail off to my right, and pushed harder. It took only a moment to hear the battle, then to smell it.

And then to emerge from the woods . . . and step directly into hell itself.

The woods edged into the cleared land of the Stone farm, furrowed rows of dirt either left fallow for the season or already cleared of whatever green they'd held. Now, in the warmth of late summer, there were only scraps of what had once been growing.

The farmhouse was on the other side of the field, white clapboard and guarded by a windbreak of trees on the opposite side, all of it on a gentle rise that offered a view of the lake.

And ten yards from the tree line, a bonfire that might have sprung from one of Dante's hellish circles. Wood and brush had been piled six feet high, and the flames licked the sky several feet above that. There'd been chairs, but they were tossed, scattered across the field along with empty beer bottles and an upturned cooler.

Some of the humans were running, screaming. Others were down, blood staining the earth and scenting the air. Five wolves—

the shifters from the firepit, including Connor—stood between the humans still on their feet and the monsters who'd attacked them.

They were wolves, but not wolves.

They were beasts. And they were enormous—twice as wide as a human, and nearly as tall as the fire itself. Their bodies were generally wolflike, if wolves stood on two legs, had claws as long and sharp as icepicks, and narrow, gaping muzzles with fangs nearly as long as their claws.

The wicked hour had come, I thought ruefully. But these were no cryptids, no myths. They were as real as I was.

There were four of them. Going by fur: silver, brown, red, and black. But their fur was matted and bare in spots, showing what appeared to be human skin beneath. For all their bulk, they were skinny enough that bone and tendon were visible beneath that thin skin.

Stringy strength, Beth had said, and I understood now what she meant.

And since blood and human and smoke and clan were the only scents in the air, they were undeniably clan, even if their magic was fractured. How had this happened?

They stood together, swatting at the wolves as if they were nothing more than irritating pests, but they didn't seem entirely certain what to do next. At least until the brown beast stepped forward, raised his muzzle to the sky, and let out a howl that lifted every hair on the back of my neck . . . and had the monster paying attention.

He threw out his hand and sent a black wolf flying through the air, until it landed with a horrible whimper on the dirt twenty feet away. It rolled to its belly, whimpered again. Then rose on shaky legs, shook off the fall, and prepared to lunge again.

That had been first blood, at least between beasts and wolves, and the battle began.

The remaining wolves jumped forward, Connor in the lead. I

had to work to tamp down my fear and let him fight his battle. And being an immortal, I pulled the dagger from my boot.

My fangs descended, my eyes silvered. Moonlight dripping down the blade, I ran forward to a human who lay facedown in the dirt, blood streaming from her arm. Her hair was long and brown, her body petite, and I had a horrible jolt at first, thinking I'd found Carlie dead.

I steeled myself, turned her gently, checked her pulse.

The woman wasn't dead, and she wasn't Carlie. There was a knot on her forehead, already purpling, and a gash across her cheek. I checked for obviously broken bones, decided she wasn't wounded enough that she couldn't be moved. I could carry her to the house, but I'd have to go through the fighting; that was too risky. I looked around, saw the remains of a small wooden structure—three sides sheltered from the wind—in a hilly patch of green. Probably a place used to feed grazing animals, and they'd plowed around it to set seeds in the ground.

I put away the dagger, picked her up, watched the fight for my chance to cross the battleground, and when the chance came, I ran. The ground was dry and hard, the furrows trip hazards that made every step dangerous. I dodged a piece of flaming wood thrown clear of the fire as the debris pile moved, settled.

I placed her beneath the shelter. She moaned when I put her down, eyes fluttering open. "What happened?"

"Just a little mishap at the party," I said with a light tone, since the Supernaturals were supposed to be a secret. "A very hairy mishap."

"What—," she began, then sat up, her eyes growing wide as she saw a beast screaming in front of the fire, the flames reflected in her eyes.

Then her eyes rolled back, and she fainted.

"Probably for the best," I said, then rose and turned to face the battle again.

The wolves had managed to separate the beasts, were taking them on individually. Connor had Brown, and they were lunging at each other, muzzles and claws already dripping with the other's blood.

As always, the monster was jealous—of the blood, of the power, of the fight. But there were monsters enough here, and the broken magic of whatever had made the beasts. I couldn't risk it. Not now.

No, I said, and tried to ignore the urgency of its pleas.

It was stronger, it assured me. It would fight better, and I had made a deal.

That I was actually having a conversation with the monster was a nightmare for another time. And yes, I could have used its strength. Probably could have used its amorality. But humans here had an odd relationship with the supernatural, and we had enough to deal with. I wasn't going to make that worse with red eyes and violence that I couldn't control.

I can't deal now. It's too dangerous.

I felt its anger then, the internal burn of fury that I was denying what it wanted. I doubled over with the sharp shock of pain.

I am dangerous, it said.

The silver beast roared, drawing my attention back to the fight. Two wolves lay on the ground, chests heaving. Red was in the same shape. Only Connor and another were still fighting, their attention focused on Brown and Black.

Silver saw me and began to move forward, the earth seeming to shudder with every step. Its paws were bigger than my head, and given those claws, it wouldn't need an aspen stake to do plenty of damage.

If it kills me while we're arguing, I told the monster, *we both die. Step back.*

I put my own magic behind the demand, and all the glamour I could muster. After a moment, the pain receded, and my mind became gloriously clear. But I knew the reprieve was temporary. I'd angered it, and while I won the battle, I had a sinking feeling that I wouldn't win the next one. And possibly not the war.

Georgia was right. It was fighting me for control. And I was losing ground. But there wasn't time to dwell on that now. The other war still raged, and I was one of the soldiers.

I pulled my dagger out again, worked to clear my mind of all but the blade and the enemy. I was vampire. I was predator. I had skills and power of my own. And I would use them.

Twenty feet away, Silver roared again, blood and saliva dripping from its fangs. There were cuts along its torso, tufts of hair and skin hanging from its legs where the wolves had gotten purchase with fang and claw.

And it looked pissed.

"Oh good," I said merrily, and thought of the lessons I'd learned in France, in the humid basement where I'd learn to fall and rise a thousand times. And where I'd learned to make the dance mine, not to let my attacker lead.

I had one skill I'd bet it couldn't master.

I sucked in a breath, moved my weight to the balls of my feet, and pushed off. I ran toward it, arms and legs pumping, then pushed up, soaring into the air, dagger extended. I landed on the animal's torso, thrust the blade into its shoulder. Its fur was crusted, and the smell was astoundingly bad—animal and dirt and a sourness that seemed to come from the magic as much as the body.

But it felt pain. It screamed, reared back. I grabbed handfuls of fur, but it twisted, and I flew, hitting the ground with a thud I could feel in every bone—and slamming my head against a furrow of brick-hard dirt.

There was a yip I recognized as Connor's, and I glanced up, found him staring at me in concern. "I'm fine," I called out, blinking until my vision cleared.

I looked up again, watched the beast pull out the dagger, the blade sliding wetly through muscle and flesh, and howl at the pain. It dropped the blade and turned, met my gaze.

And then it started running.

The movement was awkward—a wolf balancing on two legs attempting to imitate a human's running form. It was trying to move like a human, I realized. Or more accurately, like a shifter in human form.

"That is some very bad magic," I said, crawling to my feet, trying to keep the world from spinning around me.

It reached me, stretched out its awkward limbs, and swiped out. I crawled beneath its legs, kept moving toward the dagger. I heard it loping behind me, the impact of its footfalls giving me a good indication of its location. I spotted the dagger three feet away. Then two.

It swiped again, the tips of its claws burning hot across my back, and sending me across the ground. I rolled to a stop, climbed to my feet, saw it look down at the dagger as if puzzling out what to do.

It had known enough—was human enough—to pull the dagger from its shoulder. But it couldn't quite remember how to wield it. Which was fine by me.

I scrambled to my feet, lunged for the beast again, sweeping the dagger up as I raked my nails across the dirt. I kept running, putting distance between us so I could turn and face it.

And did, brushing dirt and sweat and blood from my eyes.

I bared my fangs, hissed out an oath as the gashes in my back pulsed with pain. The beast turned again, blood seeping from its shoulder and leaving a dark stain down its torso. Baring its fangs in a kind of dare, it loped toward me again, the fury evident in its eyes.

This wasn't just an animal fighting for territory. It was angry. Furiously angry. Because we'd interrupted it? Because we'd hurt it? Or because it just wanted to hurt, to kill?

I adjusted my fingers around the dagger's handle, crouched just enough to keep my center of gravity low, and moved the weight on the balls of my feet. The beast reached me, swiped, and I spun to avoid the claws, slashed down across its calf as I turned. I'd hoped to sever a tendon, to put it on the ground, but its skin was tougher than I'd thought, and this time I hadn't used my body-weight.

I still sliced, and it still screamed, the sound high-pitched and frantic, and turned around, snatching the air to get me, to stop me. I dropped and rolled, then popped up again, slashed across the front of its other thigh. I ducked to avoid its claw, but it grazed my shoulder, sending me off-balance. I hit the dirt again, but managed to keep the dagger, rolled onto my back.

It loomed over me—firelight flickering across its face—and screamed again, its breath emitting a stench as bad as the rest of it. I changed my grip on the blade to prepare for an upward strike . . . when a human voice filled the air.

"Stop, you bastard!"

There was a mighty *thud*, and the beast fell to its side, revealing Carlie behind it, scratches across her face and collarbone, and a stick as thick as a baseball bat in her hands.

"Good shot," I said, and began to climb to my feet.

Carlie smiled, dropped the stick. "Thank you! I was afraid it was about to—"

That was all she managed to say, because the beast was up again and, in the space of a heartbeat, caught her in its jaws and ran toward the woods.

The beast had Carlie.

The scream was stuck in my throat, and it took my brain a moment—too goddamn long—to process what had happened. Cold slicked down my back even in the fire's enormous heat, and I stared into the woods.

The beast had Carlie, I thought again, even as the monster insulted my fighting, my impotence. But I didn't need the guilt. She'd been trying to save me when she'd been taken.

And hell if I was going to give her up.

I ran like I was chasing hell itself, instead of the opposite. The beast's trail was, at least, easy to follow. It cut a swath through the trees, left a trail of dark blood and broken magic that was impossible to ignore.

I pushed harder, ran faster. My lacerations were screaming, my head still spinning from the knock I'd taken. But pain meant nothing. Not compared to her life.

I had to get Carlie back. There was no other option.

I could hear the beast ahead of me, breath stuttering and footfalls growing slower. It was wounded, too, and carrying a human. A small human, but still.

That I couldn't hear her screaming, didn't hear a cry for help, planted fear deep in my belly. Was some of the spilled blood hers? Had the beast's teeth pierced something vital? Would I be too late?

"No," I said, and forced myself to move faster, until the trees and leaves were blurs around me and I could barely feel the trail beneath my feet.

Ahead of me, shadows shifted and moved in the narrow beam of moonlight that managed to penetrate the trees. I saw the beast's form, dark and hulking, and knew what I needed to do.

I had to stop it. Had to get Carlie free of it, and given the gap between us, I'd have to use my dagger.

I couldn't miss.

They were sixty feet ahead of me, and I pushed again, narrowed the gap to fifty, to forty, to thirty, until my heart felt like a piston in my chest, my lungs burning nearly as badly as the scratches on my back.

Thirty feet.

I couldn't wait any longer. I held the dagger by the tip, pulled back, and let it fly. It streamed through the trees like an arrow, straight and true. I heard the punch of contact, the grunt of sensation, and the sound of something heavy hitting the ground.

"Bingo," I said, and ran toward it.

I reached the small clearing made by its fallen body.

But the beast was gone, along with my dagger.

Carlie lay across a granite bolder, her face and hands and arms smeared with blood. Her small body broken, her skin gray, and dark blood seeping from a rip across her abdomen. Her mouth was open, eyes staring.

"*No,*" I cried out. "*No, no, no,*" and sprinted forward, felt her carotid.

There was a pulse, but that was generous. It was faint and irregular, and with every pump of her heart, more blood stained the ground around her.

She was bleeding out.

I swore again, pulled off my jacket, pressed it to her abdomen to try to stanch the bleeding, even though I knew it was futile and wasn't going to help. Not when the beast had torn at her flesh like it wanted to shred her to pieces.

I couldn't call out. If I did, the beast might come back. I could lift her, carry her, but where? I was in the middle of the woods; the resort and the farmhouse were somewhere on opposite sides of me. Even if I could find a place to take her, she wouldn't survive the trip.

"Fuck," I said, and pressed harder, and blood seeped warm and wet through my fingers. There was so much.

My fangs descended, not in lust, but in reaction to the sheer volume of blood. Not even my monster was interested in her, in this death and waste and misery.

"Come on, Carlie," I said. "Hold it together. Be strong for Georgia, for Connor." But she wasn't going to hold it together. If I didn't do something, there wasn't going to be a happy ending here.

I looked up, around, had to risk a scream. *"Connor!"*

I listened, hoping to hear the sound of paws on the ground, of rescue. But there was nothing but the beat of my heart in my ears, of the *plink* of blood onto stone. Of life into stone.

There was another way. I knew it only in possibilities, in the stages that had been explained to me by my parents, my professors . . . because I was the only vampire who'd never experienced them.

The time that elapsed between her heartbeats grew longer, the beats softer, no longer a pulsing of muscle, but a sigh. A releasing. There was no more time to wait. Not for rescue. No one was coming to save her now. Which meant I had to, whether she wanted it or not.

"I'm sorry," I told her, pushing back the hair from her face.

And sank my fangs into her neck.

Her blood was a sweet song, and I was torn between thirst, desire, and guilt. But the latter couldn't matter; I had to do this, and I had to hope it worked.

The concept was simple: Bite, spreading the agent that prevented coagulation and triggered the mutation. Drain the human blood and replace it with my own blood, which would feed the mutation. And then wait for the physical transformation to be complete—three days of pain and terror as human biology transformed to vampire.

Unless it didn't.

Only Master vampires—those tested and recognized as Master vampires by the AAM—were officially considered strong enough to ensure the transformation would be successful—and wouldn't simply kill the human. They were also the only vampires considered experienced and resourceful enough to manage the emotional and psychic connection that linked the Master and the vampire he or she created.

I was twenty-three and could barely manage my own life,

much less anyone else's. But that couldn't be helped, any more than the risk could be avoided.

The beast had taken Carlie's life. Here, in the forest alone, this was her only real chance to live again.

She barely moved as I drank, neither conscious nor strong enough to fight me. And I thought it was better that way. She'd seen, experienced enough horror for the night. There was no point in adding to the burden she'd already carry.

It took only minutes for me to drink, my body hungry and depleted from the fight. She was a limp doll cradled in my arms, skin translucent, cheeks hollow, dark half-moon shadows beneath her eyes.

"I'm sorry," I said again. Full of blood and power and oblivious to pain, I snicked fangs into my own wrist so the blood welled in two dark streams. I held my bloodied wrist to her, let droplets fall upon her lips, and waited.

But she was still as a stone, an alabaster rendering of the woman I'd met at Georgia's. The woman who'd attacked a beast with a stick to save me from harm.

"Come on, Carlie," I said, and maneuvered more droplets onto her lips, the contrast between bright blood and pale lips so obvious, so terrifying.

For another minute more, there was nothing. No movement, no sound, no attempt to take the blood I'd offered her. Despair covered me like a blanket. The possibility that I had not saved her, but hastened her death.

And then her lips parted, and the blood licked away. Hope rose, and I offered my wrist again.

Her eyes flashed open, stared up at me. She dug fingers, bloodied nails, into my arm, wrenched it against her mouth, and then began to drink. The sensation was strange—not bad, not good—but strange. My own power, life force, being taken, used, to complete the transformation. And literally sucked away.

"Ow," I said as her teeth began to sharpen and dig into my skin, but I was glad of the pain. It was penance, and little enough cost for the havoc I'd be wreaking on her life.

Magic rose, cold but bracing, as it began the first stages of its work—mending what was broken. With my free hand, I pushed away the jacket I'd used to put pressure on her wound, watched as the jagged edges knitted together until the skin was whole again. Still sickly gray, but whole.

She would never see the sun again, but she'd heal quickly. Assuming she survived the rest of it.

There were footsteps, movement through the trees, and I wrapped my free arm protectively around her, gaze darting from tree to tree to find the threat.

Connor stepped into the clearing, in muddy jeans and shoes, a shirt rolled and snaked into his waistband. He must have picked up his clothes while searching for us. His torso was bloodied, punctures and lacerations tracking across his arms, his belly.

Relief crossed his face first—gratitude that I was alive. And then he looked closer, saw Carlie, my arm, her lips around my wrist.

His mouth opened, but he didn't speak, just stared at us until, I guessed, he could comprehend what he was seeing. It would have been a shock, I knew. A horror, probably, to see the girl he considered a little sister bloodied in my arms.

And to watch her drink.

But we were on a schedule, and there was no time to waste. So I had to add insult to injury and hope we'd find our way out the other side. Because while I understood the process, I wasn't a Master, and Carlie deserved more than my inexperience.

Fortunately, I now knew a vampire, a Master, a physician. I needed his help and hoped he'd be willing to give it.

"I need Ronan," I told Connor. And hoped he could see the apology in my eyes.

* * *

We waited until she stopped drinking, which took only another minute. She detached from my arm and fell back, limp; Connor scooped her into his arms and began to move through the woods.

That he wouldn't let me carry her, despite the fact that I was fed and healing and he was still injured, was an arrow through my heart. Like he didn't trust me not to do her further harm.

He didn't speak, and the silence between us seemed to stretch and strengthen.

She'd survive, I told myself. That was what mattered—that the destruction the clan was wreaking wouldn't claim another victim. And if Connor and I—the bond that had grown between us— didn't survive, I'd have to live with that. But that didn't stop the stutter of my heart or the pain that pierced it.

Connor didn't need the trail to find his way back to the resort, and we made it back in ten minutes. There were shifters every-where. Nervous, waiting, staring at the column of smoke, or at-tending to the injured shifters who'd limped their way back from the battlefield.

Cash and Everett were notably absent.

There were gasps as Connor walked past them, ignored them, and took the girl into Georgia's cabin.

"Get Ronan," he said to Georgia.

His voice was entirely alpha now and brooked no argument. And Georgia made none, at least aloud. But the grim set of her eyes when she looked at Carlie, then shifted her gaze to me, was more than enough.

Connor placed the girl on the sofa. Protectiveness—a sharp tug of it I hadn't expected—pulled me back to her. I went to my knees in front of the couch, rubbed my hands over my face.

"How long does it take?" he asked.

I opened my eyes and looked at him, saw pain and worry

etched on his face, and hated that I'd put it there. "If you mean the transformation, three days."

Assuming she didn't die along the way, but I couldn't bring myself to say that aloud. I had to believe this was going to work.

I cleared my throat, tried to push through the knot of emotions that tried to strangle me. "You said she lived with her grandmother. You might want to check on her, if you haven't already. Let her know Carlie's . . . alive."

Georgia came back in. "Ronan is on his way. He's not far from here." She looked at me. "What happened?"

"There was a party at the Stone farm," I said. "On the other side of the woods. We were at a firepit and heard screaming. We all took off and found the fight—creatures attacking the humans at their party—and fought them."

"Creatures?" she asked.

"We'll get to that," Connor said, gaze on me. "Keep going."

I nodded. "I was fighting one of them, and I went down. She tried to save me. She hit the beast, and it went down, but came up again and dragged her into the woods. It was fast. I followed it, eventually got close enough to throw my dagger. I hit the beast, and it dropped her and kept running. She was hurt, so I had to let it go."

I swallowed hard. "It ripped her abdomen open. She was nearly gone when I got to her. Her heart—"

I could hear the echo of her heartbeat again, a soft and fading whisper.

I shook my head, made myself meet his gaze. "Her heart was stopping. She wouldn't have survived if I'd tried to move her. So I began the process. I bit her, took her blood, and gave her mine. And then you came."

The only heartbeat I heard in the following silence was mine.

"Someone needs to check on her grandmother," Connor said finally, his face and tone carefully schooled.

Georgia frowned with confusion, but nodded. "We'll check on her. Make sure she's all right." She looked at Connor. "Are you going to tell me what the hell it was?"

"Unknown canids," Connor said. "Four of them. Not actual wolves, not shifters. They were bigger, taller, leaner. Walked upright. And not wild animals; they were supernatural. They were magic. They're what attacked Beth," he added. "And killed Loren."

Georgia blinked, as if trying to translate words she didn't quite understand. "Magic. You're talking about a curse? A spell?"

"I don't know." He paced to one end of the living room, then back again. "What about dire wolves?"

Georgia's brows lifted nearly to her hairline. "Dire wolves. As in prehistoric animals? Mammoths and saber-toothed tigers and cavemen? I know they existed, and they're extinct," she said, frowning. "My father was obsessed with wolves, had a big book, and he'd show us pictures of the types of canines around the world. Everything from dire wolves to Chihuahuas." She tried for a smile, but it didn't stick. "Dire wolves moved on four legs, not on two."

"Yeah," Connor said, running a hand through his hair. "I don't know what they are, or how they are, but I don't know of anything else that's big enough. Not that has existed before. Maybe this is something new. Either way, they're clan."

Georgia's eyes went wide. "No."

"Yes," he said simply. "Based on the scent, on the magic, they're clan. They've done something to themselves magically, made themselves bigger, stronger. But still clan. They attacked Beth. Killed Loren. Nearly killed Carlie."

Georgia shook her head, as if that might clear away some of the confusion. "I don't understand any of this. Who would do it? Or why?"

The who and why, I thought, were beginning to piece themselves together. This started with Paisley, and it would end with her.

"We're working on that," Connor said. "And we'll figure it out."

It took ten minutes for Ronan to burst in, two vampires behind him, all of them changing the air in the room. Georgia's mouth pinched into a hard line, either unhappy with the vampire or the fact that he was in her house.

Ronan ignored us, kneeled beside Carlie. He pulled back her lids, scanned her eyes, then put a hand on her wrist to check her pulse. "What happened?"

I told Ronan the same story I'd told Connor and Georgia as Ronan made his examination. Silence fell when I'd finished the retelling and he finalized his work. Then he looked at me.

"How long did you feed her?"

"Minutes," I said. "Ten maybe? I fed her until she let go."

"How long since you stopped?"

I had no idea how much time had passed. It felt like hours, but guilt and worry had pulled time, stretched it. I looked toward the windows, found the sky was dark. "I'm not sure."

"About twenty minutes," Connor said.

Ronan nodded, rose, looked at me. "After the initial feeding, there's a period of rest followed by supplemental feedings over the three days. So you accidentally did the right thing."

His voice was hard now, tinged with admonishment, but his words still had relief moving through me.

"She'll be all right?" Connor asked.

"We don't know that yet. Not all survive the transition, particularly when the vampires making them are not old or strong enough." He looked at me. "You are not a Master. You don't have the experience or the skill to do this."

"You may have missed the part of the story," I said, barely managing to control my tongue as guilt burned off, replaced by anger, "where I either bit her or I let her die."

"Don't imagine yourself a savior," Ronan snapped out. "She may die anyway, and there will be more pain in between."

I moved closer. "I did what had to be done in the moment. I'm experienced enough to know that giving her a shot at life was better than letting her die. I won't apologize to you for that." If Carlie demanded an apology, that would be different. But I'd have to worry about that later.

"I'm also experienced enough to know that she needs to be with you—with vampires—during the transition. Not here. I called to ask for your help. Do you want to help, or do I need to find someone who will?"

There was condescension and irritation in his eyes now. He didn't think much of me, and he thought even less of my request for help. But one of his vampires came forward, probably at his telepathic order, and picked up Carlie.

"Come with me," Ronan said, and turned for the door.

"Find Alexei," I heard Connor say to Georgia behind me, and he followed me out.

FIFTEEN

Of course he has a limo," Connor muttered as we slid into the long white vehicle parked outside Georgia's cabin. It was an Auto, a woman's voice requesting in sultry tones that we please take our seats and engage the safety belts.

Carlie had been laid on the limo's carpeted floor, a vampire holding her head, and another at her feet to help keep her stable. Connor and I took seats along the reverse-facing bench, just far enough apart that our bodies didn't touch.

Ronan sat on the side-facing seat, one hand draped over the back as he stared out the window. His vampires stared at me. Unlike the shifters, their expressions were shielded; I guessed that was due at least in part to deference to their Master. But they couldn't hide the bristling magic that peppered the air.

We drove southwest, following the old main road that paralleled the lakeshore before diving inland onto a two-lane road roofed by arcing trees.

Connor sat silently, brow furrowed, gaze on Carlie.

I couldn't blame him. I watched her, too, checking for sign of transformation or distress. But she was so still, so motionless, that it was difficult to imagine anything was happening at all. And that we hadn't lost her despite my efforts.

I knew Connor was worried about her, but it was impossible to ignore the emotional wall that seemed to be rising between us. And it wasn't difficult to imagine why he'd constructed it. I'd hurt someone he loved—used fangs and blood against her—and dragged him into a political nightmare in the meantime. I'd become exactly the kind of liability Miranda had warned me against.

"A little rebellion," Miranda had called me, "because he can't afford you." If relationships really were a kind of math—good qualities measured against bad, benefits measured against costs—tonight would certainly have changed the balance, and not in my favor. Not as long as he sat in measuring silence.

Forest bluffs gave way to rolling hills, and eventually to a shadowed house that waited on the crest of a knoll for its vampires to return.

The house was stunning even in the dark. Pale golden stone, symmetrical with white windows, tall white chimneys on each end, and a columned portico. With no other buildings nearby, it looked like a dollhouse a child had left behind. Or maybe the site of a Gothic horror novel.

Two Sup communities in this small slice of rural Minnesota, but their homes couldn't have been more different. The sprawling and aging resort, hiding among the trees beside the lake, versus this castle on a hill, a stark and unavoidable mark on the landscape.

The limo followed the drive to a covered portico at the side of the house, with more white columns and molding. One of Ronan's vampires hopped out first, opened the door. Connor and I climbed out, and then Ronan negotiated Carlie out of the vehicle and toward the house.

Quiet as ghosts, we followed him inside.

The house was clad in dark wood—floors, ceiling, paneling—and the front room was home to an enormous stairway in the same wood. Light filtered through an opaque ivory dome at the top of the first landing, and dark red velvet swagged in generous loops above the windows.

A vampire came down the stairs. She was slender, with pale skin and long raven dark hair that swirled around her shoulder in a loose braid. She wore a fitted red dress and black heels. She reached us, cast a quick glance at us before looking at Ronan. "I've prepared a room."

Ronan nodded, carried Carlie upstairs. When he passed her, the woman looked back at us. "I'm Piper," she said, and didn't ask for our names. "Bathroom's just there, if you want to clean up."

I nodded, feeling physically jumpy and emotionally numb. I looked back at Connor, found his gaze on me, concern clear in his eyes. "I'll be right back."

He nodded, crossed his arms in a way that showed off his muscles. Legs braced, he looked like a man prepared for another battle. But since two vampires followed me down the hall, I didn't think he'd be the one who'd need to fight.

I found the bathroom, closed the door, and shut my eyes for a moment in the darkness. The monster was quiet, exhausted, satiated by violence and blood.

When my heartbeat began to slow to a more normal rhythm, I turned on the light, then stared at myself in the mirror. I barely recognized what I saw. My cheeks were flushed, my lips swollen, my skin pale but for the already healing scratches of battle. My eyes were still silver, and there were twigs and leaves and probably worse in my hair.

I washed my hands and face, finger-combed my hair. And felt nearly normal when I opened the door again—if I didn't think too much about the vampires waiting to throttle me outside it, and the human somewhere above us who might not survive the evening.

By the time I made it back to the central room, Ronan stood with Piper, quietly conversing. Connor stood exactly where I'd left him, arms still crossed. *The alpha being alpha,* I thought, and joined him.

His expression was still carefully blank, but anger shimmered in his eyes. He was a man riding very close to the edge of fury. I just wasn't sure at whom he was going to direct it.

Ronan turned to us, moved closer, hands clasped behind his back. "Take me through it again," he said.

So I did, step by step. From firepit to screaming, from the clan's territory to the Stone farm, from the hell of battle to the agony of finding Carlie, alone and broken. And then I told him of the decision I'd made and what I'd done.

"What attacked the humans?" he asked.

"I don't know," Connor said. "They're clan members affected by some kind of magic, turned into wolflike creatures that attack on two legs. They aren't similar to any wild animals or Sups we know about."

"Why did they attack?" Ronan asked.

"We don't know that, either," Connor said. "The Stone farm is at the edge of the clan's territory. Maybe they believed the humans were getting too close. Maybe the magic has affected them. Or maybe they're just homicidal assholes."

"Are they dead?"

"Not that we're aware of," Connor said. "We hurt them, but they survived. They ran away from the resort, deeper inland and into the woods."

No one spoke for a long time.

Finally, Ronan broke the silence. "This will put pressure on the communities. Ours and theirs. Yours potentially. She was changed without her consent. She was changed within earshot of humans. And she was changed without my consent."

"It wasn't your territory," I said. "It was the clan's territory."

"And as Cash will certainly point out, you didn't have his consent, either."

Heat began to rise again, to speed my heart and call the monster who'd already had its fun tonight. Who was getting harder and harder to push down. "I was not going to leave her on the ground, bleeding out."

"It wasn't your choice to make."

"Wrong," I said. "It was the *only* choice to make."

"You're a vampire. You had obligations."

"To who? I don't have any obligations to the clan, and even if I did, I kept the clan from killing a human tonight. I don't owe you anything."

"You are in my territory." Ronan's voice was low and dangerous. His eyes silvered, and his fangs descended, and magic rose in the air, peppery and hot. I braced myself against the coming blow—and prepared to meet it.

I liked and appreciated rules. I liked order. But even I knew that rules sometimes had to be bent or even broken. Exceptions had to be made, or else the rules would swallow their purpose, their intention.

"I'd have thought better of your parents," he said, "that they hadn't raised you to break the faith with other vampires."

"How did I break the faith?"

"She is a friend of the clan, and you didn't have their consent. Once again, you're in my territory and didn't have my consent. Maybe your parents' wealth, their status, has poisoned you. Spoiled you. But you aren't in Chicago, and things work differently in the real world."

Now I was pissed on behalf of myself and my parents. "I was raised to do the right thing, and that's what I did. Politics is second—will always be second—to saving lives."

"She is one life. You've potentially put all of us in danger. Which is more important?"

I just stared at him. "You can't be serious. You can't tell me you'd have left her there, refused to help her, let her die."

Ronan just looked back at me. "I don't have the luxury of worrying about one human. I have a coven to consider."

"Fine," I said. "You can feel free to squander your immortality if you'd like—to not use the gifts you've been given. I don't plan to." And that included making sure she was safe from his single-mindedness. "Are you going to take care of Carlie, or do I need to find other arrangements?"

"I care for my vampires," he said. "That's precisely my point." He stepped closer. "You will not endanger my people further. You will not touch another human."

There was glamour in the words, magic in the push. And insult in both. Maybe he thought I'd changed her as a lark, as an opportunity to set up my own kingdom in northern Minnesota.

"I saved her," I said again, and it took effort to say those three words, to swim through the glamour that demanded I concede. "And I'm not going to waste any more time arguing with you. We have bigger problems to deal with."

"You will not endanger my people further," he said again, a demand for obedience that was growing stronger, more insistent. But while it may have affected me, it didn't affect the monster. It rose through my weakness, through the magical subjugation of my will, and stepped forward through me, and turned my eyes crimson.

"Get the fuck out of my way," I said to him, my voice low and hoarse and as full of anger as his had been of command. The monster was eager to back up the words with action, and moved forward.

Connor put a hand on my arm, searched my face. And the monster looked back at him.

"*Shit,*" he said, and held my arm tight so I couldn't lunge after him. "Drop the magic," he told Ronan. "You're not helping her or yourself."

"She will—"

"*Drop the fucking magic,*" Connor ordered again. And this time, Ronan didn't argue.

The glamour slipped away like the outgoing tide, and I breathed again, gained control again . . . and found Ronan staring at me, eyes wide, with absolute horror.

Even the monster was shamed.

"What's wrong with you?" Ronan asked.

Connor turned on him so quickly, I barely saw him move. He had Ronan by the shirt, shoved him back against the wall. "There is nothing wrong with her. And if you ever use glamour on us again, you won't live long enough to regret it."

"I suggest," Ronan said, his eyes like quicksilver, "that you take your hands off me."

Connor's chest was heaving, his eyes cold as ice, but he lifted his hands, stepped back. "How long until we know if she survives?"

"Not until the transformation is complete. Or it isn't."

"I'll need to see her," I said.

Ronan turned his eyes on me. "I believe you've done enough. If she desires to see you when she wakes, we'll contact you. You'll find the limo waiting outside."

And with that, we'd been dismissed.

The limo took us back to the resort, but didn't deign to drive into the compound. It pulled up to the entrance, came to a stop, and waited for our exit. We climbed out and had barely shut the door behind us before it accelerated, tires squealing in its rush to return to the coven.

"Let's get inside," Connor said quietly, scanning the road, and we walked toward our corner of the resort.

He didn't touch me, didn't hold my hand. And the distance knotted something in my chest.

"Get a shower," he said when we reached the cabin. "It will help."

I took his words to heart and dived into the hottest shower I could stand, letting the water pummel me until I'd knocked away some of the adrenaline and anger and grief. It did help, a little. But feeling like Connor was still on my side, that we were still united against the enemies we were facing, would have felt better.

I toweled my hair, came out in leggings and a T-shirt, and found him locking the doors as dawn threatened outside.

He looked back at me. "You must be tired," he said finally.

"I'm exhausted," I said. "How are you?"

"Same." He sighed, and the sound was ragged. There was a lot on his shoulders, not least the pile I'd added tonight.

"I'm sorry," I said. "For all of this."

His expression was blank, and he offered no comfort, which was a slice at the edge of my heart, sharp and keen as my sword.

"So am I," he said. "This isn't the trip I'd had in mind—or the troubles I'd expected we'd find."

I was afraid to ask whether he meant me or the monsters. But I knew, even if we couldn't talk about us—or there was no us to discuss—that we needed to talk about what had happened. "You really don't know what they are?"

He shook his head. "Based on the evidence, they're clan members who've made some kind of magical change. But I don't know how."

"I can talk to Theo, Petra. Maybe there are sorcerers in the area or—I don't know—a magical well."

There was nearly amusement in his eyes. "A magical well?"

"I'm loopy," I said.

"So's Petra."

This time, the reluctant smile was mine. "Yeah. She is. But she knows her stuff. She might just say that this is the Beast or—" I stopped, realized it was far more likely the reverse was true, and looked at Connor, who nodded.

"I just got it, too. Maybe the clan isn't being attacked by the Beast of Owatonna. Maybe the things that fought us *are* the Beast of Owatonna, or at least the latest iteration. Maybe this isn't the first time someone has used this magic. Hell, maybe that's why the magic is broken."

"All because of Paisley?" I wondered. "Her death seems to have been a trigger, maybe spread over the general unhappiness in the clan. The anger about staying closeted, about refusing to change. And Traeger is at least part of the who."

"Yeah," he said grimly. "And Traeger's connected to Georgia, which makes this even more complicated." He frowned. "Where would the magic come from?"

"Well, either something's doing the magic to them, and they don't have a choice in it—"

"Or they're doing it to themselves somehow," he finished.

"Can shifters do magic?"

"Not well," he said, "and I mean that literally. We can do a little manipulation, but not much, and not well."

"Which would explain the feeling that it's broken."

He made a vague sound of agreement; then his brow furrowed when he looked up at me again. "There could be trouble."

"Trouble?"

"Ronan isn't the only one with a chip on his shoulder. The clan will want to talk to us. If we're lucky, they'll wait until dusk."

And if not, I thought silently, they'd pull us out of the house in daylight, and that would be it for me.

"It's also possible the creatures will come back, will target us specifically. I've asked Alexei to check for trails, see if locations can be identified, to see if broken magic can be identified around the resort. And in the meantime, I'll be listening. They won't hurt you."

But again he didn't reach out, and that was another small wound.

"Get some sleep," he said. "Tomorrow we'll deal with what comes next."

Having been dismissed again, and totally unsure of my steps,

I walked back to the bedroom, closed the door, and sat down on the bed. And felt more alone than I ever had before. Alone and guilty and afraid that by trying to do something good, I'd screwed up something I'd never imagined I'd want.

I'd be damned if I'd apologize to Ronan or the clan for doing what had to be done. But I was an adult, and I understood my actions would have consequences, fair or not. Those consequences left a dark pit of fear in my belly.

Connor had said we'd deal with what came next, but that wasn't enough for me, not with this. I didn't know how to move forward, given what I'd done. So I pulled out my screen and contacted the one person I knew who'd been in my position before. Who'd changed someone because circumstances demanded it. And had dealt with the aftermath.

It took only a moment for his face to appear on-screen, and the mere sight of him made my eyes fill with tears. "Hey, Dad."

His eyes brightened. "Hello, Lis." But as he scanned my face, the smile fell away. "What's wrong?"

"I changed someone." I held back the tears, but it was a battle and nearly cost me the rest of my strength.

My father's expression remained perfectly blank. He was good at that—masking his emotions until he'd heard all the facts, or reached his decision, or considered his next steps. "Tell me what happened."

I told him about the trip, the animals, Loren's death and the tracks we'd found, the attack on the bonfire. And Carlie, pale and bleeding on the ground.

"She'd gone gray, and her heart was . . . a whisper. I couldn't stanch the wound, so I did the only thing I could think of."

"And the circle turns," he murmured. "She's all right?"

"For now. We'll see what happens in a few days. She's with Ronan, although he's not happy about bearing that burden. He's also angry I changed her without his consent or the clan's consent. He's worried at least in part about the human response, I think. Suggested it would have been smarter to let her die and save his coven the trouble. One life for the many."

"That's very old-fashioned," he said. "But he's not the only vampire who shares that attitude."

I nodded, was suddenly so tired, and not just because the sun was probably tracing the horizon.

"Do you want me to tell you that you did the right thing?"

So much, I thought. So much it made my chest ache. "Yes."

"You did the right thing," he said, his answer coming quickly. "But that doesn't mean there won't be consequences. And those can be the hardest consequences to bear—the ones we face because we've done the right thing, the hard thing."

"I know," I said.

My father nodded. "After I changed her, your mother was angry at me for a very long time. She had lived her entire life under the thumb of her parents. When she'd gone to college, then graduate school, she'd gained some independence. Particularly when she came back to Chicago. For the first time, she was able to live in her town on her own terms. And I ruined that for her. Took away her independence, at least as far as she saw it."

"You saved her life," I said, and knew immediately he'd led me right to that statement, and I'd followed right along.

"I did," he said. "But I also took something away. Both of those things are true. And, frankly, it took me too long to acknowledge my part in it. To understand what she'd lost. It had been a long time since I'd been human, since I'd felt the threat of time in quite the same way. You're younger, and you'd understand that better than a four-hundred-year-old vampire. That's one of your strengths."

I nodded, but didn't feel especially strong right now. Not when adrenaline had given way to self-doubt. "I know I've hurt Carlie, even if I didn't mean to. I've changed her life. And the thought that she might hate me for doing it bothers me."

"It's a complex situation, with a lot of gray and not much black-and-white." A corner of his mouth lifted. "You do generally prefer things to be black-and-white."

"It's easier to know whether you've done the right thing—or someone else has—when it's black-and-white."

"I won't argue the point," he said. "But we grow more when the decisions are harder. Carlie might be angry at you. And she's entitled to her feelings. They may be logical, they may be irrational, but she's entitled to them. But that doesn't change what you did or why you did it.

"She'll not be bound to you," he added. "Not if she's going to be fed solely by Ronan during the rest of the process. But you began the process, so you'll do her the honor of staying nearby and, if she'll see you, of speaking to her about it. And if she agrees to talk to you, you take responsibility for your actions. Respect your choice, the decision that had to be made. And respect the change you've wrought to her life."

I nodded. "You're right."

"In case it helps—even if your mother had decided never to speak to me again, had decided to loathe me for the rest of her immortal life, I'd have done the same thing. The world would be less without her. Same goes for you. In the more immediate sense, let's discuss your and Connor's current situation."

A flush rose hot on my cheeks.

"Are you in danger?" he asked before I could mutter out a response to the relationship question I was afraid he was going to ask.

"The clan will probably want to speak to us tomorrow, and they're going to have plenty to say. The creatures were pretty seriously wounded, so I imagine they're licking their wounds. Connor's keeping an eye out. I don't suppose you have any idea what they are?"

"None," he said. "Connor's theory—that they're clan members

affected by magic—seems entirely logical. But I don't know of any shifters who've taken that shape before or magic that would do it. I could ask your mother to reach out to Mallory."

The thought of involving Lulu's mom made me uncomfortable, like I was going around Lulu. "That's okay. I'm going to give Theo an update. The OMB has connections to the Order." The Order was the mandatory union for sorcerers and sorceresses.

He nodded. "You'll let me know if you need anything—backup or otherwise."

Whatever else fell apart, I could rely on my father, on my family. I wasn't sure if I'd ever be able to tell him how much that meant to me.

"I will."

"Get some sleep," he said. "You'll have a clearer eye tomorrow. And whatever happens, the House is here, and us with it."

"I love you."

"I love you, too. Go do the right thing."

We ended the call, and I looked down at the blank screen in my hand. I felt better about what had gone down tonight, and appreciated my father's last message.

Go do the right thing.

I'd give myself what was left of night to wrestle with the battle, the fear, the weight of what I'd done. But tomorrow, it was time to think about Carlie, and how I could help her. Starting, first off, with finding the creatures that had hurt her and making sure they didn't hurt anyone else.

I sent Theo a rambling message, explaining what had happened, what we'd seen, what I'd done. I asked him about magic, and told him he could talk to me or my father when the sun fell again. And because it was escapist and important to him and made me feel better, I told him I hoped he'd been able to snag his comic.

I meant to put my screen aside, to give myself a break from

drama until the sun rose, but I needed one more thing. So I tapped the screen again, sent a message.

YOU UP? I asked, and waited for a reply.

Lulu's response was nearly instantaneous. I TOLD YOU, RODNEY. I'M NOT INTERESTED.

HILARIOUS, I messaged. IT'S BEEN A CRAP NIGHT. TELL ME SOMETHING GOOD.

HUMANS RECORD THEMSELVES DOING STUPID THINGS AND UPLOAD THE VIDEOS SO STRANGERS AROUND THE WORLD CAN WATCH THEM.

YES, YOU'VE JUST DESCRIBED THE INTERNET.

HUMANS MAKE NO SENSE.

IT IS A TRUTH UNIVERSALLY ACKNOWLEDGED, I agreed. HOW IS ELEANOR OF AQUITAINE? I wasn't even brave enough to use a nickname or acronym over text. Because she'd know.

DISPLEASED SHE GOT CAT FOOD INSTEAD OF BLUEFIN TUNA. SHE RIPPED UP ONE OF YOUR SOCKS.

WHY MY SOCK?

BECAUSE I DIDN'T WANT TO USE ONE OF MINE OBVS.

I could fault the sentiment, and the loss of a sock, but not the logic.

YOU OK? she asked. GIVEN THE CRAP NIGHT.

NOT AT THE MOMENT. BUT I THINK I WILL BE.

GOOD, she said. BECAUSE ELEANOR OF AQUITAINE WANTS TO HAVE WORDS WITH YOU WHEN YOU RETURN. IN ADDITION TO THE CAT FOOD, SHE DISAPPROVES OF YOUR FOOTWEAR.

Of course she did. And the sock had nearly been worth the laugh I'd sorely needed.

SIXTEEN

The first time, I woke to heat, and jolted awake, thinking I was back in front of the bonfire, fending off the beasts. But it wasn't fire, or not exactly.

It was light. Sunlight—a pinpoint ray of gold that slashed across the bed like a knife.

I was half-asleep, barely conscious, but I knew enough of pain and heat to scramble away and out of the literal line of fire. I dropped to the floor, moved into a corner, and, in the darkness, slept again.

The second time, I woke in darkness, curled in a ball on the floor at the end of the bed. I rose, wincing at the quick jolt of pain, and found an angry red stripe across my thigh. It would heal, but I'd never forget the sensation. I'd been sliced by katanas, scraped by monster claws. But the searing effect of sunlight was something altogether different.

I rose and walked back to the window, still covered by the exterior shutters, at least as far as I could see from here. But something had happened. Something had damaged one of them, breaking the fortification intended to keep me safe.

And I seriously doubted that was a coincidence.

I got dressed and, given the tenor of things, belted on my

sword. The cabin was empty; I walked outside, found Connor staring at the shutter.

He glanced back. "Hey."

It was cooler today, and he wore his black motorcycle jacket over a shirt, the ensemble completed by jeans and boots. His eyes were shadowed, like he hadn't slept well or long. And I could still feel the boundary between us, the heaviness of things spoken . . . and not.

"There was sunlight in my room," I said.

"What?" He looked me over. "Are you all right?"

"I'm fine. It woke me up, so I moved into the corner."

"It woke you up," he repeated slowly, watching me carefully. "Because it burned you."

"A very small burn," I said. "Just on my leg, and it's probably already gone." I tried for a smile, but it felt odd on my face.

And then I looked at the shutters he'd been scrutinizing, and realized how the light had gotten through. They were warped and gouged around the edges, the metal rippled—like someone had tried to pry them off and expose me to the sunlight. They hadn't been successful at either, but for the split in the metal that allowed in that single shard of sunlight.

"I'm sorry," he said.

I looked back at him, guilt and apology warring in his eyes, and tried to lighten the mood. "Why? Did you do this?"

He ignored the joke. "I heard noises outside around two or three o'clock. I went outside to check, startled something coming around the side of the cabin. It ran back toward the road."

I lifted my brows. "Human, shifter, or creature?"

He pointed at the ground. "You tell me."

The ground was crossed by a bevy of marks—human or shifter footprints, animal tracks. And I was about to ask Connor to point out what he was seeing, when I realized it wasn't a group of marks;

it was a single mark with several parts. Not like the creature—with its elongated track. Not like a human, or shifter in human form, with its longer and wider pad. But a mix of the two. A long pad, with the indentation of paw pads at the top.

"Half shifter, half creature?" I asked, looking back at him.

"I'm not sure, but I think it didn't transform completely. The thing I saw—something tall, thin, sparse hair—wasn't a shifter, and it wasn't a human. It was gone before I could get a good look."

"So maybe whatever magic they're using affects the shifting—changes what they shift into, or how they do it."

"And it's not working very well," he said. "I think it's supposed to be a hybrid."

"Aren't shifters hybrids?"

"No, we're both man and wolf. Our transition is like flipping a coin—you have the wolf or the human."

"But the creatures are like both human and wolf at the same time," I guessed. "Wolves that walk on two legs."

"And enhanced," Connor said. "Bigger than both." He shook his head, looked at me with apology in his eyes. "I didn't inspect the shutters. I only checked they were still in place. I'm sorry they hurt you. And I'm sorry I allowed it."

Whatever was between us, I could give him this. "You don't owe me an apology, and you didn't allow anything. There was no reason for you to go over the shutters with a microscope. It's illogical they'd have tried to remove them."

Guilt shifted to confusion. "What?"

"This is indirect and sloppy. Maybe they think causing me pain will hurt you. They apparently don't realize vampires aren't comatose during the day; we sleep. Pain wakes us up. They'd have been a lot more successful attacking me or you away from the resort. Here, the odds are higher they'd be seen or caught."

Connor blinked, looked back at the shutters. "This was sloppy."

"Yeah, it was." But since it plainly wasn't beyond them, I'd put a blanket over the window tonight, just in case.

And something else was interesting. . . . "It ran away."

"Yeah," he said, putting his hands on his hips. "I scared it off."

"Right, but that's new, or at least different from last night. Last night they were eager to fight."

"You're right. This is more like the attack on Beth."

"Nervous around the resort," I suggested, and felt better that we seemed to be getting into our rhythm again. "So," I began, thinking it through, "they're angry about last night, they decide to get revenge, but they're wounded, tired, and maybe the shifting is broken. They aren't at full power, but they still come back here to take a shot at me, and you by proxy."

"We need to find them."

"Yeah. We do. Before they hurt anyone else." I looked around. "Did Alexei find any tracks leading from the Stone farm? Any indication of where they went? Maybe a handy path leading right to Traeger's cabin?"

"No," he said. "And no broken magic at the resort. Either they didn't come back here, or they did and the magic dispersed too quickly for him to sense it."

"If they didn't come back here, where would they go?"

He opened his mouth to add something, closed it again at the sound of footsteps.

We turned, found Maeve coming our way, three bulky male shifters behind her. They all wore leather, had guns belted to their waists. Maeve wore a very self-satisfied smile along with her leggings, boots, and leather jacket.

She ignored me, looked at Connor. "You're wanted. Both of you." Now she slid that gaze to me, with eagerness that made me feel a little punchy.

"Wanted?" Connor asked coolly.

"Cash and the elders. And Ronan and his people. They want

to talk to you about last night." She slid her gaze to me. "About what she did. Let's go."

The shifters stepped closer. In response to the obvious threat, Connor moved to stand in front of me. While I appreciated the gesture—maybe we weren't done?—I didn't want him putting himself in danger at my expense.

"You hurt her, you hurt the Apex. Understood?"

It was clear from their expressions, hard and eager, that they wanted to fight. But while they might have followed the clan's orders, they were at least smart enough not to take on the Apex while his son was watching.

"Then you'd better go with us willingly," Maeve said.

If she realized I was wearing a sword, she didn't mention it. Maybe she thought a vampire with a sword wasn't a match for a roomful of shifters. A serious error on her part.

Connor watched her for a moment, meeting her gaze directly until she looked away.

"What happened there?" she asked, gesturing to the shutters. Brow furrowed, she looked honestly confused and surprised at what she saw. "Did something hit it?"

"Something—someone—tried to pry it off," Connor said.

She frowned. "Seriously?"

"Seriously. Where do they want to talk to us?"

"The lodge."

"Then let's get this over with."

We walked in silence. Maeve walked in front. I was behind Connor, gaze drilling into his back, as if that might tell me what he was thinking and feeling—and what I was supposed to be doing about it. The beefy shifters walked behind us, just in case we might make a run for it.

"A minute," Connor said to Maeve when we reached the lodge. "I need a minute with Elisa."

She looked at me, evaluated. "Two minutes. Come on, guys," she said, and they all walked inside, let the door slam shut behind them.

"Fuck." The word was a swear and an exhalation. He ran a hand through his hair.

"They're going to confront us about Carlie."

"At least."

"You're worried about what they might do?"

"I don't get worried," he said, voice snappish, then held up a hand. "I'm sorry," he said. "I'm—not handling this well, either."

"What aren't you handling well? The monsters, the clan, or the fact that I assaulted someone you consider to be family?"

His face went hard, and my stomach roiled with nerves.

"I'm sorry," I said. And when I was steady again: "I'm not handling it well, either."

"We need to talk," he said, voice as hard as his expression had been. "But not right now. Not until we deal with this. Let me take the lead."

I looked at him, searched his face, but the mask was already in place. Angry and arrogant, and ready to face down whatever the clan put in front of us.

I understood battle, and I understood politics. But I liked one of those a lot more than the other. I wasn't looking forward to this war of words. Words were often pointless, and politics just an irritating ego game. Give me a sword any day.

"We'll talk," Connor said again, then leaned forward. He put a hand at the back of my neck, rested his forehead against mine. "Whatever happens in there, I need you to trust me."

It was a big ask, given our history, the fact that we hadn't yet talked about what had happened last night. But these were his people, and this was his turf.

"Okay," I said.

And then we walked inside.

* * *

Maeve waited inside the door. When she saw us, she turned on her heel—a soldier called to war—and headed for the stairs. We followed her, and the beef followed us. We went back up to the former ballroom, found the doors closed. But that didn't stop the magic that spilled through the walls. Shifter. Vampire. Pack and coven.

Maeve gave a rhythmic knock—three, two, three—and the door opened. We walked inside. There were at least forty shifters in the room, along with a few vampires. It smelled of heat and animal, and the air practically vibrated with magic. And heady anticipation.

The shifter portion of the crowd was split neatly in half— young shifters on one side, older on the other. A nation divided.

Cash, Everett, Georgia, and Ronan stood at the front of the room, waiting for our arrival. Miranda stood near them, and the smile on her face was triumphant. Not, I thought, a good sign.

We walked through the crowd, which parted to let us through, then closed the circle again, surrounding us. Not the best strategic position, but we didn't have much choice. At least we had Alexei, whom I spotted weaving through the crowd near the far wall.

"It seems we have a rather significant problem," Cash said when we reached the group. His arms were crossed, stance wide. And he stood just slightly in front of the others, as if the elders had again ceded control to him.

"The clan members who attacked the Stone farm last night? Yes, I'd consider that a problem." Connor's voice was hard as granite, but smooth as glass. The sounds the gathered shifters made were much more primal, much angrier. Outrage given voice at the possibility the injuries had been inflicted by their own members.

"We have no information the animals—whatever they were— were clan," Cash said. "None have been positively identified."

"As you've been advised, the attacks on Beth, Loren, the Stone farm smelled like clan."

"So you think, what, shifters learned to shift into something else? Into something new?"

"I think they're using magic—and badly—to change themselves into the creatures we saw last night. They were undeniably clan."

"If they're proven to be clan, they'll be dealt with."

"Does that include the perpetrators of the newest attack? The one that occurred a few short hours ago?"

Connor's tone was casual, and he watched Cash carefully. But if Cash knew about the shutters, he didn't show it.

"I have no idea what you're talking about."

"I'm talking about the creature—or the half-shifted creature—who tried to pry the shutters off our cabin and expose Elisa to the sun."

Cash's brow furrowed. "That didn't happen."

"Shutters are still there, damaged though they are. You can inspect them yourself." Connor took a step forward. "If you have any control over the creatures, I'd strongly suggest you . . . dissuade them . . . from attacking the daughter of one of the most powerful Master vampires on the continent." He lifted a shoulder. "But that's just my suggestion."

It was a good strategy—taking the offensive and starting with a recitation of the clan's crimes. We'd see how well it worked when Cash shifted us back to the inevitable topic.

"If anyone in the clan is involved," Cash said again through gritted teeth, "they'll be dealt with." For the first time, he shifted his gaze to me. "Our focus right now is on other crimes, including the near death of a human. Georgia," he said, and she stepped forward.

She looked at Connor with apology in her eyes. But she wasn't feeling it enough, I thought with some anger, that she'd refuse to stand with Cash and Everett.

"Sheriff Paulson came around during the day," she said. "He knew about the attack at the bonfire. Some of the other humans had called him, described an animal attack. He thought it sounded like the attack on Loren. Wanted to know our progress on that investigation, if we'd found the culprit."

"So he acted like law enforcement," Connor said flatly. "What did you tell him?"

"That Loren was killed by an animal," Cash said, pulling our attention back to him. "Which is the truth."

"It's the least important part of the truth," Connor said.

This time, Cash was the one who shrugged carelessly.

"You're surprisingly lackadaisical about the fact that one of your elders has been murdered, and several of your clan members have been attacked. Makes me wonder if you're involved."

Cash's gaze was cold and hard, his only movement the tapping of fingers against his biceps.

"And let's correct the record," Connor continued. "It was your clan who nearly killed Carlie. Elisa saved her, sparing you some very penetrating questions from the authorities."

Cash's gaze didn't waver. "Carlie was bitten and changed without her consent."

I looked at Ronan, found his expression blank, his gaze cool. I guessed he still agreed with Cash's assessment, and hadn't become magnanimous overnight.

"To save her life," Connor repeated. "Because she was attacked and left for dead by one of the clan members under the influence of some very nasty magic."

"Evidence?" Cash asked.

Connor cocked his head. "Are you telling me you can't detect the scent of bad magic, Cash? That's an important skill for a clan leader."

Cash unfolded his arms, and although he didn't step forward, the move seemed hostile. "You just have answers for everything, don't you? But your attitude, shitty as it is, doesn't change the basic facts—your little girlfriend made a vampire within our territory without our consent, and in Ronan's territory without Ronan's consent."

I bristled at "little girlfriend," especially since Connor and I had barely talked since the fight. I felt the monster's agreement. It was no mere companion, and it wasn't little.

That we agreed was an odd sensation. But not entirely bad.

"If Carlie dies," Cash continues, "or if she survives and regrets what happened to her, that will have disastrous consequences for the clan and the Pack."

"Less disastrous consequences than her dying in the woods because of your people?"

"All sorts of strange things happen in the woods," Cash said. His attitude—his carelessness toward human life—echoed Ronan's.

"You're so afraid you'd let a human die rather than save her life and face the consequences?" Connor's tone was matter-of-fact and carried a shadow of censure.

"Fuck you," Cash said. "I don't care who you are. You don't walk into the clan and call us cowards."

"I didn't call you cowards," Connor said. "I said you're afraid, and you are. I don't know what you're afraid of, Cash. Humans. Change. Pick one."

"Fuck you," Everett said.

Connor's smile was feral. "I'll offer again—you want to try me on, Everett? I'd be happy to oblige."

The crowd began to move, to shift, to talk, anticipating a fight, willing one to happen.

"Let's go," Connor said. "Me and you, right here. We don't even have to tell my father. It can be our little secret."

He pulled off his jacket, let it drop to the floor. He'd worn a tank beneath, the fabric baring slick and strong muscle, and I heard more than a few sounds of throaty appreciation in the crowd.

"Come on," Connor said, voice low and threatening, the room silent to catch every word.

Fury burned in his eyes like blue fire, all pretense of humanity gone from his expression. It was the haughty look of an angry titan, a primal god, enraged by the inanity of lesser beings.

It was impossible to deny he had the power, the authority, to be Apex. To lead the North American Central Pack and its shifters. And I bet every shifter in the room knew it.

Everett was either too dumb to figure it out or naive enough to believe he was stronger, because he curled his hands into fists, stepped forward until there was only a foot between them. That no fear crossed Everett's eyes made me think he was even dumber than I'd first imagined. "Come on, pretty boy. I've hurt plenty of men in my life. Wouldn't mind adding another to the list."

He tried to shove Connor back, but Connor was younger and stronger, and resisted easily. And the expression on his face—full of cold hatred—didn't change.

The crowd wasn't sure what to think.

"Oh," Connor said mildly. "Were we starting?" His fist shot out, snapping Everett's head back.

Everett roared, and the crowd surged forward. I had my sword in hand in a heartbeat. I moved between Connor and the advancing crowd, felt Alexei sidle along beside me, and watched surprise light in the eyes of the shifters we faced. They hadn't expected I'd be willing to fight or that a shifter would stand with me.

Ronan, for his part, merely stood by and watched, apparently content to judge, but not actually involve himself.

"*Stop this!*" Georgia's voice boomed across the room. I glanced back, watched as she muscled Connor and Everett apart while Cash looked on with a bland smile.

"This is insane!" Georgia yelled. "Everyone calm down. Everett, step the fuck back."

Everett growled, blood seeping from his lip, but he did as she demanded, working his jaw with a meaty hand.

"Connor." Georgia's word wasn't a request, but an order.

He lifted his hands, put more space between him and Everett, nodded at me and Alexei. I put my sword away, and we took positions by his side.

Cash spared Everett a look of disappointment, then shifted his gaze to Connor. "The vampire broke the rules."

"Her name is Elisa. And the rules needed breaking."

"Rules are rules for a reason," Cash said. "I'd have thought the Apex's son would have realized that. Pack law rules here. And Pack law is inviolate, isn't it?"

Connor didn't answer, so Cash looked at me.

"We have a process here. Mechanisms for justice."

Connor lifted his brows. "A process good enough for Elisa, but not the members of your own clan?"

"Members of our clan didn't make an unwilling vampire." He looked at me. "Your crimes will be heard by the clan elders, the coven, the violation of our rules considered."

My stare was flat. I wasn't naive enough to believe I'd get a fair hearing with Cash and Everett serving as two-thirds of the jury.

"A ruling will be made," Cash continued, "and punishment will be decided. And administered."

"Elisa's not within your jurisdiction," Connor said, his voice all business now. "She isn't Pack."

Connor saw the trap a moment too late. The frank admission that his romantic interest wasn't like him, wasn't like his family, wasn't like his Pack. And, more important, that she was an out-sider whom Connor had brought into sensitive clan discussions.

Miranda's smile grew wider.

"She isn't Pack," Cash repeated. "And yet here she is, accom-panying you into clan territory." He looked at me. "You have a choice. She submits to our jurisdiction and the hearing, or we can decide her fate without your input. Your choice."

"Have you lost your damn mind?" Georgia's voice was loud, cutting through the noisy crowd and silencing it. "The clan is destroying itself from the inside. Someone is killing our members, assaulting humans, and you want to bring down the wrath of the Pack and Cadogan House on us because that girl saved Carlie's life? I thought we were here to give them a talking-to, not to en-sure our damn annihilation."

"You're soft because you're family," Everett said. "I don't think you need to be part of this discussion."

"Then let's all thank the gods nobody asked you. Somebody with some goddamn sense needs to be in this discussion." She looked at Cash. "I will not agree to mutually assured destruc-tion."

"You're outvoted," Cash said. "It's time we take a stand."

Her brows flew up. "Against the Pack?"

"Against those who disrespect our rules and threaten our way of life," Cash said.

"Against the Apex's son?" Georgia persisted.

Cash's gaze flicked to Miranda, whose expression had gone intense. And I guessed Cash hadn't come to this little plan on his own. Miranda, who wanted Connor—and maybe the Pack even more now—had made her first real move.

After a moment, Cash looked at me. "Do you want your say, or don't you?"

I told Connor I'd trust him, but I wanted my say. We were going to have some very serious words about treating humans as collateral damage and the clan's total absence of authority over me. And if words weren't enough, I'd speak with steel.

I opened my mouth—and was interrupted.

"I forgot to mention," Cash said. "If she isn't comfortable agreeing to our terms, I'd be happy to invoke Obsideo."

That wasn't a term I knew, and I glanced at Connor to see if he understood. Given his furious expression, I guessed he did.

"What is Obsideo?" Ronan asked, brow furrowed.

Cash's smile was thin. "Would you like to explain it, Connor, since you're our resident Pack expert?"

"Archaic Pack law," Connor threw out, without looking at Ronan. "In a time of crisis, Pack members can summon a representative of the Apex. That rep is obliged to show up and assist in the resolution of the crisis." His eyes darkened. "And they're obliged to stay until the crisis is resolved." He turned his gaze toward Miranda, nailed her with a glance.

"*Magically* tied," she said, and her smile was reptilian. "And so handy that you're already here."

Connor looked back at Cash, and his voice was cold and hard as flint. "Obsideo isn't a game."

"Oh, we're all very serious here." He looked at me, tapped the handle of the knife holstered on his belt. "Of course, there's no need for Obsideo if you'd rather the vamp stand up before the clan, the coven."

Enough of this, I thought, and put a hand on my katana. But Connor's hand was on my arm.

"She doesn't submit to you," he said, the words nearly a growl. "Do it."

Cash smiled meanly. "If you insist. The elders of the Northwood Clan claim Obsideo."

Magic shimmered in the air, thickening it, warping it. It was hard to breathe, and I had to work to stop my rising panic—and my monster's—as my lungs constricted. Connor's fingers tightened on my arm.

"Breathe slowly," he said quietly. "The air is fine; you're just feeling the magic."

But my vision was dimming, narrowing, little sparks of light flashing around the edges.

Cash grinned mirthlessly. "Your vampire doesn't like obligation magic."

Monster and I both moved forward, and this time it took both Connor and Alexei to hold me back.

"Let me go," I managed, struggling against them, and didn't much care this time if my eyes had silvered or gone red. Didn't much care if they saw exactly how much of an outsider I really was. I caught Georgia's concerned glance, looked away. I didn't want pity now. I wanted to fight. I wanted air unspoiled by magic, and honest battle with blood and steel. Not this farce.

Then the magic snapped into place around me—and I could breathe again. I sucked in air, and as I stopped struggling, felt Connor's fingers loosen.

Obligation magic was a bitch, I thought, as I forced my heart to slow, sent the monster down again.

The magic couldn't compel me; this was shifter magic, and as Connor had pointed out, the Pack had no authority over a vampire. But if I guessed correctly, it would tie him to the clan until the "crisis" was resolved. I noted the glimmer in Miranda's eyes, wondered if she could keep him forever and give herself a clear path to Apex.

"You're all right?" Connor asked.

I nodded, for form, because this wasn't the time or the place to get into it. But I wasn't all right. I was pissed. I hadn't been planning to give in to this farce masquerading as justice. They knew damn well that I'd had to change Carlie, that the "extenuating circumstances" demanded it. So it was ludicrous that he was putting himself in danger—handing himself over to the clan—on my behalf. And it was insulting. I could handle myself, especially against Cash, whom I hadn't yet seen fight his own battles.

"You're obligated," Cash said.

"I'm obligated," Connor agreed, and turned to walk out.

I followed close behind, because Connor Keene and I were going to have some words.

SEVENTEEN

I managed to wait until we'd marched back to the cabin and stepped inside before turning furious eyes to Connor.

"I'm going to just . . . stay outside," Alexei said, right before I slammed the door closed.

I was seething, rage fountaining so hot I felt my blood might actually boil. Even the monster was angry, and I let it be. Let it rise to the surface, through insult mixed with the residual guilt about what I'd done the night before.

"What the hell was that?" I asked.

"Elisa—" He held up a hand.

"No," I said, pointing at him. "It's my turn to speak. First of all, you've barely talked to me since last night. You think I don't know what you're thinking? That you're angry I hurt Carlie? That I hurt someone you loved? And that you finally saw me for the monster that I am?"

Anger flashed in his eyes.

"And second," I said quickly, afraid to give him time to respond, "I fight my own damn battles. I do not need someone stepping in front of me, and certainly not a damn shifter. I don't need someone agreeing to be tied to this clan, which can go straight to hell as far as I'm concerned. And I don't need you stuck in Grand Bay, Minnesota, for the rest of eternity because you think I can't handle myself. Why the hell would you consent to that?"

"Do you want me to answer you, or are you going to keep ranting?"

I could actually feel my lip curl. I stepped closer to him. "Oh, I'm just getting started."

His eyes went hot in response. "Then let me respond to the first volley," he said. "First of all, my feelings don't just switch off and on like a damn flashlight. That's insulting to both of us. I've seen you in human form, and I've seen you as a vampire. I've seen your monster, and I've seen you fight. I've also seen you snort milk out of your nose."

"I was ten," I countered.

"Maybe so, but it's imprinted on my memory. All those things are part of you. And I don't take issue with any of them." He moved a step closer so there was only a breath of space between us. "You saved the life of a girl I've known since she was a child. But for you, she'd be dead."

I stared at him. "I thought . . . after you saw me with her . . . after what I'd done . . ."

"No," he said, the word so simple, so honest, that it loosened the grip of fear around my heart. "And as for last night . . . I've been trying to outthink Cash—to figure out what he might do, how he might try to milk this situation, and how to keep you safe from it. I'm sorry that put distance between us." He put his hands on his hips. "I guess I didn't handle the threat to you very well."

"I guess you didn't," I said, still trying to grapple with the new understanding. "I get that you're alpha, Connor. But so am I. I can fight my own battles. I *like* fighting my own battles."

He cocked an eyebrow. "You didn't argue when I helped you with the fairies."

"Helped," I emphasized. "This wasn't helping. This was jumping in front of me and taking the hit yourself—not just because of Carlie, but because you're in line for the throne."

"He wouldn't have stopped with you," Connor said. "He's ignoring the destruction of his clan by members of his clan, because he's decided we're the enemies."

"Because of Miranda."

"Partly," he said. "And partly because he prefers to believe it. The alternative is admitting what he's allowed the clan to become. He's dishonorable, Lis. He'd have called Obsideo even if you'd bested him. I'd prefer you not get hurt along the way."

I lifted my chin. "That wasn't your choice to make."

His gaze bored into me, as if he could see past skin and bone and straight into my soul, into the core of me. "There was no choice. Do you think I would let them lay one finger on you?"

The question was quiet, intense.

"Miranda—," I began, but he shook his head.

"Do you think I wouldn't go to war for you?"

I simply had no words, didn't know what words could be spoken in response to something so staggering.

His eyes turned stormy. "You are a very interesting package, Elisa Sullivan. Even if it took me twenty years to realize it. Last night, you had a hard choice to make, and you made it. You saved Carlie, even though you knew it was breaking the rules, would be risky for her, would be risky for me." A corner of his mouth nearly lifted. "I can only imagine the mental debate before you did the deed."

"There were a lot of considerations," I said quietly.

This time, his smile was big and genuine. "You did the right thing," he said, and the dregs of the tension slipped away. "But there's nothing right about what's happening here. They're using you because you're here, because you're a convenient lightning rod. And that's wrong. Their problems are my burdens, not yours."

I saw the misery in his eyes. He'd managed to hide most of it, but he was disappointed in his people, in the chaos they'd allowed, and the pain they'd inflicted.

"You're wrong about one thing," I said. "You aren't here alone, so you don't have to bear the burdens alone. And not just because we're . . ."

"We're?" he prompted with a crooked smile.

"Dating?" I offered hesitantly.

"Oh, at least," he said, that grin widening.

"Not just because of that," I said. "I changed Carlie, and I take responsibility for that. I'm used to fighting my own battles, and I know you are, too. And you did help me with the fairies. So let me help you here." I took his hand, squeezed it. "This isn't a fight you have to win on your own."

I distinctly heard an *"Aww"* from the patio. "And I'm pretty sure Alexei is eavesdropping, and he also has your back."

"I'm not eavesdropping" came the voice from the patio. "But yes on the back thing."

I just shook my head.

Connor watched me consideringly for a moment. "Don't underestimate how much they're intimidated by you, Elisa."

"Well, now you're just flirting with me."

His smile was sly. "You're a trained and powerful Supernatural from a trained and powerful—and wealthy—family. You have power because of your strength and your origins. They can't muster that kind of power. Just look around the resort if you want evidence of that."

"You might as well have described yourself," I said.

"Also part of the problem," he admitted. "We are privileged. They'll use that against us if they can."

"And the fact that I'm an outsider," I said.

"You aren't Pack," he said, tipping up my chin. "But I have no illusions about that, and no concerns. If this trip proves anything, it's that the clan needs fresh eyes. And a good airing out."

Which is why he hadn't worried about admitting my otherness in front of the clan.

He rubbed a thumb across my lips, looked down at me with

eyes of melting blue. "No concerns," he said again, and his eyes drifted shut, his lashes dark crescents against his skin, and moved his mouth across mine.

He kissed me, magic flaring between us, hot and bright. . . .

I grabbed a lock of his hair—and took his mouth. His hands came around me immediately, pulled me against the warm line of his body, every ounce of him toned and taut. His mouth was insistent, demanding, and I met his advance, sliding hands through his hair, and pulling him closer until he groaned with a hunger I knew was as wild as my own.

He deepened the kiss, lips and tongue skilled and tempting.

His hands slid along my waist, my ribs, and then he cupped my breast, and I nearly gasped, shocked by magic and pleasure and still, in some part of me, the fact that Connor Keene was the one providing it.

"Lis," he said, voice ragged and astounded, and I was relieved that I wasn't the only one staggered by the heat. His thumb circling, arousing. I heard myself moan, and then he turned, twisting so my back hit the wall, his free hand cradled behind my head.

That was alpha—power and will tempered by compassion—and all that power was focused on me, on desire and arousal, and for a moment, I thought I might actually catch fire. . . .

And then someone pounded on the door.

Connor growled low in his chest. When the pounding echoed again, he swore. *"Just a minute,"* he called out.

Breathing ragged, he leaned his forehead against mine, took one breath, then another, working to regain his composure, giving me time to find mine. "The Yellowstone Caldera had better have opened up," he called out, "or I'm going to have words with whoever that is."

He stepped backward, ran a hand through the hair I'd tousled, and looked at me with eyes that gleamed like sapphires, his smile cocky. "We're going to finish this."

"Oh, most certainly we are."

He walked toward the door.

"And you were joking about the Yellowstone Caldera, right? We have millions of years before that happens?"

His snort didn't make me feel better.

Connor paused at the closed door, rolled his shoulders, settled himself. Then he opened it to reveal Traeger and, wearing a grim expression, Alexei behind him.

"This had better be damn important," Connor said, his tone a challenge.

"Apparently Traeger has things to tell you," Alexei said. "About what happened."

Connor muttered a curse before stepping aside, giving me an apologetic look as he opened the door wider. "Come in," he said, "and start talking."

Traeger sat at the table, fingers knitted together, hair flopping over his forehead. He looked more harried now than he had at the cabin. There were circles beneath his eyes, and his skin was sallow and drawn.

"You want something to drink?" I asked Traeger.

He looked up at me, frowning as if surprised by the question, and shook his head. "No. I'm fine."

Connor pulled out a chair on the other side of the table and sat down. Alexei stood in the corner, glowering.

"Is it true about the shutters?" Traeger asked. "That the creatures messed with them?"

Connor's expression didn't change, and I gave him credit for that. "Yes. The creatures, or one of them, tried to tear them off and expose Elisa to sunlight."

Traeger swore, pushed his hands through his hair. "I think I know why this is happening. Or some of it. Maybe who."

"Start at the beginning," Connor said as I took the seat beside him.

"Paisley and I, like you said, were dating. We were having fun. Hanging out. Talking. She came back from the woods one night in wolf form; I was going to meet her afterward. And I saw him waiting at the edge of the woods, kind of pacing. Like he was waiting for her, too."

"Loren," I guessed. "You're talking about Loren."

He looked up at me, nodded. "Yeah. He moved away when he saw me, but I saw him talking to her, waiting for her, things like that, more often. I think he was interested in her."

Having seen the photo of the young and lovely Paisley, I understood why. But Loren was decades older, and she was involved with Traeger. This didn't sound like mutual interest.

"She didn't feel the same," I offered.

"Not even close," he said. "He was older than her grandfather, and we had a thing going on. He wasn't mean or anything. But he kept hinting around, being wherever she was expected to be."

"He was stalking her." Connor's voice was cold, the words leaching furious magic into the air.

"I don't know if it was like that," Traeger said. "But he was . . . I'd say she thought he was harassing her."

That might explain why Beth and Jae had seemed leery when Loren had approached them.

"Did she tell anyone?" Connor asked.

"She wouldn't even admit it to me. I asked if he was bothering her, and she said no. Said he was just a harmless old guy, kind of funny. Paisley was chill, and she liked everyone. But you could tell—I could tell—he sometimes made her uncomfortable." He swallowed hard. "And then she was gone."

His voice had turned hard, and when he looked up, so had his eyes. "I think Loren killed her."

Frowning, Connor leaned forward. "You have evidence of that?"

"I know what I know," Traeger said, but shifting his gaze. "No. I don't have any damn evidence. I have a feeling. I have what I saw—the look on her face."

And the fact that Loren was the last person who'd seen her alive. And she'd apparently been angry about whatever they were discussing.

"How could he have killed her?" Connor asked. "They were walking together along the old main road, right?"

"Maybe they'd had a fight, and she told him to stay away from her. He got pissed, and he pushed her in front of a car. Or maybe it was an accident; I don't know. I just know he made her uncomfortable, and then she was gone. She should have talked about it," he added. "But she wouldn't."

"But you would," Connor prompted. "You told someone you were angry. That Loren was getting away with something."

Traeger's lips pressed together. "I'm supposed to be loyal."

"To the clan," Connor said. "To the Pack. Not to the people who put them in danger."

Traeger's jaw worked as he considered, as if he were chewing over the words he wasn't sure he should say. "I told Cash."

Connor sat back. A quick glance might have made you think he was just getting comfortable, relaxing. But his hand was fisted on the table, knuckles nearly white, and the look in his eyes was nothing near relaxed.

He was angry. And working to hold himself in check.

I understood the feeling.

"And what did Cash say?" Connor asked.

"Same as you. He wanted fucking evidence. Wanted proof that Loren did anything other than be in the wrong place at the wrong time. I had nothing. And that was that. No proof of crime, so no punishment."

Maybe it wasn't so surprising that Cash had seemed pretty casual about investigating Loren's death. Give him a good memorial, a good send-off, but don't worry overmuch about the details, because whoever killed him did you a favor. Ridded the clan of a problem.

"And that bothered you."

"Fuck yeah, it bothered me." He slapped the table with the flat of his hand. "It's fucking wrong. It's the same shit different day around here. Elders are in charge, and we don't question them. Elders do wrong and too fucking bad. They get away with it."

"Did you tell Georgia?" I asked.

Traeger's combative position didn't change, but his gaze softened. "No. What could she do? Everybody knows Cash calls the shots."

"Do they?" Connor's words were barely a whisper. And I began to feel a little bit sorry for Cash and the rest of the elders.

"It's the truth, man." Traeger looked up, met his gaze. "Maybe you do things differently in Chicago or Aurora or Memphis, but we ain't in any of those places. We're here in the sticks where Cash and the others are in charge. Their way or the highway. And where else would we go?"

Connor didn't answer, just watched him.

"Here," Traeger continued, "playing at being humans while we're surrounded by wilderness. That's ironic, don't you think?"

"So, what? You thought you'd bring back a little of the wildness?" Connor asked. "Wreak a little havoc?"

Traeger seemed to go a little paler. "Not me, man. I don't have anything to do with it." But he looked away, avoiding eye contact and the truth.

"You haven't lied to me yet, Traeger. Don't start now."

Traeger stared hard at the refrigerator as he considered, worked through whatever dilemma he was facing.

After a good minute of silence, and while Connor watched him, he turned back again.

"It started with Zane Williams. One of my friends. I was pissed and blowing off steam, told him I thought Loren had been harassing Paisley. I said I'd love to take a few swings at him, but couldn't. Because he was clan, because he was an elder." Traeger cleared his throat. "Zane said things needed to change. And I said he was fucking right." He looked up at Connor. "And he still is.

"That was a few months ago," Traeger continued. "And then Paisley died, and Zane said it was too fucking bad the clan hadn't stopped Loren in the first place." He swallowed hard again. "And then Loren was dead."

Silence fell over the cabin, heavy and full of magic. Traeger's: nervy and uncertain. Connor's: barely banked anger.

"And you think Zane killed him."

"Yeah."

"Did you help?"

"What? No. Of course I didn't help."

"There were four creatures at the Stone farm, Traeger. *Four* of them. That means Zane isn't working alone."

"I'm not one of them," Traeger said, bitterness in his voice. "I mean, I'm one of his friends, but not his only friend. I wasn't included in the plan."

"Who was?" Connor asked.

Traeger swallowed hard, as if working past the guilt of betraying his friends. "He was closest to John, Beyo, Marcus. He's supposedly got some human friends in town who sell to him when he wants to get high, but I don't know their names."

"And he didn't give you any details about how they were doing it? What they were changing into?"

"Not really. He's been cagey about it."

"You were friends enough that you think he might have killed Loren because Loren hurt your girlfriend," I said. "But he didn't invite you to play with him? He didn't tell you how he was going to do it?"

"Because of Georgia," Alexei said quietly, and Traeger nodded.

Connor sat back, watched Traeger. "They weren't sure if you were trustworthy."

"Yeah," Traeger said bitterly, a flush rising on his cheeks.

"Then give us your best guess," I said.

"I don't know. I haven't even seen the creatures. Just heard about them." He seemed shamed by that, too. That he hadn't been included even that much, and even though he'd helped spark their behavior. "Zane told me he figured out a way to get even with Loren, to scare him into telling the truth. Something that would make them strong."

"Magic?" I asked.

"He didn't say. I assumed so, because you could tell their magic was . . . different . . . when they came back."

"Did any of them know how to do magic?" I asked.

"Do magic?" Traeger asked, and his face seemed earnestly blank. "Like spells and stuff? No. We aren't sorcerers." He shifted his gaze to Connor, as if looking for help in explaining what shifters are to a noob.

"It's rare," Connor said. "But there are shifters who can work spells. Not very well."

"No shit?" Traeger looked genuinely surprised. "Huh. I don't think Zane knew anything about that. He just said something about how they'd be able to reach their full potential. At first, I thought he was full of shit, that maybe he'd found some kind of energy drink. But then Beth was attacked, and Loren was dead, and the Stone farm, and then the shutters. And I haven't seen them in a few days."

"Why did they attack Beth?" Connor asked.

Traeger rubbed his arm. "They were coming out of the woods and thought she saw them. They were going to knock her unconscious, hope someone would just think she tripped or something, and wouldn't believe her if she remembered anything."

"She didn't get a good look," Connor said. "So they hit her for no reason."

Traeger just lifted a shoulder.

"Do you know why they attacked the Stone farm?" I asked.

Traeger shook his head. "Probably because the humans were always crossing into our territory. Cash didn't care 'cause Carlie's practically family, but Zane didn't like that they hadn't been punished."

"And they tried to remove the shutters because I'd changed a human without permission—a human under the protection of the clan—and I hadn't been immediately punished."

He dropped his gaze again. "That would be my guess, yeah."

So they were playing vigilante—meting out justice to trespassers who they felt hadn't gotten what they'd deserved.

"Where do we find them?" Connor asked.

"Zane lives with his mom and sister. Jude and Evelyn. They're in one of the houses at the edge of the resort, close to the road. Beyo, Marcus, and John share a cabin. Other side of the road from Zane's. You can't miss it—there's a couch on the front porch. I went by—none of them are there."

"Do you know where else they'd be?"

"I think they have another place—some kind of clubhouse."

"At the resort?" Alexei asked, pushing off the wall and moving closer as he prepared for action.

"No, in the woods somewhere. They were always muddy when they came back."

Connor pushed back his chair and stood. "Go to Georgia's and stay there. Don't leave until we come back, and don't try to find them."

Traeger lifted his brows. "Why?"

"Because you have knowledge," Connor said. "Which you just passed on to outsiders. And Zane and his friends seem to like executing their own judgments."

Traeger's face went pale.

"You did the right thing," Connor said, replacing his chair. "It may not feel like that right now, but you did the right thing— telling us. You might have saved a life tonight. That's what you should think about."

EIGHTEEN

We watched Traeger walk back to Georgia's, made sure he went inside and the door was closed behind him.

"So," Connor said as he worked on a bottle of water that had been squeezed into the fridge between the bottles of blood, "Traeger planted this seed about Loren harassing Paisley, and the clan won't do anything about it. Zane decides he'll do something about it, rounds up three friends. But instead of confronting Cash and the others, or contacting the Pack for help, they make themselves 'stronger' with some secret magic and start playing vigilante."

"And not very well," Alexei said darkly. He stood beside Connor at the island, chewing the heads off gummi bears before eating their bodies a handful at a time. "Ironic since you let Cash claim Obsideo."

Connor gave him a look. "I didn't let Cash claim anything. I made him show his cards, because he was going to do it even if he put Elisa through the clan's 'process' first."

Alexei chewed, considered. "Probably. Miranda's idea?"

"Probably," Connor said, then glanced at me. "Anything from Theo?"

I belatedly realized I hadn't checked my screen all night. I pulled it out, found a bevy of messages.

"Theo hasn't yet been able to reach the Order about the magic," I reported as I scanned them, "but no one in the OMB or its database has any information about the creatures. And it doesn't match the description of the Beast, which is more of a bear, not a prancing wolf."

"So the Beast may still exist," Alexei said as I gave Theo an update, cramming a lot of magical extortion and shifter dramatics into a few words. "It just isn't here."

"Someone has to know what these things are," Connor said. "If this quartet of idiots didn't make this magic, someone who knows about magic must have. I don't know much about spells, either, but don't you have to know what you're aiming for when you write the spell in the first place?"

"Like a recipe," I said. "You want bread, you need a recipe for bread."

"Exactly," Connor said. "Let's go talk to Jude and Evelyn." He glanced at Alexei. "You want John, Beyo, and Marcus?"

Alexei's smile was sly. "Three to one sounds like very fun odds."

"Why do you eat the gummi bears' heads first?" I asked as we headed outside again.

"So they go down easier."

Shifter logic.

Zane's house was a slightly larger version of the cabin, and the similarities in style and decor were beginning to creep me out. I understood the group wanting to live together in the resort; vampires lived in houses, after all. And maybe they'd all liked the style enough not to change it, or just weren't that interested in the aesthetics. But it was unsettling to walk in and out of same-but-slightly-different buildings. Like each was a broken reflection of the last.

Jude was a woman with tan skin and a hard-bitten look. Her hair was a cap of pale blond, her makeup strong, and her clothes decorated with rhinestones and embroidery. Evelyn was probably in her mid-twenties, with a swing of straight blond hair, simple clothes, and delicate makeup. She'd distanced herself from her mother's style, intentionally or not.

"We're looking for Zane," Connor said. "Have you seen him?"

"Not in a couple of days," Jude said. Her voice had the thick and grainy tone of a lifelong smoker.

"Would you normally see him every day?" Connor asked.

"He usually drops by, sure. But could a few days pass before we see him? Yeah. He's got his own life."

"We understood he lived here with you," I said.

"He does," Jude said, and didn't elaborate. So I guessed that was all we were going to get about her son's sleeping habits.

She sat on the couch, leaned forward. "What's it like to be a vampire?"

"Mostly dark."

"What about to live in one of those vampire houses?"

"*Mom,*" Evelyn intoned. "I'm sure you aren't supposed to ask about that."

"I don't see why not. She's a vampire. She doesn't hide it or anything. Made a new one last night, didn't she?"

"We need to talk to Zane," Connor said, trying to move us back toward the point, which had begun to fade into the distance.

The seriousness in his tone seemed to have her—finally—realizing this wasn't just a mild social call. "Why?"

"We think he might have helpful information about the trouble the clan's been experiencing lately."

Jude snorted. "He'd have information about how to be a pain in my ass. Takes money out of my purse 'cause he's on some new tear. Some new fixation. Pawned some of my good china just to get a little extra cash. He'll grow out of it," she said, and sounded convinced, "but he's in that stage."

She rolled her eyes dramatically, and didn't seem to realize that telling us her son was a troublemaker was only going to make us look harder at him. Or maybe that was what she wanted: for someone to handle her son.

"We understand he's friends with John and Beyo and Marcus."

"Sure," she said.

"What about Traeger?" Connor asked.

She laughed bitterly. "Yeah, when he's not running around doing something for Georgia. She keeps him busy." She sounded disapproving. "Kids need time to be themselves."

"Hmmm" was all Connor said.

"I think I left my screen in the car," Evelyn said, rising from her stool at the kitchen counter. "I'm going to go get it." She flicked her gaze toward the door, signaling that we should follow her.

"Thanks for your time," Connor said, rising. "If you see Zane, we'd like to talk to him."

"Sure, sure."

We followed Evelyn outside and around the house to the family firepit a few yards from the lakeshore.

"I love my mother," she said quietly, arms crossed and gaze on the water. "But mothering was not exactly her strong suit."

"Sounds like Zane causes you both some grief," Connor said.

"Rules don't apply to Zane," she said. "Or at least that's his position. He comes and goes as he pleases, takes what he wants." She shook her head, looked back at us. "I work in town, and I've got my own place. I drop by to check on her."

"You're doing her a favor by not causing her problems," Connor said.

She shrugged. "You're here because of Loren, aren't you? Because of last night?"

"Why do you say that?" Connor asked.

"Because if you told me my brother was involved, that he hurt someone, I wouldn't be surprised. I mean, I wouldn't call him violent. At least not before. But he does what he wants, and he always has."

"Traeger says he might have been angry at Loren."

"Who isn't he angry at?" Evelyn said. "According to Zane, he's the smartest guy in the room at all times. And my mother's 'boys will be boys' attitude doesn't help."

"What about Cash?" Connor asked.

"Cash doesn't care what happens around here as long as it doesn't attract human attention."

"That sounds very frustrating," I said quietly, and was glad she'd figured out a way to get some distance from the drama.

"It sucks," she said. "They're family, but it sucks."

"Do you know where we can find Zane?" Connor asked.

"No. She was telling the truth—he does disappear. Sometimes they go up or down the shore. Like she said, he gets obsessed with things. Some idea or hobby or whatever. He's been secretive lately, which is a new one for him. He usually likes to talk." Her voice was dry. "I had the sense he'd fallen into some new project. I don't know what—'cause secretive. But when he was here, he was on his screen more than usual, said he was doing his 'research.'"

"What about his friends?"

"John, Beyo, and Marcus," she said. "His own little gang."

"He was in charge?" I asked, reading her tone.

"Oh yeah. Zane doesn't take instruction well; he decides. And the others are basically zeta males. They'd do whatever Zane said."

Connor looked away for a moment, gazed at the water, brow furrowed as if considering . . . or deciding, before shifting his gaze back to her. "Evelyn, I'm going to level with you—I think your brother is involved in the attacks on Loren and on the bonfire. We need to find him before anyone else is hurt."

She just looked at him, expression blank. "I can't say I'm surprised. But I honestly don't know where he is. You could ask his friends, but even if they knew, they wouldn't tell you."

And presuming they were here, I thought, and not with Zane.

Given the attack had involved multiple creatures, the latter seemed more likely.

"Do you think your mom would let us look through his room?" I asked.

"Oh. Um, she probably wouldn't." Evelyn smiled, and there was nothing happy about it. "But I pay the rent, and I will."

"Zane borrowed something of mine," Evelyn threw out as we passed her mother, still on the couch, now with a beer in one hand and a screen in the other.

We followed her down the hallway, passing a small bathroom cluttered with knickknacks to a bedroom on the left. She opened the door, and the smell of unwashed sheets and stale beer wafted out.

"He's classy," Evelyn said, surveying the carnage.

I'd have said it looked like someone had tossed the room, except that I suspected that was its normal state. There were a small bed, a bureau, a nightstand, a desk. An entertainment screen and a closet with two sliding doors. There were clothes everywhere—socks on the floor, jeans across the bed, a pile of shirts in a laundry basket, a pile of everything spilling out from the closet floor. Empty beer bottles stood in groups in the few empty spaces not covered with clothes, like bowling pins waiting for the roll.

This was a far cry from Georgia's cabin or ours, from the house Marian and Arne shared. And farther still from the Pack's Chicago HQ.

"I'll wait outside," Evelyn said, and left us alone.

"Thoughts?" I asked. "Hazmat suits?"

"What a fucking mess," Connor muttered, and I had the sense he wasn't just talking about the debris field.

"Yeah." Giving up any hope that I'd walk out of this room without needing a shower, I dived in.

The bureau was closest, so I went there first, picked through the detritus with a fingertip. There were coins and credit tokens, pieces of gum, pens, peanut shells, and crumbs (assorted). No wallet, no notepad with scribbled secrets, no magic potion.

"He's a pig," I said.

"No argument." Connor flipped back the blankets on the bed, throwing discarded clothes and funk into the air.

I opened a few drawers, found them mostly empty but for a random T-shirt here and there. Not surprising, given most of the clothes were on the floor.

While Connor kicked through the stuff on the floor, I walked over to the desk. Here, there were glimmers of the boy Zane had been. A small yellow car, a baseball, a scouting pin, all of it scattered with the same garbage as the bureau.

I unwadded a ball of paper, scanned an old-fashioned receipt, the kind handwritten on a carbon paper pad. The store's name was printed on the receipt, the amount listed but the items identified only as "Misc."

"Have you ever been to the Crystal Inferno?" I asked him.

"Not that I'm aware of. What is it?"

"Looks like a store in town. A few weeks ago, Zane spent four hundred bucks there. Or he has the receipt of someone else who did."

Frowning, Connor came around the bed, glanced at the receipt I held out. "What the hell does this guy want with crystals?"

"Maybe that's his latest obsession," I said. "But if he bought crystals, where are they?"

"That's a very good question," Connor said, glancing around. "You find anything else?"

"No. But I haven't gone into the closet. I'm not brave enough."

He chuckled. "Let's start with the receipt and see how far we go."

We walked back into the living room. "Have you ever been to the Crystal Inferno?" Connor asked Jude.

She snorted. "I'm not wasting money on hippie crystals and herbs. We're already magic. Don't need any of that nonsense."

I guessed she wasn't aware her son's feelings were different.

"Then we'll thank you for your time and get out of your hair."

"Sure, chief," she said, and lifted her bottle in salute.

We met Alexei in a plot of green between the Williams house and our cabin.

"Anything?" Connor asked.

Alexei shook his head. "Gone. Cabin's a mess, small for the three of them, and needed airing out. It was disgusting, but they haven't been there in a few days. Smelled musty. Milk's spoiled. I dug around, didn't find anything that indicated where they might be or how they're making the transformation. You find anything?"

"Nothing about where they are or what they're doing," Connor said. "Zane's a punk—and not in the charming way I was a punk," he added for my benefit. "Family confirms he's a trouble-maker, gets fixated on things, and leads the others around."

"We did find this," I said, and offered him the receipt.

Alexei's brows lifted. "Who spends four hundred bucks at a place called the Crystal Inferno?"

"Someone buying magic supplies?" Connor offered.

Alexei nodded. "That could work. You going to check it out?"

"Yeah. Maybe we can nail down their location. In the mean-time, can you talk to Georgia? Presuming Traeger's right about the 'clubhouse' being out in the woods, the clan needs to get peo-ple out there looking, searching."

Alexei nodded. "Fat chance, but I'll ask."

"We'll meet you back at the cabin," Connor said. "Be careful out there."

"Same to you," Alexei said, then slid his gaze to me. "And be careful with that damn sword."

*   *   *

We walked back to the cabin to get the bike for the drive into town. Connor rolled his neck and shoulders as we walked, as if fighting back tension.

"Are you okay?"

"Frustrated," he said. "Shifters are allowed to live their lives without worrying about politics, drama. But there comes a point where it just seems they've stuck their heads into the sand. It makes me . . . punchy."

"Would you like to spar? I'd give you a fighting chance."

Connor snorted. "I've already seen what happens when we spar, brat. And we've got work to do."

I couldn't really disagree with that.

The drama notwithstanding, it was a beautiful night for a drive. Clear and just breezy enough. We took the old main road toward town, then veered away from the shore into the set of tidy blocks where the courthouse and post office stood. The Crystal Inferno sat at the end of the road, the slender bookend in a row of buildings that included a bar and a bank.

The store name blinked in neon letters, a crystal ball among them. It lit in stages: bottom, middle, top. Bottom, middle, top, the neon buzzing quietly in the darkness. It was late, but the store was still bright despite the hour, either for the thrill of humans dipping a toe into the occult in darkness or for the Supernaturals who apparently shopped here. Crystals hung from strings in the windows that flanked the door, and the shelves were well stocked.

"Ready?" Connor asked.

"Yep. We playing humans or ourselves?"

His smile was a little bit feral. "Oh, ourselves. Feel free to be scary if you need to."

Jude hadn't been far off. There was plenty of hippie in the Crystal Inferno, from guides to joining the world's consciousness to dreaming your way to happiness and wealth. There were lotions and oils, crystals and geodes, and a small selection of health food staples intended, according to the sign, to "increase the body conscious," whatever that meant. A woman sang in Gaelic on the store's speakers, and the air smelled like patchouli and pepper.

And beneath all the trappings was the subtle buzz of magic.

"Good evening," said a cheerful voice from somewhere deeper in the store. We followed it to the counter, where a woman with tan skin and dark hair used a scoop to portion dark seeds into small glass jars.

She was tall and curvy, her eyes wide and dark, her mouth generous. She wore a flowy dress with wide sleeves and a V-neck in a floral pattern, and her nails were carefully manicured in pastel pink.

Not a shifter, not a vampire. A sorceress. Bingo.

"Welcome," she said, without looking up. "Feel free to browse, or let me know if I can assist you. We have palm reading appointments for tomorrow, but none left tonight, I'm afraid."

She looked up, and her eyes went wide. "Well, well," she said with a laugh, and put down the scoop. "You aren't who I expected to see tonight. Connor Keene and Elisa Sullivan. I know you from TV, the screen," she said. "What brings you to our little backwater?"

"Family" was all Connor said. "And you are?"

"I'm Paloma," she said, and began to screw tiny lids onto the tiny jars. "We don't have any blood, but we've got some nice kombucha."

"We're actually just here for information," he said.

"Information? About what?"

"Let's start with why a sorceress is holding court at a shop in a backwater."

She flinched, turned her gaze to me, and there was a lot less welcome in it. "Hey," she said. "I'd appreciate if you wouldn't out me."

"You don't tell people you're a sorceress?" I asked.

"No, and you don't have to be rude about it. This isn't Chicago, and there are many reasons not to tell people, including discrimination. Humans might think of me as eccentric, but they think of me as human."

"That's fair," I said.

"Does the Order know you're here?" Connor asked.

A blush rose high on her apple cheekbones. "I'm nonpracticing, so I don't have to be registered. I run a legitimate human-oriented business, so either tell me what you want or get out."

Our questions had been pointed, but not rude. So they didn't explain the sudden nerves or high-pitched protests.

"We just want information," Connor said. "About what you sold Zane Williams."

Her lips pursed. "If he's complaining about the price, we negotiated that, and he said it was fine. It's past the return date, and we don't give refunds." She pointed to the sign beside the cash register. It did, indeed, state NO REFUNDS ALLOWED.

"We don't care about refunds. Have you seen him in the last few days?"

"Zane? No. Why would I? I know in Chicago Sups are one big happy family, but Sups don't mix up here. We keep our magic to ourselves, and I don't have anything in common with the clan."

The bell on the door rang, and we all looked back. Four humans—all women, one of them wearing a white "Bride to Be" sash. They were all giggling and immediately began pawing through the merchandise.

"A bachelorette party," Paloma said. "Just what I need."

"What did Zane buy?" I asked.

"Why do you—"

"Paloma," I said, leaning over the counter, "let me make this simple: We're trying to find Zane. We're looking for information that will help us find him so we can all get on with our evenings, okay? The faster we do that, the less chance those girls have to figure out who we are and wonder what we're doing here. So maybe knock it off with the questions?"

Her eyes widened. "Okay. I'm just— I don't get many nonlocals in here. Or many people trying to interrogate me. He bought a geode."

"A geode," Connor said quietly. "He spent four hundred dollars on a rock?"

"It was a really gorgeous rock," she muttered. "And there were a few other things." She closed her eyes. "He bought some wax and a brass seal, some essential oils, a quartz crystal."

There was absolutely no way the Zane Williams whose room we'd surveyed was going to seal envelopes with fancy wax.

"Did he buy anything magical?"

This time, all the color went out of her face. "Keep your voice down. I don't sell real magic here."

"Do they know that?" I wondered, gesturing toward the bridal party.

"Humans believe what they want to believe. Spellselling without a license is illegal." She lowered her voice. "I don't even sell charms, grimoires, because I don't want to get in trouble with the Order."

In addition to her body language and the nervous magic, that she wouldn't meet my eyes told me she was lying.

I'd play along. For now. "Why did Zane want a geode? From what we hear, he's not exactly rolling in money."

"I don't know," she said quickly. "Maybe he liked the look. Wanted to spruce up his decor."

"Paloma," Connor said, leaning over the counter, "Loren Owens is dead. And we think the person who killed him also attacked Carlie Stone and tried to attack us. We think Zane and several of his friends are involved in that. So if you have information that would help us find them, we need it. *Now.*"

"I don't know," she said again, this time defensively. "But I think Zane was hoping to sell it—to break off the crystals and pass them off as gem-quality amethysts."

No way was Zane that organized. And I couldn't imagine anyone would be dumb enough to buy fake gems from him. Who would have trusted him enough to do that?

"Why do you think that?" Connor asked.

"He asked about the stones, if you could take the stones out. I said you could probably chip them out, but why would you want to, because it would ruin the geode?"

"Do you know where he was going to do this potential selling?" Connor asked.

"No. I don't even know if he was going to do it. He was pretty keyed up when he left, but I haven't talked to him since."

We left her after that pronouncement to let her handle the bachelorette party.

"She was lying," Connor said, glancing back through the glowing window.

"Oh, completely," I agreed. "She made up the story about the geode. Not that I'd doubt Zane would pull the con, but he isn't organized enough to do it."

"And the brass seal," Connor said, shaking his head. "Because he has a lot of fine correspondence to take care of."

"Right?" I looked back. "There's magic in the air, but it's faint. I think she sold them something magical. A charm, a spell, an amulet, a potion, something that contributed to what's going on now. She may not know what it was for—or she doesn't want to know. But she's involved."

"We need her to tell us the truth."

"We can't *make* her talk."

He just looked at me, a gleam in his eyes.

"We can't *legally* make her talk," I amended. "If she's the only sorceress in the area, yeah, it's likely she's the source of the magic. But it's not positive, and we don't have any evidence she was involved other than the receipt, which could be totally innocuous."

"It's not innocuous."

"No, it's not, and she's lying. But we need more information, or something to pressure her with."

That gleam came back.

"You're very bloodthirsty today."

"Sayeth the vampire."

"I'm bloodthirsty every day. It's part of my charm. We need leverage. Maybe Theo can find something when he reaches the Order that we can use against her."

Bells jingled, and Connor looked back at the store, watched the bachelorette party walk outside, each carrying a small white bag with CRYSTAL INFERNO printed on it. They strode down the street in their short dresses and stiletto heels, then slid into the back of a waiting pink limousine.

"Why do humans do that?" Connor asked.

"Ride in limousines? Fastest way to get from point A to point B while also drinking cheap champagne."

"The sash and the giggling."

"Do you have any idea how many giggling girls I've seen you with?" I touched a hand to his arm. "'Oh, Con, you're so strong. And you're just so handsome.'"

He just stared at me with a mix of horror and amusement in his eyes. "Never happened."

"Oh," I said with a grin, "it happened. And gave me plenty of ammunition."

"You're a brat."

"So you've said."

Connor glanced at his watch, his grin fading. "I need to get back. The memorial's in less than an hour. I can give Georgia an update while we're there, make sure the search is under way." He looked back at me, frowned. "You'll be okay on your own?"

"I'll watch my back. You'll keep an eye out for Zane?"

"Oh, absolutely," he said. "We have many things to discuss."

I still wasn't sure what the memorial would involve, but he didn't change clothes, so given that—and the general nature of shifters—I assumed it wouldn't be a formal affair.

I knew it was safer to stay near the cabin, but I couldn't just sit. If I sat, I'd think. And I didn't want to think right now. Not about last night—the blood and the fire and the gore. Not about Carlie and the sickly gray of her skin, and not about the danger we were still in.

We had an idea who the creatures were and knew they'd been using magic of some type. But we didn't know the magical details or where Zane and the others had gone. We needed more information.

We needed more luck.

So I'd try to be productive. I'd start with another look at the ground near the cabin, at the shutters. Maybe I could find a trail, a scrap of fur that could be tested for magic, some bit of evidence I could ship off to Theo and Petra and, in return, get a solution.

And because I apparently had a target on my back, I'd be very careful. I found a penlight beneath the kitchen sink, and walked outside. The temperature had dropped, and the chill seemed to soak the scent of woodsmoke into the air. The resort was quiet, probably because most were attending the memorial and those who were left were subdued enough to stay quiet.

I walked around the side of the cabin, thought enough to stop and flick the light toward the ground. The tracks we'd seen earlier had been mashed and covered by others, probably clan members curious about Connor's story. I didn't see any other evidence, so I turned to the shutters.

The grooves were obvious in the sharp circle of light made by the penlight. Striped grooves where something with claws—very large claws—had gouged the metal. Not just scratching at it—although there were scratches, too—but actually trying to rip it apart with claws. Not the smartest tactic.

On the other hand, they were smart enough to try to remove the shutters. Punishment by sunlight.

I moved the beam of light around the rest of the shutters, but didn't see anything else unusual. Or at least not any more unusual than unique Supernaturals making a go at the real estate.

But then I stepped closer.

Near a shutter's top right corner, in a spot I had to stand on tiptoe to see, was a scratch in the metal that didn't look like a gouge. And it didn't look accidental. It looked like a symbol: two capital Rs standing back to back, the first letter reversed so their spines were aligned. I wondered if I was imagining it, my brain seeing a pattern in marks that were actually scattered and random. But the letters looked intentional. There were even little serifs along the bottoms.

So who was "RR"? That didn't match the initials of the shifters we believed were involved.

I pulled out my screen, took a photo, and sent it to Petra. SYMBOL AT SIGN OF ATTACK, I messaged. CAN YOU FIND ORIGIN?

It was a challenge, I guessed, that she wouldn't be able to resist.

ON ASSIGNMENT was the message she returned. RESETTLING RIVER TROLL DUE TO CONSTRUCTION AND HE IS PRESENTLY TRYING TO PUSH SUV INTO RIVER.

I stared at the message for a moment, trying to figure out if

Petra—of the dry wit and sarcasm—was joking, or if I should contact Theo and have him send help.

JUST KIDDING, she said, before I could ask for clarification. IT'S ONLY A SEDAN.

She had a unique sense of humor.

NINETEEN

I was flipping through the cabin's former guest book, which had been tucked among outdated travel guides and Minnesotan recipe books—heavy on the cranberries and wild rice—when there was shuffling at the back door.

I put down the book—having just read an entry about the owl that kept the Peterson family awake all night—and picked up my sword, then unsheathed it.

I was taking no more chances.

I crept to the door and, as it swung open, extended my katana against the neck of the person who entered.

Connor lifted his hands, grinned at me. "I'm at your mercy?"

I liked the sound of that more than I was willing to admit. I lowered the sword, tugged a lock of his hair with my free hand to pull him forward, and pressed my mouth to his. He wrapped his arms around me, then shifted our bodies so I was against the wall, his mouth hot on mine.

"Is that a sword," he asked after a moment, "or are you glad to see me?"

"Both?"

He humphed, glanced down at the katana.

"You usually come through the other door," I pointed out. "I was being careful."

"Back door was closer. And I'm glad you were being careful. It made for quite a welcome home."

"I'm feeling more myself." I searched his face. "How was the memorial?"

"Surprisingly uneventful." We walked back through the cabin. I sheathed the katana, put it back on the table.

"That is surprising."

"It's customary for all clan members to attend," he said. "But that wasn't going to happen here, and Cash knew he wasn't going to win that battle. So the elders got the memorial they wanted, and the haters got to skip it. Attendance was low."

"Interesting," I said. "Mostly Loren's generation?"

"Nailed it in one. The eulogy was about respecting your elders."

"Also unsurprising," I said. "You talked to Georgia? Gave her the update?"

"I did. She didn't like it. We had some hard words, but she said she'd talk to Cash about a search. And how was your evening?"

"I found something interesting. Come here." I took his hand, tugged him toward the patio doors.

"Why am I going outside again?"

"Because I want a second opinion." I led him to the shutter, posed him in front of it, used the penlight to direct his attention to what I'd discovered. "What do you see?"

"One of many reasons that someone is going to get their ass very handily kicked?"

"In addition to that. Be more specific."

"I don't know . . . ," he began, but then trailed off, leaned closer.

"Do you see it?"

"I see something. A symbol? A logo?" He traced it with a fingertip. "It's scratched in, by the creature that tried to rip off the shutter." He paused, looked back at me. "They left a goddamn calling card. Do you know what it means?"

"Not yet. I've asked Petra to take a look. I assume it doesn't mean anything to you? Nothing wolf related?"

"Such as?"

"I don't know. Realm of Regal Canines?"

"Yes, you've cracked it. It stands for the Realm of Regal Canines." His voice was as dry as toast.

"I knew it. I guess we can report to the elders now and go back to Chicago."

"Theoretically," he said. "But maybe first let's go check with Georgia."

She opened the door with a dish towel in her hands. "Right on time. Come in. Sit down. We're just about to eat."

We exchanged a glance and Connor shrugged, and we followed her into the dining room. The table had been set for four, but Traeger was the only other person in the room. Dinner was apparently a stack of butter-topped steaks, foil-wrapped baked potatoes, and a gorgeous baguette that would have been perfectly at home in Paris.

"Are you expecting company?" Connor asked.

"Yes," she said. "You and Elisa." She pulled out the chair at the head of the table. "I figured you'd be by. Family needs family in a crisis. And allies. I figure we're both. Sit down, and let's eat while it's hot. Then we'll talk."

I'd barely eaten a thing since the bonfire, so the food was a warm welcome.

We were famished and ate in relative silence—three shifters and a vampire refueling with some pretty magnificent steaks and my well-kneaded bread. Maybe baking could be a hobby, after all.

"I owe you an apology," Georgia pronounced when we'd stuffed ourselves silly.

"I don't disagree," Connor said, and Georgia's mouth quirked.

"You're a lot like your mother, you know. She also doesn't suffer fools."

"No, she doesn't. But while I'll agree you owe us an apology,

I'm going to save you from making it. Let's all just agree the situation is complicated."

"I can agree to that," Georgia said. "I'm sorry about Obsideo."

"It exists for a reason," Connor said. "And it's done, so there's no point in dwelling on it." As if reminded of the weight of his magical bonds, Connor rolled his shoulders. "Did Cash agree to send out teams to search?"

"No," Georgia said grimly. "He thinks that would be a waste of resources, and the clan needs to stay close to home, given the external threats against it."

"Quintet of idiots," I murmured, and Connor squeezed my hand in agreement.

"Fortunately," she said, "I have my own allies, and I've sent out some teams. They won't have the coverage we need—not given how large the area is, how deep the woods—but it's better than nothing.

"I'd heard rumors about Loren having affairs, of course," Georgia continued. "But he's a shifter and single. I'd never heard anything about it being nonconsensual." She reached out, put a hand on Traeger's. "If that's what happened to Paisley, I'm sorry for it. Very, very sorry."

Traeger nodded, but looked away, grief and anger etching lines in his face that he was too young to bear.

"Connor says the spellseller told him Zane bought a rock," Georgia said to him. "Do you buy that?"

Traeger shook his head. "He wouldn't care about a rock."

"Have you ever visited the shop?" I asked them. "Bought any magic from her?"

Georgia snorted. "I haven't been in and didn't know she was a sorceress. Is she—what do they call it—registered?"

"She says she isn't," I said, and glanced at Traeger, brows lifted. "What about you?"

"What would I want with crystals and shit?" Traeger asked.

"She's lying," Connor explained. "Maybe because she doesn't want to get tagged by the Order, or maybe because she's feeling guilty or afraid. We're hoping the Order can give us some leverage."

"We could go into town in wolf form," Traeger said. "Scare her into telling us the truth."

"Trying to scare people into doing the right thing is what got us here in the first place," Connor said. "If we get leverage, we'll talk to her again. What about a symbol made up of two *R*s?" He looked between them.

"No," Georgia said, and glared at Traeger, who shook his head. "Why?"

"We think they left it near the shutter," Connor said. He pushed back his chair. "Trae and I will take care of the dishes. But first, we're going to get some fresh air." He looked at Traeger expectantly, waited until he rose.

"Don't go far," Georgia said.

"Literally just to the patio," Connor said with a smile. "Your boy will be fine."

"I'm not her boy," Traeger muttered, but there was something pleased in his tone.

"Fresh air does a body good," Georgia said. "And you will take care of the dishes, but they can wait until you're back. And this will give Elisa and me a chance to talk."

We waited until they walked outside and the door closed behind them.

And then I was alone with her, dreading the possibility that I already knew exactly what Georgia wanted to talk about.

"Getting some attention from Connor will also do him some good," she said. "Feeling like he's heard."

"He came to us," I said. "Told us about Zane. Connor's already told him that was the right thing to do, the hard thing to do. I think he appreciates his dad's influence enough to know what it's like when people don't have good role models."

"Trae definitely didn't," Georgia agreed. "I did the best I could, but I wasn't his parents."

I nodded, looked out the window. The wind had picked up outside, and branches snapped against the windows.

"Doing the right thing," Georgia said. "The hard thing. There's a lot of that going around."

I looked back at her, wasn't sure if I'd see censure or approval. I found neither—more a kind of curiosity.

"You did right by Carlie," she said. "It's taken me some hours— some hard hours—to think through it. But it was the choice you had to make, and you made it."

"I did."

"I'm glad of it. I get the sense, Elisa, that you make a lot of hard choices."

I understood we weren't talking about Carlie anymore.

"Would you like to tell me about it? I realize I offered that before, and you declined, and events in the middle may not endear me overmuch. I don't know you very well," she said. "But you saved Carlie, and that means a lot." She smiled a little. "And I see enough of you reflected in his eyes, in the way he looks at you."

I watched her for a long time, my chest aching with emotion.

Maybe it was a weakness I shouldn't have shown. Maybe it was the debt I'd have to pay back drawing nearer. Maybe it was the combination of exhaustion and weakness. Maybe I was tired of being afraid.

Or maybe, because she was a shifter and there was trouble enough in her own family, it didn't feel as hard to be honest.

"I call it the 'monster.'"

We stayed at the kitchen table, and I told her everything. I told her about the dragon, Mallory's binding magic. The sensation that something foreign, something other, was living inside me. That it was violent and angry and powerful and strong. That it wanted out.

And that it was getting harder and harder to hold it back.

"Why don't you want anyone to see it?"

"Because then everyone would know what I am—that there's a risk I'll go crazy and hurt someone every time I fight. And everyone would know that my parents' big plan had a very big flaw, and that flaw hurt me."

"Why do you say it hurt you?"

"It makes me crazy. It makes me fight like a berserker."

"It makes you fight like a predator."

"It makes me a monster."

"It makes you a vampire."

This was beginning to feel uncomfortably like a trip to a therapist's office, not a casual chat with my boyfriend's aunt. I didn't feel good about mixing those streams. I walked to the windows, folded my arms, looked out.

"Even if your parents' plan was a failure," she said quietly, "do you think they want you to suffer? To bear the guilt over something none of you could control?"

"I think there's no reason for me to add to their guilt when I can bear it."

"Then I guess those are the questions you have to ask yourself: Are you bearing it? Or are you just getting by?"

She paused, seemed to organize her thoughts. "I think Supernaturals, because we focus on our unusual strengths, don't spend nearly enough time discussing our weaknesses. I think we should all talk more. Be forthright and honest about who we are and what we're feeling. If the clan had, if we hadn't forced the younger shifters to suppress their anger, to hide their feelings and push them down, maybe we wouldn't have lost people.

"I like you, Elisa. And I don't want you to end up like that—

pushing down your feelings, living for your anger, until you're consumed by it."

"I don't know what to do. I don't know how to avoid that. There's no one I can ask. No book I can read. No screen page with information. I've found a few things that help—yoga, office work—that keep it quiet."

"I think you have to ask yourself why you have to keep it quiet."

I just shook my head.

"Have you asked it?"

"Asked it what?"

"Who it is? What it wants? What it can do for you?"

"I know what it can do for me. Violence."

"You can do violence well enough on your own. You don't need the monster for that."

I shook my head.

"Maybe I'm wrong," she said, sitting back and crossing her arms. "But even if it was foreign before, it's not foreign any longer. It's part of you, and you're part of it. You're stuck together. So figure out how to live together."

"That's what Connor said."

"He occasionally has a good idea." Her face softened with kindness, with sympathy. "I know you feel like you took a risk telling me this. I can feel it. But consider the possibility that I'm not the only one who wouldn't judge you. Based on what I know, your parents love you, and they'd want you to let them help. They wouldn't want you to bear something so heavy on your own."

I thought about the talk I'd had with my father, how he'd been the first one I'd talked to about biting Carlie.

"Sometimes the hardest thing we can do is be honest with those we love about who we are. Sometimes it's also the best thing we can do."

"I'll think about it," I said. Because that was the most I could promise right now.

* * *

Overly tired, I left Traeger and Connor to help with the dishes, promised them I could make the forty-yard trip back to the cabin safely.

The resort was as quiet as a graveyard. No firepits burning tonight, no raucous parties. Instead, the cabins were lit from the inside and out, even the bravest of shifters inside with doors locked. Even if they hadn't believed us—or the other shifters who'd fought—about the creatures who'd attacked, they weren't taking any chances.

I reached the cabin, was surprised to find Alexei on the steps.

"Hey," I said, walking to the porch. "You waiting for Connor?"

"Nope," he said. "I'm on guard."

"On guard?"

He glanced up and back. "I'm going to keep an eye on the place while you sleep. Because of the shutters."

I simply stared at him. "You're going to guard the cabin."

"That's the plan."

I considered walking inside, leaving him to his work. But I thought about what I'd shared with Georgia, the lightness I felt for making my confession. So I took another chance and sat on the step beside Alexei.

"I appreciate that you're looking out for Connor. And I appreciate that you're looking out for me."

He nodded.

"I grew up in Cadogan House. Always guarded, always big shutters on the windows. In Paris, there were guards, but no shutters. Just big velvet curtains. They were beautiful—this deep blue that was the same color as the sky at midnight. But they were curtains. I'd trained one night for twelve hours—it was winter—and practically fell into bed when dawn came. And I didn't check the curtains first."

He was quiet for a moment, insects filling the silence. Then he asked, almost tentatively, "What happened?"

"My legs were exposed for, we think, about ten minutes before I screamed myself awake. There was a human guard in Maison Dumas, and she heard me, came running. She got the windows closed, bandaged me. I had to convince my parents not to fly to Paris. And learned my lesson about checking the curtains.

"I healed," I said, "being a vampire. But it took a good week, and nothing cut the pain in the meantime." I looked over at him. "I know your standing guard isn't just about me. But I appreciate it. I just wanted you to know that. So, thank you."

He nodded. "You're welcome, Elisa."

It was the first time I'd heard him say my name.

TWENTY

I need to buy Alexei a pound of gummi bears," I said at dusk as we prepared to leave.

Connor snorted, crunching an apple of brilliant crimson. "Flirting with him isn't going to endear you to me."

"Sugar flirting isn't emotional flirting. And it's not actually flirting at all," I corrected, belting on my katana. "It's payment for services rendered."

"Still sounds like flirting."

"Have you updated your dad?"

"I'm not comfortable with that segue."

"I'm not going to buy him gummi bears."

"Well, that's a relief." He walked toward me, offered his apple. "Bite?"

If Eve had been half as tempting as Connor Keene with a Red Delicious, I felt a sudden sympathy for Adam.

"I'm . . . fine," I said.

He cocked an eyebrow, smile spreading slowly. "Are you?"

"I am. Why are you flirting with me? Do you need gummi bears?"

He snorted, took another bite of his apple. "Yes, the Pack has been updated. Pops is irritated by the Obsideo, but fine with the result."

"You fix the clan?"

"No," he said, and took a final bite. "We fix the clan."

* * *

We found Alexei still on the steps, chewing on the end of a scarlet red rope of licorice. And staring at a wall of gleaming white aluminum.

"What is . . . ," I began, taking in forty feet of vehicle. "Why is there a motor home parked in front of our cabin?"

"It arrived two hours ago," Alexei said, taking another bite. "Hasn't done anything since it arrived."

"So it's probably not an immediate risk?" I asked flatly, as he chewed, watched the door contemplatively.

"Not unless you're waiting to be attacked by retirees."

The door opened, and we looked into the green eyes of a very pissed-off-looking cat.

"Shit," Connor muttered, stepping behind me. "Devil cat."

Eleanor of Aquitaine hissed at the sight of him. Which made me feel a little better about our tumultuous relationship, but didn't make me any less surprised to see her sitting there.

"Did she open the door?" Connor's question was soft, and there was a cautious edge to it. Smart boy.

"I doubt she's mastered that without opposable thumbs," I said. "She does look pissed at you, though. What did you do?"

"I exist. That seems to be enough."

As if in agreement, the cat swished her tail while Lulu stepped behind her. She wore a white ringer T-shirt with red at the collar and sleeves and "Lovers Love Minnesota" across the front.

"Hello, Minnesota!" she said brightly, then looked down. "Pardon me," she said, and the cat turned around, flicked its tail in the air, and trotted deeper into the RV.

"Your cat?" Alexei asked.

"Ah, he deigns to speak to me. And no, Eleanor of Aquitaine does not admit to ownership. She allows us to live in her loft."

"You brought a cat into a compound of shifters," Connor said.

"She brought herself," Lulu said, stepping onto the asphalt. She opened her arms, and I gave her a hug.

"I'm really glad to see you," I said. "But why are you here?"

Theo stepped into the doorway. "We're the roaming Ombudsman's office."

"Anyone else in that clown car?" Connor asked.

"Just us," Theo said, stepping onto the asphalt. He nodded at me and Connor, then at Alexei.

"Alexei, Theo," I said, introducing them. They exchanged nods. "And why is the Ombudsman's office here?"

Theo glanced at Connor. "It was his idea."

"Was it?" I asked.

"I thought we could use some allies," Connor said. "I just didn't think they'd come in . . . that."

"Recreational vehicle," Lulu said.

My heart sighed at his sentiment. "Thank you," I said, and Connor smiled back. "But is it safe for them to be here? All things considered."

"No safer than for us." Connor smiled, lifted a shoulder. "But no less safe, either. We're a team on this one. And we could use some investigators."

"That would be me," Theo said, raising a hand. "Although I did fill in Lulu and Eleanor of Aquitaine on the basics during the trip."

"Which you should have done," Lulu said, punching me lightly on the arm. "Lot of drama."

"That's why I didn't tell you," I said. "And since you don't like drama, why are you here?"

"It's a recreational vehicle," Lulu said again. "I'm here to recreate. Or recreationally work, anyway. I brought my supplies, and I'm going to do some plein air painting. I want no part of your magical drama. But I am available for cheese curds and hot dish."

I was glad to see her but worried, too. "You have to be careful. Most of the county is pissed at us."

"I take it seriously," she said, shifted her gaze to Connor. "And I take him seriously. He's not going to let anything happen to you."

"No," Connor said as if she'd been asking him the question. "I'm not."

I pushed down irritation, because I knew she meant well. "I don't need protecting."

"Two Sups are better than one," she said, then shifted her gaze to Alexei. "Usually."

She stared at him. He stared back at her, silently.

I just watched them, fascinated.

Beside me, Connor said, "Alexei."

"Yes?"

"Have you met Lulu?"

"Sure."

Another moment of silence passed.

"Classy," Lulu said.

"Moving on," I said, looking at Theo, "do you have anything to report?"

"Wait," Lulu said, and held up a hand. "That's my cue to not be here." She pointed east. "Lake that way?"

"It is," Connor said. "And that's our cabin if you need anything. Keep your eyes and ears open."

"I will."

But as she walked past Alexei, he took her arm. "You shouldn't go out there alone."

She looked down at his arm, then slowly shifted her gaze to his face. "I go where I want. And I suggest you take your hand off me."

Alexei watched her for a long, smoldering moment before raising his hands, holding them both up as if showing his innocence. "My apologies," he said, and we all exhaled.

"I'm walking right there," Lulu said, and pointed to the shore-line. "If any large monsters appear in the darkness, you have my permission to rescue me."

Alexei watched her walk away. "What's her problem?"

"You're assuming she can't handle herself, for one," I said. "Be-cause trust us—she can."

When he opened his mouth to object, I held up a hand. "I know you meant well, but until we figure out what's going on, we're all vulnerable to attack. Theo told her what's happening here, and she'll take care of herself. But she won't sit in a cabin and wait it out any more than we would."

"This isn't a fight you're going to win," Connor said, and clapped Alexei on the back.

"She's being illogical," Alexei said.

"She's an artist," I told him with a smile. "Get used to it. If you want to stand guard, go for it. But I wouldn't let her see you."

Alexei looked back. "Maybe I'll just stand on the patio."

"Good luck and godspeed," I said, squeezing his arm.

"With that topic closed," Theo said hopefully, "you should come in." He climbed the stairs back into the vehicle.

"Is the clan going to give you trouble about the RV?" I asked Connor as we followed him.

"Probably. But we'll handle it. I want them close by."

"Because you want to keep an eye on them?"

"Pretty much," he said with a smile. "They're helpful and kind and capable. But they aren't shifters. We're all in enemy territory, relatively speaking. I'm sorry that it's come to that, but that's where we are."

I was sorry, too. Not just for us, but for him, as someone who loved the Pack, Cassie and Wes, whose child's initiation would always be scarred by the memory of what had happened after-ward, and for those who disagreed with Cash, who'd apparently had no way to argue or to correct their situation.

"It smells like feet and Cheetos in here," Connor said.

"The RV already smelled like feet. Cheetos are my driving fuel," Theo said. "And Eleanor of Aquitaine's been stealing them and hiding them around the RV."

But for the smell, the vehicle's interior was nice. Burled wood and pale leather, and fancier than I'd have thought the city of Chicago would spring for.

A lot fancier.

I looked at Theo, narrowed my gaze. "This was in the OMB budget?"

"What's that, now?"

There was further narrowing until my eyes were suspicious slits. "Theo, did my parents pay for this RV?"

"No," he said. "Of course they didn't pay for it. They just, you know, contributed a little."

I just looked at him.

"Some," he amended.

I lifted my eyebrows.

"Okay, most of it." At my narrowed stare, he held up his hands. "Not my call or my doing. Your father and Yuen talked. And then I talked to Connor and passed that along, and decisions were made."

I sighed, both appreciative my family had wanted to help and irritated that they thought I'd gotten into something that required a rescue team.

"I think this would be a good time to show our worth," Theo said. He slid into the small dinette, began to work a tablet. "You there, Petra?"

"I'm here!" We heard her voice first, then her torso began to shimmer in midair in front of the table.

"Augmented reality features," Theo said, gesturing to her floating head. "The RV is loaded."

"Petra is a tech whiz," I said, and offered a wave. "Hello, Petra."

"Hello, Elisa and Theo and Connor and Eleanor of Aquitaine."

The cat jumped onto the counter opposite the dinette, tried to paw at Petra's image.

"I know, pretty girl. I miss you, too."

Eleanor of Aquitaine meowed coyly.

"You're friends?" I asked, staring between them.

"Of course," Petra said, shifting her gaze back to us. "Are you not?"

I had to work not to show fang.

"All righty," Petra said. "I have a mediation later tonight—the sedan did not survive its dunking in the Chicago River—so let's get this going."

"Did you find anything about the symbol?" Connor asked.

"Of course. Its source and possibly some of the explanation for what you're seeing." She glanced down at Theo. "If you would?"

"Sure," he said, and swiveled the tablet on the table to face us. On its screen was an image of the symbol I'd found on the shutters, the lines jagged and cut into what looked like gold.

"A carving?" Connor asked.

"A signet ring," Petra said, and the image zoomed out, showing a gold ring with a round flat top on which the symbol had been carved. The ring looked like an antique, but not an antiquity.

"How old?" I asked.

"This ring is from the nineteen sixties," she said. "From a cult called the Sons of Aeneas, Aeneas being the heroic ancestor of Romulus and Remus, the twin founders of Rome."

"And suckled by a she-wolf," Connor said, and she nodded.

"And they supposedly took in all the power of the wolf in that process," Petra said.

"That explains the 'RR' on the ring," I said, sitting on the sofa across from the table. "What was the cult about?"

"The group was started in the nineteen forties during World War Two. A quartet of friends from New York was about to ship off to some really hairy fighting in France. Someone made a joke about how they needed to be heroic and strong like wolves, and they started the club. All but one of them survived the war, and when they came back, they formalized the group."

"And how did it become a cult?" Theo asked.

"Evolution," Petra said. "The original founders died, and you add in a little gang warfare, a little cocaine, and a social club becomes something a lot darker. Instead of just using the wolf as a symbol, they start to worship wolves. And it spreads across the country. Local dens start to open up. They pretend to be just another fraternal society, something like the Freemasons, and they put on a good face about charitable works and community service, and maybe that was true in some of the dens. But not everywhere."

She looked away, eyes scanning as if she was reading from a source. "They took mythology very seriously, created their own tracts and treatises about wolves and their particular favorite— werewolves."

"The wolf illuminati," Theo said.

"Not unlike," Petra agreed. "The cult bought into the Romulus and Remus mythology, decided werewolves were the perfect union of human and wolf—the chocolate and peanut butter of the human and animal kingdoms, if you will."

"Hybrids," I said, and she nodded.

"These humans weren't wolves, or anything close to it, and they wanted to be. So they did a deep dive into Roman history and records, and found a spell intended to bring the power of the wolf into the human body, just as Romulus and Remus theoretically did."

"Bingo," Connor said. "Zane and the others found the spell, and they found a spellseller who was more than happy to do a little magic without telling anyone."

"There are SOA dens in Minnesota," Petra said, "and I found

all this stuff online with not too much hacking, so it's pretty likely your shifters could find it, too."

"They found it," Connor said, "and decided the dogma made sense and wanted to try it."

"Dogma," Petra said with a smile. "Nice."

I looked at Connor. "How did the Pack not know about this cult?"

"I have no idea. Did it ever work?" he asked Petra. "Was there ever evidence the spell did what it was supposed to do?"

"Not in the public records," she said. "A few SOA chapters said they were successful. They did the spell during closed sessions, claimed Keith or Carl turned into a werewolf, but it was never verified outside the chapter meetings."

"That's probably why they didn't know," Connor said. "Assuming the magic worked at all."

"We have to go back to the spellseller," I said. "We know Zane and the others didn't do magic, and she does. She must have made the spell for them. If we can confirm how the magic was done, maybe we can figure out some way to fix them. Or stop them."

"She refused to talk to us last time," Connor pointed out.

"I believe that's where I come in," Theo said. "I talked to the Order's registrar. They know of Paloma, but she isn't registered to practice. It's like being on an inactive list. And, interestingly, there aren't any other sorcerers in this part of Minnesota—registered or otherwise."

"So the spell could only have come from her," I said.

"So the spell could only have come from her," Theo said with a nod.

"Nice work," Connor said, and clapped him on the back.

"Thank the very talkative registrar. She's new, and I don't think she's learned yet how little information the Order actually likes to share."

"I'm guessing Paloma will suddenly become a lot more cooperative," I predicted, "especially with a visit from Chicago's Ombudsman."

"Could we have a little break before we leave?" Theo asked. "We've been in this vehicle for ten hours, and I'd really like to stretch. And not smell feet. She wouldn't let us stop."

"Lulu?"

"Eleanor of Aquitaine."

The RV's door opened. Theo, Connor, and I all reached for weapons. But it was Lulu carrying three cans of tuna.

"That was a quick trip," I said.

"The shoreline is, like, twenty yards away, and it's dark. Not a lot of land to scape, you might say."

"So you raided our larder instead?" Connor asked.

"She's displeased with my travel-food selections," she said dourly. "Except for the Cheetos. What's the status in here?"

"It's possible," Theo began, "the assholes—and that's a technical term—found out about a cult dedicated to this wolf-human hybrid idea and borrowed a spell they came up with."

"We're going to talk to the spellseller and hopefully blackmail her into telling us the truth," I said brightly. "But first, we're going to take a break."

"Excellent," Lulu said. "That will give us a chance to catch up."

"Will you be discussing anything interesting?" Theo asked.

"Menstruation, feminism, and acai bowls."

"I'm out," Theo said, and headed for the door.

Silently, Lulu loaded the tuna cans into a narrow cabinet. When she'd closed it, she looked back at me.

"So," she said, "you changed a human without her consent and didn't want to tell me that."

"No-drama rule," I protested.

She narrowed her already angry eyes. "You didn't make the drama. You just reacted to it."

I couldn't seem to help it. I'd kept up a strong face, even for my father, but here with Lulu, the emotion—and the words—just flew out. "What if she dies, Lulu? What if I did this thing, and caused all this trouble, and she dies, anyway?"

"No." She pointed at me, her eyes hard and hot. "No. You do not get to regret that, and you don't get to take it back. You saved her life. Period. If you want to regret anything, regret that the beasts made her a victim. Do not regret doing the right thing. That's vampire hindsight."

"My mother—"

"*Lived,*" Lulu said. "She lived because your father saved her life. Period. I know she had some issues to work through, and that's fair. That's her right. But he did the right thing, and so did you. That's who you are, Lis. You're their kid, and you're a good egg. You think I'm going to be friends with a sociopath? No."

"No-drama rule."

"No-drama rule," she agreed.

It helped, hearing her say it. She was my best friend, but that required more honesty, not less. And if I'd done the wrong thing, she'd tell me, then do whatever she could to help me get out of it.

"Thank you. Connor and my dad said the same thing."

Her lips curled upward. "Good. They're right. And since I'm allowed to assume you did the right thing, being your bestie, I wasn't asking about that." She smiled. "I was asking about him and you and the progression with Connor."

"I'm not going to kiss and tell."

"Elisa Sullivan. You may be a vampire, but you are not a good liar. You've told me about every kiss you've ever had. And the times you didn't get kissed."

"What? That doesn't make any sense."

"Michael McGregor."

"Michael McGregor and I went to second base."

"Michael McGregor accidentally brushed your boob while you

were showing off Krav Maga moves. Then you threw him to the floor and broke his arm."

"Nose. And it wasn't on purpose. He just had a bad landing."

Her mouth twitched. "Whatever. The point it, you enjoy sharing details with me. So how's the trip going vis-à-vis the romance?"

"He's into me, and I'm on the same page. I'm just trying to . . . let it happen. In between attempts to kill me."

She reached out, squeezed my arm. "My little girl is growing up."

TWENTY-ONE

Connor borrowed Georgia's SUV, and Theo and I climbed in for the trip into Grand Bay proper to threaten the spellseller. Apparently a glutton for punishment, Alexei opted to stand guard at the cabin, keep an eye on Lulu.

"Is it just me," Connor asked when we were on the road, "or is that cat unnerving?"

He pushed a hand through his hair like a man who'd just survived a standoff.

"Unnerving," Theo agreed from the backseat.

I glanced back at Theo. "You're a former cop and an excellent shot"—then I looked at Connor—"and you're a wolf. We're chasing down magically enhanced shifter hybrids because you're required by arcane Pack magic, and you're unnerved by an eight-pound cat?"

"I didn't say it was logical," Connor said. "I just said I was unnerved."

I wasn't unnerved by her so much as flummoxed.

What did Petra have that I didn't? I'd fed her. Called her by her full name. Attempted to pet her, although admittedly that hadn't gone well.

"For an eight-pound cat," Theo said, "she sure requires a lot of energy. Maybe she's one of those psychic vampires."

I opened my mouth to argue, tell him that wasn't a real thing.

But we were chasing down the rogue spellseller who had probably turned a bunch of twenty-year-olds into those monster hybrids.

So I just saved my breath.

"It's not a bad downtown," Theo said when Connor had parked and we were walking along the brick storefronts. "Cute, with the flower beds and the signs and the happy couples."

"Everything's perfect in Grand Bay," Connor said. "Until you consider the asshole Supernaturals."

We turned the corner to reach the street where the shop was located—and stared at one of those asshole Supernaturals.

The black hybrid.

My heart began to thud, blood speeding from the possibility of battle, and the memory of the last time I'd faced this particular monster. My monster watched the scene warily, but hadn't yet decided if it wanted any part of this particular beast.

"What are we calling them now?" I whispered.

"I think the nomenclature is not the most important consideration," Theo said. "And I'm going to just take this opportunity to say 'holy shit.'"

"Asshole Supernatural works for me," Connor said, and I got a minor warm fuzzy for having thought the same thing.

"It's alone," I said. "I wonder if it's headed for the same place we are."

"It looks like it could use another dose of whatever candy the spellseller is handing out," Theo said. "I mean, I know I'm the relative newbie here, but it looks . . . sick?"

It still bore cuts and scrapes from the fight, and it still fit the "stringy" description. But Theo was right—it looked thinner than it had at the bonfire, bone and tendons standing out in sharp relief.

"The magic isn't doing him any good," Connor guessed. "It's tearing him apart."

Magic had a nasty way of doing that to the uninitiated. It was power, and anyone who failed to respect that usually suffered the consequences. I wondered if that explained why my monster hadn't yet reared its head. It was attracted to power, but there was degradation here.

"And where the hell are the other three?" Connor asked.

We waited for a moment, watching the other roads for the other beasts to come loping toward us.

They didn't, but the humans who'd just come out of the bar at the other end of the street screamed. One couple ran back inside; another pulled out their screens to record the scene for posterity.

The beast turned at the sound, swiping out an arm and flipping a bench so it tumbled down the street like a toy.

"Shit," Connor said. "Anybody by chance have an idea which shifter this is?"

"None," I said.

"So let's try them all. Zane! Beyo! John! Marcus!"

He paused between each name, and the beast seemed to flinch when he said, "Beyo," but it roared again, swiped a planter this time, sending it careening into a bar's window. Glass shattered, and more humans screamed.

This was about to get very, very nasty.

"I'll go around through the alley," Theo suggested, "and come at him from the other side."

"Do that," Connor said. "But get the humans inside first."

Theo nodded, then jogged around the building and out of sight.

"Over here!" Connor called out, and waved his arms, trying to get the beast to move away from the bar, from the people inside.

It lifted its head, bared its fangs at us, and began moving toward us.

"Are all your vacations this fun?" I asked, unsheathing my sword.

"Only the ones with hot vampires," he said, and pulled his own blade—a wicked-looking thing with gnarled edges. Now on the other side of the monster, Theo guided humans into the bar.

"Go low," I told Connor. "I'll go high."

"Roger that," he said, and as the distance between us grew shorter, we raised our blades in preparation for the fight.

The creature lifted its muzzle, and I crouched, anticipating the howl that would precede its rush forward.

"Ready," Connor said quietly, and I nodded.

The howl was unearthly, sending an electric chill down my spine. This wasn't a beast on the hunt, or even the fury of a clan member who wanted revenge. It was the scream of a wounded animal—and a trapped human.

The beast began to claw at its chest, its arms, still howling, spittle falling from its lips.

"What the . . . ?" Connor asked, and started to move forward, but I held him back with my hand, not wanting him to get too close to the magic.

"Wait," I said.

Light flashed—not the bright glow of a shifter switching forms, but a sharp and fractured bolt that put the scent of something chemical in the air. With each flash came a concussion of magic, as the boy's body was racked, pulled, fur displacing skin until there was a final burst of light, and he fell to the ground in front of us, pale and naked and skeletally thin.

"Help me," he managed, and curled into a fetal position.

"Jesus," Connor said, and we ran forward.

I caught movement in the spellseller's window, watched her watch us and make not a single move to help. "Asshole," I muttered, and caught Connor's surprised glance.

"What?"

I gestured toward the window, watched his expression go dark. He muttered a curse that was much less mild than mine.

"What's your name?" he asked, turning back to the boy as Theo made his way toward us.

"Beyo . . ." was all he managed before he passed out.

Connor stood up as a siren began to wail in the distance. "We need to get him out of here. I'm going to move the vehicle around. I'll be right back."

"I don't think we're going anywhere," Theo said.

The SUV squealed to a stop in front of us barely a minute later. Connor climbed out, leaving the door open and the motor running, and came around while Theo opened the back door.

"I've got him," Connor said, lifting the young man into his arms as if he were nothing, then placed him in the backseat, closed the door. "I'm going to take him back to the resort," he said. "I'll have Georgia keep an eye on him."

"We'll talk to the spellseller," I said. "Maybe witnessing this will have jogged her memory a little."

Connor nodded, looked at Theo. "Don't be afraid to show your badge. I'll come back when he's settled."

"Be careful," I said, and pressed a kiss to his lips.

"Same goes for you, brat."

He drove off, and we turned back to the woman who stood in her front window, still wringing her hands.

A pretty good metaphor, I thought ruefully. "Let's go ruin her night."

Paloma blanched when she saw us coming, then tried to play casual by flipping the "Open" sign to "Closed."

"Wow," Theo said. "I don't know if we should go in now that she's turned that sign around."

"Yeah," I said, pushing open the door. "It's a real obstacle."

There was a handful of humans in the store, most near the windows and on screens, reporting what they'd seen—or trying to figure out exactly what it had been.

"I'll keep an eye on her," I said. "Can you take care of them?"

"My pleasure." Theo pulled his badge, raised it. He didn't have any jurisdiction here, but it wasn't like anyone was going to read the fine print. "Sorry for the interruption," he said, "but we need everyone to vacate the premises, please. If you could just all step outside and be on your way."

Helpfully, he held open the door, waited for them to file out, and closed it again. Then he flipped the lock, turned back to us.

"What are you doing?" Paloma asked, skittering behind the counter as we walked toward her.

"We're here to get the truth," I said, idly picking up a geode, examining the crystals inside, then setting it down again. "Because we're very sick of being lied to."

"I don't know what you mean," Paloma said, but her hands were shaking. When she realized we'd noticed, she crossed her arms, hiding her hands.

"I didn't introduce myself," Theo said, taking out his badge. "I'm with the Ombudsman's office. Do you know who they are?"

"Yeah, I know. You don't have any jurisdiction here."

"No," he agreed, "I don't. But what I do have is information. You also have information, Paloma. And you're going to give it to us."

"I don't know anything."

"Oh, but you do. Because you're the only one who could." Theo looked at me. "Did you know I spoke with the Order earlier today?"

"You don't say," I offered, feigning surprise. "And how are things in Milwaukee?"

"Efficient. They keep really good records, and our Paloma here is the only sorceress—registered or otherwise—in the area." He turned to Paloma again. "This begins and ends with you, Paloma. Would you like to be honest now, or should we just call the Order and let them deal with you?"

She turned her gaze to the window and looked absolutely miserable. "I didn't know they'd turn into . . . that," she said, then looked back at me. "That's the absolute truth."

"You'll pardon me if I don't believe you," I said dryly. "Especially since, despite your powers, you stood there and watched. You didn't even try to help."

"There was nothing I could do."

Theo looked at me, brows knit in false puzzlement. "Nothing she could do, Elisa. Doesn't that seem strange?"

"It really does," I agreed, enjoying the banter more than I probably should have, given what was at stake.

"You don't have to believe me," she said. "Maybe I wouldn't believe me if I was you. But again, it's the truth."

"We'll believe you if you tell us the truth," I said.

Paloma rubbed her forehead. "Can we—can we go sit down? I'm getting one hell of a headache. It's the magic. It gives me migraines."

She rustled through a bead-covered doorway along the back wall.

We followed her down a hallway that led to a restroom and a small office. The office held a desk and two visitors' chairs. It was organized but full of boxes, paperwork, and collectibles. A paper lantern hung from the ceiling, and a poster demonstrating yoga poses was stuck to the brick wall. And the room was thick with old magic, pungent layers that seemed to permeate the air and the furniture and left the air feeling oily.

She sat down behind the desk, closed her eyes, and rubbed her hands over her face. Then she sighed heavily, seeming to contract in the room, and put down her hands again. She looked tired and miserable. Unfortunate those feelings hadn't pushed her to find us before.

"He came to me because he had a problem."

"He who?" I asked.

"Zane. He was alone, and he was frustrated. He came in near midnight one night, roamed around the store, seemed nervous or agitated. I watched him, because I thought he was going to steal something. He had that kind of jitteriness. But then he came up to the counter. Handed me a piece of paper and said he needed that."

"And what was on the paper?" Theo asked.

Paloma swallowed. "A spell. Ingredients for a potion, instructions for use, an incantation."

"And what was the spell for?"

"I don't know," she said, and jerked when Theo leaned forward. "I don't know," she said again, but didn't meet his gaze. "I know how to follow directions, but I don't, like, have a degree in spell theory. Based on the ingredients, I thought it was supposed to make them stronger."

We let silence fall in the wake of that statement.

"Do you believe that?" Theo asked, glancing at me.

"I'm not sure yet," I said, and glared at Paloma.

She put her hands flat on the desk, leaned forward as if to work harder to convince us. "I swear to god, that's all I knew."

"And what did you tell him?" Theo asked.

"I played it off at first, said I didn't do any real magic, and then that I wasn't licensed. He didn't believe any of it. Said he could feel my magic. I said fine, even if I did magic, I didn't do dark magic. I wouldn't make a compulsion spell. Couldn't do it, as I didn't even stock those kinds of ingredients. So I asked him what the issue was, if there was any other way around it."

"Because you wanted to sell him some real magic," I said, my irritation rising.

"Because I want to pay my rent," Paloma countered. "He said someone was hurting his family, and he wanted to stop it. So I made the potion, told him to follow the instructions and say the incantation."

"So you gave him the potion that night?" Theo asked.

"No, he had to come back for it. I had the ingredients on hand, but you still have to be careful in the making. There are steps you have to take, stages you have to follow. You can't just dump everything in and expect to get a good result."

"How long until it was done?" Theo asked.

"Maybe a week?" A faint flush rose on her cheeks. "It was done faster than that, but he hadn't been able to get all the money together, so I held it."

"Do you know where he got the money he used to pay for it?"

"No. Why? Should I?"

Not if you were willfully oblivious, I thought. "So you gave him a weapon."

"I gave him the magic he paid for. I didn't have control over what he did with it afterward."

But her eyes skittered away from mine, focused on a stack of papers on the corner of her desk. She wasn't telling the truth, or at least not all of it. But we'd get to that. . . .

"How did he pick it up?" Theo asked.

"He came back to the store with three of his friends. Beyo and"—she squeezed her eyes closed, as if trying to remember—"I'm not actually sure of the others' names."

"John and Marcus?" I offered.

"Maybe."

"What do you know about the Sons of Aeneas?" I asked.

Her eyes widened. "The cult? I had a treatise on them—a little paperback. I keep some materials on the occult—kind of a 'true crime but paranormal' version. We get a lot of demand for that around Halloween. Mostly kids looking to be entertained."

She sounded so absolutely certain of it that I both pitied and disdained her. She'd armed Zane, and who knew who else, with weapons as sharp as any blade, as powerful as any gun.

"Can we see it?" Theo asked.

"Oh, sure," she said. "I'll go get it." Then she squeezed around the desk and our chairs and into the hallway.

"Odds it's gone?" Theo asked. "Pilfered by Zane and the others?"

"High," I said. "Nice little bit of background for his growing obsession."

"Yeah," he said, then looked up when she entered again.

"It's gone," she said as she stepped back into the room. She was wringing her hands, working her fingers over and over as if that would solve her problems.

"Oh, my god, shock," Theo murmured.

"Zane or the others probably took it," I said. "What do you know about it?"

"Not much, other than what's on the cover." She wedged behind her desk again. "It's a small book, paperback sized but much thinner. Blue-and-yellow border on the cover. It's from a press in North Carolina. They did an entire series on cults and paranormal groups in the late seventies, and they've been reprinting them since. I think the Sons of Aeneas must have been around that time period, because there was one of those 'ripped from the headlines' type stickers on the book. Like, 'Hey, check this out. It's going on right now. You just heard about it on the news' or whatever."

"But you don't know what they did?"

"No. I didn't read it."

Another irony—that the woman who operated the magic store seemed to have very little understanding of how it actually worked.

"Did Zane talk to you about the SOA? Or anyone else?"

"Not to me, and not that I'm aware of to anyone else."

"Do you know Loren?" I asked.

She swallowed, began to shuffle a stack of papers into a precisely aligned block. "The clan leader who died? Why do you ask?"

I glanced at Theo, got his small nod. He'd also seen she wasn't telling the truth. I watched her until the silence stretched taut and tense as a wire. I was tempted to push a little magic into the air, use my own glamour just to nudge her along. But it proved unnecessary.

"I knew him," she said.

"You don't say," Theo said, tone flat as the documents she'd just organized.

This time, her eyes went hard. "You don't know me. You don't know anything about me or who I am."

"You're right," I said. "We just know you're selling unlicensed magic, and because of that magic, one shifter's dead and others have been injured."

"I didn't know they'd become monsters."

"You've said that," Theo said. "But you knew they were angry, that they wanted to be stronger, that they wanted to hurt someone. And you sold them the weapon they used."

"It was just a potion."

"It was a *weaponized* potion," I said. "You knew exactly what they were going to use it for. You might not have known the mechanism—that they'd become monsters—but you knew they wanted to punish someone."

Tears welled, and she looked away, face tight with anger. "A few years ago," she said, "I had a friend in the compound. We'd have dinner every couple of weeks, maybe play cards or fish. I was walking back to my car one night, and Loren found me. He said he saw me across the yard, wanted to make sure I got back to my car safely. And when I did and tried to unlock it, he cornered me against the door. Said I was beautiful, and I deserved better than someone who made me walk around by myself after dark. 'There are wolves in the woods,' he said."

She nibbled at the edge of her lip, as if working over the words, then looked back at us. This time, a tear tracked down her cheek. "He put his hands on me, moved in to kiss me. Slid a hand up my skirt and . . ." She cleared her throat. "He assaulted me. I managed to get the door unlocked, told him to get his hands off me or I'd scream. He raised his hands and stepped away, smiling the whole time. I left the resort, had to stop on the old main road to be sick."

She swiped beneath both eyes. "I made it home, lost it. And I haven't been back to the resort since."

Theo leaned forward. "I'm very sorry that happened to you. He had no right to do it, and he should have been punished for his behavior."

"Yeah, well. I told the sheriff. He said he'd talk to Loren, and did, and Loren told him it was just a misunderstanding. He told the sheriff he'd been worried about me and had a witness who'd confirm he'd walked me back to the car, said good night, and that was it. The sheriff recommended I let it drop."

"I'm sorry for that, too," Theo said.

"People looked at me funny for a good month afterward. I just said I'd had a nightmare and got confused, and it wasn't a big deal. I didn't talk to him again after that. But I heard rumors that I wasn't the only one he approached. Zane told me what he'd done to Paisley. That he'd killed her. So I gave him what he asked for."

"And you didn't tell us about that last time because you didn't want them to get into trouble?" I guessed.

She blew out a breath, took in another, then squared her shoulders and looked at me. "I'm not licensed to make the magic, and I wasn't exactly sad to hear Loren was dead. Is that what you want me to confess?"

"We don't hand out absolution, Paloma. We're just trying to find the truth." *And a solution to the problem,* I thought. "Is there some kind of antidote?"

She just looked at me, expression blank. "An antidote?"

"Isn't there usually some way to reverse the effect? To get the shifters back to their normal condition, normal state?"

"Maybe theoretically. But like I said, I'm not a practitioner. Not really. I just dabble now and again. I don't keep grimoires or spell books in here. I just pick up things here and there—a charm on a message board online or whatever—and work from that."

"Do you have any of the potion left?" I asked. If there was any chance to correct the magic, we'd probably need it.

"No," she said, and again seemed confused by the question. "Why would I have kept any? I made it for them."

That was as much bafflement as I could stand.

Anger rode heavy in my blood, pushing the monster to the surface and sending its anger spilling over mine. But mine was stronger, hotter, more bitter.

I was out of my chair and heading for the door in seconds.

"You know how to reach us if you think of anything else," I heard Theo say behind me. "Here's my card. If they come back, lock yourself in back here and call me, okay?"

I didn't hear her response, and I walked outside, the bell ringing on the door as I let it shut behind me.

Once outside, I closed my eyes and gulped in fresh air. Even the whisper of broken magic that remained out here was better than the sad miasma inside.

I belatedly realized that I stood alone, that there were no more humans on the street, no law enforcement. If the sheriff had bothered to investigate the incident, he'd already packed up and moved on.

The bell on the door rang again. "You okay?" Theo asked when he reached me.

"I will be," I said, and opened my eyes. "Sorry I bailed. I reached my limit, and it was stifling in there. There's magic," I added, given his confused look. "She's lying about only dabbling in it. There were layers upon layers of old magic. I didn't sense it until we were in the back room, so I assume that's where she's working."

Theo whistled. "Any of it dark?"

"I don't think so, but that's not really my expertise. Either way, the Order will have plenty to discuss with her. She was victimized, and Loren should have been punished. But not this way. And not by building lies upon lies. Are you going to turn her in?"

"Oh yeah," he said slowly, as if savoring the words. "I don't generally like to be a narc, but in this particular case, I'm going to look forward to that contact. In fact . . . ," he began, then pulled out his screen, tapped out a message. "And done," he said after a moment, putting his screen away again. "I imagine she'll be hearing from the Order very soon."

"She may run for it."

"She may," he said. "But that kind of magic can be traced, at least according to the Order. She won't be able to pretend anymore."

"Good," I said. "And I forgot to ask. Did you win the auction for the comic book?"

"I did," he said. "All in all, a pretty interesting week."

A vehicle pulled up, and we both turned, ready to respond to an attack. But it was Connor in the SUV. We climbed inside.

"Any luck in the search of the environs?" I asked.

"Not according to Georgia," Connor said, then pointed to the go-cups tucked into the drink holders. "I got you both a coffee. Figured you could use a boost. There's also muffins."

"Not going to argue," Theo said, pulling one of the cups from a drink holder and taking a plastic-wrapped muffin bigger than my fist.

I took a sip of coffee, then rested my head back on the seat. "Oh yeah. That hits just the right spot."

"No comment," Theo said from the backseat. "But also yes. Thanks, man."

"No problem."

We sat in the vehicle for a moment, sampling our drinks.

"This is the best coffee I've had in a long time," Theo said.

"Same." I slid Connor a glance. "And it only took being attacked, defamed, and threatened to get it. The least you could have done was get this for me three days ago."

His eyes glittered with humor. "I wasn't aware you were cheap enough to be bought with a cup of coffee."

"It's spectacular coffee," I said. "So not entirely cheap. But also yes," I said, repeating Theo's phrase and settling in for a little bliss.

Theo updated Connor as we drove back to the resort, explained what the spellseller had said.

"Loren was an asshole," Connor said, turning into the parking space in front of the cabin. "And Cash should have handled him or called someone who would."

I turned around to look at Theo. "The clan and the sheriff have a financial arrangement. The clan helps fund his election campaigns, and he doesn't mess around in clan business."

"Gross" was Theo's assessment. I agreed.

"I don't like Paloma," I said, "and I don't respect her. She may have been victimized, and that was wrong. But she knew exactly what she was doing here. And there's something pitiable about the way she thinks about magic and revenge—that she never had any choices."

"That nothing was her fault or her responsibility," Theo said.

"Yeah. Exactly." There seemed to be a lot of that going around.

We found Georgia sitting at the kitchen island with Lulu, who balanced a sketch pad in the crook of her arm, was drawing a cluster of pinecones and birch bark she'd arranged on the kitchen island.

"I was just chatting with your sassy roommate," Georgia said with a smile.

"Her," I asked with a grin, "or the cat?"

Georgia's smile faded. "That cat's a goddamn menace."

Connor smirked at me, and I just rolled my eyes.

"You pronounced 'majestic' incorrectly," Lulu said, smirking as she swept pencil across paper in long, fluid strokes.

I sat down at the island to finish my muffin, lost half of it to Lulu, who nipped a chunk before I could slap her hand away.

"Beyo?" Connor asked.

"Cleaned up, unconscious, and under guard," Georgia said. "He's in one of the empty cabins. When he wakes up, he'll be restrained. We'll let you know so you can talk to him."

"Good," Connor said with a nod, nipped another chunk of my muffin.

"Dude."

"I didn't get one for myself."

Georgia smiled, seemed to enjoy the byplay. But the smile faded quickly enough, and she looked at me. "What did you learn?"

I gave the replay this time, telling Georgia about the cult and the magic. "Zane learned about the SOA, found her, paid her to make the spell. She knew they wanted to take on Loren, and claims he assaulted her, so she didn't ask any questions. Says she didn't know they'd turn into something, just thought they'd get stronger."

"This cult ring any bells for you?" Connor asked.

"This wouldn't be the first time humans tried to turn them-selves into werewolves. I don't know of any times it was actually successful—that someone transformed or became this hybrid you've mentioned."

"Maybe that's one reason it's all gone wrong," I said. "I mean, not just because the magic may not be good in the first place, but because they aren't humans. They're shifters. It would have af-fected them differently."

"I bet you're right," Connor said.

"We need to update the clan," Georgia said.

Connor looked at her for a quiet moment. "You know there's

a good chance Cash won't believe us. That we will lay out for him exactly what his shifters have been doing, and why, and he'll continue with his denial."

Georgia looked away, irritated by the words or the fact that she knew he was right. "The truth will out. And we'll see what happens then."

TWENTY-TWO

Georgia left to request an audience. Ironic, given she was an elder as well, but Cash and Everett apparently had some superior claim to that title. Based on what I'd seen so far, that seemed mostly the case because they had Y chromosomes.

"I'd like a favor," I told Connor when we were alone again in the cabin. Lulu planned to binge-watch a fashion competition in the RV, and Theo was cleaning his service weapon. Just in case.

"Anything."

I smiled at the quickness of his answer. "For the last few days, whenever we've been around Cash, I've played the guest, the girl-friend, the colleague—and that's fine. I'm comfortable being all those things. But I'm not just any of those things, so I've been playing this . . . role . . . for their benefit."

"And what's beneath the role?"

"Vampire. Not of the biting variety," I said, "given the clan has already seen the aftereffects of that. But the fighter. The swagger. I think it's time to show that side to the clan."

He watched me for a moment, considering. "We'll piss people off."

"Only if we're lucky," I said with a grin. "Like you said, the clan needs a little airing out. A disruption. Maybe a vampire in regalia will wake them up a little. And besides—you may be required by the Obsideo to solve their crisis, but they can't keep you from doing it on your own terms, right?"

"You have a point," he said. "And not just the katana."

"Or the fangs."

"Or," he said with a smile, "you be the vampire and I'll be the alpha, and we'll see what happens."

I hadn't brought many clothes, but I didn't need a closetful.

Black jeans. Black tank. Black boots. Simple, dark, powerful. I unraveled my braid, tossed my head, and shook out my hair. When I flipped my hair back, it made a long and wavy halo of soft gold around my shoulders. Lipstick of deep crimson, and my sword in hand. No scabbard, no belt. Just gleaming steel.

The rest was up to me.

When I walked back into the room, Theo, Lulu, Connor, and Alexei were waiting.

"About fucking time you showed a little fang," Lulu said, nodding as she looked at me. Theo and Alexei had similar looks of approval.

I'd have summed up Connor's expression in a single word: *Yes.*

"That's going to make quite an impression," Theo said.

"That's the idea," I said, wiggling my fingers around the corded braid of the katana handle, feeling for just the right grip. And enjoying the satisfaction when my fingers settled into just the right places.

I hoped I wouldn't need to use it to shed blood in a room of Connor's Packmates and kin. But that didn't make me a little regretful I wouldn't be able to use it at all.

They were assembled in the main room. Everett and Cash leaning lazily against the fireplace with cigars. The rest of the clan exuding nervous energy and plenty of anticipation.

Georgia joined Everett and Cash, while Alexei and Theo slipped into the back. Connor and I cut straight through the middle of the room, to the shock, surprise, and fury of several clan members.

There were outbursts from shifters, and I caught "blade" and "bitch" thrown around by some of them. I glanced back over my shoulder, met every gaze in turn, and dared them to step forward. To transform talk into action. And knew that none of them would.

"Quite a dramatic entrance," Cash said, then puffed on the cigar. "You want points for flair and originality?"

"We have an update," Connor said, voice flat and all pretense of politeness gone. And then he laid it out.

"Beyo, John, Zane, and Marcus," Connor said. "Members of your clan who've become interested in a cult called the Sons of Aeneas bought magic from the spellseller in Grand Bay in order to change themselves into more powerful creatures. They did that in order to punish Loren for his harassment of Paisley and his role in her death. The magic turned them into human-wolf hybrids, and they're responsible for the recent attacks, Loren's death, the Stone farm attack."

Behind us, the crowd erupted with noise. I didn't turn around, but could feel their anger at my back, the magic as hot as fire.

Everett's face showed every expression—shock, disbelief, anger. Cash remained stoic, his only movements the occasional puff of his cigar.

"That's quite a story," Cash said, raising his voice to be heard over the crowd. "And an interesting way to turn attention from you and your . . . *paramour*," he said, giving me a look so twisted with loathing and lasciviousness, it made my skin crawl, "to the clan."

He stubbed out the cigar in a glass ashtray on the high mantle, then turned to Connor, hands on his hips. "In other words, you blame us for the crisis. That's not going to release you from the Obsideo."

"We blame no one," Connor said. "We're just presenting the facts."

Cash snorted. "The facts always depend on who's telling the

tale. You have actual, biological proof that Zane and the others turned into these 'hybrids'?"

Connor arched an eyebrow. "Four members of your clan were present at the attack and saw the hybrids."

"And saw no transformation."

"Beyo transformed on a public street in town," I said, and Cash just rolled his eyes.

"Beyo is unconscious and hasn't told his side of the story. Bring me a clan witness, and we'll talk."

"You want DNA samples?" Connor asked.

"I'm asking you for anything other than this tall tale you're dumping at my door. Look, Zane's a problem child. We know it. We'll deal with it. But there is absolutely zero chance he pulled something like this off."

"And his visit to the spellseller?"

"You think a two-bit, third-rate sorceress is telling you the truth?" Cash's laugh was a humorless bark. "She sells garbage from China and has no appreciable skills."

"Okay," Connor said, crossing his arms. "I'll bite. What's your theory?"

"I have no idea," Cash said. "But all this started when you walked in that door. I don't know what kind of witchcraft you brought into our home. I won't let you turn this clan against itself. I won't let you use it to win political points with your father"—he looked at me again—"or the Houses."

Casually, he put an arm on the mantle. "We'll see what Beyo has to say. Then we'll know the truth, at least as far as Beyo is capable of giving it."

"And if someone dies in the meantime?" Connor asked.

Cash's gaze was hard and brutal. "Then we'll wonder how you managed to predict what would happen. You want to be released from the Obsideo, I suggest you go back to the drawing board."

* * *

We walked out of the lodge, assembled again in the clearing near the horseshoe pit.

"He's using you to cement his own power," Theo said. "Clever. Dickish but clever."

"Yeah," Connor said. "It's not a bad spin for short-term thinking. Spin the problem as caused by us, or complicated by us, or unresolved by us. Problem is, it falls apart in the long term."

"Because the clan falls apart in the long term," Georgia said grimly.

"Yeah," Connor said again. "We already know he doesn't trust the younger shifters, and we've handed him proof he was right. If he was smart, he'd use this situation to cement the elders' power—call it proof the younger generation isn't fit to rule. Instead, he's focused on Chicago versus the clan or vampires versus the clan."

"Outsiders versus the clan," Theo said, and Connor nodded.

"Exactly. Even if we're going, the intraclan struggles will still be there, simmering. Eventually, that pot boils over." He looked at Georgia. "You should consider putting more guards on Beyo."

"I want to object and say Cash wouldn't try to hurt him. But that would be a lie."

I nodded. "He's an eyewitness. The only certain link between clan and creatures."

"Beyo has responsibility here," Connor said. "But he's not responsible for everything. Cash takes Beyo out, and he's got a very tidy answer to his very thorny problem."

"Blame it on the spellseller and the bad egg," Theo agreed. "And everything's hunky-dory until the hybrids come back."

"Short term," Connor said again. "He's just arrogant enough to think that if he can solve the immediate problem, he'll have plenty of time to address the rest of it."

"A fucking disgrace," Georgia said, gaze narrowing at the lodge. "This clan has become a fucking disgrace."

"Unfortunately," Connor said, "I'm inclined to agree." And he watched warily as Maeve approached us. She was alone this time, and the obvious malice in her eyes was gone. Her expression was blank, so it didn't give me any idea of what she was actually thinking.

She nodded at Georgia, then turned to Connor. "That was quite a story you told."

"Not a story," he said. "The absolute truth."

She looked pained, but nodded. "I don't want to believe it, but I know Zane and the others. They're arrogant, sometimes stupid, and always complaining about the elders."

"Do you know anything specific about the creatures?" I asked.

She shook her head. "We weren't friends. Just acquaintances. It's not the kind of thing they'd have talked to me about." She looked away, then back at me. "Could we talk?"

I lifted my brows. "About?"

"You're going to make me say it aloud in front of everyone?"

I watched her for a moment. "Could you give us a minute?" I asked Connor.

He watched Maeve just as I'd done, considering, then nodded. "All right. Meet us back at the cabin."

"Sure." I waited until they'd walked away, then lifted my brows. "Well?" I asked Maeve.

Her eyes flashed, but this time I thought I saw respect in them. "You're a hard-ass—you know that?"

"I'm a vampire." I gave her a toothy smile. "So that's a compliment."

"Fair enough." She cleared her throat and didn't make eye contact for a long moment. "Miranda was rude about the Connor thing. I thought she had information about you—knew something about you using him. I don't know you very well—"

"You don't know me at all," I said.

"That's fair," she said after a moment. "I only know what I saw in the media, and what I've heard."

"From Miranda."

"From sources," she said. "There were rumors this was just a game for you. And I took those rumors for fact, because I didn't take the time to, you know, talk to you about my concerns. To be up-front. I just assumed and accused and was wrong, so now I look like the asshole. Because it's pretty obvious that you aren't using him."

"Finally, something we can agree on."

A corner of her mouth quirked. "I don't like you, but I kind of like you."

"I'd say the feeling's mutual."

She offered a hand. "Truce?"

I watched her for a moment. This hadn't been my fight. But we were going to need all the allies we could get. "Truce," I said, and we shook on it.

Georgia asked around the resort, and no one had seen Marcus, John, or Zane in a few days. And no one had any idea where to find them. Apparently, the comings and goings of twenty-something shifters weren't monitored.

With no trails to track the beasts and no more leads until we talked to Beyo, we gathered in the cabin. Lulu sat on the patio, using a white pencil to sketch the landscape on dark paper. I cleaned my sword while Theo worked remotely on his screen. Connor lay on the couch, eyes on the ceiling, frowning as he considered, evaluated, debated.

There was a knock at the back door, and we all looked warily at it. "I'll get it," Connor said, rising. "Elisa has a tendency to threaten people with her sword."

"It's not a tendency," I said, sliding a piece of rice paper down the length of the blade. "It's training."

Alexei was preceded by the smell of meat and sauce, and he walked into the kitchen, holding a tower of pizza boxes. "I ordered dinner."

"There are only five of us," I said as Lulu came inside, apparently drawn by the scents. "How much pizza do you think we're going to eat?"

Alexei placed the pizza on the island, began to spread out the boxes, and shrugged. "One of us is a vampire."

"All right," I said, holding up my hands. "We need to clear up this vampire eating thing."

"The thing where you eat everything in sight?" Lulu asked, peeking beneath a lid.

"I literally do not do that. I'm very discerning."

"*Picky,*" Lulu mouthed.

"So not constantly voracious," I said. "I'm not going to eat an entire pizza, and I don't think anyone else in here is, either."

"Speak for yourself," Theo and Connor said simultaneously, then looked at each other, nodded fraternally.

"This is not a war you will win," Lulu said, putting an arm around me. "So let's just eat and be merry and wait for someone to tell us where the bad guys are."

"Aw," I said, leaning into her. "You've been paying attention."

"As minimally as possible. Where's the pepperoni?" She flipped up a lid. "Bingo," she said, and grabbed a slice, began eating from the point.

"I also have beverages," Alexei said, pulling a bottle of honey-colored liquid from his jacket.

"I wouldn't say no to some mind erasing," I said. Unfortunately, it wasn't in the cards. Alcohol didn't work the same way for vampires as it did for humans; I could relax, enjoy a pleasant buzz. But that was usually the end of it.

"What is it?" Connor asked, and Alexei passed over the bottle. "Hell's Glen Fifteen," he said, then looked approvingly at Alexei. "Good choice."

Theo whistled. "That's quality."

Connor nodded, looked at me. "This will be good for your training."

"Training?" Lulu asked suspiciously.

"The wolf thinks I need to learn to appreciate good Scotch."

Lulu snorted, chewed pizza. "Good luck with that. She drinks chocolate wine."

Connor scowled, bit into his own slice of supreme. "So I've heard. It's a disgrace."

"Hey, we found something to agree on!" she said cheerily, and gave him a high five.

"You're both hilarious," I said, but was secretly pleased they weren't sniping at each other, even if at my expense. Since I didn't really care what I drank, it was a low-drag bargain.

"Found another option," Alexei said, looking through one of the kitchen cabinets. He pulled out a tall bottle. "Moscow's Own is not a vodka brand I recognize."

"Hard pass on that one," Theo said as Alexei found glasses in another cabinet, handed them out. "Light or dark?" he asked, holding up the bottles.

Lulu held out her cup. "Light me up, so to speak."

Alexei twisted off the screw cap—a sure sign of quality liquor—and poured a finger's worth.

Lulu just looked at him, cup still outstretched. "Don't be stingy."

He poured another finger, which apparently satisfied her. She took a drink, winced. "Good lord. Is there a basement beneath the bottom shelf? Because this is awful." She smacked her lips. "Like if someone burped legitimate vodka and bottled that."

"Then you can find the next bottle," Alexei said, brows raised.

"Great. I'll find something halfway decent."

"If your stomach isn't strong enough," Alexei said, "you could always pour it back into the bottle."

Eyes on Alexei, Lulu tipped back the cup, finished it off, then held it out again. "Next."

Alexei poured her another finger.

I crossed my arms, watched them. "I'm not sure if it's better or worse that she's found someone other than you to fight with."

Connor chuckled. "It does make for a change. And he's still a shifter, so at least she's keeping it in the family."

Since neither whiskey nor vodka sounded to me like a good match for pizza, I grabbed a bottle of blood from the fridge.

Theo cleared his throat. "So, at the risk of being a complete asshole, could I try a sip?"

"Sure," I said, and offered him the bottle.

After a heartening breath, he took a drink, then winced, handed it back. "Not for me. It's like drinking pennies."

"I've never eaten a penny, so I'll take your word for it." I took the bottle back, finished it in a single gulp.

Then realized the others were watching me.

"Sorry," I said, and wiped my mouth with the back of my hand. "Too vampiric?"

"No," Connor said with a light in his eyes that was hard to mistake.

"It's cool," Theo agreed, then cleared his throat again, looked down at his slice. "And I should probably just eat this pizza."

"Wise choice," Connor said with a grin. "Wise choice."

We ate and talked like normal people—not a collection of Sups trying to solve a problem and release a handsome prince from an evil spell.

The Scotch was poured, sipped. "Jesus," I said between coughs, fairly certain someone had replaced the alcohol with gasoline.

Lulu snorted. "I told you. It's not her thing."

"Take even tinier sips," Alexei said, ignoring her. "Just enough to wet your lips. You'll taste the caramel that way."

I sipped again, barely touching tongue to liquid. And, okay, if I breathed just right, I could detect a mellowness that wasn't awful. But liking it might be a challenge that required immortality.

"At the risk of blowing up this great party," Theo said, swirling the whiskey in his glass, "do you think Cash is going to be satisfied with whatever you tell him?"

"Words?" Connor asked. "No. Evidence? Maybe. Ultimately, Cash will believe what he wants. But he can't avoid Beyo forever, and we're going to find the rest of them. The clan will see the truth, and there's a pretty good chance it will change the balance of power."

"In that case, we look forward to the big reveal," Theo said, tipping an invisible hat in Connor's direction.

"Have you heard from Ronan?" Lulu asked.

"No," I said. "It's day two, so they'd still be feeding her. I think he'd tell me if she hadn't made it, at least so he could blame me for it."

"Lot of guilt throwing in Minnesota these days," Lulu said. "What happened to Minnesota nice?"

"Only applies to humans," Theo said.

"I guess."

"Will you be able to . . . control her?" Alexei asked.

It was the kind of question that might have rankled, if there hadn't been genuine curiosity in his eyes.

"No," I said. "Even Masters don't control the vampires they make. They usually have a telepathic connection, and a Master can call the other—make them come to the Master. From the way my father tried to describe it, there's a more general connection. Not parent and child, exactly, but something protective. But she didn't have much of my blood, so that probably won't happen here."

It wouldn't be tested unless Ronan allowed me near her again. And he didn't like or trust me.

"Sup life is hard," Lulu said, taking a sip. "That's why I opted out."

"You could use your power for good," Alexei said, and the look she gave him had nothing friendly in it.

"I beg your pardon?"

"You've got good magic. I can tell." He lifted a shoulder. "It's a waste for you not to use it."

Lulu stiffened. "You don't know anything about me or my magic."

"I know enough," he said.

"I think you should mind your own business. Power corrupts," she said. "It changes the person who uses it. It changes the people around. It becomes a bargaining chip, something to fear. Just look around," she said, spinning a finger in the air to indicate the cabin. "This entire resort consists of shifters who don't want humans to know what they are. That's not so very different from what I've done."

"They're still shifters in private," Alexei said.

"And I am who I am," Lulu said. "I can't change it. But I'm not the only person in the world with a skill they aren't using. Humans who speak multiple languages don't get chastised because they enter into careers other than being translators. And if humans are allowed to have gifts and not use them, so am I."

I couldn't argue with that—and wouldn't, even if I'd wanted to. Her magic—her genetic gift and burden—was hers to carry.

Alexei just watched her, quiet and still, then nodded once. An acknowledgment of what she'd said.

"So," Theo said, breaking the awkward silence that followed, "what was it like?"

"What was what like?"

"The biting. And this isn't prurient interest," he added, hands raised in innocence as he smiled at Connor. "I'm just curious."

"It was . . . odd," I said after a moment's consideration. "Mentally, it felt like a violation—given the circumstances. But physically, it felt natural. It felt vampiric. I've bitten vampires before—two of them. Both in Paris, but it wasn't like this."

"Who'd you bite before?" Connor asked with a heavy air of "Who do I need to beat up?"

I shifted my gaze to him, grinned. "A single vampire in Paris is going to be a single vampire in Paris."

He humphed. "Have you ever tasted a shifter's blood?"

The heat rose to my cheeks so quickly, I might have been on fire. On one level, we were having a perfectly average conversation about our normal biological processes. But beneath it was something more—curiosity, anticipation, interest.

"I haven't," I quietly said, and kept my gaze on him. "Are you offering?"

"Things are getting warm in here," Lulu said, rising from her seat, "and that is very much our cue to exit."

Connor just smiled . . . wolfishly.

"Do we have a plan for tomorrow?" Theo asked.

"We check if the searches have found anything," Connor said, "and we talk to Beyo and we see where that leads."

We walked to the cabin door. They'd moved the RV to a larger lot about forty yards from the cabin.

"You want me to walk you back to the RV?" I asked. "Or Connor can."

"Oh, I'm not going back to the RV."

I shifted my gaze to Connor, lifted my brows. "Why not?"

"Because I'm not going near the cat." He looked up, then toward the window. "She was staring at me through the window."

"She was looking outside," Lulu said. "You just happened to be there."

"She had malice in her eyes."

"She always has malice in her eyes," Lulu said. "It's her nature." She rose. "Come on, Lis. You can walk me back. You're brave enough to face her."

"I live with her," I said. "She knows where I sleep. Seeing her through a window's the easy part."

The air had cooled by the time we walked outside, a nice breeze flowing off the lake. It was a hint of the winter to come, which would be even harsher here than in windblown Chicago.

Theo stayed a few paces behind me and Lulu, giving us space to talk.

"He's afraid of her," Lulu said as we walked across a field of overgrown grass. I worked to not think about what might be sliding through it.

"He has no reason to be afraid," I said. "He's enormous, as a man and a wolf."

Lulu snickered. "Like you'd know."

"Context clues," I said with a grin.

"Look, from a psychic standpoint, when you get down to the attitude and the magnificence, she weighs a ton."

I glanced at her. "Why are you kissing up to the cat?"

"I'm doing no such thing. I merely recognize her worth. And her very acute sense of hearing."

I looked up toward the RV. Eleanor of Aquitaine had planted herself in a windowsill, watching, waiting. "She hid something again, didn't she?"

"I have no idea what you're talking about."

I laughed, low and easy. "She did. She hid something you need, and you're trying to get it back. What was it?"

Lulu rolled her eyes. "My screen, okay? She took my screen, and I have no idea where she put it."

"Of course she did."

*   *   *

I deposited Theo and Lulu in the RV and made my way back to the cabin and was shocked to meet Arne and Marian, the shifters we'd met on the way to Grand Bay, coming up the path. They both wore light jackets, carried to-go cups of fragrant coffee.

Why had they driven all the way out here? I wondered, and hoped the violence hadn't spread to their home.

"Hey," I said, walking toward them. "Is everything okay?"

"I think we need to ask you that," Marian said, giving me a hug. "How are you and Connor?"

"Okay for now," I said. "What are you doing here?"

Arne held up his cup. "We're taking a turn on shutter duty today."

"Shutter duty—" I began, and it took me a moment to figure out what he'd meant. "You drove up here to stand guard?"

"We did," Marian said. "Connor is important to us, and you're important to him. Alexei put in a call, so we came."

Probably hearing voices, or because he was making sure I'd made it back from the RV lot, Connor walked out of the cabin and looked as surprised as I probably had. "Everything okay?"

"They're guarding us today," I said, saving them the second explanation. "Alexei asked them to."

"You didn't have to drive up," Connor said, giving them both hugs. "But I appreciate that you did." He gestured to their cups. "You've got enough caffeine?"

"We're fine," Marian said.

"We've got pizza if you're hungry," I said. "Someone ordered too much."

"We're good, but thank you."

"How were the girls' recitals?" I asked.

"A few tears," Arne said, "a few blank stares, and a whole lot of cute. I might have gotten a little teary-eyed."

"Same," Marian said. "Misty Copeland they were not, but they had a lot of fun. And we took a lot of pictures. We'll send you some."

"I'd love to see them," I said, for some reason imagining the girls dressed as dancing fruits and vegetables.

And speaking of food . . . "I think you've got more provisions on the way," Connor said, gesturing to the mulch path.

Ruth, Rose, and Traeger walked toward us, Traeger carrying a plastic cooler. Rose limped a little, her right leg in a sturdy brace, but she was upright and moving.

"How's the pin?" Connor asked, putting a hand on her shoulder.

"I won't be bowling for a while," she said with obvious frustration. "But I got to kick some monster ass, so that helped."

"What's all this?" I asked as Traeger put the cooler on the patio.

"Beverages," Ruth said with a smile. There was a bruise on her forehead, a healing cut on her face, but she looked much better than she had the last time I'd seen her. "Saw you in the lodge," she said. "You looked good with the sword."

"Thank you."

"We figured," Rose said, "if we're going to guard this place, we might as well do a little recreational day drinking." She opened the cooler, pulled out a can of beer. "Let's get to work."

We repeated our cold pizza offer, which Ruth and the others declined. But they accepted hugs and heaping thanks before settling themselves in.

"It's going to put them at risk," I said when we'd gone inside. "I don't like that."

"I don't, either," Connor said. "But you need sleep, and I can't stay awake twenty-fours at a time. So we'll let them help us and be grateful for it."

"I wish I baked."

He arched an eyebrow. "What?" he asked, a smile lifting one corner of his mouth.

"I wish I baked so I'd have something useful to give them. Muffins or something to say thank you." I frowned. I didn't really have any hobbies other than yoga and dealing with supernatural drama, which was practically a job, anyway. "I need a hobby."

"Two separate conversations," Connor said. "They don't need a gift. They're being generous because they want to and because that's the type of people they are. They don't need us to validate that. And hobbies, yes. Everyone should have a hobby. I have Thelma."

"I'll think on it," I said.

"Perhaps you could . . . play the vampire."

"What?" I looked up at him, found his lips parted, his eyes hot and intense. I cocked an eyebrow. "Enjoyed that, did you?"

Before I could respond, his body was pressed against mine, and it was abundantly clear just how much he'd enjoyed it.

I wrapped my arms around his neck, kissed him well and thoroughly. And I would have raked fangs against his neck if there hadn't been five keen-eared shifters outside.

"Vampire and wolf," I said when the kiss cooled, and I rested my head against his chest, was calmed by the beating of his heart. "Who'd have thought?"

"Nature," he said simply.

TWENTY-THREE

It was early when I rose, the world just going dark. The sun had already slipped below the horizon, which was marked in brilliant shades of yellow and orange. I walked outside and stretched, considered going for a run. Last night's breeze had apparently been a harbinger of fall-like weather, as the temperature had dropped again during the day. A low fog had descended in the chill, rolling across the lake like smoke.

And I saw Lulu beside the lake, a small shadow against the marked sky.

I walked her way as birds shuffled in the trees and fires began to crackle on the other side of the resort.

She sat on a low stool, knees together and ankles spread, a wooden box on an easel in front of her. She dabbed orange paint on a canvas the size of a postcard. Half a dozen more canvases—the sunset in various stages of production—littered the ground around her.

"I'm trying to grab the light before it's completely gone," she said without looking up. "It's hard to capture the sky when it keeps changing."

"Looks like you're doing a good job of getting each stage." Careful with the edges, I picked one canvas up. It had been finished just before dusk, the sun a globe of light at the edge of the world, the sky just beginning to blush.

"This is gorgeous," I said, and wondered—not for the first

time—what it would have been like to see a sunrise or sunset from beginning to end.

"Thank you," she said, frowning as she switched to a buttery yellow, began to place highlights among the clouds. "I'm only going to have a couple more minutes before it's gone."

"I'll wait," I said, and stared quietly across the lake. Watched the waves move hypnotically toward the shore, and let myself relax. It might have been the first time on this not-vacation that I'd done that. But my mind didn't slow. Not just because of everything that was going on here, but because of the decisions I knew I had to make when I went back.

I'd grown up with martial arts classes, piano lessons, tutors. In Paris, I'd started school again, had lessons. My life had been scheduled, regimented, and I'd liked it that way. Graduation, then service to the House of vampires; my nights had still been ordered around my obligations.

Now I was the guest of a friend, a temporary Ombud, and a woman—for the first time in her life—who didn't really have a mission.

"I need a hobby."

"Well aware," she said as the sky darkened, orange flaming against purple.

"Maybe I could learn to paint."

"No."

Her answer was just fast enough to be insulting. "Why not?"

"Because you're literal. You like rules. Art—even realistic art— is about pushing past boundaries, perception, concepts."

I didn't like the answer, even if I found no basis to disagree with it.

"I also need a new mission," I said.

"There we go," she said. She dabbed the brush in liquid I knew was mineral spirits, then wiped it on a towel. "I knew this trip was

going to help you start asking questions." She glanced up at me.
"Before now, you were waiting."

"For what?"

"To make peace with the life you thought you'd have so you
can move on to the next one. We've already discussed that you
shouldn't be a bureaucrat. Speaking of the OMB, did you know
Theo can juggle?"

"I did not. He gave you a demonstration?"

"Accidentally. It's a long and cat-vomit-filled story." She waved
that away. "But that's a road trip tale for another time. We're discussing your ennui."

"I don't—," I began to argue, then realized she was right. She'd
been right when we talked in Chicago, even though I hadn't liked
hearing it. "I still don't know what comes next. How do I figure
that out?"

"If it was me, I'd start with what *doesn't* come next. You don't
like working for the OMB. Why?"

"I don't not like it. But I wouldn't call it fulfilling."

She smiled, as if pleased by the admission. "Good. You seem
to enjoy supernatural drama, as much as I detest it."

"I'm not sure if that's a compliment."

"It's neutral. But the OMB, from what you've told me and approximately two hundred complaints from my father, is about ten
percent drama and ninety percent paperwork. So you need a job
that tips that scale." She looked at me. "Have you had fun on this
trip?"

My instinctive reaction was to say no, to protest that there'd
been too much violence, too many people hurt, too much frustration. But that wasn't the full truth.

"Yeah," I said. "It's been . . . thrilling. Even with the bad parts,
I've liked being out here with him, digging into this crisis."
Watching people, I thought silently. And deciphering what I saw

there. "But there's no alternate career path for fixing magical drama. That's just the OMB."

"You could be a supernatural special agent."

"I think I need a covert government agency for that."

"You could create one."

"I'm confident, but not 'I am my own country' confident."

"You know what I mean," she said. "Look, you care about Supernaturals. You care about what happens to them. And apparently you're pretty good at figuring out why something is wrong and fixing it." She shrugged. "You just need a title and a client willing to pay your rate structure. Which will be very, very generous."

"So your solution is I should invent a job for myself and find people to pay me a lot of money."

"I mean, in a few words, yes."

There were footsteps behind us. We both glanced back, found Connor on the path.

"Did they find the hideout?" I asked.

"No, but Beyo's awake," he said, eyes narrowed in purpose. "Let's go see what he has to say."

Another cabin, another round of shabby decor. We found Alexei standing in front of the open fridge, back to us as we came in.

"Suspect security," Connor said. "You can't even be bothered to lock the door?"

"I'm the one who told you to come," he said, closing the door and turning while he unsealed a soda bottle. "And I knew you'd opened the door, because her magic's different."

Connor just humphed, because he couldn't really argue with that. "How is he?"

"Looks like shit. Had a sports drink, some aspirin."

"Any flashbacks?"

"Not so far. But we haven't let him shift."

"You can do that?" I asked, brows raised.

Alexei took a drink, nodded. "Shifting takes magic. We have a method to block that."

"The Apex can do it alone," Connor said. "But without the Apex, it takes a few."

"And there are at least a few of us on the side of right and justice these days."

"Anyone else come by?" Connor asked.

"Everett and a couple of others came by earlier, looked like they were in a fighting mood." He gestured to the shotgun on the table. "I told them they were welcome to come in if they wanted."

"Did they want to talk to him?" I wondered. "Or did Cash tell them to come?"

"That's the question," Alexei agreed. "Cash hasn't been here yet."

"We are," Connor said.

Alexei gestured toward the hallway. "He's in the bedroom. I'll stay here."

Connor squeezed his shoulder, and we walked down the hallway. A bookshelf had been moved in front of the back door, presumably so Alexei only had one door to guard. A door to the left was open, and we looked inside.

Beyo lay on a bare mattress in a room empty but for a stack of boxes in one corner. His arms were extended at his sides, cuffed to the steel supports of the bed frame.

Alexei had been right. Other than his skin having a little less gray pallor, he didn't look any healthier than he had the night before. He wore jeans and a T-shirt that bagged on his gaunt frame, raw scrapes and bruises visible where cotton didn't cover.

His eyes were open, staring at the ceiling. He jerked when Connor knocked on the doorframe, lifted his head before dropping it back again.

There was misery in his face, mixed with what I thought was guilt. Feeling guilty was probably his first good decision in a very long time.

"Beyo," Connor said. "You know who I am."

"Yeah."

"I take it you're one of the Sons of Aeneas?"

Beyo's head popped up again, surprise in his eyes. "You know."

"We have pieces," Connor said. "The Sons, the spellseller, Loren. We don't have the full story. And you're going to tell me, right now, or we're going to have an even larger problem than we already do."

Beyo swallowed, lay back again. "It started with Paisley. Or she was the first time we got serious."

"Got serious about?" Connor asked.

"Making changes. Fixing things around here. Cash, Loren, Everett, the rest of them. We've been pissed for a long time and tried to get someone to pay attention, to do what needed to be done around here. But they're living in the past. And then Paisley happened." He looked up again, and anger was a fire in his eyes. "He killed her."

"You have evidence of that?"

Beyo muttered something. "How the fuck were we supposed to get evidence? You think Loren didn't fix things? Didn't arrange things just so to cover his tracks? He was the last one to see Paisley alive, and then she was dead. He has a reputation around here, you know. For getting whatever he can from the women of the clan and taking what he can't get willingly."

Connor didn't ask for evidence this time, presumably because he had expected the same answer. "So you decided to get even," he said.

"We decided to get stronger," he said. "Cash, Everett, Loren, they're all old. Their time is done. We were going to work together, take the lead."

"Because none of you were strong enough to take him individually. None of you alpha enough to challenge him for the clan. So you decided to cheat."

Beyo rose up, strained against his bonds with enough force to make the metal creak in protest. "What the fuck do you know about it? You're in Chicago, living it up. We're out here. Pack but not really, right? Barely making it."

"We are Pack," Connor said, each word bitten off as his anger and frustration grew. "Pack takes care of Pack—if we know there's a goddamn problem. You could have come to us. You could have come to me."

"Whatever," Beyo said. "We did what we had to do."

Connor pulled a hand across his jaw, visibly worked to maintain his control. "You learned about the Sons of Aeneas."

"Zane was screwing around online, trying to find a way to make us stronger. He learned about the SOA, how werewolves were descended from Romulus and Remus. They founded Rome. That just proved we were powerful. That we were supposed to be leaders. That we weren't supposed to be in goddamn hiding. We did some more digging, found they had this spell that got passed down from generation to generation to turn humans into wolves. Hybrids. Since we're already shifters, we figured it would just make us more powerful. So we went back to the shop. Told her what we needed. At first, she didn't want to. Said she didn't do that kind of thing, didn't have magic, but we knew that was bullshit. She's a sorceress, right? And she had a book on the SOA, even. She eventually made the stuff."

"Did she know why you wanted it?" I asked, curious how much of what she'd told us had been the truth.

Beyo went silent.

"Answer her," Connor said.

"She knew we were pissed at Loren. That's why Zane picked her—why we went to her. He's got a friend who's a friend of hers. Said he'd tried to hurt her one night. So he mentioned we had some issues with Loren, wanted to be able to face him down. She gave us the potion, and we drank it."

"And transformed," Connor said.

Beyo closed his eyes. "It was fucking amazing. First time we shifted, boom! We were huge. Strong. Fierce. Had all this energy, all this power. That was a few weeks ago. Only takes a drop of the potion each time, so we were careful with it."

"And you made a plan to kill Loren."

"We destroyed him," Beyo said shamelessly. "Left his body at the waterfall so it would be found. So Cash and Everett and the others would know they weren't invulnerable. That there was something out there stronger than them."

"We already know you attacked Beth because she saw you."

"We didn't want to hurt her," Beyo said. "She didn't do anything wrong. But we had plans, and we didn't want anyone to know about them."

"And the Stone farm?" Connor asked.

"Zane told us what they were doing—encroaching on our territory. Trying to take our woods a few yards at a time. He heard them partying, and he lost it. We figured he knew best, so we went with him. And he went crazy."

"Did he?" Connor's tone was flat, unimpressed.

"At first, we were going to scare them off. Douse the fire. Make sure they'd leave our land alone next time. But there was blood in the air, and he just lost it. John and Marcus just lost it."

"And did you lose it, Beyo?" Connor moved a step closer. "Is that why Carlie was ripped to shreds? Because you couldn't control yourself?"

"Zane did that."

Connor's laugh was hard and mirthless. "You're all fucking cowards."

"We're not cowards. We're doing what needs to be done." Beyo shifted his gaze, now furious, to me. "We found out you bit Carlie. We went back into the woods, could read the blood on the ground. You changed her and still didn't get punished for it. That was more of the same—more bullshit by the clan that refuses to stand up. So we went for the shutters. That didn't work, and the next night the clan went fucking easy on you. I was going back to the store, was going to scare that woman into giving us more potion, fixing it so the transformation was easier. And then saw you."

"And saw an opportunity," I guessed. "But couldn't control the transformation, fell out of the hybrid form too quickly."

"Yeah."

"Cowards," Connor said again. "You all nearly killed Carlie, and Elisa saved her, and you want her punished for that? What kind of fucking sense does that makes, Beyo? And then—and then—because you're cowards, instead of calling Elisa out and fighting her, you tried to kill her in her sleep. And when you saw me, you just ran away. Wouldn't face me, either."

"We're the only ones who can fix the clan," he said, but without much conviction.

"You're killers," Connor said, disgust in his voice. "You hurt people because you're too weak or cowardly to call a challenge, call a vote, or call the Apex."

He moved forward again, until his shins grazed the edge of the bed, until he leaned over Beyo. "Loren was a predator and a disgrace. And I'd have liked to get my hands on him, to explain to him—very clearly—what it meant to be Pack. Now I can't do that. The Pack can't do that. He should have been made to understand what he'd done. To make amends for it, to be stripped of his Pack membership and turned over to the humans. Because you played judge, jury, and executioner, he won't get the years of punishment he deserves. Do you know how that makes me feel, Beyo?"

Beyo just looked away.

"Angry," Connor said. "Very, very angry." He walked away, put space between him and the bed.

"Where are Marcus, John, and Zane?" I asked.

No answer.

"If she has to ask again," Connor said, "we're both going to regret it." There was a threat in his words—a danger—that I hadn't heard from Connor before. A ruthlessness that said he understood that leadership often meant unpleasant things in order to protect the collective.

"Beyo," I said quietly, "you helped us tonight because you knew what they were doing—playing vigilante—was wrong. You know their hurting Carlie was wrong. Don't let them hurt anyone else. Let us find them before they hurt someone else and before they're too far gone to come back from this. Tell us where they are."

Beyo swallowed. "There's a cavern out by the waterfalls. You follow the trail that runs past the creek. When the trail ends, you follow the creek for a while, and there's a cave back behind some boulders. The local SOA chapter has a Web site, and it talks about the cavern—that's how we found it. It was used for some of their rituals. We said we'd make the cavern legit. Not just a club, not just a cult. But real. The Sons of Aeneas, like meeting our destiny." He sighed heavily, chest rising and falling and so thin, I could see the outline of his ribs through his shirt. "If they're thinking like humans, they'll go there. Lay low until the coast is clear. And if they aren't there, I don't know. It's getting harder to come back."

"What do you mean?" I asked.

"Every time we change, it gets harder to remember who you are. Harder to not feel like you're just the wolf. Only the wolf."

A chill snaked up my spine. That was a feeling I could very much relate to, and it was a little unnerving to hear it described so well.

"Broken magic," Connor said quietly, and I nodded. "Who will they attack next?" he asked.

"I don't know."

"Will they try again for Elisa?" Connor asked. "They've already failed twice."

"You and Elisa," Beyo said, and Connor's eyes went wide. "She's your responsibility. Zane said you should both be punished."

Connor's look was a mix of pity and anger. "Who else?"

"I don't know," Beyo said. "Whoever hasn't done right by the clan."

Defined, I thought, *by a bunch of narcissistic and magically damaged twenty-year-olds with savior complexes.*

Connor looked at Beyo for a quiet moment. "Anything else you want to tell me?"

Beyo shook his head. "I want to sleep now. I just want to sleep."

We left him alone, returned to the living room. Alexei sat in a dining room chair he'd turned toward the door, crossed his ankles on the table. He looked back over his shoulder when we walked in, then kicked his feet down again, rose.

"You get anything?"

"Explanation and possible location. Magic's gone bad, twisted them," Connor said. "They're having trouble coming back from the shift."

"What will happen to Beyo now?" I asked.

"Whatever the Pack decrees," Connor said. "Given one Pack member is dead by his hand, others injured, he may not survive the punishment."

The Pack lived by its own code, which was probably one of the reasons Connor had been so angry at what Beyo and the others had done. The Pack was there to enforce, to protect. Beyo and his friends had tried to bypass that system and hurt other Pack members in the process.

"You think Cash will believe all this?"

"Oh, I wouldn't worry about that." Connor slid his screen

halfway from his pocket. "Had the recorder function engaged." He slid it back again. "But I'm thinking about not telling him."

"Interesting choice," Alexei said.

"They used a cavern out by the waterfalls," Connor said. "You know it?"

Alexei shook his head. "No. That where the others are?"

"Maybe. Maybe not." Hands on his hips, Connor looked out the window. "I'm trained to defer to leadership. Here, that's the clan, the elders. But what happens when shit goes bad? When the elders go bad?"

"Oh, that one's easy," Alexei said. "When the elders go bad, you call in the big dog." He clapped Connor on the shoulder. "In this case, my friend, that's you."

TWENTY-FOUR

We walked outside, breathed deeply of fresh night air. Connor moved away from us, stared into the darkness with hands on his hips, strain around his eyes, and anger still tightening his jaw.

"We'll meet you back at the cabin," I told Alexei.

He watched Connor for a moment, probably to be sure leaving him was the right move, then nodded. "There any pizza left?"

"There is. And it's yours if you'll give Theo an update." I'd totally forgotten to grab Theo before we'd come to talk to Beyo. On the other hand, Beyo probably wouldn't have spoken so candidly with another stranger in the room.

Alexei nodded, walked toward the cabin. I waited until we were alone, then asked, "Are you okay?"

Connor's responsive grunt was heavy with misery.

"Anything I can do?"

He looked back at me, brows lifted. "My Packmate just confessed he'd tried to kill you because, long story short, he thought my family was useless. And yet you offer to help?"

"I . . . care about you," I said.

His grin was charming, wicked. "How much did that cost you?"

"A lot, punk. So don't push it."

With a laugh that rang with relief, he pulled me into his arms. "I can hardly call you a brat right now."

"Then save us both the trouble," I said, and relaxed into him, let the warmth of his body burn away the disgust.

I didn't have my mother's appetite, but there was no denying the scent of leftover pizza was intoxicating when we walked back into the cabin. Theo, Alexei, and Lulu were already around the table, tucking into folded slices.

"Thanks for waiting," I said, and grabbed a slice of pepperoni from the nearly empty box.

"It's fine," Lulu said. "I painted Theo sprawled like an ancient god."

I chewed cheese and meat, looked speculatively at him. "Really?"

"No." Theo sipped a soda. "I talked to the Order—which is on its way to Grand Bay to have a very long conversation with Paloma."

"Good," Connor said. "She needs oversight from someone. She's too dangerous on her own."

"What did you learn?" Theo asked.

"We're looking for a cavern," I said, and gave the group the brief version of Beyo's story. "Supposedly there's a cave past the waterfalls used by a prior Sons of Aeneas group. Beyo and the others found it online using information they took from the spell-seller, and they made it their HQ. They might still be there."

"Oh," Lulu said, swallowing a bite. "I've seen this."

We all looked at Lulu.

"You have?" Connor asked.

"Sure. I was doing some research on the way up, figuring out where I wanted to paint. I was considering the waterfalls because there are photos online of the trails, and they looked cool. There are a few videos, too, and I actually watched the video for this one. It looks like snake city. Sorry," she added at my involuntary whimper.

"I'm sure it's fine," I lied.

"She won't even eat udon," Lulu said, pity coloring her voice.

I looked at Connor. "This is private property, right? The waterfalls and surrounding area."

"It is," he said. "But I seriously doubt they asked for permission. And we're going to bypass that for the time being. Apologies later instead of asking first."

"If we find them there," I asked, "how do we get them out again?"

"Unconscious?" Theo offered. "Worked well for Beyo."

Connor smiled. "That would be my preference. Easier to move. And if Beyo's any indication, they won't be very heavy." His voice was grim but determined.

"You want me here or there?" Alexei asked.

"You'd better stay here," Connor said. "Just in case they show up before we do." And then he nodded surreptitiously toward Lulu, got Alexei's answering nod.

Since I appreciated the gesture, the fact that Alexei would keep a protective eye on her, I didn't argue with the method.

"You think you could guide us?" I asked Lulu.

"I'm not going on a monster hunt."

"No," I said, "you aren't. But you know this place and apparently the virtual tour. You can guide us." I held up my screen. "Electronically. Assuming you found your screen?"

"I found it. And I'm not willing to go into further detail. You'll let me know if there are any painting-worthy spots?"

"Absolutely."

"You want to tell Cash before or after you go out there?" Alexei asked.

Connor sat back, linked his hands behind his head. "I don't know. Frankly, we're probably likely to get the same result either way."

"Denial," I suggested.

"Yeah," Connor said. "But I have to think our chances of success are better if we come back with Zane and the others in hand."

"Then let's get to it," I said.

We drove the same road we'd taken the night of the initiation, parked along the road near the trail. Ours was the only vehicle, and I hadn't thought to ask Beyo how they'd gotten this far into the woods. It had to be at least ten miles between the resort and the waterfalls; had they run all that way?

We took the trail, passing the waterfalls and the spot where Loren had been found, and traveled deeper into the woods. After five more minutes of walking, the trail dwindled, disappeared.

"To the right," Lulu said, voice ringing through our screen-linked earpieces. "There's a pass up ahead, and we go through that, then over the boulders. That's a bit of a scramble."

"On that," I said, and we veered toward the right. The terrain was relatively flat here, the ground soft and loamy, with silver birch towering above us.

"There are some really great rock formations on the other side of the waterfall, up the bluff a little. All right," she said after a moment. "You're getting close. It's about twenty or thirty yards around that bend. Just hug the rock, and you'll see it."

"I'm going to take the lead," Connor said. "Elisa behind me," he whispered. "Sword out. Then Theo."

"The cheese stands alone," Theo said, and I gave that the sad trombone sound it deserved.

We slipped through the woods, keeping the bluff to our right, until we could hear the soft ping of water against rock.

Connor held up a hand, and we waited in silence, ears perked, listening.

There was no sound, no movement, no magic, or at least not recently.

"They're gone," I said quietly.

"But we stay careful and alert," he said, and moved forward . . . and stared at the gaping maw in the earth.

"Cavern," I asked, "or hellmouth? You be the judge."

"Hellmouth," Lulu and Theo said simultaneously.

The cavern was a low, long gap in the face of the bluff, the stone red around the edges. The sound of water grew louder, a few insistent drips, as did the echoes of water on rock.

"Let's go in," Connor said, then turned to Theo. "Can you stay out here and talk to Lulu?"

"I was just going to suggest I stay here," Theo said. "I'm not crazy about cramped spaces."

"Good," Connor said. "Keep an eye on the perimeter. If you see them, fire one in the air. We probably won't be able to use comms with all that stone."

"Done," Theo said.

"And be careful!" Lulu said. "Especially with snakes."

"Bringing it up isn't making it better," I told her. But we made our way in.

Stone arced above us, the ceiling just high enough to stand in. The ground was carpeted in pebbles and looked dry. The water was somewhere in the distance, in the shadows ahead.

I followed Connor across the space, feeling my way over uneven rocks. The cave was probably forty feet across, then narrowed to a damp hallway of seeping, mineral-streaked rock that was cold and a little slimy to the touch. And would be a very unfortunate bottleneck if we found the shifters at the other end of the tunnel and had to get out again.

The ceiling dipped, grew lower, so we had to crouch to move through. I wasn't claustrophobic, but the sensation of moving through and under solid rock caused cold sweat to slip down my spine.

I was alternating my gaze between my feet and Connor's back, and still nearly tripped when we crossed a threshold into another room.

"Damn," Connor said, standing straight again. "Look at this."

I wasn't sure if he meant the space or what was in it. Because both were extraordinary.

We'd entered a chamber cut into rock, the ceiling forty feet above us. The room was roughly circular, cut by wind or water or the movement of the earth into what seemed now like a geological cathedral. White stalactites dripped down from the ceiling and glittered in the beam of our flashlight. The walls were brown and ocher stone. They'd been marked by wind and rain, as well. But also by humans.

There were paintings—not the Paleolithic variety, but made by modern hands. Two stylized humans suckling from a she-wolf, and "Sons of Aeneas" painted in sweeping colors. An altar had been made of one stone formation, covered by a red cloth now stained by time and geological processes.

"I'm guessing this is the cavern," I said quietly, touching fingers to the painting. "Chalk," I said, rubbing the grit through my fingers. "It requires less equipment than painting."

Lulu would be proud that I'd learned something.

"They've been sleeping here," Connor said, and I glanced back. He was crouching near a depression in the wall. "Sleeping bags, camping supplies. No dust. It's been recently used."

"But not tonight," I said. "Beyo's been gone a while. Maybe they panicked, changed hiding places."

Something glinted in the dirt. I kneeled, brushed away dust, and picked up my dagger. The one I'd lost at the farm; the one that had been buried in the back of the silver beast.

"They've been here since the bonfire," I said, and cleaned off the dirt, held the dagger up for Connor to see. And where were they now?

* * *

"Empty," I told Theo and Lulu when we emerged from the cavern. "They've been using it, but not tonight. Any sign out here that they might have gone anywhere else?"

Theo shook his head. "No footprints other than the tracks we've already made."

I frowned. "They couldn't have passed us. We'd have seen them."

Connor swore, and I looked back at him. He was staring at the trail, toward the direction of the resort.

"What?" I asked.

"We drove part of the way, but they can't drive in creature form." Although that did present a mental image that had us all smiling.

"So there has to be a trail that leads back to the resort," I said. "And we haven't been on that trail."

"That's a long way back," Theo said.

"Yeah, but it's the only way back," Connor said. "And they'd have figured out Beyo betrayed them, that he'd give them up."

"They'll go back to the resort," I said. "Back to where it all started."

"And back to Beyo, to offer up a little of their precious revenge."

We ran back to the car, making surprisingly good time over crappy terrain, and managed not to twist any ankles, break any legs in the process.

"I'll drive," Theo said. "You've got calls to make."

Connor tossed him the keys, pulled out his screen and we climbed into the vehicle. He had Lulu pass the comm over to Alexei, then called Georgia, asked her to alert Cash and the entire resort and make sure Beyo was well protected.

"Call the sheriff and the state patrol," I said when he finished the calls. Connor looked at me, pained by the suggestion. "The only way this stops is if someone puts a stop to it. We have to be that someone."

He cursed but made the call.

Theo drove like a bat out of hellmouth, and why wouldn't he, given it was the middle of the night, there was no traffic, and the single county sheriff probably didn't bother to issue traffic citations?

We drove into the RV lot, checked on Lulu.

"Lock yourself in," I told her, "and don't come out unless it's one of us."

"I'll literally keep the motor running and run them down if I have to. Be careful."

"We will," I said, and watched, waited until she'd closed and locked the door again.

The cabin was our next stop. There, we'd rendezvous with Alexei and Georgia and prepare to move on foot to Beyo's cabin.

"The resort on alert?" Connor asked, frowning at the glinting firepits at the edge of the lake.

"There's no one out there," Georgia said. "Just a little show. We didn't want to alter things from normal too much, in case we scared them away."

"Everyone's in the lodge," Alexei said, "which is locked and guarded. Except Beyo. We considered moving him out of the cabin, but figured leaving him—and his scent—there would help narrow the field."

And keep the creatures focused on their target.

"I've got friends positioned on the opposite side of the resort," Georgia said. "They'll keep an eye on the perimeter, and give me a signal if they see anything."

"You seem to be enjoying the operational element," I said with a grin.

"Feels good to shake out the fur now and again."

"Cash and Everett?" Connor asked.

Georgia's mouth twisted. "They're in town playing pool," she said bitterly. "We've left messages."

"Very responsible," Theo said. "They've got quite an interesting leadership style."

Alexei snorted.

"Let's go," Connor said. "And let's end this."

We moved silently across the resort, sticking to the darkest of the shadows as we approached the cabin. We stopped in the shadow of the cabin that stood thirty feet away from Beyo's.

Adrenaline was already pumping, the monster looking for a foothold, an opportunity to come forward. But I'd already made a decision about that. And I took Georgia's advice.

I reached out for it and asked it a question. *Do you want to fight?*

At first, there was silence, and I thought maybe the idea that we could communicate anything other than need and violence was ridiculous.

And then . . . *Fight.*

Okay, I told it. *Be ready.*

The monster answered with a stretch that sent a delicious warmth through my veins.

"Probably should have done that a long time ago," I murmured, and could have sworn I heard it chuckle.

Somewhere in front of us, a single firecracker popped and sizzled.

"I'm guessing that's the signal?" Connor whispered.

"That's it," Alexei said. "You ready to move?"

"Go," he said, and Alexei and Theo split off to give us another angle of attack.

"I'm going to let the monster fight," I whispered, and Connor looked back at me. The wariness I'd expected to see was nonexistent. I found only a grin.

"Are you?"

"It's stronger. But I'm better with a sword. So I'm going to try fighting with it."

"Good," he said, and kissed me hard. "I like having the better weapons."

The earth shook before I could answer him. The hybrids stepped onto the lawn between the lakeshore and cabin. Silver, red, and brown.

If Beyo was telling the truth, Zane was the silver beast. The one who'd attacked Carlie, and stolen my dagger in the process.

Ready? I asked the monster, and felt its answering thrill. *Go,* I told it, and stepped back to let it take control.

It stepped into my skin, this predator, and moved into a crouching stance with flawless accuracy. I raised the katana, moonlight gleaming along the blade, and prepared to move.

The silver hybrid lifted its muzzle.

Yes, we thought together. *We're here. And this time, we'll take you down.*

The red beast moved toward Beyo's door.

"Go!" Connor shouted, and chaos rolled across the resort.

We jumped up from our positions, surrounded the wolves.

"Zane!" called my voice, and we ran toward it, my monster directing my feet, my pumping arms, and me swinging the katana forward.

I had to ignore the fact that Theo and Alexei and Connor were running into danger, too, and focus on the beast in front of me.

"Hey, asshole!" I said, and it curled its lip, began to lope forward and away from Beyo's cabin.

Not the brightest bulb, I thought, and felt the monster offer its agreement.

The hybrid reached out, and I slid between its legs, sliced a long strip from its calf. It howled, overbalanced, and nearly landed on me as it fought for control. I scrambled to my feet and swung the katana again, gestured it forward.

"Not impressive, Zane. Want to try again?"

It loped forward but, instead of swiping to grab me, stuck its arm out to slap me backward. I spun to dodge the blow, but it corrected, sent me flying.

This time, I'd learned my lesson. I rolled, which softened the blow of the landing and helped me get to my feet faster.

"Lis!" I heard Connor's voice over the sounds of battle, and despite whatever horror he was facing.

"I'm fine," I called out, and faced the beast again.

The monster was angry. And unless I was wrong, feeling a little sting of pride.

We go again, I told it, and sucked in a breath, ran toward Zane. This time, we jumped, took air and skimmed over the top of his head, spittle flying beneath us as we moved. We pivoted, slashed down, and pierced the beast's shoulder, slicing through tendon and sending it to its knees.

The monster felt victorious, and I reveled in its pleasure.

We turned again, ready for another strike. But light began to flash, that bitter-smoke scent filling the air. Magic pummeled the beast, spasming through his body, revealing a pale man, body brutalized by battle and the weight of the spell he'd been carrying.

Revealing Zane.

Weakened though he was, the transformation didn't stop him. Naked and thin, he came at me, arms swinging like those of a boxer on the ropes.

"Bitch," Zane said. "Ruining this . . ."

"Oh, spare me," I said, and knew what the monster wanted to do. It punched out—sharp jab, hard uppercut—and then a front kick that had him flying through the air.

Zane hit the ground, skidded twenty feet, and came to a stop. Chest still rising and falling, but head lolling to the side.

Good girl, I told the monster and, for the first time in our relationship, felt it preen with delight—and realized it had feelings just like I did. It wasn't just a well of anger, but a creature—somehow bound to me—that also hadn't asked to be in this situation. And I was going to have to learn to work around that.

I rose, looked around, found half the resort—including Theo and Georgia—was watching Connor finish off the brown hybrid.

"It's impressive," Theo said as Connor plunged a dagger into the creature's calf, pinning him into the ground.

We both winced.

"What's impressive?" I asked.

"Watching the future Apex in action." He slid me a glance, grinned. "You ready to be the future Mrs. Apex?"

"Watch it, friend." I tapped the blade of my sword. "I'm still armed."

Theo snorted.

"What the fuck?" Cash exclaimed as he and Everett ran toward the field of battle, stared at the scene in front of them.

"What the fuck are those?" Everett said, face a mask of horror as he looked over the creatures.

"The hybrids," Connor said. "Or the ones left. John and Marcus. Zane's over there," he said, pointing. "They're here to kill Beyo, which we didn't let them do, and to take out me and Elisa, if they could manage it. They didn't," he said good-naturedly.

Cash didn't speak, just looked over the beasts, his eyes wide and staring . . . and his mind probably reeling to figure out how he was going to manipulate this to his benefit.

Magic flashed, and he threw up a hand to shield his eyes, then watched as John and Marcus began the transformation back into human form. And just as with Beyo and Zane, it was an ugly process.

"What the fuck have you done to my people?" Cash asked when the shifters were revealed again, pale and sickly and thin.

"Obviously nothing," Connor said. "They've done this all on their own."

But Cash had made his decision, picked his path, and wasn't going to be swayed from it. He strode toward Connor, fury in his eyes.

"Oh, for fuck's sake," Connor said and, when Cash reached him, pounded his fist into Cash's face.

"Good show," Alexei said as Cash hit the ground. "That was a nice one."

Everett tried to step forward in Cash's stead and make his own run at Connor, but Gibson held his arms back.

"No, thanks, old man. You've had your chance."

Connor nodded with approval. "This is the hell you have wrought in this clan. The destruction, all because you were so goddamned determined to hold on to power you hadn't earned. Those days are over."

"Over," Georgia agreed, stepping beside them. "This has gone on too long," she said to the growing crowd, over gasps and shock as they surveyed the damage.

"You have no power—," Everett began, but Georgia just held up a hand.

"Save it. Given that you've been faced with indisputable evidence the hybrids exist, they're deadly, and they're members of your clan, I think we can safely say that Elisa's actions were reasonable and she acted in order to save Carlie's life in the best way available to her. The only person she needs absolution from is Carlie." She looked at me. "You have our apologies." She shifted her gaze to Connor. "As do you."

"I appreciate the gesture," Connor said. "And, Georgia, you're family. But you all wrought this. None of you are innocent. You knew Loren was a predator of the worst kind, and you ignored the victims. You knew something was hurting your people, but you ignored the evidence. That's unacceptable. The North American Central Pack hereby names Georgia McAllister as leader of this clan. She's in charge unless or until the clan votes otherwise."

"You can't fucking do that," Cash said, climbing to his feet. "We don't release you from the Obsideo. You're still obliged to us."

But Connor's eyes stayed bright. "Cash, you are an idiot. When you claim Obsideo, you have to specify the problem. Otherwise, you leave the choice up to the person who's obligated, which would be me. The problem in this clan is its leadership. And I've just solved that problem."

As if the magic somehow agreed with him, it released its hold, power spilling through the crowd like water through a broken dam, swirling around our feet.

Connor turned to me, his smile satisfied and smug.

"Connor Keene," I said. "That little bit of strategy was positively vampiric."

"I'm going to assume that's a compliment."

"Oh," I said with silvered eyes, "it absolutely was."

"Good," he said, then pulled me toward him. "Let's try a little more vampire drama."

He kissed me with abandon, let his magic mingle with the eddies of power at our feet, let the others feel the power, the attraction, the emotion. And when he pulled back, his breathing was hard, and there was a mix of amusement and desire and alpha confidence in his eyes.

"Aw, keep going," Alexei shouted. "I'm recording this."

We turned to look his way, found him holding up his screen.

"Why would you do that?" Connor asked.

"Because it was a good kiss, and someone will pay good money for the footage."

"Alexei." Connor's voice was flat.

They watched each other for a second, and Alexei smiled first.

"Because the Pack will want to know who she is and who you are. She may not be a shifter. But I think they'll like what they see."

I arched a brow. "That's the best compliment I'm likely to ever get from you, isn't it?"

"Probably," Alexei said.

"Then I'll take it. And thank you."

His cheeks actually pinked a little.

Blue and red lights flashed as Sheriff Paulson's vehicle pulled into the parking lot. He got out, looked around. "What the hell is happening out here?"

"We're just visitors," Connor said, and we limped back to the cabin. "Talk to Cash. He's got all the answers."

EPILOGUE

I woke to a single message, the one I'd been hoping for—and dreading at the same time: SHE'S AWAKE. That was the bat signal, the green light for Connor and me to drive back to the coven's house.

I was nervous about the trip. Not sure of the expectations, of my beloved rules. Not certain what I'd feel for the girl I'd changed so profoundly. And I didn't relish the idea of playing politics with Ronan.

"It's like he's playing at being a vampire," I said when we were in Georgia's SUV and driving toward the house. We'd decided it would be safer, all things considered, to take a vehicle that offered more protection than his bike.

Connor glanced at me. "What?"

"Sorry. Finishing a conversation I started in my head. He talks about doing what's necessary to keep his people safe, but when I made a hard choice to protect someone—in the way only vampires can protect them—he accused me of disloyalty. Of threatening his kingdom. Isn't that hypocrisy?"

"I imagine he's not well-versed on how well-socialized vampires behave. Not as isolated as they are."

"Maybe," I said. But I guessed that was just one of the many dysfunctions caused by the coven's isolation.

We pulled beneath the covered drive, and I looked up at the dark and imposing doors.

One of the vampires who'd accompanied Ronan to the resort opened the door, escorted us into the house.

I didn't want to go back inside, to feel oppressed by red velvet and dark wood—or the emotional weight that layered over it. But I recognized that feeling for what it was now. It was the magic that had been laid down, frosted over the house and seeping into the furniture and fabric, designed to dull the senses of humans and keep their questions at a minimum.

"The spellseller did this," I said to Ronan, who waited in the foyer.

He wore a dark suit today with a low collar over a V-neck shirt. "Yes," he said, nodding at me, at Connor. "To protect us."

"And are you better for it?"

He looked at me for a long time. "Let's go upstairs," he said by way of answer, and moved to the staircase.

Despite their obvious age, the treads were silent as we walked upstairs. Perfectly built or magically honed? Their inconsistencies wiped away or the sounds muffled?

Light shifted as we walked beneath the dome and rays of moonlight that filtered through the iron bars that held the glass in place.

We reached the landing, took another impeccably paneled hallway, and then turned into a room on the right. It was simpler by far than the rest of the house. A small rectangle of a room, with a window opposite the wall, a bureau, a desk, a small four-poster bed. Moonlight streamed through the window, cutting across the dark furniture.

The room was lit by a Tiffany-style lamp, or maybe an original, whose glass shade matched the style of the dome and cast soft gold-tipped light.

She sat cross-legged on the bed, a burgundy T-shirt over dark leggings. Her feet were bare. A book was in her lap, her gaze focused as her eyes tracked the lines of print.

Carlie looked up. She was still pale, but that was an improvement over the gray pallor she'd worn when I'd last seen her. She looked stronger—not just healthier, although, being immortal and now self-healing, she almost certainly was. But a little more sculpted. Cheekbones slightly rounder, muscles slightly tighter. It happened to most who were transformed—bone and muscle rearranging to make the package just a little more beautiful. All the easier to capture a wary human.

"Carlie," Ronan said quietly. "You have a visitor."

He stepped to the side as Carlie looked up, revealing me behind him. I made myself meet her eyes and braced myself for anger, for hatred, for the lash of words—and, depending on how angry she was, for fangs.

Her eyes went huge, went silver, and she leapt off the bed, was in front of me before I'd even considered grabbing a weapon.

She was fast. So fast.

And she wrapped her arms around me, embraced me with fierce strength she probably didn't yet know she had.

"Thank you. Thank you, thank you, thank you."

"I— Okay," I said, and patted her back, could practically feel my bones creaking beneath her embrace. "You're welcome, I guess."

"Let's give them a minute," Connor said behind me, and I could hear the relief in his voice.

Ronan opened his mouth to speak, probably to ask Carlie if she was all right to be left alone with me. But he held his peace, probably when he saw the expression on her face. They left us alone, closed the door behind them.

She stepped back, linked her fingers together. "I'm sorry. You don't even really know me, and I'm probably just overwhelming you."

"It's okay. I'm—I'm a little surprised you aren't furious with me."

Her brows popped up. "Why would I be mad at you?"

What sounded like genuine confusion in her voice loosened some of the tension in my chest; bindings of fear unbuckled.

"Because I changed you—or started the process—without your consent."

She snorted. "My consent was bleeding all over the freaking ground. I knew, when that thing picked me up, that I was a goner. I could feel it kind of"—she looked away, emotion welling in her eyes—"bite through me. There was so much pain. He was running, and every time his feet hit the ground, it got worse. And then I got cold, and I got tired, and I felt like I was floating. He jerked and put me down, and then you were there."

She looked back at me, her smile so beatific I wanted to cry. "I heard you talking to me, and then you took the pain away. When you bit me," she added, as if I hadn't already committed every second of that night to memory.

"And then I was gone for a while, and then you began to feed me, and I came back. It was sudden, like I'd been thrown right into my body again. And the blood was . . . weird but amazing. You saved my life, but if you need my consent now, then you have it, lady. You freaking have it."

She grinned. "Besides, do you have any idea how dull it is to be a human in Grand Bay, Minnesota? To smell like doughnuts all the time? Even the Sups are dull. I mean, I like Georgia, but the resort is a dive, and all the pretending to be human? Why would you do that?" She pointed at herself. "This looks a lot more fun."

I smiled. "I think we'll be seeing some leadership changes there. And the monsters have been caught. So they won't bother you anymore."

"Good," she said with a nod.

"So, do you think you'll want to stay in Minnesota?"

She bit her lip, looked apologetic. "I don't want you to be mad or anything, but yeah." She looked around the room. "I kind of like it here. The vampires seem nice, and the house is really cool, and Ronan said I could stay and still work at the shop at night. But if that's not cool with you—"

"That's fine with me," I said. "Absolutely fine. I mean, we can stay in contact as much as you want, and you can maybe come visit me in Chicago sometime. But things have changed for you so quickly, and you don't have to be in a hurry to make a decision. Your life is here, at least for now. I think you should see what that looks like for you as a vampire, and then decide."

"That sounds good. Would it be okay if I gave you a hug?"

"Of course," I said, and she embraced me and nearly broke every rib.

"Gently," I said. "You've got to learn your strength."

"Crap, sorry," she said, and pulled back. "That's what Ronan said. Did I break anything?"

"Nothing that won't heal." I rose, knowing I needed to let her go, to find her way.

"I know you didn't come up here to make a vampire," she said. "And I had to explain that to Ronan, because, damn, it would have been easier to find a person in Chicago. But I'm really glad you did."

"I'm glad, too," I said, and meant it. "I should go. We're getting ready to head back to Chicago."

She nodded. "Thank you again."

"You're very welcome," I said, and left the room feeling much lighter.

Ronan and Connor waited for me downstairs, twenty feet between them. Fast friends they were not.

Connor looked at me, and I nodded. "We're good here," I said.

His smile looked as relieved as mine had been.

"Before you go," Ronan said, "there are some things I should say. Privately."

I arched an eyebrow. "Anything you have to say to me, you can say in front of him."

Connor brushed the tips of his fingers against mine—the lightest touch, but full of emotion. Of promise.

"I suppose I had that coming," Ronan said.

"At the least," Connor said.

Ronan didn't spare him a look. "I underestimated you. Or perhaps I should say I prejudged you. I believed I understood who and what you were, what you would be. And I believed I understood what had happened with Carlie. I was wrong on all accounts."

"Were you?" My question didn't sound very sincere.

"I believed you had made her without thinking. Perhaps because you'd been raised to take what you wanted. Or perhaps because you simply wanted a vampire of your own. And then I spoke with her."

"And she told you the same thing I did." My tone was desert dry.

"She did," he said, guilt darkening his eyes. He walked to the windows, pushed back the curtains with a finger, looked out. "Regardless, she survived, and that's what matters."

"Carlie said you'd invited her to stay here. You'll take care of her?"

"She is one of us now," he said simply, with a certainty that made me feel better about returning to Chicago.

"If she needs anything—if she needs me—you can reach out."

"I will," he said.

And that was the best détente we'd reach for now.

Back at the resort, we gathered outside the RV. It still smelled like feet and Cheetos.

"Thank you for coming to my rescue," I said, giving Lulu a hug, then Theo.

"Technically, our rescue," Connor said, shaking Theo's hand. "And thanks all around."

"We're family," Lulu said. "You'd probably have done the same for me."

"Absolutely would have done the same," I said. "Down to the cheap vodka and spelunking."

"You do know how to woo a girl," she said, then slid her gaze to Alexei, just looked at him with raised brows.

He stared back at her wordlessly.

"No emotional goodbye?" she asked.

"We live in the same city."

Lulu just rolled her eyes, climbed into the RV. Theo followed, giving us a wave before closing the door behind them.

Alexei pulled a candy bar from his pocket, began to unwrap it as he walked to the bike he'd already prepped and loaded. It sat beside Thelma, which held our bags and helmets.

"You sure you don't want to ride with them in the RV?" Connor asked.

"I'm sure." I looked back at Thelma. "I want Thelma."

His smile was broad and very, very pleased. "Grab the helmet and come sit right here." He patted the leather seat, the look in his eyes suggesting he wasn't entirely focused on the bike.

I smiled at him. "You misunderstand. I don't want to ride," I said with a grin. "I want you to teach me how to drive it."

He just looked at me for a long moment. "Are you seeing anyone else?"

The sudden change of topic made me take a moment. "I— What? No. Why?"

He cupped my face in his hands, kissed me until the tips of my fingers tingled. "Because I want you all to myself."

I grinned up at him, watched the answering glow in his eyes. "Okay."

"Okay," he said, then kissed me again, sealing the deal.

He threw a leg over the bike, patted the seat in front of him.

"Come on, Elisa Sullivan. We've got a long way to go."

Read on for an excerpt from the first
Chicagoland Vampires Novel,

SOME GIRLS BITE

Available now

ONE

The Change

At first, I wondered if it was karmic punishment. I'd sneered at the fancy vampires, and as some kind of cosmic retribution, I'd been made one. Vampire. Predator. Initiate into one of the oldest of the twelve vampire Houses in the United States.

And I wasn't just *one* of them.

I was one of the best.

But I'm getting ahead of myself. Let me begin by telling you how I became a vampire, a story that starts weeks before my twenty-eighth birthday, the night I completed the transition. The night I awoke in the back of a limousine, three days after I'd been attacked walking across the University of Chicago campus.

I didn't remember all the details of the attack. But I remembered enough to be thrilled to be alive. To be shocked to be alive.

In the back of the limousine, I squeezed my eyes shut and tried to unpack the memory of the attack. I'd heard footsteps, the sound muffled by dewy grass, before he grabbed me. I'd screamed and kicked, tried to fight my way out, but he pushed me down. He was preternaturally strong—supernaturally strong—and he bit my neck with a predatory ferocity that left little doubt about who he was. What he was.

Vampire.

But while he tore into skin and muscle, he didn't drink; he didn't have time. Without warning, he'd stopped and jumped away, running between buildings at the edge of the main quad.

My attacker temporarily vanquished, I'd raised a hand to the crux of my neck and shoulder, felt the sticky warmth. My vision was dimming, but I could see the wine-colored stain across my fingers clearly enough.

Then there was movement around me. Two men.

The men my attacker had been afraid of.

The first of them had sounded anxious. "He was fast. You'll need to hurry, Liege."

The second had been unerringly confident. "I'll get it done."

He pulled me up to my knees, and knelt behind me, a supportive arm around my waist. He wore cologne—soapy and clean.

I tried to move, to give some struggle, but I was fading.

"Be still."

"She's lovely."

"Yes," he agreed. He suckled the wound at my neck. I twitched again, and he stroked my hair. "Be still."

I recalled very little of the next three days, of the genetic restructuring that transformed me into a vampire. Even now, I only carry a handful of memories. Deep-seated, dull pain—shocks of it that bowed my body. Numbing cold. Darkness. A pair of intensely green eyes.

In the limo, I felt for the scars that should have marred my neck and shoulders. The vampire that attacked me hadn't taken a clean bite—he'd torn at the skin at my neck like a starved animal. But the skin was smooth. No scars. No bumps. No bandages. I pulled my hand away and stared at the clean pale skin—and the short nails, perfectly painted cherry red.

The blood was gone—and I'd been manicured.

Staving off a wash of dizziness, I sat up. I was wearing different clothes. I'd been in jeans and a T-shirt. Now I wore a black cock-tail dress, a sheath that fell to just below my knees, and three-inch-high black heels.

That made me a twenty-seven-year-old attack victim, clean and absurdly scar-free, wearing a cocktail dress that wasn't mine. I knew, then and there, that they'd made me one of them.

The Chicagoland Vampires.

It had started eight months ago with a letter, a kind of vampire manifesto first published in the *Sun-Times* and *Trib*, then picked up by papers across the country. It was a coming-out, an an-nouncement to the world of their existence. Some humans be-lieved it a hoax, at least until the press conference that followed, in which three of them displayed their fangs. Human panic led to four days of riots in the Windy City and a run on water and canned goods sparked by public fear of a vampire apocalypse. The feds finally stepped in, ordering Congressional investigations, the hearings obsessively filmed and televised in order to pluck out every detail of the vampires' existence. And even though they'd been the ones to step forward, the vamps were tight-lipped about those details—the fang bearing, blood drinking, and night walk-ing the only facts the public could be sure about.

Eight months later, some humans were still afraid. Others were obsessed. With the lifestyle, with the lure of immortality, with the vampires themselves. In particular, with Celina Desaulniers, the glamorous Windy City she-vamp who'd apparently orchestrated the coming-out, and who'd made her debut during the first day of the Congressional hearings.

Celina was tall and slim and sable-haired, and that day she wore a black suit snug enough to give the illusion that it had been poured onto her body. Looks aside, she was obviously smart and savvy, and she knew how to twist humans around her fingers. To wit: The senior senator from Idaho had asked her what she planned to do now that vampires had come out of the closet.

She'd famously replied in dulcet tones, "I'll be making the most of the dark."

The twenty-year Congressional veteran had smiled with such dopey-eyed lust that a picture of him made the front page of the *New York Times*.

No such reaction from me. I'd rolled my eyes and flipped off the television.

I'd made fun of them, of her, of their pretensions.

And in return, they'd made me like them.

Wasn't karma a bitch?

Now they were sending me back home, but returning me differently. Notwithstanding the changes my body had endured, they'd glammed me up, cleaned me of blood, stripped me of clothing, and repackaged me in their image.

They killed me. They healed me. They changed me.

The tiny seed, that kernel of distrust of the ones who'd made me, rooted.

I was still dizzy when the limousine stopped in front of the Wicker Park brownstone I shared with my roommate, Mallory. I wasn't sleepy, but groggy, mired in a haze across my consciousness that felt thick enough to wade through. Drugs, maybe, or a residual effect of the transition from human to vampire.

Mallory stood on the stoop, her shoulder length ice blue hair shining beneath the bare bulb of the overhead light. She looked anxious, but seemed to be expecting me. She wore flannel pajamas patterned with sock monkeys. I realized it was late.

The limousine door opened, and I looked toward the house and then into the face of a man in a black uniform and cap who'd peeked into the backseat.

"Ma'am?" He held out a hand expectantly.

My fingers in his palm, I stepped onto the asphalt, my ankles wobbly in the stilettos. I rarely wore heels, jeans being my preferred uniform. Grad school didn't require much else.

I heard a door shut. Seconds later, a hand gripped my elbow. My gaze traveled down the pale, slender arm to the bespectacled face it belonged to. She smiled at me, the woman who held my arm, the woman who must have emerged from the limo's front seat.

"Hello, dear. We're home now. I'll help you inside, and we'll get you settled."

Grogginess making me acquiescent, and not really having a good reason to argue anyway, I nodded to the woman, who looked to be in her late fifties. She had a short, sensible bob of steel gray hair and wore a tidy suit on her trim figure, carrying herself with a professional confidence. As we progressed down the sidewalk, Mallory moved cautiously down the first step, then the second, toward us.

"Merit?"

The woman patted my back. "She'll be fine, dear. She's just a little dizzy. I'm Helen. You must be Mallory?"

Mallory nodded, but kept her gaze on me.

"Lovely home. Can we go inside?"

Mallory nodded again and traveled back up the steps. I began to follow, but the woman's grip on my arm stopped me. "You go by Merit, dear? Although that's your last name?"

I nodded at her.

She smiled patiently. "The newly risen utilize only a single name. Merit, if that's what you go by, would be yours. Only the Masters of each House are allowed to retain their last names. That's just one of the rules you'll need to remember." She leaned in conspiratorially. "And it's considered déclassé to break the rules."

Her soft admonition sparked something in my mind, like the beam of a flashlight in the dark. I blinked at her. "Some would consider changing a person without their consent déclassé, Helen."

The smile Helen fixed on her face didn't quite reach her eyes. "You were made a vampire in order to save your life, Merit. Consent is irrelevant." She glanced at Mallory. "She could probably use a glass of water. I'll give you two a moment."

Mallory nodded, and Helen, who carried an ancient-looking leather satchel, moved past her into the brownstone. I walked up the remaining stairs on my own, but stopped when I reached Mallory. Her blue eyes swam with tears, a frown curving her cupid's bow mouth. She was extraordinarily, classically pretty, which was the reason she'd given for tinting her hair with packets of blue Kool-Aid. She claimed it was a way for her to distinguish herself. It was unusual, sure, but it wasn't a bad look for an ad executive, for a woman defined by her creativity.

"You're—" She shook her head, then started again. "It's been three days. I didn't know where you were. I called your parents when you didn't come home. Your dad said he'd handle it. He told me not to call the police. He said someone had called him, told him you'd been attacked but were okay. That you were healing. They told your dad they'd bring you home when you were ready. I got a call a few minutes ago. They said you were on your way home." She pulled me into a fierce hug. "I'm gonna beat the shit out of you for not calling."

Mal pulled back, gave me a head-to-toe evaluation. "They said —you'd been changed."

I nodded, tears threatening to spill over.

"So you're a vampire?" she asked.

"I think. I just woke up or . . . I don't know."

"Do you feel any different?"

"I feel . . . slow."

Mallory nodded with confidence. "Effects of the change, probably. They say that happens. Things will settle." Mallory would know; unlike me, she followed all the vamp-related news. She offered a weak smile. "Hey, you're still Merit, right?"

Weirdly, I felt a prickle in the air emanating from my best friend and roommate. A tingle of something electric. But still sleepy, dizzy, I dismissed it.

"I'm still me," I told her.

And I hoped that was true.

The brownstone had been owned by Mallory's great-aunt until her death four years ago. Mallory, who lost her parents in a car accident when she was young, inherited the house and everything in it, from the chintzy rugs that covered the hardwood floors, to the antique furniture, to the oil paintings of flower vases. It wasn't chic, but it was home, and it smelled like it—lemon-scented wood polish, cookies, dusty coziness. It smelled the same as it had three days ago, but I realized that the scent was deeper. Richer.

Improved vampire senses, maybe?

When we entered the living room, Helen was sitting at the edge of our gingham-patterned sofa, her legs crossed at the ankles. A glass of water sat on the coffee table in front of her.

"Come in, ladies. Have a seat." She smiled and patted the couch. Mallory and I exchanged a glance and sat down. I took the seat next to Helen. Mallory sat on the matching love seat that faced the couch. Helen handed me the glass of water.

I brought it to my lips, but paused before sipping. "I can—eat and drink things other than blood?"

Helen's laugh tinkled. "Of course, dear. You can eat whatever you'd like. But you'll need blood for its nutritional value." She leaned toward me, touched my bare knee with the tips of her fingers. "And I daresay you'll enjoy it!" She said the words like she was imparting a delicious secret, sharing scandalous gossip about her next-door neighbor.

I sipped, discovered that water still tasted like water. I put the glass back on the table.

Helen tapped her hands against her knees, then favored us both with a bright smile. "Well, let's get to it, shall we?" She reached into the satchel at her feet and pulled out a dictionary-sized leather-bound book. The deep burgundy cover was inscribed in embossed gold letters—*Canon of the North American Houses, Desk Reference.* "This is everything you need to know about joining Cadogan House. It's not the full *Canon*, obviously, as the series is voluminous, but this will cover the basics."

"Cadogan House?" Mallory asked. "Seriously?"

I blinked at Mallory, then Helen. "What's Cadogan House?"

Helen looked at me over the top of her horn-rimmed glasses. "That's the House that you'll be Commended into. One of Chicago's three vampire Houses—Navarre, Cadogan, Grey. Only the Master of each House has the privilege of turning new vampires. You were turned by Cadogan's Master—"

"Ethan Sullivan," Mallory finished.

Helen nodded approvingly. "That's right."

I lifted brows at Mallory.

"Internet," she said. "You'd be amazed."

Photo by Dana Damewood Photography

Chloe Neill—*New York Times* bestselling author of the Chicagoland Vampires novels (*Blade Bound, Midnight Marked, Dark Debt*), the Dark Elite novels (*Charmfall, Hexbound, Firespell*), the Devil's Isle novels (*The Beyond, The Hunt, The Sight, The Veil*), and the Heirs of Chicagoland novels (*Wild Hunger*)—was born and raised in the South but now makes her home in the Midwest, just close enough to Cadogan House, St. Sophia's, and Devil's Isle to keep an eye on things. When not transcribing her heroines' adventures, she bakes, works, and scours the Internet for good recipes and great graphic design. Chloe also maintains her sanity by spending time with her boys—her favorite landscape photographer (her husband) and their dogs, Baxter and Scout. (Both she and the photographer understand the dogs are in charge.)

Ready to find
your next great read?

Let us help.

Visit prh.com/nextread

Penguin
Random
House